Michael Jecks is the author of the bestselling Templar series, comprising thirty-two novels starring Sir Baldwin de Furnshill and Simon Puttock, and the acclaimed Vintener trilogy starring Berenger Fripper. *Pilgrim's War* is the first instalment of his new Crusader series, following two families separated by a blood feud.

He is a past Chairman of the Crime Writers' Association, helped found the Historical Writers' Association, and founded Medieval Murderers. He has been a Fellow of the Royal Literary Fund, helping students at Exeter University.

Michael lives in northern Dartmoor with his wife, children and dogs.

To find out more about Michael and his work, please visit his website at www.michaeljecks.co.uk, where you will find links to his Twitter, Facebook, YouTube and Wordpress accounts.

MICHAEL JECKS

PILGRIM'S WAR

**SIMON &
SCHUSTER**

London · New York · Sydney · Toronto · New Delhi

A CBS COMPANY

First published in Great Britain by Simon & Schuster UK Ltd, 2018
A CBS COMPANY

Copyright © Michael Jecks, 2018

This book is copyright under the Berne Convention.
No reproduction without permission.
® and © 1997 Simon & Schuster, Inc. All rights reserved.

The right of Michael Jecks to be identified as author
of this work has been asserted in accordance with sections
77 and 78 of the Copyright, Designs and Patents Act, 1988.

1 3 5 7 9 10 8 6 4 2

Simon & Schuster UK Ltd
1st Floor
222 Gray's Inn Road
London WC1X 8HB

Simon & Schuster Australia, Sydney
Simon & Schuster India, New Delhi

www.simonandschuster.co.uk
www.simonandschuster.com.au
www.simonandschuster.co.in

A CIP catalogue record for this book
is available from the British Library

Hardback ISBN: 978-1-4711-5000-5
eBook ISBN: 978-1-4711-5003-6

This book is a work of fiction.
Names, characters, places and incidents are either a product of the
author's imagination or are used fictitiously. Any resemblance to actual
people living or dead, events or locales is entirely coincidental.

Typeset in Times by M Rules
Printed and bound by CPI Group (UK) Ltd, Croydon, CR0 4YY

MIX
Paper from
responsible sources
FSC® C020471

Simon & Schuster UK Ltd are committed to sourcing paper
that is made from wood grown in sustainable forests and support the Forest
Stewardship Council, the leading international forest certification organisation.
Our books displaying the FSC logo are printed on FSC certified paper.

For my wife, Jane,
for her understanding, patience and generosity,
all of which were sorely needed in
the creation of this book!

And

In loving memory of
Roy George (Peter) Jecks
1920–2017

LONDON BOROUGH OF WANDSWORTH	
9030 00005 9000 9	
Askews & Holts	01-Mar-2018
AF HIS	£20.00
	WW17017647

BOOK ONE

The Gathering Storm

CHAPTER 1

Sens, Monday 24th March, 1096

The news rippled through the market like a flame running along a strip of cloth. People stopped and listened, and began to leave the stalls of food and wine, and made their way to the square before the great church, where the cool breezes tugged at cloaks and hats. Many looked up at the steeple, struck with the symbolism of that stone finger pointing towards the heavens as they waited. This was a great day, a day no one would forget. They had been waiting six months for this.

Sybille disliked large crowds. She felt someone jostle her, and slapped the hand at her backside, turning and glaring at the grinning, bearded man behind her. Josse stepped between them, truculently shoving him away with his staff.

'Thank you, Josse,' she said, shielding Richalda as best she could from others in the square. She wouldn't put it past these uncouth churls to try to fondle Richalda too, even though the girl was not yet eight years old. There were some who would fondle a flea-bitten cur after too much wine, and the air reeked of sour wine from the breath of those about her.

Josse nodded; he stood only a little taller than her, with the fair hair of a Norseman and pale grey eyes. He had a slight build, and his face was as lined as an ancient peasant's. Her husband, Benet, had found him, an unemployed sailor at the Parisian docks, and Josse had been as loyal as only a fellow rescued from a life of poverty could be. His staff whipped out, and a man cursed and took his injured hand away.

It was the way of things. Women who joined a throng like this were considered fair game, especially in a town square. Sens was a big town, and with the buildings ringing the part-cobbled, part-grassed area, it felt like a huge baiting pit. For a woman, it was dangerous to be in such a crowd alone. Not only humiliating, with men touching and fondling her body like fruit in a grocer's basket; worse could happen. It was the way of the lower classes that they would view any woman as available if she were to walk among them, which was why Sybille tended to avoid large crowds, but today should have been different.

They were here to listen to the preacher.

He had arrived yesterday: a ragged man clad in filthy clothes, with a hunched figure and a face long like that of the donkey he rode. He only ever drank wine and ate fish, apparently, and after his extensive travels he was as emaciated as a scavenging cur, but his piety gleamed in his eyes, so they said, and Benet was determined to come and hear him speak.

Darling Benet. He was seven years older than her, and since they had married he had aged and looked much older. It was difficult to make money as an apothecary, and several times in the last fourteen months they had come close to having to sell their rooms and find a smaller place from which to continue his profession. No matter what he tried, though they scraped a living, money was always tight.

Partly, she knew, it was his nature. Of an evening he would gamble with his friends at the taverns, whether on cock-fights, dogs or a game of chance. It was what a man would do when drinking. There was nothing she could do to prevent him. In the past Sybille had rescued her family by pawning or selling her jewels, but there were few enough left of them now. The next time Benet saw a guaranteed opportunity, or a wager that he thought could make them secure, she just hoped he would be right. And that he could stay away from playing dice.

The crowd began to jostle forward; there were shouts and cheers, and Sybille felt a thrilling in her breast: this was the man they had gathered to listen to, the man who would explain the Pope's proposal. All wanted to get closer to him, to hear the words that were said to come straight from God.

She could see nothing over the sea of heads and hats, but the people were moving, and she was sure that the man known as *the Hermit* would soon be speaking. Where was Benet? She hoped he had not gone to the wine shop to drink and see his friends again.

There was a sudden clamour, and she glanced about, hunting for Benet. When she looked back towards the church at the farther side of the square, a small man stood on a crate, his arms held up to the sky for silence. From this distance it was hard to see him clearly, and Sybille hoped that he would speak distinctly, but even as she had the thought the crowd was stilled, as though all were simultaneously struck dumb.

The small figure began to speak.

For two brothers to appear so dissimilar made many suspicious, especially since their mother had been, as all acknowledged, far too friendly for her own good when a maid. It ensured that they were the source of much quiet mirth while children.

The folk had some cause for their gossip.

Odo, the elder, was a full three inches taller than Fulk and ascetic in appearance. He had mousy-coloured hair and green eyes like his father. By contrast Fulk was wiry, with dark hair and pale grey eyes that marked him as different. Still, his fists had a whip's speed, and he had a temper to match, as many neighbours had learned. In any case, while some declared that Odo's narrow face and long nose was reminiscent of the local priest when the boy was born, none could say that Fulk's strong, square jaw was like any man other than his father, the miller. Besides, no one wanted to insult either boy. Early on Fulk was marked out as a fiery spirit who was quick to take offence, whether to himself or his brother – although he was equally swift to forgive and apologise. As he grew older, his stormy temperament was tempered with a generosity and warmth that appealed to all. At the same time Odo grew more serious, a youth whose interest was sparked more by piety than by the pleasures of the flesh that so inspired Fulk.

Fulk's engaging smile, quick wit and charm made him known to all the more cautious fathers of young maids long before the two left to travel to Sens: Odo to work in the great church's bakery, Fulk to learn his trade at a blacksmith's. Most of the village approved of the brothers' departure. All the men agreed that Fulk was a wastrel and malcontent who would deprive a score of maidens of their virginity and end on a gallows. Their wives agreed that he was no better than his mother, while casting thoughtful glances at his powerful shoulders, his regular features and ready smile, that had little to do with defending their daughters.

'What's he saying?' Fulk demanded now.

'I can hardly hear a thing.' Odo frowned. He burped quietly, tasting sour wine in his throat, staring fixedly at the preacher as the man lifted his arms to signal silence.

'Aye, well, with the noise here, that's hardly surprising,' Fulk said. He uncorked his wineskin and took a good gulp. This was a day off for him, and he intended to make the most of it.

'Drinking again?' Odo said.

Fulk passed him the skin and Odo drank deeply.

Fulk grabbed it. 'Hey! Don't finish the whole skin!'

'Just saving you from yourself, little brother,' Odo said loftily.

Fulk took another swig for luck, and then cast his eye about the crowd. At the fringes of the crowd, he saw her. A tall, dark woman, a young girl before her, and a thin, wiry man behind her who stood close enough to know her, but far enough away that Fulk was sure he was no husband. A servant, then. And a woman like her, with the elegance of a queen, would surely have to be chaperoned wherever she went.

'I wouldn't mind hearing what *she* has to say,' Fulk said with a grin.

'Eh?' Odo said, distracted.

'Nothing.'

'Quiet, then!'

'All right, Odo. We aren't in church now,' Fulk said mildly. He turned his attention towards the crowd on the steps where Peter the Hermit stood.

He was an unprepossessing character, in Fulk's view, even at this distance. A shabby-looking man, thin and wretched, grubby and tatty, like many of the pilgrims loitering behind him. Fulk could easily understand the desire to escape a life of toil and drudgery – there were few jobs more guaranteed to make an intelligent man seek adventure than one which involved rising before dawn, making a fire, and then working

7

hard all day until night-time. Worse, the smith was a lazy, drunken brute who despised all apprentices, and looked on Fulk as nothing more than cheap labour. Fulk was keen to see life, to experience *adventure* – but Peter the Hermit was not the man to tempt him, he decided. Unlike the woman: she could tempt him any day.

'That's the Hermit, then?' a man asked.

Odo was straining to hear, but Fulk nodded. 'Yes. That's the one. What's he saying now, Odo? Can you hear him?'

'He's saying that the man to his side is Sir Walter de Boissy-Sans-Avoir, a bold knight who's keen to serve pilgrims,' Odo said. 'Fulk – shut up! He says pilgrims used to be able to travel all the way to Jerusalem, but the last time he tried to go, he was turned back. The heathens who stopped him mocked him, he says.'

Fulk shrugged, and started to turn back to the woman in the crowd, but something in the speaker's tone made him frown and peer at the men on the steps.

The Hermit's voice was swelling.

'They stop Christians from visiting the site of Jesus's crucifixion, but that is not the worst of it! These heathens do not stop at that! They persecute the poor Christian souls who live there! These poor people suffer all the cruel privations and torments their cruel rulers can conceive. Some are forced to give up all their belongings and wealth; those in Jerusalem itself are barred from taking part in our holy ceremonies. They are bullied, enslaved, their women taken from them and compelled to consent to all manner of . . .' his voice dropped to a low growl '. . . vicious and unnatural acts. The Christians are taken and have their private parts cut off to make them unsightly in the eyes of God, or have their bowels ripped from their bodies while they are alive, so that the heathens can learn whether they have swallowed gold or jewels. *All this in the Holy Land where Christ was born!'*

This last was bellowed in proof of his horror. He stood with his arms upraised, fists clenched as though demanding that God Himself listen. Gradually his taut figure relaxed. His arms fell slowly and he gazed about him with weary insistence. He lifted his hands, now cupped as if begging for alms, and held them out as though pointing at the crowds.

'This is why, my friends, this is why, when the Emperor of the Eastern Empire, our friend in Constantinople, begged that we should help him fight the predatory fiends who encroach ever nearer to his city, our Holy Father, the Pope, became so affected. He hears the voices of our brothers in Christ, and has prayed and reflected hard, searching for an answer. And God has answered him! *God has told him what to do!* My friends, we shall march on the Holy City itself, and wrest it back from the foul invaders who stole it! Even as I speak, hosts are gathering all over France and the Holy Roman Empire, and will soon make their way to the Holy Land. There they will fight all those who stand against us! We shall fight with these heretics, and kill all those who refuse to submit to God's will! Men are marching under the banners of bold men like Sir Walter here, for wherever the Pope's authority is respected, men will obey him. What, are the men of Sens less bold than those of Paris? Of Toulouse? Of Bordeaux? Nay! You will march too, will you not?'

A roar of agreement and approval came from a thousand throats. Fulk looked about him and saw the poor lifting their fists and shouting, while behind them merchants cast subtle glances one at another. They would be unlikely to risk their own hides, he reckoned.

'Women, children, all will be welcomed, for all your sins will be forgiven if you join this holy endeavour. If you come, be you never so tainted with sin, you will be rewarded in Heaven!'

'He's a persuasive orator,' Fulk said cynically. 'He knows how to get the attention of the townsfolk!'

The hermit lifted his fist again. 'Will you join me? Will you help our cause? This is God's will! God asks it! God demands it! *God wills it!'*

His words were taken up as a chant, and Fulk heard it reverberating around the square: *'Dieu le veut! Dieu le veut! God wills it! God wills it!'*

'Very persuasive,' he said. The sight and the sounds were thrilling, he could not deny it. 'I feel sorry for the fellows they will attack.'

'Well, they are godless heathens, brother,' Odo said sharply. 'They deserve punishment for the crimes they have committed against God.'

'Someone should do something about it,' a man near Fulk said.

He was a scruffy tranter or carter, Fulk thought as they introduced themselves. The fellow introduced himself as Gidie. He had a belly like a barrel, which he was filling from the drinking horn in his hand; his other gripped a heavy-looking staff. His hosen were splattered and stained with the mud of a hundred villages, his tunic faded from green to pale brown where the sun had sucked the colour. With a face wrinkled like a prune, but a nose as round and purple as a plum, he looked like any contented villager.

Fulk nodded to him encouragingly. 'You want to? March all the way to Jerusalem on this great . . . what does he call it, Odo?'

'He said it is to be a great *iter*, a pilgrimage, a walk across the lands to Jerusalem, to demand the right to visit the Holy City, and take it back from these heathens so that Christians might live there safely once more,' Odo said.

There was a sudden roar from the crowds. It sounded like the massed baying of a pack of hounds, Fulk thought.

'Dieu le veut!'

Odo added thoughtfully, 'He said, "All those who march will have remission of all sins."'

'That'll persuade some.' Fulk shrugged.

'With your lifestyle, I'm surprised it doesn't appeal to you,' Odo said tartly.

'Me?' Fulk said innocently, but Odo wasn't listening.

The Hermit concluded: 'No matter what your age, no matter what your crime, your Pope, your Holy Father, has promised that you will be forgiven. All those who die on this blessed pilgrimage will ascend to Heaven immediately! *Dieu le veut*; God wills it. Who can refuse such a glorious end? Give your money to support the pilgrims, or join the pilgrims as well! What do you have to lose, compared with all you will gain?'

'Aye?' Gidie said. He spat eloquently into the street. 'Reckon there'll be enough willing to go and do that, does he?'

'He says he is gathering a great army to join him and wrest the Holy Land from them.'

The tranter looked at his belly, then Odo and Fulk up and down. 'I think he's going to be happier with you two youngsters, rather than an old fart like me, don't you?'

Emersende listened carefully. A man pressed against her, and she felt his hand on her hip. She turned and grabbed his crotch and laughed. 'Come on, you want to fuck with me, little man, you need more than a little *cornichon* like that!'

The fellow's face darkened, and he knocked her hand away, bunching his fist as though to attack her, but immediately Emersende tilted her pale face and stood arms akimbo. 'Try that, and you'll regret it. I have friends here.'

Her words were not in jest. Already three men had taken to watching the man. 'Jacques, you see this man? He likes to touch me up, but doesn't like me talking about it.'

The fellow spat a curse at her, and stalked away through the crowds. Emersende chuckled to herself. 'I think I could let you have a cup or two of wine when you visit us next, Jacques,' she said.

He nodded with keen anticipation. Jacques knew he could expect special favours when he went to see her next.

Emersende rolled her shoulders. Last night she had slept badly, and her muscles were aching. If she could, she would have remained in her cot until later, but today she had been persuaded to come and listen to the preacher. Well, she was here, and frankly she thought she was wasting her time.

'He's not very impressive. I had thought to find a strong man, a knight, who could gain the attention of the people all about,' she said.

Beside her, young Jeanne tucked a stray blonde curl beneath her coif. Guillemette glanced at Emersende and shrugged. 'You know what they can be like, some of these scrawny types. Look like they'll die at the first spend, and then keep you rutting all night. Perhaps he has more stamina than you think.'

'He had better, or else he'll fall over,' Emersende said dismissively.

'I think he looks quite nice,' Jeanne said. She was not yet two-and-twenty, a slim, fair woman with a long, heart-shaped face and pale blue eyes.

Emersende pulled a face. 'A runt like that?'

'He's not as bad as some I've serviced,' Guillemette said. She was older than Jeanne, and at the upper limits of her appeal, where her technical skills were beginning to be outweighed by fading looks. She swore that she was but eight-and-twenty years old, but Emersende knew she'd been saying that for at least three years now. If she had to guess, Emersende would think that Guillemette must be at least two-and-thirty, and more likely two years older than that. Emersende had a good eye for the age of her fillies. A woman running a brothel had to.

'He reminds me of a man I knew once,' Jeanne said. 'He was kind.'

There was a reflective tone in her voice, and Emersende knew that she was thinking of her husband, Edmond. He had been kind to her at first. Men often were in the beginning. Sadly it had not lasted; Jeanne still hoped he might revert, but Emersende was better acquainted with his type.

It was a strange truth that often women with looks as good as hers would marry brutes who would treat their dogs better. Jeanne had been wedded when only sixteen years old. To woo her, Edmond had been charm itself. That ended almost as soon as the priest had folded his alb, yet Jeanne still did not realise that her husband saw her only as a chattel, to be used or sold as he saw fit. She was too trusting.

Emersende knew the story well. She had seen Jeanne in a tavern and, seeing how Jeanne ensnared a couple of men, taking them outside for a fumbling knee-trembler in the alley behind, she had approached the girl with a view to offering her the protection of a bed in her establishment. As so often, when she saw the girl close-to, she saw that Jeanne's eye was badly bruised, her lips puffed. 'Who did that?' she asked.

'My husband,' Jeanne said quietly.

'Come with me and talk,' Emersende said.

'I can't. He'll see. If he sees me stop to talk, he'll do more of this,' Jeanne said, eyes downcast, a finger touching her eye.

'You are truly married?' All too often a prostitute would have a partnership with her blade. He would take the majority of the money she earned, and in return would offer her protection. The other side of the coin was, if she stopped working, he would often beat her senseless.

'Yes. He loves me . . . I think – but we need money.'

'Is he here now?'

'Yes. He's watching us.'

'Point him out to me.'

It was unnecessary. Her man, Edmond, was a heavily bearded fellow who stood with a group of other men near the doorway, as though to stop her from escaping his clutches. He was glaring at Emersende like a judge eyeing a convicted felon.

Emersende nodded and looked to Christoph, her guard, making sure he saw the man too. Then she said, 'You have skill in beguiling men. I would like to have you work for me.'

'Edmond would not allow it. He . . .'

'I will offer him more money than he makes now.'

And it had worked. Edmond declared himself content with his share of the money, while Christoph loomed over him, and in return Emersende had made him swear that he would no longer beat Jeanne.

Looking back at the Hermit now, Emersende said, 'I don't think that bag of piss and bones would keep you occupied more than five minutes, and that includes haggling over the price.'

Guillemette feigned injured pride, bridling as though this was a challenge to her abilities. 'I could have him five times in an evening, if I wanted,' she declared.

'Would you want?' Emersende said.

'I would prefer a stud half his age and double his weight,' Guillemette admitted with a giggle.

'Hey! Shut up! We're trying to listen to the preacher,' a man called.

Emersende turned to stare at him, frowning, until her face cleared as she recognised him. 'Don't you tell me to shut up, Georges, or I'll tell your wife what you asked for last week,' she said.

The man reddened while his companions laughed at his embarrassment, and Emersende smiled to herself. 'I've seen enough here.'

She led the way back to the brothel, proudly thrusting her bosom forward like a knight bearing his shield into battle, Guillemette thought. Emersende knew her place in the world. Once, like Guillemette and Jeanne, it had been mostly on her back, but now Emersende was a businesswoman of status. She ran her brothel with kindness and compassion. There were few women so independent, and fewer still with her income. She was proud of her status, even if she was looked down upon by the matrons of the town. They could try to look down on her if they pleased: Guillemette knew that Emersende was no one's plaything. She could sell herself or her girls as she pleased, but for profit; she was owned by no man.

'What's he saying now?' she asked as they reached the edge of the crowd. There was a sudden burst of cheering.

'That anyone joining the journey can be reborn,' Guillemette said. She gave a twisted grin. 'Bit late for us, eh, Em?'

'Yes,' Emersende laughed.

Neither woman noticed that Jeanne didn't join in their mirth.

CHAPTER 2

Sens, Monday 24th March, 1096

'There!' Benet said as he returned to his wife and daughter. He was a man of middle-height, and had a broad smile that made his blue eyes all but disappear in a way that never failed to melt Sybille's heart.

She returned his smile as the crowds began to empty from the square. The old church at the top of the square loomed over them, and she glanced up at it, making the sign of the cross. It was a habit, but today it felt necessary, as though she had a need to ward off evil. All about them the crowds were repeating the same chant, fists raised and punching the air as they cried: *'Dieu le veut; Dieu le veut; Dieu le veut.'*

At the far side of the square, under the wall of the old church, she saw women hurriedly stitching brown fustian crosses to the left breast of those who had taken the oath to march to Jerusalem, while clerks scribbled notes of names or took gifts to help the people marching. Many were happy to pay, she thought, rather than undertake such a perilous journey.

'You know, I have been considering,' Benet said. 'Josse? Would you take Richalda and walk on ahead?' He waited a moment or two, until he was sure that his daughter was out of earshot before taking his wife by the arm and leading her away from the crush. 'The preacher spoke well. Perhaps we ought to think about joining his great pilgrimage.'

Sybille felt a cold clutching at her breast. He gave a broad smile and opened his hand: in it lay a fabric cross. A shiver ran down her spine, and she gave an involuntary glance all about her at the town, the people, her home. 'What, you mean to leave us here and go off on pilgrimage? How long would it take you to travel all that way? We would not know whether you would ever return. No, husband, please do not do this.'

'No, I mean you and Richalda to come with me,' Benet said. He was still smiling, his eyes twinkling. 'This hermit, Peter, is gathering a huge army. Not just the scrags and tatters of the villages about here, but many thousands, from all the towns and cities in the kingdom and beyond. His military adviser is Sir Walter de Boissy-Sans-Avoir, and the Pope is speaking with other knights to have them join. They will bring their feudal hosts with them, so armies will march from all over Christendom! The Hermit says that he will lead his own army of the poor and meek. It is they who will inherit the earth, and it will be the common folk who will show the path of righteousness to the others. Imagine! An army of men and women dedicated to the support of God and winning back His land! And it is not only Peter. There is a host of preachers, all criss-crossing the lands and persuading Christians to join this great campaign. Even the Pope is engaged with this cause. It is the greatest issue of our time!' He smiled, his excitement palpable.

'Benet, it will mean a journey of hundreds of miles,' Sybille said. 'How could we afford such a—'

'Hundreds? It will be many hundreds, perhaps thousands! My

love, this will be the beginning of our future,' he laughed. 'I will sell the house, and with the money we will buy all we need for the journey. If we carry gold, it will be easier to hold about our persons. I will hold it in my scrip, wife. And then, when we have taken Jerusalem for God, we can settle there and enjoy a new life, a simpler life.'

'Benet, how will it be simpler? We shall still have to buy food. We will need money!'

'And we shall make money, my love. Just think! These people are innocent, they think only of the long march, but when they get there, what then? I will tell you! They will need to take on the land and make it fertile. When we have Jerusalem, there will be a need for men such as me, who can trade and deal, who can sell tools and food, who can help to make the city work.'

'What of Richalda ? Do you think she will cope with such a journey? She is only seven years old, Benet! What if I die on the journey, who would look after her then?'

'Woman, now you are being deliberately difficult!' Benet said, perhaps more shortly than he intended.

Sybille stood a little straighter. 'Difficult? Husband, you are not thinking about the dangers. Look at me! Would you risk my life? Richalda's life?'

Benet gesticulated, pulling a grimace and taking a deep breath. 'Sybille, my love, why do you never give me credit for having a brain? This could be the greatest opportunity of our lives, the chance to save Jerusalem! We would be the first to settle in a new Christian kingdom here on earth! Think! We could be among God's most favoured people, and forge a new life in that most glorious land! We would be like kings, living out there. God Himself would look kindly upon all that we did. That is what the preacher was saying, that we should all benefit, if we would go with him.'

'So you think we should sell everything and leave here on the word of that man? But he said that he had never been to Jerusalem himself, but that he had been turned back.'

'Yes, but so what? It is Jerusalem, woman! *Jerusalem!* The land where Jesus lived. We would be living there in memory of Him! God would protect us from all dangers for that. You trust in God, don't you?'

She nodded, but all the while she held a picture of her daughter in her mind. 'Of course.'

'Then we must prepare to leave. I shall sell the shop, you must procure the basics for the journey, and we shall set off as soon as all is packed and ready.'

'Yes, husband,' Sybille said as he pulled at her hand.

'It will be good, believe me! We shall walk there, and at the sight of our host, all the heathens in the city will flee,' he said. 'They will not dare to confront the army of God!' He grinned broadly, and then punched the air.

'Dieu le veut! Dieu le veut!' the people cried. To Sybille, their calls sounded like the giggling and jeering of demons.

'What is it, Jeanne?' Emersende asked.

Jeanne had dragged behind as they walked from the square, and now Guillemette was a short distance ahead, seemingly alone with her thoughts. It left Jeanne and her mistress alone.

'It is Edmond. He wants me to work more. He says I'm lazy. Because my money is going to you, I should work the streets again. He wants to sell me to his friends in the tavern.'

'He promised me that he would leave you to work with me and only me,' Emersende said, her voice cold.

Jeanne shivered. When Edmond had confronted her this morning, she had been terrified. It was like the old days. He was drunk still after an evening with his friends, and he wanted her

19

to go straight to them in the tavern near the river, but she had insisted that she couldn't, and fled, hoping he would be asleep or sober when she returned.

'Jeanne, you cannot come and work for me if you have bruises again,' Emersende said. She had a disinterested tone.

Looking at her, Jeanne was struck with a sudden cold fear. Emersende met her gaze and smiled, but while there was sympathy in her eyes, there was absolute conviction too. 'What can I do? If he hits me, I cannot help myself.'

'I cannot help you if you turn up battered and bruised. I need my sluts willing, eager and able to service the men. If you turn up beaten, the men won't want you.'

'What can I do, then?'

'Don't go back. Stay with us. I'll have Christoph look after you, and when you go out, take him with you.'

'But Edmond will be angry!'

'Edmond will be drunk,' Emersende said firmly. 'He usually is. But I will not have you shared with a group of sweaty bar-drinkers who are but one step from the gallows. You know as well as I do that his friends are brutes, not like the customers that I bring.'

'Yes.'

'So you must stay in the brothel where we can protect you. If you want, I can send Christoph to gather your things when Edmond is not there.'

'Would you look after me?'

Emersende's voice could have greased the city's town's gates. 'Child, you are one of my girls. Do you think I would desert you? You are worth a lot to me.'

'Thank you, Emersende,' Jeanne said with tears springing afresh.

Her mistress smiled and shook her head like a matron chiding a foolish child, but there was a hard glitter in her eyes that Jeanne did not see as she wiped the tears from her own.

Cerisiers

As Gidie the tranter clattered up the stony track to his home late that evening, he could not help but pause and look about him at his village.

This was a good land. Here, on the hill overlooking the deep valley of the River Yonne, all he could see was green pasture, trees and verdant plains. It was a wonderful place. Once he had hoped to raise his children here, but all he hoped for now was a life without mishap. He was too old to worry about women. His main interest in life was his wine, of which he was inordinately proud.

He shut his donkey Amé in the stable with a manger full of good hay, and made his way to the house, pouring a cup of wine and diluting it with water from his spring before sitting on his stool. There, he stared at his bed. It held memories for him.

It was a broad bed, made by his own hands. They had conceived their child in that bed, and she had gone into labour in that bed, and she had struggled with the pain and fevers, and gradually she had succumbed and died in that bed. A neighbour had offered to take the bed, but he wouldn't let it go. It was a symbol of his marriage, and he detested the thought of it being used by someone else. He could have burned it, but only a fool would burn a perfectly usable bed which would have to be replaced at some expense later. Better by far to keep using it. And although he was not a particularly spiritual man outside of church, he did sense that keeping the bed in some way kept his Amice by his side.

But there was nothing else in this house that could hold him. It was a shuttered little place, with a cold, unwholesome heart. Gidie had never thought of it before, but now, as he glanced about him, he realised that it was like him: loveless, chill and closed up. He rarely spoke to others, and when he did it was to dicker over the price of transport, or the cost of goods he should carry to market. There was no one he could call a friend here, and he had not possessed a lover since the day of his wife's death. That experience, watching her die, mopping her blood, had killed all lust in him.

What, he wondered, was his life worth? If he were to die tomorrow, who would hold up a scales to his life and pronounce it good or bad? How would he weigh in the balance? God and all his angels could shrug and mutter that he hadn't been a terribly bad man, but who would speak for him? Why would anyone speak for him?

Gidie stared about the room again, and as he did, his eyes fixed on the cross over the bed. For some it was the sign of salvation and hope. For him it was only a reminder of his faithlessness and God's punishment. God had punished him by taking Amice from him. His soul was blackened.

The words of the preacher came back to him. What if he too could be forgiven?

Sens, Thursday 27th March

It was three days later that Fulk met his brother again.

He walked into the tavern, ducking under the low lintel, and peered about the smoky chamber. The two brothers met here often. It was not far for either of them, and what the wine lacked in quality it made up for in price. Inside there were benches set out at the walls, and old casks served as tables. It was full of men already, and it was hard to see the far side of the chamber because of the press and the smoke.

Fulk saw him.

Odo was on a bench at the far wall, further away from the fire roaring in the middle of the room, and Fulk pushed through the crowds. Seeing a maid dispensing drinks near the fire, he asked for a large cup of mulled cider from her pot. He sniffed his drink, smelling sweetness from the honey and spices that had been thrown in, and his mouth watered at the odour. With a broad grin on his face, he made his way across the room to Odo, trying to sneak around to his side without being spotted, but as he approached Odo turned at the last moment. 'You're late.'

'God save you, brother. I hope I find you well?'

'God give you a good day,' Odo responded. He looked Fulk up and down. 'You look well, brother.'

Fulk shrugged and grinned. 'I have been fortunate. God has shone his face on me! I've found extra work, and I have been promised more money if I complete it all on time.'

'No wonder you look smug,' Odo observed. He knew his brother was always desperate to earn more. Fulk's master was notoriously tight-fisted. 'How did you manage that?'

'Me?' Fulk said innocently, sitting upright and trying to look hurt, like an abbess accused of theft.

'Your smith would rather have his teeth pulled than pay you an extra *denier*,' Odo said.

'I am worth every sou he pays me,' Fulk said.

'He does no work himself, so he should appreciate you, if you are to be believed,' Odo said.

Fulk joined his brother on the bench. 'The whole kingdom is in an uproar. It seems almost everyone is to join Peter the Hermit's pilgrimage. Many of them are demanding weapons, and my master cannot be bothered to make them, so I have asked at another smith's forge, and he'll pay me plenty to make arrowheads, swords and long knives. That hermit could not have come at a better time.'

'I am glad for you.'

Fulk looked about him in the room. The tavern was filling with raucous men with cloth crosses stitched to their breasts. 'Look at them,' he said. 'The fools are celebrating the fact that they are going to risk their lives! They have no idea what they will face while they are on their way, what hazards they will meet, what weather, what dangers from enemies and wild animals!'

'No. They must be fools,' Odo agreed. A faint glower puckered his brows.

'They will probably half of them never come back,' Fulk said. He thought of that: never have to wake early to light the fire; never be told what time to be back in his miserable, hard, cold palliasse; shivering at night, rather than staying out with friends at an inn where the wine flowed like liquid sunshine, and the women smiled on him. 'They must be fools,' he added, but less convinced.

'They march to the Holy Land, which is to be praised. They have the conviction and determination. God will honour them.'

'I have no doubt He will.' Fulk saw a woman who was glancing about the chamber with a speculative look in her eye. 'Meanwhile, there are many women who will need comforting when their menfolk are gone. We will be lucky!'

Odo gave him a cold look. 'You would try to ravish their women while they march away to war? That would be a callous, disgraceful act.'

'It would be a kindness! Think of those poor women, deserted, desperate, keen to find a little solace in a cruel, lonely world,' Fulk said virtuously.

'You are a man with no soul,' Odo said. He was frowning.

'Me? I am just a man trying to support those who will be left behind,' Fulk said lightly, but then he gave his brother a serious nod. 'And some will need support, Odo. Think of those who will die on the journey, or who will die in the wars out in the Holy Land. Their wives and loved ones will not hear of many of their deaths. Some may never know what happened to their men, but will remain here, growing older and more frail, wondering always whether their men have died, where they might be buried, or whether they simply deserted their families, and remain in some foreign city.'

Odo shook his head. 'That is no excuse for you taking advantage.'

'You will too, when you see the young women throwing themselves at you. Even you won't be able to refuse them a little comfort in their sadness.'

'I would certainly refuse them.'

'You think so? I'll bet you will change your mind when the first wench pleads with you, clinging to your sleeve and begging for the solace of your company. Although, to be fair, she needs must be entirely desperate to seek comfort from you!'

'I would not. I will not be able,' Odo said, more quietly. He was staring into his drink like a man suspecting poison.

'What, you think you would be able to maintain your hard, firm exterior? As soon as a little maid like that blonde one over there started pleading with you with tears of frustrated lust in her eyes, your heart will melt!'

Odo look at him with exasperation. 'I will not, no, because I will not be here.'

'Why? What does that mean?'

'Fulk, open your ears! *I won't be here!* Listen: the world is changing. There are people out there who need our help to defend them and the Holy Land. This could be the time for all Christians to come to the help of Jerusalem. Perhaps it will be the end of time. Maybe the—'

'Odo!' Fulk's face had become a mask of shock. 'Don't say that you have taken up the cross?'

With a shamefaced smile, Odo reached into his purse and pulled out a large cloth cross.

Fulk winced at the sight. 'You can't! Look at you, you don't even own a decent knife, let alone a sword. You don't know how to hold a weapon or fight. You've spent your life making bread!'

'God will give us the strength we need. He will guard us on the march, and He will protect us in our battles.'

'If we stay behind, we can help to look after the town! With all these men leaving, there will be a need for men with brains and intelligence. We could make a fortune here, Odo! I could make money enough to start my own forge; you could buy a shop in Cook's Row, or a bakery of your own! Don't throw it away to go on a fool's errand!'

'Fulk, my mind is made up. I have already told my master.'

Interest broke Fulk's tirade. 'How did he take it?'

Odo winced. 'Not well. He threatened me with a peel.'

Fulk grinned. 'I hope there was no bread on it at the time!'

'It is decided. I shall go.'

Fulk frowned. 'You are mad. Worse, you are a fool. Going all that way, on the word of a hermit you've never seen before.'

'He spoke the word of God.'

Fulk pulled a face. He looked like a man who had bitten into a sloe berry. 'Well, there's only one thing for it.'

'What?'

'I'll have to go with you. It would be impossible to leave you all alone for such a long journey. You would get yourself into trouble trying to cross the market without me to help you.

Besides, I'm the one who can fight. No one would accuse you of being the one to get into scrapes. That has always been my forte.'

Odo shook his head irritably. 'There are lots of things you have not considered.'

'I will soon pack and be prepared.'

'You? I remember that time when you planned to meet a maid, and forgot you had already agreed to meet another at the same place.'

Fulk winced. The ensuing battle was still painful to recall. 'Aye, well, that was embarrassing, but—'

'And the time your master left you in charge of his business for a day, and you drank all his strong ale and wine, and he found you hog-drunk in the—'

'I confess, that was a mistake.'

'Mistake? It all but cost you your apprenticeship.'

'Yes, well, even apprentices have their foibles.'

'I will have your life on my conscience. I am glad to be responsible for myself, but not you too, Fulk.' Odo shook his head grimly and finished his cider.

'I am responsible for myself. Now, buy more drink. I'm coming too.'

'Are you sure?' Odo asked, his eyes searching Fulk's face.

'Yes.' Fulk finished his drink and held out his empty cup. 'Come, let's drink to our journey! It will be an adventure. And you're so determined to protect the women of this town against my lusts, the least you can do is buy me another cup.'

'If you're determined to go, well, I suppose I cannot stop you. It is said that the grand *iter* is to begin on the second Monday after Easter. I suppose that gives us time to settle our affairs.'

'I have to join you. After all, knowing you, you'd wander in the wrong direction entirely,' Fulk said lightly.

'Wait! This is a serious undertaking, Fulk. It is a pilgrimage. If we go, we have to go understanding that we are pursuing God's will. It is no light-hearted jaunt. You must be sober, and no fornicating on the way.' His eyes glazed over as he seemed to stare into an uncertain future. 'We must be aware of the serious nature of the task before us.'

Fulk glanced at the crush of people near the bar. The woman he had seen earlier had disappeared. He was sad for a moment.

'Odo, you could make even a feast taste sour! Cheer up, brother, and buy me more drink. I think I will need it, having agreed to this.'

Sens, Thursday 3rd April

Jeanne pressed the latch on the door nervously. The latch was wood, and stuck, and when she forced it, there was a loud click. She warily pushed at the door, peering around it into the room beyond. It was dark, and she was struck with the idea of stepping into Hell itself. The door with its leather hinges was a gaping maw, and she shivered involuntarily.

She had not brought Christoph. He had been busy removing a drunk when she set off, and she didn't wait in case her courage dissipated. Instead she had come here alone, and she was regretting that now as night drew in. She felt terribly vulnerable standing here, on the threshold of her home.

Stepping inside, she was about to cross the room when she heard a sound and froze. It was the noise of a stool scraping on the packed earth of the floor.

'You thought you'd find me gone, you bitch, didn't you?' he said as he swung his fist.

In the dark Edmond's blow was misplaced, but while it glanced off her jaw, she felt her teeth crash together. Blood filled her mouth while lights flashed and sparked in front of her, and she fell to the floor like a corpse. She had no sensation in her legs or arms, only an all-consuming pain at her mouth and skull that seemed to envelop her head.

'You've been living at the brothel for the last few days, you bitch! You didn't think of me, did you? You want to leave me, *wife*, is that it?' he said, and now he was closer.

She could see his boots, and saw one draw back, but couldn't speak to complain or plead. Instinctively she tried to retreat from him, for she knew what was coming, but her body would not respond, and the kick caught her right breast. She gave a harsh grunt from deep in her throat. The agony was so intense, she was reduced to hacking sobs, curling like a child while tears flooded her eyes. She was aware of his kneeling beside her, and she could smell his breath, sweet and sickly like the wine he had been drinking, and then she saw something shining with a sickly grey gleam in the dark, and she whimpered. The sight of his knife was enough to spark energy in her muscles, and she tried to push herself away. She scrabbled with her hands, trying to get purchase, but he caught her tunic at the neckline and gripped it hard, pulling her towards him, lifting her to her feet.

'If you try to escape me,' he said, bringing his knife's blade up and resting it on her nose, 'I'll mark you so that no man will ever want you again. I'll cut off your nose, your ears, your lips, and no man will even look at you, let alone pay for you. Look at you! A *slut*! A *whore*! You're lucky I keep you in my house. But from now on, you'll do what I say, and just now, I say you'll service my friends. You owe me, *bitch*! You're my wife, and you'll do as I say!'

He thrust her away, and when her head hit the wall, it was mercifully enough to make her lose consciousness, but not for long enough.

When she woke, her nightmare really began.

CHAPTER 3

South Tawton, Thursday 3rd April, 1096

Roger de Toni rode through the vill at the head of the seven horsemen, his father at his side, and stared down at the peasants labouring in the filth in the fields. A young man in his early twenties, he was still new to the land here. His hair was the dark brown of his people, his eyes a pale grey, the same as his mother's. His build was much like his father's, and typical of a warrior who had trained with sword, shield and lance since the age of six. His shoulders were broad and strong, his belly narrow, his right arm powerful as befitted the son of a knight, and he rode like the messenger of death and war that he was.

'Look at them! They hate us,' his father said.

Roger glanced at the villeins without interest. One or two dared to meet his gaze, but for the most part men, women and children looked away. Cowed, pathetic, these folk were inconsequential. 'What of it?'

'Always be aware. These people still dream of removing us.

They were beaten less than a generation ago, and it would take little for them to rise up again.'

'And be cut down again. Really, they are cattle to be herded.'

'Cattle? Have you never seen an angry bull?'

Sir Radulph used a sharp tone as he spoke. 'Do not mistake our position here. These fools may be ignorant but there are many of them. If they wished, they could kill us all.'

'What of you, father? Do you hate them in your turn?'

'Me? What would be the point? It would be like hating the sheep in my flocks, or the cattle in my herds. They are not worth hatred.'

'No,' Roger agreed. He did not hate the people here either: he despised them. They were weakly, pathetic. Once they had been a proud nation, but since the glorious campaigns of King William they were destroyed and only of use as workers.

'You dislike this land, don't you?' his father said.

'There is nothing to like,' Roger said. 'Look at it! It is green, yes, but only because it rains every day. There is little sun or warmth such as I knew at home in Normandy.'

'Your brother will take Conches-en-Ouche,' Radulph said. 'The castle there is the family's, and we have to keep that as the centre of our family's authority. But, given time, this little collection of hamlets will become equally as valuable, I swear. The land is rich and fertile, you have good woodland, and you have power.'

'This is a border territory. The men of Cornwall seek to foment trouble at all times. We will have to fight them to keep their unrest stilled,' Roger said.

'Then do so. Show them the iron fist,' Radulph said. He turned to his son. 'This land was taken by me and I will not cede it. If the people need to be beaten into acceptance of my rule, they will be. You must control them as you would a rache: a hunting dog is not subdued by kindness; it is brought to obedience by the club and the whip. The people here are no different. You will have to use all means to keep them controlled. Do so.'

'I would prefer to remain in Conches,' Roger said. 'I want warmth. This cold, miserable land is draining to a man with ambition, and I have plenty. I don't want to be stuck here like a hazel twig planted in this damp soil.'

'What would you do, then?'

They had reached the little wooden fort that was their home. In defence against outlaws and brigands the gates were routinely kept locked. A loud bellow at the porter soon had the men scrabbling to unbar the gates and, with a graunching of iron, they were opened. Sir Radulph led the way into the castle's court, the donjon on its small hill before them.

The men dismounted with a clattering of steel and Roger followed his father up the hillock to the hall.

To Roger's surprise the local priest was waiting for them.

'There is urgent news, my lord,' he said to Sir Radulph.

'Speak!'

The priest bent his head in a deep bow. The knight demanded proofs of respect from those who lived on his lands, as much from priests as from villeins. While his father gruffly welcomed their guest, Roger de Toni moved to the cupboard and jerked his head to the steward for a cup of wine, almost draining it as the steward took a second to his father. It was rude to drain his own first, but Roger was thirsty and out of sorts. This wooden hall was cold, and although the peasants had filled the gaps in the walls with daub, still the wind howled through. The flames in the middle of the floor moved, the smoke gusting and dancing with every breeze outside.

What he wouldn't do to escape this foul, chill island.

The first thing he would do when he owned this fortress at the extreme of civilisation would be to build a stone castle. Not to protect from enemies, but from the wind. These walls offered no more protection from gales than a mail shirt.

'I have a message, my lord,' the priest said. He was an elderly man and spoke haltingly in the presence of his Norman overlord, for Radulph's short temper and violence were well known in the parish. 'It is from your cousin, Stephen, my lord. He asks you to join him.'

'Me?' Radulph stared frowningly. 'What is this? Join him why?'

'The Pope has declared a great expedition, a journey to the Holy Land to liberate the poor Christians of that land from the cruel Saracen oppressors who treat them like stones to be crushed underfoot,' the priest said.

'Well? What of it?'

'Your cousin has decided to join in this great pilgrimage, and he will join the Pope's forces. He asks, will you join him with your feudal host, to help take Jerusalem from these Saracens, and bring the city back into the light of God's grace.'

The knight drained his cup and held it out to be refilled. 'Read it.'

The priest began from the top with the lengthy, polite salutation, but Radulph grumpily gesticulated with a hand, waving it around and around until the priest skimmed over the rest and got to the meat of the message.

'This he says: he is collecting a force to fight under his banner. He will leave at Easter, and proposes to meet with you and others at Rome. From there, he will take the road to the coast and take ship and make his way to Constantinople, and thence pass into Anatolia, and by stages march to the Holy Land and Jerusalem as the good Pope has asked.'

'To the Holy Land?' Radulph shook his head, and then walked to his great seat on the dais and dropped into it. He cast an eye about the whitewashed walls of his hall, at the tapestry of which he was so proud, and which was succumbing to the weather, at the small collection of plates on his sideboard and the tables against the walls. 'It is many leagues to Rome,' he said pensively. 'A great many. I knew a man who took up the pilgrim's garb, and he said he reached Rome, but that it was still further to the Holy Land. He never made it.'

'Father! Let's go! It will do me good to travel, just as we were saying. This would give me the opportunity to travel while doing God's work. It is the perfect opportunity. Let's go together and take our swords to recapture the Holy Land!'

Radulph smiled down at his son with a slight perplexity on his face. 'Roger, you have little understanding of what you suggest. You have no idea of the distances involved, and still less of joining in a host such as this must be. It is a hazardous thing, to travel so far. Better if—'

'This is God's own work!' Roger said.

'And holding our lands here is *our* work!' Radulph snapped. 'If I go off seeking out Saracens to slay, there may be no castle here on my return. Do you want to have to win back our lands from the peasants just because we took time to journey all the way to the Holy Land?'

'If you won't go, at least allow me! Let me take a small force, perhaps ten men-at-arms, and I will go and win renown for you. I swear, I will come back with glory!'

Radulph eyed him doubtfully, then threw a look at the priest. 'What do you say, priest? Should my son go in my place? Do you think him old enough to command?'

'I have known your son only a brief time, my lord,' the priest said carefully. 'He is a most competent warrior, I am sure, but does he have the skills to weld men to his ambitions? A commander who cannot command is a poor thing in battle.'

'You say? Aye, I daresay you were a priest with the men who went to stand against King William when he stormed the beaches. Well, this is a cause in which it will be easy to keep the men together. There is only one purpose, the greater glory of God, and by the cross of my sword, I am sure that he will acquit himself bravely. Perhaps you should go with him, if you think that he would benefit from your counsel?'

'Me?' The old man looked shocked.

'I jest, old man. You would scarcely make it to the coast, let alone across the Channel. But if my son is to go, he will need to have good counsel if he is to make it to Rome. I will send a good man with you, Roger. A man who has skill and knowledge. Someone who can guard you and guide you. You are too hot-headed on occasion, and you fret when you do not get your own way. This journey will cure you of that, I hope. But before you leave, you will be knighted. I will not have a son of mine depart for Jerusalem without being given his rank.'

Roger bowed to his father. There was a thrilling in his blood: he would be knighted! A warrior in his own right at last! And then away from this boring, wet landscape, off to find excitement and adventure!

His father eyed him sourly. 'You will return here with a fresh outlook on the world, and perhaps the size of your position in it.'

Sens, Friday 4th April

Guillemette was pulling on her chemise again as her latest client walked from the room. Last evening she had been kept busy until the early hours, and she had remained in her bed till late this morning, until the first client arrived at almost noon. Now it was time for food, her belly was telling her.

She had a cup beside her cot, and she filled it from the jug of wine she kept handy. Some days, it was the wine that kept her sane. The older, rougher men who came in stinking like ferrets, with hands as coarse as unsmoothed floorboards, were enough to drive any woman to wine, she thought. She was considering a second cup when the door opened, and she saw Jeanne.

'Hello, Jeanne, I . . . God's mercy, what happened?'

Jeanne walked in unsteadily. Her face was bruised and scratched. There were tooth marks on her throat, and she shook like a fine birch in a gale.

'Jeanne, come in and sit down,' Guillemette said, pushing aside the dirtier sheets. Guillemette sat on the edge of the cot and patted the mattress beside her. When Jeanne sat, Guillemette put her arm about the slim shoulders. 'What happened? Were you attacked?'

'My . . . my husband did this. He slapped and beat me, and kicked me when I was on the floor, and he made me . . . he made me lie with his friends . . . he shared me with them like a barrel of ale,' Jeanne said. Her voice was low and calm, even as her body shuddered.

'He sold you to them?' Guillemette said coldly.

'I went home to fetch some clothes, but he was waiting, and he . . . he did this.'

Guillemette felt her chest constrict with rage. It was almost difficult to breathe, she was so angry. 'You wait here,' she said, and hurried from the room to fetch Emersende. She was soon back, with the madam of the brothel and Christoph.

'Look at her!' Guillemette said, flinging a hand at Jeanne. 'You can see what he's done to her.'

'What happened, Jeanne?'

Jeanne, her eyes downcast, spoke haltingly about her return to her home, how Edmond had grabbed her and beat her, and then passed her to his friends. 'They all took me,' she said, 'and then Edmond grabbed their money and left me there.'

'He swore to me that he would not misuse you,' Emersende said. 'I cannot believe that he did this to you.'

Guillemette nodded. 'To do this to her, it's shameful.'

'I'm surprised you went back against my advice,' Emersende said. 'You did say you would stay here.'

Guillemette, listening while she tried to calm Jeanne, heard a new note in her voice. She turned to peer up at the madam.

'I had to fetch a fresh chemise and . . .' Jeanne whispered.

Emersende shook her head with finality. There was no cruelty in her face, only a cool disinterest, like a woman deciding not to buy when a vendor would not drop his price to accommodate her. 'Well, clearly I cannot use you like this,' Emersende said. 'You must go home again, and don't come back until the worst of your injuries are healed.'

'Wait!' Guillemette said. 'But surely you don't mean to desert her? Emersende, she needs help, a place to stay where she will be safe—'

'I am not here to provide alms for women with bad husbands,' Emersende said with finality. 'If her husband is to do this to her, she's no use to me. If he wants to make money from her without my help, then he can have her back. It will be an expensive mistake on his part.'

'You won't help her?'

'Don't be foolish, Guillemette,' Emersende said. 'Now get back to work. There must be a desperate man out there somewhere. Go and find him. Christoph, send her home.'

She withdrew from the room humming a tune, and as if for the first time Guillemette saw her as she really was. Although she could put on a kindly act when it suited her, she was yet a businesswoman. Her interest lay only in how much money she could win from her clients, and that meant the value of her stable of women.

Guillemette stopped Christoph. Jeanne looked as though she could not fully comprehend Emersende's dismissal. She was stunned, and barely aware of her friend even when Guillemette took her hands in her own. 'Jeanne, did you fetch your things from your house?'

'No.'

'Is there anything you need there? Really need?'

'No ... Guillemette, I don't want to go back there. I can't! I can't live with him any more.'

'You won't, Jeanne,' Guillemette promised. 'You'll never have to go back.'

BOOK TWO

The Grand Pilgrimage

CHAPTER 4

Sens, Friday 4th April, 1096

Guillemette hefted the pack over her shoulder as the two trudged eastwards. She was sorry to be leaving Sens, for the town had been good to her over the years, but that could not change her feelings towards Emersende. Her casual dismissal of Jeanne at the time Jeanne needed her help most had shocked Guillemette. Emersende owed Jeanne protection. That was the job of the madam of the house, to protect her girls.

'You didn't have to come with me,' Jeanne said.

'Don't flatter yourself,' Guillemette said. 'It wasn't only for you. I couldn't trust her again, if she could throw you back to Edmond after this.'

Jeanne sobbed quietly and Guillemette threw an arm over her shoulder. 'Come, now! We can find another brothel. With my skills and your looks,' she added, throwing a doubtful look at the bruised and battered face beside her, 'we shall surely find work soon.'

They had been walking for hours, and the roadway was hard on Guillemette's feet. The soles of her shoes were thin, designed for walking about town rather than heavy work. Jeanne was very quiet, and Guillemette continued prattling – in part to keep her friend's spirits up, but also to buoy her own. For all her cheering comments, she knew it would be difficult to find a safe berth. Most brothels were tough, difficult environments. Finding a place run by an accommodating madam was not easy. All too often they were controlled by brutish men who had no more interest in their women than a farmer for his cattle. Whores were there to bring in money, and as soon as they ceased to do so, their livelihood could be taken away from them. Still, she had heard that there was a place in Troyes, two days' walk to the east, and she would bend her way there in the hope that she and Jeanne could be secure.

'You're safe now,' she said.

Jeanne sniffled and nodded. 'I couldn't go back to him,' she said. She was limping a little, and not only from the rapes. Guillemette would have to take a look at her back and flanks and see the bruising. She wondered whether Jeanne's injuries could be worse than she let on.

'Of course not. You won't have to. We'll find another home, don't worry.'

They had encountered a few men and women on their way, but now they found a thick straggle of people overtaking them, all cheerful and excited as they marched. At their head was a preacher who strode along like a bailiff in search of a peasant's tax. He turned and peered at them, noting their dress and comportment. 'Are you joining with us?'

Guillemette glanced at the people behind him. 'Where are you going?'

'Have you not heard Peter the Hermit? He has spoken to us, and we obey his call to go to Jerusalem and liberate the people there.'

'Yes, we heard him,' Guillemette said.

'Your friend. Has she been attacked?'

'Yes.'

'A brigand? Or . . .'

'Her husband. He beat her like a dog, and then did the worst thing a man could do to his wife.'

The man gave a nod of polite incomprehension, and smiled. His look irritated Guillemette, as though the injuries to a woman like Jeanne were not deserving of sympathy. She said, 'He sold her to his friends. They took their sport with her.'

At that, the preacher gasped, visibly shocked. It was more satisfying to Guillemette than his earlier complacency. He shook his head and made the sign of the cross over her. 'That is appalling. A disgrace! Madame, did you not inform your priest? Your husband should be punished for such an act! I am sorry to hear of your victimisation.'

'I live, Father,' Jeanne said. Her head was downcast.

Guillemette was glad to see how the priest was affected. He shook his head. 'He should be made to realise his failings. Where is he?'

The man was gazing about as though expecting to see Edmond in the trees nearby.

'He is back at their home,' Guillemette said.

'You have left him?'

'Yes! I have left him,' Jeanne cried, and there was a fractured note in her voice, as though her very sanity was threatened.

Guillemette heard the break and put her arm about her again, just as the tears began once more. 'We will walk with you a way, if you don't mind, Father,' she said.

'You can stay with us for as long as you wish, child. Even if you wish to walk with us all the way to Jerusalem itself.'

'The Holy City?' Jeanne said. 'God would not want such as us to go there.'

'For your sins?' the man said, and smiled. 'We are all sinners, child, but if you go to Jerusalem you will find your offences washed away. You will be innocent once more, like a newborn babe. The Pope has promised it. We are a part of his army, marching under the banner of Peter the Hermit, God bless him!'

'God wouldn't want us,' Jeanne said sadly.

Cerisiers, Saturday 5th April

Gidie pulled at the reins of Amé. His donkey stared back truculently. Gidie considered using his birch to beat the recalcitrant beast, but he knew from experience that the creature would grow more stubborn if he did. He should have reached home by now, and be sitting down with a cup of ale. Instead he was here, stuck on a grassy roadway at least two leagues from his cottage.

He slumped to the ground and stared resentfully up at the beast. 'Well, Amé? What do we do now? Wait here until the Day of Judgement?'

The beast shook her head free of flies and settled to cropping the grass of the verge. Gidie gave a 'Tchah!' of disgust, flung the reins away from him and leaned back against the grassy bank. 'I'll sell you to the tanners, you useless old devil,' he muttered.

He was still there a few moments later when a man appeared in the distance. There was a small party of men and some women following on behind him, and Gidie peered at them, but he knew none of them. He had never visited the brothel where Guillemette and Jeanne worked. The man in front walked barefoot, and wore the melancholy demeanour that marked him as a religious man.

Seeing Gidie, he smiled. 'Are you well, my friend?'

'I would be happier if this brute would move.'

The preacher looked at Amé and patted her head. For a moment Gidie thought she would bite his hand, but then she lowered her head as the man scratched her between her eyes and behind her ears. 'She is a handsome animal. We have need of such as her. And you.'

'Who are you?' Gidie said, but he could make a guess.

'We are pilgrims. We go to free the people of Jerusalem,' the preacher said, and launched into a well-rehearsed peroration about the benefits of the pilgrimage. 'Have you not considered joining us?'

'Jerusalem?' Gidie said scornfully. 'I can't walk that far.'

'God will give you strength. It is His desire that we should all go to Jerusalem and free our poor brothers and sisters in Christ.'

This was God tormenting him. Gidie shook his head. 'I am not the sort of man God would want.'

'My son, He wants all those who are prepared to make the journey. The Pope himself called for all those who could go to join in. We need all the Christians we can find.'

Gidie shook his head. The preacher could argue all he wanted, but the man would not want his company, if he were to learn more about Gidie and his offences. They were sins; he knew that, but he could not regret them, no matter what.

The preacher shook his head sadly and made the sign of the cross over him, before setting off along the road. Gidie was about to haul on the reins when Amé began to follow the pilgrims.

'You see, my friend?' the preacher called with delight. 'God has shown you He wants you and your beast to join us.'

'Amé won't want to walk all that way,' Gidie said. 'But I am glad that our path goes with yours for a way.'

But when they reached the parting of their ways, Amé refused to take the road homewards, and instead pulled Gidie on behind the preacher.

The sun was already low in the sky, and at this rate Gidie would not reach home until dark. Seeing his distress, the preacher called a general halt and walked back to Gidie.

'My friend, you are disconsolate. Tell me, do you have a wife who will miss you?'

'No, but I—'

'You said that you are not the sort of man God would want to go to Jerusalem. Would you like to share your crime with me?'

Gidie's face darkened. 'What makes you think I've—'

'Why else would you think yourself unfit?'

Gidie looked down. 'I know I'm unfit. If you must know, and want me to divulge my crime, you have to swear to hold my confession in confidence.'

'I so swear.'

'Very well. You must know, then, that I was once in the priesthood. I was given a chapel in a small village, and I was content.' Gidie could remember those happy times now in his mind's eye: tending his small garden; speaking with his little flock in the tavern or at the church's gate; fresh births and baptisms; young brides so bright and optimistic, grooms the worse for the cider or wines they had drunk; funeral services with sad-eyed men and women comforted by his words. The annual round of ploughing, planting and harvesting, each important, purposeful tasks that lent meaning to the life of the village.

But it was Amice who made his life worth living. Amice, his wife, his lover – his sin. Gidie could not find the words to unburden himself.

'I left my chapel. That is all you need to know.'

'In Jerusalem you will find peace. God promises you eternal life, the remission of all your sins, if you only do this one thing for him.'

Gidie looked at him. The certainty in his voice rang firm

and true, like the honest truth of a cathedral bell. Perhaps the man was right. Gidie had nothing to hold him here now. Perhaps . . .

Troyes, Monday 7th April

'Do you think he could be right?' Jeanne said.

They had been with the pilgrims for three days now, and at last the city of Troyes was before them. Every so often, through the trees lining the roadway, the dark smudge of a city's smoke appeared in the sky. It was all Guillemette cared about, this idea of a city. It held the promise of wine, a river to soak her feet, a fire before which to rest her aches and pains.

As they walked, the pilgrims accreted more and more people. It was like fine droplets of water on a metal bowl. First there were many tiny ones, but these gradually touched others and grew and grew, until there was a smaller number of large drops, and these joined until there was a single great pool.

Men and women heard of the approach of the pilgrims, and came to meet them. As they passed through a village, the preacher would speak and people would join them; as they walked beside a field, workers would drop their tools and become part of the growing column.

Guillemette found that the constant tramping dulled her senses. She was moving along with a roll in the hips like an ancient peasant, her eyes fixed on the distant bend in the road. It would be only another few paces to that corner, she was thinking, and then there will be another straight section of roadway to the next corner, and then another . . .

She grew aware that Jeanne was speaking and listened, but without comment.

'Perhaps Edmond was right to think I should go back to him. He was always so loving to me in the beginning.'

Guillemette had heard it all before. Jeanne had told her soon after arriving that her husband had been a kind, generous man until the day they needed money and he suggested that she offer herself to others for money. At first, Jeanne thought he was joking, she said, but then he began his persuasion with his fists and she learned swiftly that there was nothing humorous in his proposal. It was a story that Guillemette had heard before, not only from Jeanne, but from other women trapped in marriages with men who were more keen on ensuring the steady flow of wine to their mouths than the wellbeing of the women they had married. All too many of her friends had told the same story.

It reminded Guillemette how lucky she was. She had been married, once, and would never submit to a man again. He had been another Edmond, just as vicious. Paul had enjoyed hitting Guillemette whenever he was drunk. So one day, Guillemette had done what she should have done long before. She took a knife, and now Paul would never hit another woman again and Guillemette was free. She could enjoy what remained of her life.

'I shouldn't be here,' Jeanne mumbled. 'I should be with my husband.'

This was the first stage. Guillemette had seen so many women in the brothels of Sens and she recognised the signs. 'Jeanne, don't.'

'Don't what?'

Guillemette pulled her from the column of pilgrims and dropped her bag. She put her hands on Jeanne's shoulders and stared into her eyes. 'You can't go back, Jeanne. You're feeling miserable and scared because you've left everything behind, but it will get better. If you go back, he will beat you again, and he'll sell you to his friends again, and he'll keep you for as long as you can win him money, but as soon as you're too old, or too scarred from his beatings, he'll beat you one last time, and that time you won't get up again.'

'But I don't know where I'll go,' Jeanne whispered.

'Nor do I, Jeanne. But wherever we go, it's better than going *back*. I know. I've been in the same position as you, I know what it's like. Everything ahead is scary, whereas if you turn around and go back to him, at least you know what you're in for. But you can't. If you go back, you'll get the biggest beating of your life, and he may kill you, if he's drunk. I know the road ahead looks terrifying, but the road behind you is worse.'

Jeanne nodded. 'But what will become of me?'

'I will look after you,' Guillemette said. 'I swear it.'

They were still there when Gidie passed by. The tranter paused, and then pulled the reluctant Amé over to them. 'Ladies, you look exhausted,' he said. 'Please, ride my donkey. At least one at a time can be rested. Amé is not the most comfortable beast, but she is better than wearing out your feet for no purpose.'

Gidie was not a young man, but the smile Guillemette gave him made him feel twenty again. He knew he would remember her smile all the rest of his days.

East of Sens

Fulk and Odo were at last on the road, Fulk striding along with his small bag, a rolled-up blanket over his shoulder and a long staff in his hand. He whistled as he walked, ignoring Odo's grumbles that the sharp noise was enough to make a man beg for a knife to end his sorrows. Odo had a few belongings thrown into a small sack, which he had bound to his own stick and dangled over his shoulder.

They were not alone. Departing Sens that day, and following down the river, there were many men, as well as several women and children, for not all had deserted their families. There were tears and wails enough as the cavalcade set off, with women standing in the roads and waving, others clinging to their menfolk and giving piteous cries. Fulk saw one neighbour taking leave of his wife while she gripped the doorframe, desperately exhorting him to stay. Her mother was with her, hands on her shoulders, and her three children clutched her skirts as they watched him stride away. Excited and eager to take part in the venture, he looked like a youth on his first hunt; his wife looked as though she knew she would never see him again. Even if he were to return, there was no knowing how long it would be before he could put his feet up before his fire again, and in the meantime she would have to work every hour to ensure that their children were fed.

She was not the only woman in distress. Up and down the streets there was the sound of sobbing or wailing. To travel so far would often mean death in a faraway land, and the womenfolk knew it.

Now Fulk gazed at the others on the road. 'There're not many warriors,' he commented.

Odo gave an emphatic shrug. 'What of it? Most of the people here are strong in their belief, and with that and God's grace, we will crush any foe that dares stand before us.'

'The Saracens are said to be mighty warriors,' Fulk said.

'So now you grow fearful of battle?' Odo laughed. 'Brother, you are inconsistent at the best of times! Be bold, be courageous, and believe in yourself and these others all about you. This is a great pilgrimage! Look around! With so many, how can we fail?'

'Brother, I look and see too few fighting men. I don't deny that the Hermit's a good orator, but there's not one knight or man-at-arms here. How many bear swords?'

'The Lord will provide all that we need.'

Fulk nodded. 'Yes, Odo, I believe He will. But He'd not object to our saving Him some effort. At the next city we'll buy ourselves swords at the very least.'

'What, and carry them all the way to the Holy Land?'

'Yes. Because if we reach Constantinople without a weapon, and have to buy them just as all the other pilgrims arrive looking for their own blades, we'll find that either we'll have to buy the most expensive cutlery in Christendom or do without. And besides, I would prefer to have a weapon for defence during our walk!'

'I suppose that does make some sense,' Odo admitted reluctantly.

'Look! There's a good armourer, I've heard, who lives in Estissac. It's not more than a day's walk from Sens.'

'Why didn't you think of this before?' Odo grumbled. 'We could have got some good steel from Sens before we left, and made sure that we got the best we could, rather than coming all this way and visiting a smith from the wilds who probably has little better idea of making a blade than I do!'

'I am the apprentice to a smith, remember? All the smiths talk of this man. I did think about our need for some metalwork before we left, Odo, and I decided very soon that the best thing to do was to visit this smith. He knows the best working and the best quenches to make the most robust blades. Trust me. Other pilgrims will waste their money on the garbage made by the smiths in Sens—'

'Your words, brother!'

Fulk gave him a glare before continuing, 'As I was saying, while others will wait till they reach Constantinople, and there they will lose all their money to unscrupulous foreigners who seek only to enrich themselves at the expense of others.

Meanwhile, you and I will have the best metal that money can buy, and at a fraction of the cost.'

Odo scowled at his brother. 'You had best be right, brother of mine, because if you're not, I'll test the strength of the blade by smacking your arse with the flat all the way to Jerusalem.'

CHAPTER 5

Estissac, Tuesday 8th April, 1096

It was afternoon when Odo entered the village with his nose covered by his kerchief against the dust. Along the roadway, the people had spread out, many walking on the soft verges, but here in the village, where men, carts and horses were forced into a narrow funnel, the dry weather meant that the dust rose and filled a man's mouth and nostrils in no time, and his head was aching from heat and thirst.

'Brother, you had best sit and . . .'

Odo snatched his arm away from Fulk's restraining hand. Fulk looked fine, as usual. Not for the first time, Odo felt irritation. His younger brother never suffered like him.

'Do you not know where this master smith lives?' he demanded sourly.

Fulk asked a woman at her door. It was typical, Odo thought, that Fulk's first thought would be to go to a woman. He was too frivolous, too interested in the pleasures of the flesh. He would have to learn to curb his natural desires.

'It's over there,' Fulk said, and led Odo down a side street towards the river. There was a grey building made of old timbers beside the water, and as they drew nearer the noise of hammering came to them. 'See?'

Odo peered around the open door. There was a large space inside. The chamber went on along the river's bank. In the middle stood a stone-walled square forge, with coals glowing red and orange in the middle. A pair of youths, shirtless in the heat, were working two great bellows, pulling for all their worth, while before them was a man with no hair but a thin pepper-and-salt beard, clad in a thick, scarred leather apron. He gripped a bar of steel in a pair of pincers, and as the steel glowed and spat tiny sparks he pulled it from the forge and took it to his anvil, where he began to beat it with a large hammer.

'Enter and state your business, unless you're just here to watch, in which case, piss on you and close the door after you,' the man said conversationally, not looking in their direction.

Odo bridled, but Fulk smiled and strode inside. 'I am apprentice to Master Jean, the smith of Sens, and I am—'

'No apprentice if you're here, unless Master Jean kicked you out for being an idle, churlish fool,' the smith said, his hammer ringing rhythmically. He paused and stared at the metal, nodded to himself, and set it back into the flames. 'So what do you want?'

'We are to join the great march to Jerusalem.'

'Oh, so you want weapons,' the man said, turning his attention back to the steel and turning it in the coals while his two apprentices worked. Sparks began to shoot up from the metal. He limped slightly on his left leg, Fulk saw. 'Wouldn't your master sell you anything half-decent?'

'Every man who knows the quality of steel knows you are the master,' Fulk said ingratiatingly.

'That's true enough,' the smith said. He took the steel back to his anvil and began his hammering once more.

'Well?' Odo asked. 'Do you have something that would suffice to slay the heathens?'

The smith said nothing for a short while. He beat at the glowing metal until it had dulled to a drab blue-grey colour, and then thrust it back into the coals. He spoke while his eyes were fixed on the metal. 'It takes a couple of inches of steel to end a man's life. I could show you how to do that with a breadknife, if you want. But if you want a good blade that will end the life of a Turk with ease, I may have the tools for you.'

Odo was about to speak, but Fulk put a hand on his breast to silence him. He could sense that the smith would not respond to harsh words – more than that, he was sure there was something in the man's mind. He caught a quick glance from the smith, a shrewd, sly, sidelong look that seemed to measure the pair of them.

'Come back at dusk, and I'll consider.'

Dosches, east of Troyes

Guillemette and Jeanne paused in their march when they saw a small wine shop at the side of the road.

'How much further do we have to go?' Jeanne asked.

She was fretful after so many miles, and Guillemette herself was becoming waspish as pebbles dug through the thin soles of her shoes and into her feet. They had entered Troyes full of hope, but their welcome had been as frosty as a mountain's ice. By gradual stages they'd gone from one brothel to another, but none had any interest in a battered young woman or Guillemette. One brothel-keeper looked them up and down and considered he might take the daughter, but not her mother. Guillemette was so shocked and angry, she had turned and stormed from the place.

'Just because Troyes has nowhere for us doesn't mean others won't,' Guillemette said. She quelled the fluttering of fear in her belly. Perhaps she was too old for this life now? 'We will go as far as we must.'

Jeanne sat beside the road and pulled off a shoe. She upended it, tipping out grit. 'I just want to have a stool to sit on. I'm so *tired*!'

'You think I feel any better?' Guillemette snapped. 'I've walked just as far!'

There was a steady stream of people passing by. They had lost the first group as their speed diminished, and Jeanne eyed those marching past now. Some peered back with casual interest, but most were exhausted and trudged on, eyes fixed on the road ahead. Many looked as though they had marched a thousand miles already, while others looked as fresh as men out for a stroll on a Sunday in summer.

A woman in her middle years was walking with a child of ten years or so, and she hesitated, then made her way to them. 'Do you need anything? Are you hurt?' she asked, looking at Jeanne's bruised face.

'We're well enough,' Guillemette said. Jeanne petulantly ignored the woman.

'If you're sure,' the woman said. 'Are you joining the pilgrimage?'

'What, walking all the way to Jerusalem? No! We are on our way to the next town.'

'I'm not. I heard the preacher speaking, and he made me feel more hope than I've felt in all my life.'

'Hope for what?' Jeanne said.

There was a sneer in her voice, but the woman seemed not to notice. 'Why, of everlasting life. What else matters? I used to have a black soul, maid. I was a whore, and I sold my soul for a few pennies and a cup of wine every night, but when I heard the preacher, he changed something inside me. He told me that I could join the journey and wipe my soul clean of all the sinfulness I had gathered. Look at me! The only good thing I ever did was look after this child, my little Esperte here. She was the daughter of a friend of mine in the brothel who died, and I swore I would look after her if I could. But even with her soul in my safekeeping, I was prone to drink too much wine and try to tempt men into bed with me. I know you will find it hard to believe, but I used to be very successful as a courtesan.'

Jeanne pulled off her other shoe, uninterested, but Guillemette urged her to continue. The woman, whose name was Mathena, had a conventional story. Widowed while young, she had drifted into selling her body as a means of supporting herself. As she aged, she had to find another way of surviving, and so she had persuaded the child to pilfer what she could, taking fruit or vegetables from market stall-holders.

'And then I saw the preacher, this man they call the Hermit. And suddenly I saw what I was doing, what I had done. He showed me that I was heading for Hell, and that I was dragging poor Esperte with me. And the preacher said to me, that I could save myself and Esperte, if I would follow him and go to Jerusalem.'

'Why, to fight?' Guillemette asked.

Jeanne gave a sardonic chuckle. 'Or give support to the men who're fighting?'

Mathena was offended. 'Not that kind of support, no. I'll help the injured, nurse the wounded, and give the men all the support I can, but I won't go whoring again. I am on pilgrimage, and God will see me in Heaven for helping His army. I believe that, truly. Peter the Hermit told me.'

Peter the Hermit, Guillemette thought: the scruffy preacher they had seen at Sens. He had said something about rebirth and being renewed, as had the priest they had met on the road. 'Do you really think it's true?'

'The Pope said so. Who would argue with him?'

Jeanne shrugged. She pulled on both shoes and stared at them while she wiggled her toes. The child, Esperte, stood at her side and stared at her shoes moving and giggled.

'Are you going all the way to Jerusalem, then?' Jeanne said to her.

'I'll go with *maman*.'

Jeanne's gaze moved to the people walking past. 'Look at them all. Do they all think they'll erase their sins?' she said wonderingly.

'Of course they do. It's been promised. God wills us to go to Jerusalem and win it back for Him. Everyone who helps will win eternal life,' Mathena said.

Her simple conviction was touching. Guillemette looked down at Jeanne, but found her attention fixing on Esperte instead. She was young, fresh and faultless, and Guillemette found herself wanting to rediscover that sort of innocence. What if it was true, and she could become reborn, as guiltless as a babe? Perhaps she could begin her life over in Christ's own city? It was a wonderful idea.

Guillemette lifted her gaze to the steady stream of people. In their faces was weariness, but yet there was hope and determination. They would reach the Holy City, because all believed in the Hermit. He had given them something to aspire to. He had given them a cause.

'I will join you, Mathena,' she said.

*

Gidie plodded on grumpily. The preacher who had tempted him to join the pilgrimage had appeared several times, and on each occasion looked at Gidie with that questioning smile that said, 'Come, unburden yourself.'

There was no need. Gidie was content. If there was something good at the end of this march, he would be satisfied. He certainly felt no desire to break his silence with this fool of a preacher.

Finally, today, he had enjoyed some peace. The preacher did not appear all day. Then, as the light began to fade, and the people were breaking their march for the evening, Gidie saw the preacher kneeling at the side of the road. The man saw him and beckoned. 'Help me, brother.'

'What is it?' Gidie said, but then his eyes fell to the ground at the preacher's knees. 'Oh.'

There was an old man. He was shivering like a man with the ague, but from the grey-green pallor of his features, it was clear that he would not be around much longer.

'Please, sit with us. It will not be long,' the preacher said. 'I wish there was someone near who could give him the *viaticum* properly.'

Gidie felt the weight of responsibility fall on his shoulders again, an unimaginable weight. 'I can,' he said.

They were there for long enough. The old man had eyes the pale grey of a sky at evening when the clouds are not too heavy: pale and washed out. He could speak only in a whisper as he clung to Gidie's hand, desperate as a sailor clasping a spar in a storm. Gidie gave him what comfort he could, repeating the Paternoster and listening to the old man's confession. And then he remained kneeling at the old man's side. For some reason the old fellow began to weep, and Gidie found himself repeating the words he had said so often to himself in the past days: 'You have tried to get to Jerusalem. You will be honoured. You have a place in Heaven already. Your soul will ascend and you will be greeted by the angels.' There was a sudden intake of breath that seemed to last forever, and a slower sigh of release, and Gidie removed his hand, folding the old man's hands over his breast. He remained there a moment, his hands on top of the dead man's, his eyes closed.

'You were a priest,' the preacher said.

Gidie wanted to rise and turn away, but he couldn't.

The preacher spoke quietly, 'My friend, we many of us have committed grave offences. Yet your words comforted that man because they were true. Did you not feel the balm of God's forgiveness as you spoke them?'

'I cannot,' Gidie said.

'Tell me your tale if you think it would help. You are here, so you are forgiven, but perhaps telling another will help make you feel so?'

Gidie shook his head, but the words came anyway.

'I was happy as a priest,' he said. 'The village was prosperous, and the men worked hard, but I became enamoured of a woman: Amice.'

The name was inadequate. It gave no indication of her fineness, her beauty, the subtle perfection of her smile, the auburn tints in her hair where the sun caught it, nor the heart-stopping brilliance of her smile.

He could remember the first time he saw her. She was seventeen summers then, slim and fine as an ivory wand. He saw her deferential obeisance as she entered the church, and he was impressed with her piety. She moved like an angel: lightly, elegantly, with economy. Not that it mattered to him. He was a priest.

'Her father was the manor's bailie, a man of authority in his middle forties who commanded the respect of all who knew him. I grew to know Amice well. She was keen to learn, and she visited often to speak with me. Hah! She called me her "personal chaplain", as though I held an office of high rank. But I did not object to her teasing, nor her occasional bursts of rage at her father, unseemly though they were. Yet I found her companionship increasingly uncomfortable as the weeks wore on. And then my feelings towards her changed.

'During the Feast of the Innocents I heard she was to be married. Her father had promised her to a wealthy widower twice her age, and Amice was desperately reluctant. She visited me to ask how she might escape her destiny. Not that I could advise her. You know how such affairs are. I could propose that she go to a convent, but a nun should be devoted to God, not escaping from life because of . . . Well, I was duty-bound to advise her to go ahead with the marriage, to respect her father's wishes, and to look to God for sympathy!'

He knew his admonishments would not work. In all conscience, he could not try hard to persuade her. So, as Easter approached, he held a service to witness Amice and her groom making their oaths before God at the church door, and as the delighted wedding group returned to the hall to celebrate, he joined for a while before making his way back to his church. There, he lay on the floor and begged for understanding, because he could not believe that marrying that young woman to a man so vile was in any way a good outcome.

He took to praying for her regularly. Every morning the couple would come to his church for Mass, and he would have to try to ignore what he saw. For her husband was a brute: grossly fat, loud, obscene in manner, and vicious.

'He was the sort of man who would kick a dog and laugh to see it scamper away in pain. In that way, he treated his wife.'

Seeing Amice became torture. Every day she was reduced.

Her face lost colour, and she became drained and weary, like a plant denied daylight. Even as the flowers began to bloom, the contrast between them and her was startling. By the time the trees were putting forth their first leaves, Gidie thought she must wither and die, if nothing was done.

Accordingly, one day when she came alone to church, Gidie drew her aside and spoke gently to her. He spoke with affection, and she smiled thinly. Then she admitted her secret: that she hated her husband; that she would poison him, if she could.

'I knew my duty. I tried to speak to her reasonably, but all the while, my own hatred of her husband and, yes, my jealousy, interrupted me. No matter what I wanted to say, the words clogged in my throat, and I found myself declaring my own love for her.'

To his delight, and horror, she admitted that she felt the same for him.

From that, it was but a short step to escape. He should have wrestled with his conscience, he should have prayed for strength, and he should not have taken another man's wife. All his learning told him that women were dangerous, that ever since Eve they were responsible for all that was wrong and sinful. Yet nothing had prepared him for his feelings for Amice. Any risk was worth the opportunity to spend even a short time with her.

So he threw away his career, his livelihood, and his soul, to live with the woman he loved.

'I see,' the preacher said sadly. 'You took her and ran away?'

'Yes.'

'Where is she?'

Gidie wiped his eyes.

'We were happy. I found a small cottage and worked the land. But her husband discovered us. Fool that he was, he came to take her back, thinking a puny priest like me could not stop him. But

I could not bear the thought of life without her; the idea drove me to distraction and violence.'

He barely remembered grasping the haft of an axe, nor the mad rush into the cottage, but he did recall Amice's white, terrified face, and the blood that curdled on the floor about her husband's shattered head.

'So, not only am I the reason Amice became an adulteress, not only am I a renegade priest, I am guilty of murder as well.' Gidie wiped his eyes again and turned to the preacher. 'So do you still think me suitable for your pilgrimage? I am a moral and social leper. None should want to be near me. God Himself punished me by taking Amice from me in childbirth. He knows how valueless is my soul.'

'Then rejoice! All those who join with the pilgrimage will find eternal life. Your sins will be forgiven, Gidie; all your past offences will be forgotten and you will be as a child. You will be renewed! Come with us and find everlasting life, just as this poor fellow here has.'

Gidie found himself sobbing. He was so desperate to believe the preacher was right.

Estissac

The brothers were back at the smith's as the light was beginning to go down behind the trees of the forest to the west.

'Come!' the smith bellowed when Fulk knocked tentatively on the timbers of the doorway.

'You want some ale?' the smith said, seated on his anvil, his left leg stretched straight before him, and raised a large jug in his blackened hand. His skin looked as though a carpenter's adze would be blunted by an attempt to hack through it, Fulk thought.

'I'd be grateful for a cup,' he said. Odo made no comment, but ducked his head in acquiescence as he took his seat on the besooted wall of the forge.

When the three had brimming cups, the smith raised his in a toast. 'To your grand journey.'

They all drained their cups and poured more ale. Now the smith cocked an eye at Fulk. 'So, boy, you want a good sword to attack the Turks?'

Odo leaned forward. 'We had not thought to buy weapons yet, for we have many miles to go before we reach our destination, but it does make sense to purchase what we need before we reach a place where the pilgrims before us have bought all the stocks.'

'You wouldn't want to go to the city without a weapon, would you?' the smith said. 'Have you ever been to the lands over there?'

'No,' Fulk said.

'You called them heathens, yet you know nothing of them. You have no idea what they are capable of.'

'You do?' Odo said, barely concealing the sneer.

'Aye, boy.' The smith rose and lit a pair of rushlights as the darkness swallowed the light outside. As he scraped sparks into tinder, he continued, 'After I finished my apprenticeship, I went east. I spent time in the great city of Constantinople, and had thoughts of going farther, except I got into a fight and did this,' he said, slapping his leg. 'I was lucky, though. To earn some pennies I got to working with a Saracen master metalworker, who showed me some of his skills.'

'You think they are worth knowing?' Odo said. 'What can you learn from a heathen?'

The old smith looked over at him. 'First, that they know how to make swords that can hold an edge like a razor; second, that just because they are heretics doesn't make them fools; third, that they are men, just like any other.'

'You say we should learn from the enemies of Christ?' Odo sneered.

'I say that you should learn wisdom where you find it,' the smith said. 'Whether it is an older Christian, a follower of Mohammed, or a dog.'

'A dog?' Fulk asked, while his brother clicked his tongue and looked away.

'Yes. If a dog learns that stealing food from the table earns it a kick, he will stop stealing. Dogs learn. A clever man learns from his mistakes.' He looked at Odo. 'A wise man will learn from other men's.'

'Do you have swords we can use?' Odo interrupted.

'I suppose so,' the smith said. He did not move, but contemplated Odo before looking across at Fulk. 'Under the canvas over there.'

Fulk walked to the far side of the room. On top of a low table there was a square of oiled cloth. He lifted the corner, and found himself looking down at three swords.

'Bring them here,' the smith called, refilling his cup. Fulk took up the three in his hands.

Two were identical. They had strangely grey blades, Fulk thought, but then, as he peered closer, he saw that the steel had little striations, like inked lines or etchings. The pommels were curious, made of steel with the same marks as the blades, but formed into teardrops, smoothly polished, that seemed to appear from the grip itself as though they had been extruded like pine resin from within.

The smith studied the two swords with a small smile before he passed them to the brothers. 'These two were made by me under the teaching of my old master. They are light, they are keen, and they will cut a man in half, if you find him without armour.'

'That is good,' Odo said, his eyes sparkling as he took up one of the swords. He hefted it, chopping it before him as though an enemy stood there. 'It is a bit short, isn't it?'

Fulk said nothing. He took the hilt in his hand. The grip was slim, but comfortable.

The smith ignored Odo's comment, but drew the third sword. It lay in a simple wooden sheath that was wrapped about with plain leather, as though it was a sword of no value or importance, but when it caught the light, Fulk gave a little gasp of surprise.

'Pretty little thing, isn't it?' the smith said, turning it in the light. 'This is the kind of weapon you'll find out there in the deserts, boy,' he said. 'Sharp as a great cat's claws, and as dangerous. See the silver ripples through the metal? The Saracens fold the metal of their blades over and over, with different metals, and then weld them all together. Beautiful, isn't it?'

'It has a fascinating curve to it,' Fulk said.

'Watch,' the smith said, and picked up a strip of cloth from the table at his side. He held it dangling in his hand, and then whipped the sword across. The strip was sliced cleanly in two.

Fulk's mouth fell open. 'How can . . .'

'They call this Damascene, this steel. It is like nothing you will ever see again. Not until you reach the country where they make this. This is the steel that the armies of the Saracens bear.'

Odo shrugged. 'Pretty enough, but we will have the word of God to protect us.'

'And mail,' Fulk grinned. 'For when He is resting.'

Odo scowled at his blasphemy, but the old smith set his head to one side. 'You think these swords are only good for slicing silks? This blade will go through ordinary steel just as easily as it cut that cloth.' He indicated the blades they held. 'Keep good hold of those swords, and you will be safe. I made them in a very similar way to this. Those blades may look just the same as any knight's riding sword, but in truth, you hold weapons that will shatter many blades that come against them. They will last you both your lifetimes and your sons'.'

'You swear?' Odo said. 'They look very short to me. All the men-at-arms I've seen wear swords longer than this.'

Fulk held his to the light of the nearer rushlight, and studied the patterns in the metal. They were less pronounced than those of the curved sword in the smith's lap, but showed clearly in the light.

'The longer the sword, the heavier it must be,' the smith said, 'or the metal will be brittle and break at the first battle. The heavier it is, the more you have to carry. You will have to purchase mail as it is, boy, and that will be a weight for you to carry across deserts and mountains. These will last you and preserve your lives. But handle them with care. These are not toys.' He looked at Odo. 'And do not use them wildly or without thought. It is easy to take life, less easy not to take it.'

'What does that mean?' Odo asked.

'You are going to a foreign land, where the people are different. The culture is different. Don't think you can walk in and destroy everything they know and love. You will be entering a place where you can learn much. Just as I did when I learned how to work metal to create these blades.'

'What can we learn from Saracens?' Odo sneered.

The smith eyed him coldly for a long moment, then turned to Fulk. 'What of you?'

'I will be happy to learn what I may,' Fulk said. He weighed the sword in his hand again. He swung it experimentally, turning his wrist and watching the steel whirl at either side of him. It felt like a living thing, as if it had taken hold of his soul and had become welded to him, an extension to his arm. It was so intense a sensation he was chilled, as though the steel had entered his marrow. A shiver suddenly ran down his spine.

The smith was watching him closely, and now his eyes creased into a smile. 'You don't have to say anything. That sword has chosen you.'

CHAPTER 6

Near Reutlingen, Saturday 3rd May, 1096

Fulk left Odo to fetch water. There was a small stream not far from where they were camping, and once their evening protection was erected – a pair of cloaks spread over a length of twine between two trees, the corners weighted with stones to hold them, and a small fire near the entrance to keep them warm – Fulk left Odo setting about preparing food. They had leaves and some salt sausage they had bought at the last hamlet, and now Fulk fetched water to make a pottage, thickened with a little barley he had bought in a market earlier, casting occasional doubtful glances through the trees at the small castle on the hill over the town.

Often they would try to get to towns before nightfall, and beg for a bed in the hayloft of a stable, but today they had arrived too late to plead entry to the town, and Fulk felt exposed and threatened by the shadowy building. At least with so many other pilgrims on the road it was unlikely that he would be a victim of brigands or greedy men-at-arms.

They were making good time. Since collecting their swords they had marched every day, excepting Sundays, because Odo had declared it would be shameful in the eyes of God. Taking the route the smith had described briefly to them had been easy. The simple truth was their way was clear. It lay in trampled grasses and mud, as an ever-growing river of people swelled and ebbed along the way. Every day more people joined and overtook them, walking on with the speed and strength of those who had not already covered a hundred miles or more. The proof of the pilgrim army was here, in the roadways turned to mire by the passage of so many feet and hoofs.

It was a never-ending surprise to see so many people each evening. They would stagger to the side of the road and make what they might of the grassy verges, or push on in among the trees in search of a comfortable space. Even when Odo and he were walking in comparative loneliness, every evening they would find the same huddles of people on the ground.

Tonight they were lying on every available space, for the most part wrapped in cloaks against the dew with their backs to the trees. Children lay snuggled on their parents' laps, some few curled up together like small packs of puppies. All about was the quiet murmur of the exhausted, an occasional sharp crying from a child, but mostly just muttered comments amid the hiss and crackle of the little fires. Some were cooking. More were too weary to hunt for suitable sticks. Fulk looked about him as he went, wondering what were their stories, what had led them to join this band, what misery or grim poverty could have tempted them to leave homes, hearths and loved ones. Was it the pure desire for excitement, like him, or by the laudable ambition to do God's work?

He filled his leather flask and made his way back to his encampment with Odo, but on the way he tripped over a young child. She lay rolled up in a dark russet cloak, and if he had been looking more where he was going, rather than at all the other people about, he would have seen her.

'Ow!' She glared up at him. 'That hurt!'

Fulk looked about. There were three women nearby. One, an older woman, was blearily rubbing the sleep from her eyes, while two others were already sitting up and staring at him.

'I am sorry, ladies,' Fulk said. 'I didn't see her in the gloom.'

The younger of the women, he saw, was bruised, with fading black and purple marks that marred her fair features. He noted that she looked embarrassed. The other women were less vulnerable in appearance. The older of them was in her middle years, perhaps forty-five, Fulk estimated, and had the shrewish look that older, widowed and unwanted women could wear. She was up and cradling the child already, so he wondered if the girl was her daughter. The other woman was over thirty, he guessed, but still had the slim good looks of a woman who was in her prime. She eyed Fulk with a measuring stare, her chin raised. It made him uncomfortable, as though he was a bullock being appraised at market. Still, she was a handsome woman, and he decided to make himself appealing to her, at least.

Putting on his most winning smile, he asked for their names, and although the one called Jeanne remained sitting, looking grumpy, the two others were prepared to be companionable enough. Fulk grinned broadly at them. 'I am Fulk. My brother is over there somewhere, a scruffy, ugly churl you wouldn't want to meet. We're walking to save Jerusalem. Are you all joining the pilgrimage?'

Guillemette nodded. 'There was nothing to hold us back,' she said.

Fulk's smile widened. She had the confidence and lack of embarrassment of a woman who had sold herself often enough.

When she looked at him there was no shame in her eyes, only a worldly comprehension, and when he cast a glance over her body, she didn't recoil with anger, but eyed him as if considering how much he would pay. 'Do you lack for anything?' he asked.

'We need food,' Jeanne said. 'We came with very little, because . . . because we were in a hurry, and we don't have anything to eat.'

Fulk looked down at the girl. She was too young for a journey as long and fraught with dangers as this, he thought. Odo would be angry, he knew, but . . . 'Come with me. We do not have much, but it will warm you a little if you share with us.'

'Why?' Mathena asked.

'I wouldn't want to see a chit like this starve,' Fulk said with quiet honesty, looking at Esperte. She was painfully skinny.

Guillemette tilted her head so that her throat was exposed. It was a deliberately coquettish movement, and Fulk could not help but let his eyes slide down the delicious line from the point under her jaw, along its length to the V of her collarbone, where he was sure he could see the pulse racing. From there on all was concealed by her tunic, but he could imagine the perfect curves of her breasts, and just now, after so many days of abstinence, the sight of this woman was overwhelming.

'I will come with you,' she said. 'Jeanne, Mathena, wait here. We don't want to lose our place.'

Fulk led the way, all the while revelling in the close company of Guillemette.

She stopped him when they reached a small clearing, a hand on his arm. 'What will you want for this food? We have no money.'

'Lady, I had no . . .'

She nodded. 'Yes, you did. Well, you can have me if you want, if it'll bring in a little food for us.'

74

'Your honest simplicity is refreshing,' he said.

'I'm not so proud that I'll starve for no reason,' she said.

He moved toward her, his hands reaching for her hips, but she slipped away. 'Oh, no!' she said, and while there was a chuckle in her voice, there was no mistaking her seriousness. 'Food first – then you can have me, if you want.'

Vöcklabruck, Thursday 22nd May

Even now, some eight weeks after the arrival of Peter the Hermit in their city, Sybille was angry. It was a constant rasp on her soul, to think that they had given up everything to join this great cavalcade, and every new day picked at the scabs of the wound. She could barely open her mouth without snapping at Benet. He was entirely to blame for their being here. She had no idea how long the journey would take, but she was worried for Richalda. Their daughter was so young for such hardships.

'Do not fear, lady. I will protect you,' Josse had said to her as they set off. Sybille had been in a towering rage that day, seeing her house sold off, all their prized possessions, few as they were, auctioned to their neighbours so that they could leave with as big a purse as they could. She wanted to snap at someone, and Josse took the brunt of her anger that day, but he only smiled and reassured her, as though he understood her better than her own dear Benet. Perhaps he did.

Some pilgrims were moving south, aiming for Rome and the coast where they would take ships to cross the seas to Constantinople. Others were gathering, apparently, in order to walk the majority of the way. The Hermit had his own group, and Sir Walter de Boissy-Sans-Avoir another. Benet had chosen to trudge along with the earliest he could, so as to reach Jerusalem with the first pilgrims, and for now that meant that they were with the army of Sir Walter.

They had passed into the plains between the mountains, and now were travelling through lands in which, to Sybille's ear, the guttural tongue clogged the back of the throat. It was a strange, horrible language, she thought, with harsh clicks and glottal noises so thick-sounding, sometimes she felt the people must choke. A villager had agreed to sell this pony, though, and although Benet had baulked at the price, Sybille had been determined. She was not going to walk any further. Already she had worn out the soles of two pairs of her shoes, and although they had found a cordwainer who could repair them, her feet felt every mile. Besides, it was better for Richalda to be able to rest more often.

'Is it much farther?' Richalda asked now.

She was seated before her mother on the pony, and Sybille smiled down at her. 'It is many, many leagues, little bird. We have a great many lands to see before we reach the land of our Lord Jesus.'

'Trust in Him,' Benet said. He trudged along at Sybille's right knee. She noticed that he was limping a little, favouring his left leg. She must stop soon and give him an opportunity to ride and rest, she thought, even if he deserved pain for bringing them here. But it would do her good to use her legs, and Richalda would benefit from a run around, too.

'It will take us another month or more,' a man beside them said on her left.

Sybille nodded, but as she looked over at him, she found herself torn.

He was a grizzled old peasant, who bore a long pole over his shoulder and a bill at his belt. A stranger, he yet looked friendly enough. His eyes were calm and blue, but wrinkled as a piece of ancient leather, and he wore a cap with a tassel dangling from a cord. At home, she would have ignored a man such as this, and continued riding without response, but here, with strange lands about them and an indefinite destination, it was a relief to talk to anyone. All pilgrims were friends.

'You know the way?' Benet asked over the body of Richalda's pony. He saw Josse glower suspiciously, edging closer. Benet held up his hand. Josse would not trust the Pope himself with Sybille and Richalda, and Benet knew it was best always to keep his servant under observation in case of accidents, just as it was best to keep a hound on a tight leash to stop it biting people.

'I have been along this way before, aye. It is a weary journey,' the man said. He did not look up at Benet or her, but kept his eyes on the horizon, as though the act of staring could reduce the distance.

'How far did you go?' Sybille asked.

'As far as the great city of Antioch, mistress. But never with so many others.'

She looked about them. Everywhere were people. They streamed off before them and trailed behind, an unimaginable number. They ranged on either side, even here where the road was not broad. Carters and sumptermen travelling in the opposite direction had a hard way of it, there was such a press. Thousands, tens of thousands, all driven by the same religious desire to bring the Holy City back into the hands of the Christians who deserved it. It was their city, after all.

'Were there not so many when you came this way before?'

He glanced up at her and gave a little grin. 'Nay, mistress. I was all but alone. I had my father and a priest, and that was all. I never thought to see such a multitude as this! And they say this is but one of the armies.'

'There are more?' Sybille said. If there were more, the whole of Christendom must be emptied, she thought. 'Some have said that this could be the end of all things,' she said more quietly. She glanced at Richalda.

'End of the world? No, it's the beginning of a happier time,' he said, and patted the bill at his belt. 'We will take back the city, and then will be a time of plenty and happiness for all, you'll see!'

Sybille was glad to hear the certainty in his voice. Many were apocalyptic in their descriptions about what would happen when they reached the Holy Land and it was refreshing to hear his stolid conviction.

'So long as your servant doesn't try to kill me first, of course,' he added.

Sybille glanced back. 'He is safe, Josse. You don't have to worry about anyone here in our company!'

Josse nodded and fell back a half-pace, but then turned to peer over his shoulder at the sound of shouts and cries. Sybille felt a quick trepidation in case it might be an attack from ruffians. There were many stories of outlaws who did unspeakable things to their captives in these strange lands, but even as the fear rose in her breast, she saw that it was only a group of soldiers who were trotting along briskly, pushing other pilgrims from their path.

She saw the heavy figure of a knight in the midst of his company, but did not recognise Sir Walter de Boissy-Sans-Avoir any more than she would have known the King of France.

Near Vöcklabruck

Odo strode on amid the throng with a determination that was, to Fulk, frankly appalling.

'Do you not feel tired, brother?' Fulk called. Then, 'Would you like a rest?'

Odo continued stomping on.

'Odo! We have been marching for days! Do you not wish to rest a while?' Then, when his brother paid him no heed, 'Odo, in the name of all the saints, *please*!'

'You should hurry, Fulk,' his brother called over his shoulder. 'We shall not get there any the sooner by strolling like a maid with her lover at the riverside in harvest time. We are here for an urgent cause.'

'Can't you stop being so ... so *relentless*?' Fulk said despairingly .

Fulk knew that his great failing was his impetuosity and occasional anger, but at least that was better than Odo's sulking. He had always nursed a grievance in bitter silence. He was sorely tempted to beat it out of him sometimes, but not today.

To his relief, Odo stopped and turned to look at him. Fulk pulled the stopper from his flask and drank a little water. It tasted of the pitch used to seal the leather. His head hurt, and his feet were complaining: they had blisters on blisters. The weight of the sword on his back was an annoyance; the cord that he had used to bind it over his shoulder had rubbed the flesh raw from his collarbone to his neck, and all in all he felt about done in.

'What's the matter with you, Fulk?'

'I am weary,' he said, barely holding back a curse as two more pilgrims barged past him. 'We have been marching for weeks now, and I'm weary. Aren't you?'

'*I* did not stay up so late last evening with the young woman from wherever she hails from,' Odo said shortly.

'That's it? You are jealous that I—'

'I am *jealous* of nothing! But this whole *iter*, this journey of pilgrimage, is based on a religious ambition. Can you not understand that, Fulk?'

'What of it? We will be granted absolution for our sins for making this journey.'

'But if you fornicate and wallow in drunkenness, you will imperil it!' Odo snapped.

After sharing their food, Fulk and Guillemette had found a man who carried a wineskin. His wine had refreshed them both, and then Guillemette had accommodated him while standing with her back to a large oak. Now Fulk gazed at his brother in genuine surprise. 'Is that what you think? I had thought that no matter what we did on this journey, we would be granted—'

'Then you need to think again! How would God react if the men who reach His Holy City were the dregs of all the thieves, cut-purses, wantons and malcontents of Christendom? He wants those with higher ideals, those who deserve His peace and salvation!'

'What was the point of the priest telling us we'd be given absolution, then? He must have assumed that there would be some like me?'

'Perhaps he thought you could keep your tarse in your braies for the course of a journey,' Odo said tartly.

'What does that mean?'

'You think I haven't noticed you slipping away at night to meet your little wench?'

Fulk shrugged shamefacedly. 'It's not been that often.'

'Every time you lie with a woman, you imperil the pilgrimage!'

'Consider me aware that I've been reprimanded,' Fulk said. He had taken to visiting Guillemette as often as he might. 'I am sorry, Odo. I didn't think of it in that light. I was looking on this as a great adventure, perhaps the only one I shall have in my life.'

'It is – but it is a *holy* adventure, not some glorified market-day festivity! Come, you need to keep up. We have many more miles to cover before evening.'

'Then go more slowly! How far is it to the next town?'

'From the look of you, an evening in the open air would be better for you,' Odo said without sympathy, but he pulled a face. 'About another four or five leagues, I think. I asked a fellow a little while ago, and think that was when the sun was a full hour lower in the sky. He said six leagues. We should have covered two leagues since then.'

Fulk nodded. 'And then only another ten thousand leagues to Jerusalem.'

'Not that far,' Odo said, setting off once more. 'Only, perhaps, nine thousand leagues.'

'You cheer me greatly.'

'Good.'

Fulk could see little that was good about things. However, as they walked, soon they came to a small brook, at which they refilled their skins and flasks, and shortly after that they reached a hamlet, in which a farmer's wife took pity on them and gave them a hunk of day-old bread each. It was enough to give them the energy to continue a little further, and Fulk found he could ignore his blisters and his shoulder after a while. The pain did not dissipate, but he was more aware of the resolution of plodding on, lifting one foot and setting it down again. The constant, unremitting nature of their journey was enough to dull all his senses.

Odo appeared to feel none of his pain. His brother, instead, concentrated solely on arriving at Jerusalem in the shortest time possible. He wanted only to reach the city before the place could fall to the Christians. Whenever he could, he had tried to set a faster pace, and Fulk had to force him to slow down like an anchor. 'If we get there too late, what then?' he muttered every so often.

It was a relief when they saw a knot of people ahead. There was a clutch of people walking, and a man on a pony who rode a little over the rest.

'I think I know that face,' Fulk said, but he wasn't looking at the man on the horse. It was the woman walking at his side whom Fulk had noticed, the woman from the marketplace at Sens when they had all heard the preacher.

Odo glared at him. 'You're not already thinking of another slut?'

'No!' Fulk said, but he could not help throwing another quick glance at the woman. She was worth a second look, he thought.

Sybille had given up her seat on the pony to her husband and was walking happily enough on the grassy verge. It was soft and easy underfoot here, and she had pulled off her shoes to let her feet enjoy the cool, long grasses, but there were too many men about her here. She had to pull her skirts decorously down. Many men would become inflamed at the sight of a woman's ankles, she knew. She was aware that several were eyeing her covertly. It was better to be down here, off the beast, for while in the saddle she was subject to glances from all directions. Here at least she felt protected from most of them.

A man near her was bemoaning the confusion of finances. 'I had to change much of my money for these shitty little things. Obols, they call them. Apparently there are two to a pfennig, in this benighted land, but they aren't the same as the obols at home. What is the point of all these silly coins, when they could use the same as we do? I wouldn't trust these foreign coins as far as I could throw them, if it weren't for the fact we need them here.'

'They'll be different in the next town, too,' his friend told him.

'Rome has its own currency, and Venice another, so I've

heard,' a third voice piped. 'We just have to hope we all have enough to last us to get to Constantinople. There we'll have help.'

'Are you sure?'

'Of course,' the first said. 'It was their Emperor who asked the Pope to send men to help him put down these heretics in his Empire. He must want to help us, when we reach him.'

The third sounded wary about this. 'So long as you're sure. I've known people ask for help, and be grateful, until the time for reckoning comes along, and then they suddenly remember other commitments and try to weasel their way out.'

'The Emperor of Constantinople would hardly do that.'

'You think so?'

Sybille listened with only half an ear. Further away someone was singing a sweet little song about a lady who fell in love with a knight who left her in search of adventure. It left Sybille feeling melancholy, and a little sad to have snapped at Benet earlier. She was a poor wife, she thought. He had made a hard choice for them to leave their home, but no doubt it would all turn out for the best. She had to believe that. He was her husband.

Theirs had been a marriage of love. She had met him when she was still only a maid, and he was an apprentice, but their love had grown swiftly, and she had never regretted her choice. He was kind, and a good man; he always helped those who needed alms, for example. If he had a weakness, it lay in his attempts to provide for his family. He had tried to expand his business, but that had failed, and almost cost them their house. Soon afterwards he thought to have secured a patron, but that man proved notoriously bad at paying his debts, and poor Benet had lost more money. All their lives together had been a struggle seeking money when the latest venture failed. He had grown old before his time.

This would be different. He was convinced that at last they would find their fortune and be able to make money. She just hoped and prayed that he was right. With God's help, if He thought they were serving His purpose, He might bestow some good fortune on them.

There were more people overtaking them now, and she cast a glance around. One, she saw, was a good-looking fellow. She liked the way that he strode, the way that his eyes were on her as he passed them, the way that his lips moved in a slow grin, before he continued on his way, but as Fulk walked on past, she averted her gaze, lifting her chin haughtily. She was a married woman, not some wayside wench.

BOOK THREE

Lothar
The German Pilgrim

CHAPTER 7

Mainz, Sunday 25th May, 1096

'Who instructed you to hold the gates against us?'

Lothar heard the ice in his lord's voice. Count Emicho of Flonheim sat easily on his horse, but Lothar knew that his Count was never more dangerous than when his tone took on that cold, precise note. Staring at the Archbishop's barred gates was not improving his temper. After all, theirs was a holy task.

It had taken them only a few days to reach the city of Mainz from Worms. The Count had been inspired there, hearing so many talking about joining the armies marching to Jerusalem. He had a dream: a vision. Many were keen to help even if they did not join the pilgrimage themselves. There were miraculous events spoken of, and pilgrims of all ages and qualities. One girl had claimed that her goose was infected by the Holy Spirit, and had led her to Cologne Cathedral. There, at the altar, she declared that the bird was aware of her ambition to walk to Jerusalem and was determined to join her.

But for all the thrilling stories of those committed to joining the pilgrimage, others turned their thoughts to the funding. Congregations donated money, thinking that their contributions would give them a heavenly reward, but many considered that the wealthiest should pay their way. Since the richest were Jewish merchants and money-lenders, the Count made it clear he believed they should support the pilgrims; in addition they should accept the Christian faith and baptism. He tried to persuade the Jews of Worms, but they had refused. It showed that they were of bad faith, so the Count ordered his men to slaughter them all.

Worms was cleansed, but Mainz had its own Jewish population.

The cathedral rose over the city like a tower reaching to Heaven itself, with its great stone walls. Workers laboured over the final works on tall, spindly larch scaffoldings, while stone-carvers plied their chisels and hammers on statues and gargoyles below before the treadmill cranes hoisted them into position. All the while fresh timbers and stones were brought to be worked and installed inside. And even as the Count's men waited, this tiny force stood barring their path with their weapons.

At Lothar's side, Heinnie gave a little chuckle. He was taller than Lothar, but his shoulders were not so broad. With his raggedly cut blond hair blowing free, his blue eyes looked brighter in contrast. He grinned now as Lothar caught his eye. 'They don't know how dangerous it is to upset our Count! Never upset a Rhinelander, if you want to keep your—'

'*Who*, I asked,' the Count said more loudly. He edged his horse nearer to the three men who stood before the Archbishop's palace. 'I would know who instructed you.'

'It was our lord, the Archbishop. He commanded us to hold the gates against you and your men,' one of the men said. He looked like the sergeant of the group, but although he spoke bravely enough, he was pale and anxious.

'Against us? We do God's work! We are here to speak with

the Jews, to persuade them to accept holy baptism. We are here to save their souls.'

'Like you did at Worms?' the man said. 'You robbed the Jews there and slew them.'

'Some were happy to help fund the pilgrimage to Jerusalem,' the Count said. Lothar and the others could hear his disdain. Some of the men began to chuckle. The Count continued: 'Now, open the gates! You can tell your Archbishop that you have followed his commands to the best of your ability.'

The guards did not move. They gripped their spears tightly, and although they were not pointing at Lothar and the Count, neither were the men stepping aside.

'You will get out of my way,' the Count said, and then leaned forward to shout, 'because, if you do not, I will have all three of you skinned alive, and have your hides nailed to the gates! Now *move*!'

Lothar dropped from his horse. This was no way to enter an Archbishop's palace, demanding entry at the point of a sword. 'Guards, you cannot win here. You have done all required of you. There's no point dying for no reason. Stand aside. We do not seek to despoil your master, only to speak with him.'

'What about?' the nervous guard said.

'That is between the Count and your master.'

The guards conferred, but then there came a shout from above.

'Who are you who come and disturb the peace of the holy precinct?'

Looking up, Lothar saw a man in archbishop's garb. The man held his shepherd's crook like a weapon, and his knuckles were as white as his face.

While Lothar and the others were distracted, a wicket gate opened and the guards slipped inside. Heinnie gave a shout, but he and Lothar were too surprised to move in time. Before they could spring forward the wicket snapped shut. For a moment Lothar expected the gates to swing wide, but then he heard bolts and bars being rammed into place. As he stood muttering a curse under his breath, the voice called again from the gatehouse above.

'Well?'

'I am Count Emicho von Flonheim. I represent the pilgrims who march on Jerusalem to rescue the Christians of the city from the cruel oppression of their heathen masters. I call on the Jews of this city to support us in our holy cause.'

The Archbishop nodded grimly. 'You mean to rob them. You may not. The Jews of the city are here under my protection.'

'Your *protection*?' Emicho spat. He curbed his temper and smiled coolly. 'Then allow us to speak to them. We march to rescue the Holy Land from the Saracens. The Jews should wish to support us and pay at least a part of our expenses.'

'I will call the Rabbi of the Jews here and you can speak with him.'

'No! Open the gates and allow us to talk to him.'

'My gates are closed to you, Count. We have already heard how your "talk" proceeded at Worms. I will not have murder here. This is a place of God.'

'We will speak with you, Archbishop.'

'From here, yes. But if you attempt to break into my palace, I will have you excommunicated, Count. You will be denied entry into the Kingdom of Heaven, and you will suffer forever at the pleasure of Satan. You will not—'

'Can we not enter if we swear not to harm anyone?'

'Harm no one? I do not believe you, false knight! You would forswear yourself! You would perjure yourself before God!'

'You take a haughty manner, Archbishop! I will swear that all I wish to do is save their souls. If they will submit to baptism, they can leave here freely. I will not harm a Christian. Save them! Let me in for *their* sake!'

'No, begone! You leave me no option. You say you wish to join the pilgrims to Jerusalem. Go and join them! The way is there,' the Archbishop said, flinging out his arm.

'Give me the Jews!'

'You will neither enter here nor harm those who are here under my protection!'

Mainz, Monday 26th May

The following day, Lothar was bored and walked about the city. To a farmer's son like him, inactivity was anathema. He made as close an inspection as he could of the walls surrounding the palace. They were much like a castle's walls, thick and impregnable without the machinery of war, and the Count had no stone-throwing weapons. It would be an impossible task, to break in here.

There was a small tavern at the side of the wall, and Lothar took a cup of wine there. The keeper was not communicative when Lothar asked about the palace wall and whether there could be a way inside. The fellow shook his head mutely and walked to the dark at the rear of the tavern. Soon the door at the back slammed.

Lothar was finishing his cup when the tavern owner's wife appeared. She was a short woman, but her belly was big enough for any glutton. She had a gross, red face, and there was grease on her lips from eating a heavy stew.

'Mistress,' he said, ducking his head.

'God give you a good day,' she said. She had a large ham in one hand, a barrel over her other shoulder. While he watched, she set the barrel on a trestle, then reached up and hooked the ham over the fire where the smoke could rise to it, before turning to him and fixing him with a beady eye. It was like being stared at by a crow. 'You are with the Count, I suppose?'

'Yes.'

'Here to kill the Jews? Some say they deserve it. They've done little enough for the town. Sitting in their great houses and making money, while poor folk suffer. What are you going to do if they won't open the gates?'

Lothar shrugged. 'We will have to move on, I suppose.'

'It's said that the Jews have boxes of gold, each family,' the women said. She licked her lips like a glutton eyeing a feast. 'A man could do much with a box of gold.'

'A woman who showed us how to get to the people inside there would be amply rewarded,' Lothar said. He watched her slyly. Her husband may not wish to help, but this woman was willing, he was sure.

She wiped her mouth with her sleeve, glancing behind her towards the storeroom before nodding. 'I can show you.'

Mainz, Tuesday 27th May

As dawn broke, Lothar and Heinnie, along with four other well-armed men, slipped into an alley. There was no one in the streets at that time, and the guards inside the palace had no warning as Lothar and the others stepped to the farther end. In the wall was a sturdy wooden door, but it was designed to keep thieves out, not to defend against a determined force of men-at-arms. Lothar carried a long iron bar, and he thrust the lever into the gap between door and jamb. He and another man pressed against it and there was a loud splintering. They moved the bar down, pushed again and, with a loud crack, the door gave way, the lintel rent apart. Lothar kicked at it, and the door shattered into pieces.

Secrecy now was pointless. They could hear voices, some half-asleep, others bright with alarm. Lothar bellowed, 'Come! This way!' and ran across the great courtyard. Two sentries and an elderly Jew were at the gateway, but they were soon dealt with, the Jew struck on the head with a maul while the guards were pushed back with swords at their throats. It was there, at the gatehouse, that Lothar felt it: a shadow, cold as a witch's kiss, and he shivered as though it was a foreboding of evil. He pulled the bars from their iron staples and slid them from the way, pulling at the gates until they were wide. Outside the Count and the men on foot hurried forward.

'You have done well, Lothar,' Emicho murmured, leaning down before standing high in his stirrups and shouting: 'Look! God has opened the gates for us! Today we shall avenge the blood of Christ that was spilled by the Jews. Kill them all!'

Lothar trotted in behind the main company. He was happy on foot, with his sword in his hand.

There was no reason why he should feel a premonition of evil. He knew what they were to do here. It was a simple matter of exterminating the Jews. He had been at Speyer, where the bishop had intervened and prevented the Count and his men from killing all the Jews, but at Worms they had achieved their aim and left the bishop's palace reeking of blood. Here they were to do the same. Lothar felt the edge of his sword. He was his Count's most trusted servant, after all, and they were doing God's will. He was sure of it, because Count Emicho had told him so at Worms: the Count had been given a divine message.

It came to him in a dream, he said. He must gather an army, he was told, and ride to Jerusalem, where he would become Emperor, and thus would begin the End of Days as foretold in the Gospels. Before that, it was said that St Paul would return, and all Jews would be baptised. So the Count had a sacred duty: to convert all the Jews in the Holy Roman Empire; those who would not accept baptism must suffer the consequences.

It all made sense to Lothar. He was a loyal servant of the Count and was deeply religious, and now he did all he could to hasten the Day of Judgement. First there must be war, and his Count was to bring it about.

There were already screams and shrieks of terror before Lothar reached the inner courtyard. There he found the Count pulling off his mailed gauntlets, gazing about him at the buildings that encircled the court with the rest of the men, when an elderly priest erupted from a small chapel, his hands held high as he shouted at the men.

'What do you think you are doing in here? This is the Archbishop's palace! You have no right to be in here! Begone before I call Christ's vengeance upon you and see you blasted by God's anger! Begone, I say!'

'Where is the Archbishop?' the Count demanded. 'Bring him to me.'

'He is not here.' The old man's face cracked into a smile. 'He escaped with the Rabbi and many of the poor fellows. You think they were foolish enough to wait? You never meant to save their souls, only destroy them all. The Archbishop saw through you as easily as looking through a window!'

Behind him, Lothar saw the first of the crowd. Men, women and children, some clad in the finest of clothing, others as bedraggled and tatty as the peasants in his own town, but all of them marked out for their race. He felt the stirrings of excitement in his belly.

'Escaped? The Archbishop chose to save the Rabbi?' Lothar saw the Count stare angrily at the priest before nodding towards

Heinnie. There was a flash of steel, and the priest slumped, blood trickling from his temple, where Heinnie's sword pommel had struck him. There was a moment of silence. The mass of Jews stared at the Count and his men, and an air of expectation enveloped the court. Lothar could feel the blood pounding at his temples, and he felt that he must soon have a headache. There was a hissing in his ears, a tingling in his fingertips, and a fluttering ran up and down his spine, like a rat on tiptoes. A baby cried, and the sound acted on Lothar's nerves like a knife slowly cutting into his skin. He shuddered.

'Men! Companions! Friends!' Emicho cried. 'Kill them. Kill them all, in the name of God!'

One or two of the Jews had weapons, but nothing that could give a difficulty to the Count's trained warriors: knives, staffs, a couple of swords, little more. The women were pushed to the rear, while the men stood to the fore with determined expressions, one little more than a boy, others with tears pouring down their faces as the Count's men drew their swords or hefted axes and spears in their hands, and began to pace forward.

With a bellow, Lothar sprang forward, sword in his hand, and slashed at a man. It was a poor cut. He felt the drag of the edge as it opened the man's jaw, and then slit open his tunic and cotte, the blood showing at the fellow's breast, but then Heinnie was at his side and effortlessly thrusting his sword into the man's breast. Heinnie gave that little giggle – he always did in a fight – and soon Lothar and he were at it side by side, stamping forward, and with each stamp of their legs they punched out with their swords, impaling the Jews who stood in their path, while other men on either side used axes and daggers to end the squirming of those who fell without dying immediately. Lothar and Heinnie, the two Rhinelanders, always fought together.

Lothar opened a man's throat, and had to wipe the spray from his eyes with his gauntleted hand. It was then that he saw there were bodies behind the Jewish men before him. Even as he hacked the limb from the man in front of him and stabbed again, he saw two women, one bearing a child in her arms. The second stabbed the baby in the breast, while the other sobbed, and then the mother was herself put out of her misery, and fell to join her child on the ground. Finally a man went to the remaining woman, embraced her, and pushed a knife into her heart before rejoining the men fighting the Count's soldiers.

There was a cold determination in the Jews' faces now. All that they had valued was lost to them. Their wives, their children, all were gone, and they fought with renewed vigour. One even managed to take a piece from Lothar's padded jack, nicking his jaw to the bone as he did it. It was an instinctive thing to bring his sword up to hold the man's blade high, while pushing his dagger into the fellow's belly and angling it upwards to find the heart, twisting the knife to kill more swiftly. The Jew winced at the pain, and a little frown puckered his brow as though he was surprised to realise he was dying, and then he toppled onto Lothar. Lothar had kicked him away and off his blade, and stood, panting, surveying the courtyard.

It was a butcher's scene. All about the Archbishop's yard there were dead or dying Jews, with an occasional sob or rattle of breath to show where the injured lay. The Count's men moved among them, ending the lives of the wounded with sweeps of their knives over exposed throats. One was laughing as he stumbled over an outflung limb and fell onto the bodies. Walking over the dead was always difficult, as Lothar knew. Arms and legs would move treacherously, as though the bodies were attempting to make their killers stumble and join them on the ground.

'Why did they do that?' he said to Heinnie.

'What?'

'Didn't you see the women? They killed their children, and then each other!'

'What do you expect? They aren't like us. That's why they had to be destroyed. They killed Christ. What more can you expect of them? They're barbarians and heathens.'

'Yes,' Lothar said, but still it made no sense to him. It troubled him.

Some had barricaded the doors to a hall, and now screamed abuse at the Count's men from the safety of their refuge. Although the men tried to hack in through the doors, they were too massive and strong for their axes, and soon the men moved away to find easier targets. In two houses several Jews were found, and the men slaughtered them with no quarter offered.

It was then that a great cry went up and one of the Count's men blew three blasts on a horn and, when all were looking at him, he held aloft a cup brimming with wine. 'Look what the good Archbishop has left for us, to pay us for ridding his palace of this scum!'

Count Emicho's soldiers followed him into the storage chambers where barrels of wine and ale stood racked against a wall. Lothar filled his own flask, carefully stoppering it before wandering back outside.

It remained fixed in his mind, that memory of the two women who had slain the child and then themselves. It was against the natural order of things for women to behave in such a way. Perhaps Heinnie was right. These people were not Christians; they thought differently. But although Lothar knew that the Jews were different, even though he knew that they were cursed because of the way they had crucified Our Lord, the sight of women murdering their own children was so alien, so abnormal, that it jarred.

97

He walked to the yard. The two women still lay there. The child lay back with its chubby mouth wide as though reaching to suckle, while the woman who must surely have been the mother had fallen on her back, her eyes wide. He was sure he could see horror in her face, as though even now she could scarcely believe what she had done, participating in her child's death. Nearby was the second woman who had killed them both. The man who slew her was not far away.

Lothar drew the stopper and drank deeply.

It was late in the night when they had finally broken into the last stronghold of the Jews in the palace grounds. It was a large hall, accessed by one narrow stair that made breaking inside more than usually difficult. Some had taken ladders to try to scale the walls, but the ladders were too short, and most of the men already too drunk to clamber all the way to the roof. Instead, a series of men had attacked the door with axes and steel levers, until at last the timbers gave way and they could enter.

Inside, they found a slaughterhouse of bodies. Each of the Jews had killed each other and themselves, just like those women. They preferred to die than to be forced to accept the Christians' faith. The sight shook Lothar. He left that room and returned to the undercroft where the Archbishop's wine was stored, and he drank a great deal to try to expunge the sight.

Mainz, Wednesday 28th May

The next morning Lothar came to with a jerk.

He was sitting on the floor in the Archbishop's hall, slumped with his back against the wall, and his hand gripped a large mazer of sycamore chased with silver. Most of the contents were now seeping into his groin where it had spilled. Blearily rising, he drained the cup and stared down at it. Memories were returning gradually, crowding into his mind, and with them came confusion about what he had seen the day before. The scenes were too raw in his mind and would not leave him. He felt tainted.

Out in the court he could hear shouting, and then a horn was sounded. Welcoming the distraction, he walked out, stuffing the empty mazer into his tunic.

He found the Count marching with Heinnie and his body-guards, bellowing for their horses to be brought, while a few men wandered, clearly very drunk. One was sitting at a wall with a leather costrel that he drank from regularly, interspersing each glug with words of a bawdy song. Another man was lying full length on the ground, passed out.

The Count climbed on a mounting block to clamber into his saddle.

'Sir Emicho? Where do we ride?' Lothar called.

'The Archbishop took the other Jews with him. Now we know where they've gone, we ride to catch them!' The Count made his horse wheel. 'Set this place afire! The Archbishop will regret trying to save these scum!'

CHAPTER 8

Rüdesheim, Thursday 29th May, 1096

Bodies were already being piled up by labourers as Lothar and the Count's forces approached the Archbishop's retreat at Rüdesheim. Another fifty, Lothar counted, to join the thousand or more they had left at Mainz. He sat on his horse and stared down at the figures being dragged from the Archbishop's yards, to be flung onto a growing pile outside the gates.

Count Emicho eyed the peasants. 'What happened here?'

Lothar edged his pony forward to listen, Heinnie following close by, as the peasant bowed and tried to respond, stuttering and gurning in his terror to be questioned by the leader of such a force. As he spoke, he kept ducking his head as though trying to beat his forehead on the ground.

'Your honour, it was the chief of the Jews did it! It was them! The good Archbishop tried to persuade them to accept Holy Baptism, but they wouldn't, and when he told them they'd have to, the Rabbi started to threaten the Archbishop. The Archbishop had to call on all his men to protect him, and that sent the Rabbi wild! He killed his own son and wife, and then tried to attack the Archbishop, and that was when the Archbishop's men killed the Jews to protect his Grace.'

'He killed his own son?' the Count said. He shrugged and stared down at the figures being pulled out and discarded. 'He saved the Archbishop that much effort, then.'

Lothar dropped thankfully from his mount, massaging his inner thighs, where the saddle had rubbed his flesh raw. He was aching, and desperate for a cup of wine or two. The journey here had taken longer than any had expected, and the dust from the roads had settled in his throat in the dry air.

As the other men dismounted and began to traipse inside, searching for food and bellowing for attendants to see to their horses, Lothar walked back the way he had come, pulling his mount behind him. He had spied a small wine shop in the shadow of the Archbishop's wall, and Lothar was convinced that there he would find refreshment faster than his companions who were already bellowing for food and drink in the Archbishop's courtyard.

It was a small tavern made for the peasants who lived in this town. Lothar walked in and beckoned with two fingers at a maid standing at the bar. She looked terrified at the sight of him, he thought, and he smiled to himself. Nothing was so guaranteed to earn a man respect as the sight of him arrayed for war. There were no chairs, but one worn and rotting bench lay at a wall, and he made his way to it, sitting with a grunt of satisfaction.

The woman had not moved. He looked over at her with a feeling of grumpiness. She should have brought him his wine by now. He was about to call to her, when something about her made him hesitate.

She was slender, dark-haired, and had the olive skin of a Galician, he thought. Her cheekbones were high, but not so much as to make her face heart-shaped. Rather, she had a long face with a narrow chin. But it was her eyes he noticed. They were a dark brown, full of intelligence and fire, but even as he looked at her, they were filled with dismay.

'Wine, woman!' he called. Surely she could hear him? It was unlikely that she could not tell he wanted to be served. He was about to rise to his feet, when he saw her grasp a knife. 'Wait!'

But she did not attack him. As he stood, fumbling for his sword, she backed away, crouched over her knife, and then she grabbed at something – a small boy, dark-haired, large-eyed, who stared at Lothar with terror.

Lothar lifted both hands and sat down again. 'Woman, I have no quarrel with you, and I don't have the energy or desire to bed you. Just bring me wine.'

She said nothing, but there was a sudden scuffle from behind her, and a large, buxom woman, her coif all awry and her round, red face perspiring, burst into the room.

'Master! My apologies for keeping you waiting! Wench, back into the buttery with you! There's more churning to be finished off. And take that rascal with you! He shouldn't be out here playing when there is work to be done! Come, be off with you! Do you think there is time to dawdle all the long day? Begone! Now, master, let me serve you a good portion of ale, or would you prefer a wine? I have the best of both, and I can serve you some sliced cold ham, if you wish, that's been preserved well over the winter, with a loaf of good bread?'

'Wine, and some meat, yes. What was the matter with that child?'

'The boy? Nothing, he's just not the fastest rat in the sewer, master!' she chuckled, but even as she moved quickly about, pouring a jug of wine, selecting a dried leg and slicing off a few cuts, he could see that her eyes often slyly lingered on him.

'I meant the mother. I assume it was his mother, not an elder sister? Are they your children?'

'Bless you, sir, no. She and the boy are brother and sister. They're here from a village a few miles away.'

'But she drew a knife to keep me away.'

'Nay, master, she was scared! Look at you! With your leather and steel! She was of course anxious in your presence. Who wouldn't be?'

'You.'

She laughed at that. 'Me? I fear no man. I run a good tavern here, and any man who tried to—'

There was a loud clattering behind her, and she gave a fleeting scowl, then hurried out to the back room.

Intrigued, Lothar stood and followed her.

The girl and the boy stood far away in the corner of the room. A broken pot smashed to pieces on the floor, its contents spilled everywhere near an open shutter, told a story: the two had been trying to flee. The woman of the house was remonstrating, and as Lothar walked in, she whirled around as though to conceal the two.

'Well,' Lothar said.

As he spoke, the girl whipped her knife up in his direction again, while the older woman squeaked at her to put it away.

Lothar slowly pulled at the buckle of his belt and let his dagger and sword fall to the ground, before holding up his hands. 'Tell the child I'm no threat to you or her, mistress,' he said. 'I'm unarmed. But if she tries to scratch me with that little knife, I'll break her neck.'

The woman was right. Both children were terrified. Lothar found a small barrel and sat on it, waiting.

'She is scared of men of war like you,' the mistress said defiantly. She had her chin sticking up so she could look down her nose at him, but Lothar didn't care. He kept his eyes on the girl with the knife.

'Well?' he said.

The girl's eyes went from him to the woman, unsure.

'She is a young chit, that's all,' the woman said. 'Leave her alone. If you don't go from my buttery, I'll call for help. You shouldn't be here. It's not right.'

Lothar ignored her. 'She's a Jewess, yes? If she will accept the true faith and be baptised, I will see her safe.'

'And what if she doesn't want to become Christian?' the woman snapped. 'Have you seen what they did to the poor souls in the Archbishop's fine house up there? Slaughtered them because they wouldn't agree to submit to being baptised!'

'What would you do with those who don't follow God?' he demanded.

'The Jews have lived here in our town for a hundred years or more. They've never harmed us! They've been good neighbours – better than most!'

Lothar crossed himself fervently. 'You should be careful of such blasphemy, woman! The Jews have been given opportunities to save themselves by paying, or agreeing to become baptised, but if they refuse to help us with our holy *iter* to Jerusalem, we are justified in punishing them.'

'Punishing them? You mean murdering them all!'

'Woman! We have been told to kill all the Jews. You know that they were guilty of the murder of Christ, but you would defend them?'

In answer, she took the girl's shoulder. 'Look at her! This child has done *nothing*. But her parents have been killed. Her mother was raped in front of them, and these two were knocked down and their house set aflame about them. It was a miracle that they were saved. Her brother here? Look at him! How could he be responsible for a crime at his age?'

'She should be taken to the Archbishop to be baptised,' Lothar said.

'No! If you do that she will die! You will be guilty of her murder as much as any other.'

That stung. 'Guilty? How dare you, woman? There is no crime a pilgrim can commit that will not be expunged by his march to Jerusalem. We win life eternal for killing the heathens who are tormenting the peoples of Christ's city.'

He reached down to his sword belt, and as he did the girl dropped the knife and burst into tears. She fell to her knees and pulled the boy to her side, weeping all the while.

Lothar buckled on his belt, trying to avert his eyes. 'Child, it will all be well. Come with me and be baptised and your life will be much improved. Come!'

She collapsed, folding in on herself as if she could compress her frame to the size of an ant, still holding on to the boy at her side. It put Lothar in mind of Mary Magdalene. Surely she would have looked the same, clinging to the bottom of the cross on which Jesus was crucified? It was an uncomfortable thought. Lothar rested his left hand on his sword hilt. A sudden vision of the two Jewesses returned to his mind. The one holding her child to be stabbed, and then willingly exposing her breast to accept the gift of death from her friend.

He forced the thought away. 'Come, child. The Archbishop will be compassionate, I am sure.'

CHAPTER 9

Rüdesheim, Thursday 29th May, 1096

It was much later and growing dark when Lothar left the tavern. In that time, he had happily accepted the hospitality of the landlady and drunk two pints of wine while she cajoled, pleaded and occasionally berated him. She had brought a loaf, some cheese and a portion of dried sausage to eat, refilled his jug, and gave him a second loaf for his journey, until in the end he succumbed to her persuasion.

'Very well, mistress. I will leave her here with you. But I swear, she should accept the Word of our Lord. What does she fear from our faith?'

'She has seen her parents and the rest of her family slain because of our faith. How would you feel if you were forced to deny your religion and accept another, after seeing it shed the blood of your friends and family?'

'Me? That's different! No one could make me forswear the one true faith!'

'Perhaps,' she said soothingly. 'I hope you never have to make such a choice. You are a good man, Lothar. I will never forget

your kindness today. She and her brother are too young to understand, but she will grow to love you like her own lord.'

'There's no need for that,' Lothar said with a belch.

He did feel comfortable. The woman's wine was refreshing, a
strong, dark red that washed down the cheeses and meats she had
pressed on him. He had intended to bring the girl and her brother
to the Archbishop, but after the fourth and fifth cup of wine his
determination had been eroded, and by the time he had seen the
jug refilled and had taken a little more, he was feeling mellow.
If the girl really objected to seeing the Archbishop, who was
Lothar to demand that she should? After all, most of the Jews of
the town were dead already, and he was reluctant to see these two
also slain. Those who had not been killed by the Archbishop's
men in the scuffle in his court would have been hunted down by
now. As he left the tavern, he saw smoke rising from a building
further down the road. Later he heard that one Jew had agreed
to be baptised and underwent the ceremony, but then went to the
synagogue ravaged with guilt and self-loathing, and set it ablaze
before throwing himself on the flames. That smoke was likely
caused by the synagogue, the pyre of the Jew who had recanted.
These Jews were determined to cling to their mistaken beliefs,
Lothar thought, shaking his head.

Heinnie saw him as he approached the Archbishop's house.
'Where have you been?'

'I found a good tavern,' Lothar said, jerking a thumb back the
way he had come. 'The mistress was very amiable.'

'You've been drinking away the afternoon, you mean,'
Heinnie said.

Lothar shrugged, but could not prevent a broad grin from
encompassing his features.

'You son of a whore!' Heinnie said with a low growl of jealousy. 'You found a wench there?'

'Just a young woman. And no, I didn't do that. All I had was wine from her.'

'Perhaps she didn't find you satisfying enough. She needs a man with a longsword, not a fruit knife,' Heinnie laughed.

Lothar smiled, but less broadly. He thought again of the girl and her brother, but now he was thinking of the woman in the tavern. She had not seemed a heretic, but she was shielding the young Jews from the men of Lothar's group. It was peculiar, but he felt as though he shouldn't reveal her complicity. He didn't want to see the Jewess hurt, and as for the boy, what was the point of hurting him?

'So, where is this place?' Heinnie asked. 'I should go and show the woman what a real man looks like!'

Lothar smiled again. 'My friend, if you took off your braies and showed her what you're made of, she would hold all men to ridicule. No, better that we should go and see what the good Archbishop will give us for our efforts in protecting him and his people from the scourge of the heathens in his towns.'

The reek of burning wood, material and flesh was all over the town when Lothar left the Archbishop's compound later that evening.

Smoke from a burning house caught in his throat, and he coughed, wafts stinging his eyes and making them water profusely, and he was fain to wipe them clear before he could continue on his way. When the wind changed direction, he carried on, but before he had gone far he found himself confronted by four bodies outside a building that billowed smoke. Flames belched from a window, and he could see a body dangling, arms stretching towards the ground as though desperately reaching for safety, but the hips were gripped in the bars of the window. The poor soul had been burned alive.

He scowled and continued onwards, but always with a nagging doubt in his mind.

It did not make sense. The girl in the tavern was guiltless of crimes against Christ. Punishing her was no more than a symbolic gesture against her race. Was there some inherent evil in people who were born Jewish? He found it hard to believe. If there was some evil in the girl, surely he would have sensed it?

He walked slowly down the lane, occasional fumes making him wipe his eyes again. The child in the tavern was determined to defend her brother, to the death if need be. She deserved respect, not punishment. His thoughts returned to Mainz: surely the two women knew that to kill a child was the most foul crime, and to kill themselves was just as evil?

From along the roads he could hear shouts and occasional screams as the Count's men searched for more Jews. He hurried his pace.

And came across Heinnie.

The man-at-arms was leading six others, all battering at the doors of the tavern Lothar had visited earlier. As he watched, the door began to give way, and he heard Heinnie's high giggle over the screams of the people inside: the girl, the tavern-woman, the boy. Lothar gave a roar, and began to run, but as he did he saw the first of three men approaching Heinnie's men. Two held swords, one had a spear and a small shield, and they ran at the flank of the soldiers, surprising them. Lothar saw a sword rise and fall, and one of Heinnie's men dropped, but before the townsmen could take advantage of their position, they were being pressed back, with Heinnie's men stabbing and cutting at them. There was no doubting the outcome. The townsmen were not as experienced in fighting and killing as the Count's paid men. One soon lay dead. More would have followed him, had Lothar not run and joined them.

'Enough!' he shouted. 'These are not Jews, and nor are the people in that tavern.'

'We have been told that there is a Jewess and a boy in there,' Heinnie said. 'And they didn't open the door when we demanded.'

'I wouldn't open a door to you in this state,' Lothar said. He kept before the townsmen, protecting them, but aware that they could at any time attack him. They had no reason to trust any of the Count's men after the harm already done to the town. One was a younger man, who panted angrily, grey eyes flitting over the men with Heinnie.

'Lothar, come, let us search the house together,' Heinnie said.

'No, leave it. I was here earlier.'

'This is your brothel? I didn't realise! Then I can check the quality of the service for myself!' Heinnie laughed.

'My friend, I ask you again, leave it.'

'There is something here, Lothar, or they would have opened their door when I asked. Why should they hide if they have nothing to fear? If they cower inside, it is because they have something to conceal. You perhaps did not see them, but we have informers who said that a young woman and boy are in here. So we have to look.'

'Heinnie, I give you my word, there is nothing in here.'

'Lothar, you are my friend. Don't get in our way.'

Lothar braced himself, but just as he thought Heinnie would attack him, his companion grinned broadly, held up his hands, and retreated a pace.

It was a relief. Lothar felt the tension ebb, and in its place he knew only a heavy weariness. He glanced at the townsmen and urgently signalled that they should go and leave the body of their friend, shaking his head as they stood warily. Something sparked an alarm, and he turned to see Heinnie's fist. It struck his face, and Lothar staggered backwards, tripping over the body of Heinnie's man and sprawling headlong, his head cracking painfully on the stone of the road. Sparks and flares flashed in front of his eyes, and his jaw felt as though it had been kicked by a donkey. While he was down, one of Heinnie's men booted him in the ribs and he felt a fresh agony like a blossoming flower spread all over his breast. His nose had been broken, the blood running into his throat and choking him, and he tried to roll, attempting to climb to his feet, but Heinnie was there. He planted a boot on Lothar's chest and pressed down gently, resting his sword at his throat.

'Rest back, Lottie. You don't have to get involved. Look what good it does you, heh? Stay there and let us do what Count Emicho has ordered.'

Lothar could not move. Blood was filling his throat, and he could feel it clotting in his moustache. He could do nothing as he heard the shrieks and wild screams from inside the tavern, the squeal of the boy, and the tormented, wracking bawling of the Jewess as she was raped, before her final murder.

Lying back, spitting out the blood that thickened in his throat, Lothar stared at the man above him.

'I will kill you.'

'Oh, get over it, Lottie,' Heinnie said, and as Lothar made as though to rise again, he slammed his fist down into Lothar's face. Lothar fell back, his head striking the cobbles, and felt himself slide down into a thick, oily darkness speckled with bright flashes of scarlet, like blood sprayed over a wall at night.

CHAPTER 10

Rüdesheim, Friday 30th May, 1096

Lothar had come to during the night as a fine misting of drizzle spat down on his face. It was cool, and each gentle drop touching his nose felt like a tender kiss from the heavens. He grunted as the bruises made themselves known, and winced as he rolled over onto an elbow and levered himself upright with an effort.

The heat from the burning tavern was scorching and he was forced to avert his face. There was nothing left of the happy home he had seen yesterday, only a shell of stone where the roof's spars were exposed like the ribs of an enormous beast. He remained there in the roadway, staring, thinking of the scared Jewess and her brother, the tavern-woman who'd sought to protect them. It was not only her, for he had seen the men of the town attack Heinnie's men as though they were determined to defend the tavern and the Jews inside. These people, who knew the Jews best, were so convinced of their innocence that they were prepared to risk – yes, and lose – their lives.

He was badly battered. His head hurt, and his flank where

he had been kicked. Walking to a doorway, he huddled out of the spitting rain, pulling his cloak about him. His sword was no longer in its scabbard, and his knife too was gone. He would have to find new ones. Even as he had the thought, sleep overtook him again.

When he woke, it was full dawn. The body of Heinnie's man had been taken away, and only an oily smear on the cobbles showed where he had bled and died after the townspeople's attack. Lothar stood, his hand on the nearest wall, hissing with pain. His eyes turned back to the ruined building briefly, and then he took three stumbling paces before halting, panting, his hand on the lower right of his breast. He could feel a sharp pain there when he breathed in. His lungs seemed incapable of inhaling fully, and he was forced to try to breathe more slowly. He lifted his chin and stared ahead. Ahead of him, he knew, was the Archbishop's residence, where Count Emicho and the men were housed. Heinnie was there.

With determination, he lifted his boot and set it down. A first step, and then a second, and soon he found he could walk almost as fast as usual, although with a series of pauses to catch his breath. He hawked and spat a gobbet of blood and his breathing grew easier. His chest hurt, and he suspected a cracked or broken rib, but it was bearable. When he swung his arms, loosening the muscles, there was a sharp pain in his left shoulder, but that was minor compared with how he had felt on waking.

Lothar continued on his way to the Archbishop's compound. The gates were still shut, and Lothar had to beat on the timbers to alert the porter to his presence. Usually, this early the gates would not have been opened, but today was not a usual day. The porter peered out, saw Lothar's blood-encrusted face, and quickly let him in. A man dressed like one of the Count's men was not going to be questioned today.

'What happened to you?'

'Waylaid by thieves. They even took my sword and knife. Where is the armoury?'

He was pointed to the chamber and he crossed the court, opening the door and peering along the racks and shelves of weapons, finally selecting a short sword with a straight-edged blade and wide fuller that extended for two thirds of the length. There was a small dagger that he fitted to his belt, and then he made his way over the court to the hall. There he sat at a bench and remained, staring up at the lightening sky.

It was the second hour after dawn that Heinnie appeared at the top of the steps leading to the sleeping hall. Lothar watched him stand at the top and stretch, yawning widely, but made no move to rise. He could feel the pain in his flank still, but he was sure that it would not disable him too severely.

Heinnie's eyes suddenly caught sight of him, and he grinned. 'You look like shit!'

'I want to speak with you,' Lothar said.

'Wait until after I've broken my fast.'

'It would be a waste of food. This is a matter that will not wait. I challenge you, Heinnie.'

'Challenge me? Why?'

'Because you slaughtered three innocents last night and then beat me for no reason. You will pay, here, in full sight of the men here and in the sight of God. I swear you are a coward and thief, and I will have your blood.'

'Lothar, they were just a Jew and her brat.'

That, Lothar thought, was the problem. Heinnie did not see humans when he looked at others. Only creatures. The three he had killed last night were as irrelevant to him as sheep or feral cats. And Lothar himself had been the same, until he saw the women killing the child and themselves. They welcomed death at their own hands, rather than give pleasure to men like Heinnie. Lothar felt cleansed by the knowledge.

'Come here and defend yourself,' he said. He rose, drawing his new sword and flinging the scabbard aside. 'Their deaths must be avenged.'

Heinnie took a sword from a guard nearest him, and danced down the stairs surprisingly lightly on his feet, giggling as he came. He took up a stance with the sword over his head, both hands gripping the short hilt, legs bent in the familiar fighting pose, but Lothar walked to him with his own blade whirling about his wrist, watching Heinnie.

'You don't have to fight me, Lottie,' Heinnie said. 'This is all a misunderstanding, I think. We had our orders, that's all. If you want, we can forget this and go celebrate with a horn of ale or wine.'

Lothar ignored his words. He was watching Heinnie's arms and face. Heinnie was always obvious when he was about to attack. He would narrow his eyes momentarily, just before he brought his blade down. Lothar knew. And he knew that Heinnie would know his own little signs, too, and just now Lothar didn't care. He stood before Heinnie, the sword at his belly's height, his left hand gripping the pommel level with his belt, ready.

He saw Heinnie's eyes dart to the side and he had his sword rising in an instant. Heinnie's blade came down and slammed into Lothar's, but Lothar had moved his hands and now his left gripped his blade near the point, like a man fighting with a half-staff. Lothar thrust hard with his right hand, trying to strike Heinnie in the face with the cross-guard, but missed. Heinnie's blade was pushed up and away, and when it slid along Lothar's weapon, Lothar took his hand away, returning it to the pommel, but as he did so Heinnie tried a quick slash across Lothar's belly. Lothar bent his body away and swept his blade right, knocking Heinnie's past, and as it went Lothar stabbed forwards. His blade met Heinnie's at the cross, close to his hand grip where Heinnie had little leverage or control. Heinnie's eyes showed sudden panic. Their edges were meeting, but Lothar had the weight of his body behind his, and Heinnie was already off balance. He could do nothing as Lothar pushed.

'I yield!' Heinnie shouted.

'I can't hear you,' Lothar spat.

'Lottie! Don't!'

But he was too late. Lothar pursed his lips and shoved, twisting his blade. He jerked it, and the edge caught Heinnie's brow, and Heinnie kicked up with his knee, desperate to break Lothar's grip. His knee missed Lothar's cods, but caught him high on his thigh and he stumbled, but as he did he punched hard with his left hand, catching Heinnie on the chin. He fell, and Lothar slashed down once, catching Heinnie across the face.

Lothar picked up his sword and held it high over his head. A number of men had gathered about them, and they were watching in silence. He looked about him at them. None of them were worried. He might kill Heinnie, he might allow him his life; it was nothing to them. Some were eating, masticating bread or dried meat, watching with almost bovine disinterest.

It was tempting to bring his blade down and finish Heinnie once and for all, but there was a part of him that still remembered Heinnie as a comrade and friend. The sword thrilled in his hand, demanding Heinnie's blood, and it was with an effort that Lothar slowly let the sword drop.

'I am no friend of yours,' he said. He picked up his scabbard and sheathed his sword. Without looking behind him, he made his way through the gates, past the gaping porter and out through the town. There was a small bridge over the river and he took it, crossing to the town of Bingen, and thence south.

He felt empty. He had lost his friend, his lord, his life.

South of Bingen

The newly knighted Sir Roger de Toni could not lose the feeling of excitement as he rode down the road, filled with the new sounds and smells and sights in this land of broad plains, heading towards the steep mountains to the south.

It was all exciting to him. Already they had been travelling for weeks – over a thousand miles, he reckoned. The initial preparation had taken two weeks, and then weather held them up at the coast, and they were still many miles from their destination in Rome – which lay another week behind the mountains, so he had heard from guides and other travellers. Not that their help was very useful in many cases. Everything here was new and confusing. The money was different, and they must convert coin at different stages; he was glad he had brought gold and pewter, which was easy to exchange along the way. Not only that, even the measures varied from one district to another. Crossing the land of the Flemings, he discovered that when the people talked of a mile, they meant an English league: three miles. Here in the Holy Roman Empire, the people spoke of one mile as an Englishman would speak of four, whereas he had heard that the people towards Rome calculated a mile as only some two-thirds of an English one.

It was an awesome journey that they were undertaking, and he was only now beginning to dimly appreciate just how far this pilgrimage was, and how long it would take them to reach the great Roman city of Constantinople, let alone the Holy City. But for now, considerations of that nature were overwhelmed by the inundation of sensations that were overwhelming him, from the sights of the immense flats beside this enormous river, to the smells of curious spices and tastes of different foods.

His men were for the most part quiet during the journey. They were a mixed group, led by the sergeant picked by Sir Roger's father: Gilles. Although Roger had attempted to tease Gilles into conversation, the man had remained resolutely taciturn and uncommunicative.

'Have you ever seen a river so broad, Gilles?' Roger tried now. He jerked a thumb over his shoulder towards the great sweep of the Rhine.

'Yes.'

Gilles was a shortish man with a barrel for a chest and hair that was shorn so close to his head that from any distance he looked bald. He had a shrewd gaze when he looked at a man, but it was not the look of friendship. Rather, it was the measuring glance a joiner would give when judging the size of a coffin. When Radulph had first taken the manor for his own, Gilles had been with him. That was some twenty years ago, and he had been Sir Radulph's mercenary every since, a reliable, stalwart man who would fight for his knight through all adversity. He liked Sir Radulph. He was not yet certain of Roger, but he would serve his interests as best he might.

Roger turned in his saddle and peered back at the men. They rode as men will, three with heads down, dozing in the warm air, two staring about them at every bush and tree in search of danger, one riding with his foreleg crooked over his horse's withers, his face bent as he muttered a prayer over his rosary. One at the rear was chewing on a chicken's leg. 'They haven't been here before, either, have they?'

Gilles eyed them briefly. 'The furthest travelled is Eudes, I think. He came from near Rheims. The rest are Breton like Guarin, or Norman.'

'What of you, Gilles? Did you travel before you joined my father?'

'I never had a need to.'

'You didn't feel the need to go on pilgrimage?'

'Not then, no.'

There was a finality to his voice that discouraged further questioning, but Roger pressed him. 'There is now, then?'

'Every man may do things he comes to regret,' Gilles said. Feeling pressed, he continued, 'I don't. I'm here to protect you, master, and I'll serve you as I may for Sir Radulph, but I am not here to tell you of my life. It's my concern, not yours.'

'But you will win redemption when you find yourself in the Holy City,' Roger said. He set his face to the mountains once more. 'They say it gleams, that it is a city of gold.'

'Who does?'

'Others who wish to go there.'

'If the city was built of gold, it would have been razed to the ground by now,' Gilles said, and spat into the road's dirt. 'You view this *iter* as an adventure. Well, it may be: perhaps we'll enjoy a pleasant ride to the Holy City and no danger; however, more men die by underestimating their enemies than by respecting them. I will respect an enemy I have not met.'

'These men are heathens,' Roger laughed.

'They are men with swords, axes, bows and arrows. And they will know how to use them.'

'You think we should fear them?' Roger grinned. He was Norman and, to Gilles's embittered eye, as incapable of appreciating danger as a puppy.

'When I meet them, I will expect them to be as dangerous as the Saxons I fought with your father. We knew we had God on our side that day, but it didn't make us treat Harold's shield wall with any less respect. You would do well to remember that.'

'Your spirit is as sour as six-month ale! It is the city of God,' Roger remonstrated.

'But it exists in the world of men.'

*

Sir Roger saw the man far off in the distance.

'What is that?' Gilles said.

'A man, walking. What of it?'

'Not him. There, riding down from the slope.'

Following his pointing finger, Sir Roger saw a band of six men on sturdy ponies. They had been riding at a moderate pace over to the left, but now they saw the lone walker and set their beasts towards him at a trot.

Sir Roger de Toni had come for excitement and adventure. 'They are brigands! Follow me!' he cried, and raked his spurs down his mount's flanks. His horse shook his head, half-bucked, and then gave a great lurch forward, his muscles moving with an uneven, ragged discordancy, he was so unused to speed after so many weeks of walking.

Gilles was surprised by his action. As Sir Roger's mount settled into his long, striding canter, Gilles remained on his beast with his mouth wide. Then he recovered, bellowing to the rest of the men to keep close while he set off after Sir Roger at full speed. In an instant, he had overhauled Roger, his hand dropping to his sword hilt and sweeping his weapon out. Sir Roger bent lower to come level, pulling his own weapon free. He held it aloft, his mouth pulling into a grin as he gave a loud, wild shriek of pure exultation.

The lone man turned and, on seeing the riders, pulled his own sword from the scabbard and threw the casing aside, gripping his sword with both hands, ready to receive his attackers.

'Look at him,' Sir Roger said to himself. 'He fears no one.'

The brigands were almost on him now, and they circled him, some closer than others. One approached too near and yelped when the man's sword slashed and cut into his thigh. The others drew away, but they would soon charge. With so many, he must be knocked from his feet, and then he would be at their mercy.

Sir Roger swung his sword, loosening his wrist, and rode in fast, striking one man on the back of his head with the flat of his sword. There was a dull thud, and he felt the hilt jerk in his hand, and the man went tumbling to the ground like a stunned rabbit. The other men shouted and turned to face Sir Roger, but then Gilles and the rest of the men were there, and the five men still ahorse retreated in the face of the superior numbers.

'Who are you?' Sir Roger demanded.

The others looked confused, but one answered in passable French, 'We are with Count Emicho of Flonheim. This man is a traitor, and attacked a comrade.'

'So you would kill him on the road like an outlaw?'

'We have the right. He all but killed one of our own.'

'You! What is your name?' Sir Roger demanded.

'I am called Lothar. He speaks the truth. I challenged a man this morning, and I bested him. But it was a fair fight. He had killed when I told him not to. I punished him.'

'What people?'

'Children,' Lothar said. He would not say more than that. Words clogged his breast.

'He must come back with us,' the man said.

'You can fight us for him.' Sir Roger grinned and moved his horse forward a little, between Lothar and his assailants. These men were warriors, it was clear, but he did not like to be ordered by common churls. He was a knight, and he would defend his right in the face of these scruffy peasants.

The men exchanged glances. It was clear that they did not like the odds of fighting against double their number.

'Take your companion and go,' Sir Roger said. 'If you try to assail this man, you will answer to me, Sir Roger de Toni. Now, go!'

He watched them as two men helped their fallen comrade

121

back into his saddle, shaking his head groggily, blood dripping from his nose and a gash on his brow, and then slowly rode off northwards. When they were disappearing over the brow of the next hill, Sir Roger finally turned to the man they had saved.

Lothar stood and watched the men warily, wondering whether he had escaped his companions only to be overwhelmed by a fresh group of brigands. 'I thank you for saving me. I could not have fought them all off.'

'You were willing to try, my friend,' Sir Roger said. Lothar was no better bred than the six he had driven off, but the fact that he had been prepared to risk his life fighting them spoke of his courage.

'Where do you go?' Sir Roger asked.

Lothar shrugged. 'My companions were to join the march to Jerusalem. I think they will follow the route to the east. They were to join the Hermit's pilgrimage to Constantinople.'

'So do we, but we head south,' Sir Roger said. He glanced at Gilles.

Gilles grunted, 'We make our way to Merano, over the mountains, then to Rome, where we will meet with the other members of our pilgrimage, and on to Constantinople.'

'You would be welcome to join us,' Sir Roger said. 'Another sword is always welcome in a land full of brigands.'

'What was the cause of the dispute?' Gilles asked suspiciously. He sat on his horse, bent over, his arms crossed over the pommel.

'Children. My companions killed them. They were young. They were innocent, and had no one else to protect them.'

'You knew them?'

'I had met them, but I didn't *know* them. I had not even heard their names,' Lothar said, and he was surprised as he spoke it aloud. It seemed so curious that he had burned his bridges with his company for a pair of children and a woman tavern-keeper whose names he did not even know.

'Yet you were prepared to suffer hardship for them?' Roger said. 'You showed chivalry, friend.'

'Perhaps. It was the right thing to do, so it seemed.'

'You didn't kill him?' Sir Roger said.

'Perhaps I should have,' Lothar said. 'It was a fair fight; a matter of honour, I would say. But when I won, it was clear others saw it in a different light.'

'So, now you can join with us,' Sir Roger said.

Lothar saw Gilles shoot a look at Sir Roger: Gilles knew that a fellow found at the wayside could be an unreliable companion. There might be more to his story than he had told them.

Gilles winced, but Lothar nodded gratefully. 'My lord, I would be glad to join you. If you would give me food and water for the journey, I will gladly be your bondsman,' Lothar said. He made a bow, and thus were their fates joined.

BOOK FOUR

Welcome and Rejection

CHAPTER 11

River Danube, near Zemun, Tuesday 3rd June, 1096

Odo woke as the sun rose and opened his eyes slowly. He put his arms behind his head.

'There was a time when I used to wake happily and look forward to breaking my fast with a fresh loaf, warm from the oven, dabbing it into beef dripping, and feeling only the satisfaction of a day's work to come.'

'I didn't,' Fulk said. His eyes were still closed as he continued, 'I hated getting up, knowing the old smith was going to strike me with a strap for every infraction of his rules. If there was a chisel out of place, he'd slap me; if the fire didn't get hot quickly enough, if the wind blew the smoke back into the smithy, if the iron didn't weld, if the steel didn't quench well, no matter what, I got a slap. I used to dream of staying in bed until late.'

'You always wanted to stay in bed late. Especially with one of the sluts from the town.'

'That's not fair!' Fulk protested.

'Why?'

'Some were good women.'

'Which?'

Fulk screwed his eyes more tightly shut. 'Never you mind.'

'And now you've found another wench on this journey.'

'I won't do it again,' Fulk muttered, although Guillemette's face intruded into his thoughts. He wished she were here now; he wished Odo would shut up.

Looking over at Fulk, Odo felt a burning resentment. Fulk looked so relaxed, whereas Odo was aware only of the responsibility. The weight of the ambition of this pilgrimage was a heavy burden and he felt as though he bore it alone. Fulk seemed to consider this a mere stroll in the sun. Even now he wore a small smile. He was *infuriating*! A pound to a penny he was thinking of a woman again.

Odo sat up. Other people in the encampment were already up. He and Fulk had joined with these people weeks ago, still in May, and the two brothers had been buoyed by the thousands on all sides. But they had been marching hard. Now, he studied his brother dispassionately.

Fulk was more wiry than he had been. Odo assumed they all were, for constant travel and little food had hardened them. At every town or city they bargained for food, but often the prices were higher than they would have been at home, and several of the pilgrims were finding it hard to acquire the food they needed. Odo felt most sorry for the children. There were many of them here, both girls and boys. Some were with their parents, but many had come on their own.

Odo shook his head at the thought of all the long, dusty, weary miles already covered. He stood, stretching, glancing about him.

In the distance he saw Guillemette. The sight made him glower. He had guessed her trade the first time he saw her with Fulk. She was so assured; too much the bawd. The other woman with her was far more appealing: a slim, fair woman in her early twenties. He admired her long, heart-shaped face and pale blue eyes. She had a stray ringlet of blonde hair at the side of her coif, and he saw it dance in the faint breeze. She looked less confident. He could imagine being married to a woman like her. A sweet-natured woman who would cook for him, sew his clothes, and keep his bed warm of an evening. That she was here surely showed that she was pious, too.

Fulk farted.

Odo looked down, tempted to kick him. 'Are you getting up?'

'Why? So we can stomp onwards? I could rest a little longer, without it having a huge impact on the rest of the campaign. What's the hurry?'

Odo pulled at a blade of grass. He held it out and touched Fulk's nose gently. His brother waved a hand at the air near his face. Odo tickled again, and Fulk irritably slapped at it. The third time, he glowered at Odo. 'What did you do that for?'

'It saved me booting you.'

With a bad grace, Fulk rose to a sitting position. When he did, he saw Guillemette and waved.

'Leave her alone. No more whoring!'

Fulk grumpily snapped, 'It's only Guillemette and her friend Jeanne!'

'They are a distraction,' Odo said, but his eyes went to the younger and fairer of the two even as he spoke.

A half-mile behind them, Benet was already preparing the pony when Sybille wearily opened her eyes.

She had not slept well. Richalda had been sick overnight, and Sybille had been forced to sit up for much of the evening, soothing her as best she might, until the shivering and dry-retching had ended. Now the child looked entirely peaceful, and Sybille knew that she herself must look drained and unkempt. She so missed the comforts of home. Now, after a month and more of sleeping out in the open, of tree roots in her back, of midge and mosquito bites, of endlessly exhausted legs and feet, of constant weariness, her reserves of good humour were all but used.

'Come, my darling,' her husband called when he saw her rising and patting the grass and mud from her tunic and skirts. 'Help get this beast ready.'

She stilled the retort that leapt to her lips. In all these days she had not resorted to the cruel tongue that tried to fight for dominance. Instead, she obediently rose and went to him. On the way she touched Richalda's face. The child frowned slightly in her sleep, but as Sybille took her hand away, she was aware that her daughter had become warm. Her face felt hot to the touch. It made her bite her bottom lip.

'Pass me that sack,' Benet called.

'Husband, where is Josse?'

'He is fetching water for the journey. Come, wife, please!' She left Richalda and went to join him, lifting the bag he indicated and holding it to him.

He smiled. 'You look tired out, Sybille. Soon we shall be at the great city of Constantinople, and then you'll see! It is supposed to be the greatest city in the whole world, perhaps even than Jerusalem.'

'Then what are we doing this journey for?' Sybille snapped.

'Darling—'

'Don't "Darling" me, husband! I've endured, God knows, the weary leagues from Sens without complaining, but if you tell me that we are here to see wondrous sights of a great city, I will . . . I will beat you with the cookpot! We've come all this way at such a hideous cost!'

'It has not cost us much, my love, and we will soon make it all up when we help take Jerusalem. Just you wait! I have a dream, my love. No more scrimping and saving, no more hardship. When we get there, we will be the first to set up a stall selling the best of goods from Sens and Paris, and the people will flock to us to buy our wares. I shall be the first to create a merchant's dynasty in Jerusalem itself!' His eyes took on a distant stare, and a smile creased his lips. 'We will be able to afford a great house, with a large garden. We will have servants, and you can rest, rather than working your fingers to the bone. Richalda will have a brother or two to play with, who'll grow to be men who can take over the business when I am old, so that you and I can enjoy our last years in contentment and comfort, and—'

'And all that is far in the future, and meanwhile we have yet to reach even Constantinople. Will we all reach the place, though? I doubt it! Look at Richalda! She was sick all last night, husband, and still she shows every sign of weakness. Look at her! You have done this to her!'

'She is young! She will soon mend.'

Sybille stared at him. 'I hope so, husband, for if she does not I will never be able to forgive you for bringing us here to watch her die,' she hissed. She picked up another sack and flung it at him, before flouncing back to her daughter.

Richalda opened her eyes and smiled weakly. Sybille returned it, but she was worried. In recent years famine had struck all Christendom, and she had seen other women's children sicken and die. Richalda was displaying the same feverish symptoms that those children had exhibited.

The Sava River

It was lunchtime when Fulk and Odo stopped at last. The army had been walking down the western shore of the River Danube for some days now, following its western bank down to the city of Zemun. Here there was another river, the Sava, that separated Zemun from Belgrade.

Fulk lurched to the bank and stood on the shoreline, his bare feet in the slow-moving waters. 'Urgh, this feels horribly good!' he called back to his brother. His sword was hanging from his shoulder by a thong, and now he drew it free and set it on the ground beside him, rubbing his shoulder where the cord had chafed his skin. He opened the flap of his scrip and peered inside. There was little enough there. He had a small portion of bread left over from two days ago, and a slice or two of dried meat that had gone greasy and smelled more rancid than smoked. Still, when he bit and chewed, it tasted good enough.

There were many people here. He could see Zemun, a large town, that lay on this side of the river a mile or so downstream, while on the opposite bank a still larger town, or perhaps a city, lay. The river was enormously wide, and a number of boats of various sizes ploughed their way across the waters.

'You should try the water too!' he called as a shadow fell across him. 'You smell like a hog, after all, Odo!'

'Perhaps I shall,' a voice answered, but it was a deeper voice than Odo's, and Fulk leaned back to look up, almost falling over. In his upside-down vision, he saw a knight with the cross sewn onto his left breast like so many who had taken oaths with the first of the pilgrims.

Fulk almost fell over in his urgent scramble to his knees. 'I am sorry, my lord, I meant no harm, I thought you were my brother,' he babbled, ducking his head.

'You gave me no insult. There's no need for fear in my presence,' the man said. 'I am Sir Walter de Boissy-Sans-Avoir.' He lifted his gaze and studied the river and the city at the opposite bank.

'Sir Walter!' Fulk said, bowing his head still lower until his brow was almost on the ground.

All the men knew of Sir Walter. He was Peter the Hermit's military adviser. Sir Walter had gathered together a large force of the stronger and more capable male pilgrims about him.

'Who are you?'

'Fulk – a smith, Sir Walter. I am with the pilgrimage, and my brother too. We hope to be at your side and Peter the Hermit's as you enter the gates of Jerusalem.'

Sir Walter nodded, still staring at the two towns. 'That is good. We have a long way to travel first, though, and Peter is not here. He delayed and is bringing up the next group of pilgrims a few weeks behind us.' He looked down at Fulk. 'You look strong enough. But hungry.'

'It is hard to buy food at a reasonable price,' Fulk admitted.

'But you do have a sword.'

'Yes,' Fulk said, and allowed a little sharpness into his tone. 'But I am no thief.'

'I didn't say you were. I was considering that you could be of use to me. You and your brother both have weapons?'

'We bought them before we left France.'

'A good idea. Others will regret not demonstrating the same foresight before long,' the knight said. 'When did you last have a full meal?'

'Not for a few days,' Fulk said. He felt the stirrings of hope.

'Your brother is in the same position?'

'He is hungry, my lord, yes.'

He considered Fulk, and then seemed to come to a decision.

'Find your brother and have him join you. You can both enter my company and share in the food I have. I would have more men like you in my party. We will need men with strong arms before long.'

Approaching Zemun

It was that same day that the catastrophe happened.

Sybille and her husband continued their journey without speaking. She was in a filthy mood with him, and although she tried to divert herself from the bitterness that was in her heart, she could not. He was a good man, a loving, caring father and husband, yet just now she wanted to hit him. Even his words, intended to calm her, failed. When she rode the pony, she cradled Richalda, who seemed to doze much of the time. There were a few moments when Sybille found herself nodding too, and more than once she jerked awake as she was beginning to slide from the saddle.

They were following the riverbank, keeping to the road made by the passage of all the other pilgrims earlier, when she first saw the great camp made by Sir Walter. There were many men and women creating makeshift tents with blankets and cloaks hanging from trees. The people had already sent for help from the nearer of the towns, and some traders had set up their stalls, shouting incomprehensibly while standing on the boards of carts, holding loaves or pieces of meat aloft. A butcher had brought cattle with him, and was energetically poleaxing them one by one, while others flayed the carcasses before a group of men-at-arms. Sybille thought that they were sure to be as tough as old leather, but her mouth watered at the sight of the bloody hunks of meat nonetheless.

Finding a small space, Benet set up their camp a short way from the water, and Sybille started to prepare dough to make bread. She had some maslin, a coarse mix of flour and ground peas and beans, and she added enough water to allow it to work, and set it in the cookpot to settle before making a fire. Benet watched her for a while, and then walked away. She didn't speak. There seemed nothing to say.

The day was warm. Sybille had Josse set up a blanket to create shade, and placed Richalda beneath it, but the child was still feeble and fractious. It was enough to increase Sybille's nervousness. But then she realised that the shadows were growing, and suddenly her fears focused instead on her husband.

She stood and gazed about her, peering in all directions, and took three paces in the direction in which he had left her, but even as she did, Richalda gave a moan. Torn, Sybille stared ahead as though she might see her husband returning at any moment.

'Benet?' she whispered, but there was no sign of him. Sybille turned back to her daughter. Richalda needed her. Surely Benet was off drinking wine and talking great stories about how he would become a rich trader when he reached Jerusalem. She crouched and took Richalda's hand in her own, using a scrap of her skirts dampened in river water to wipe at her little girl's brow. She needed herbs for Richalda, she needed food, she needed a warming drink, but most of all, right now, she needed her husband.

Josse stood irresolute, staring down at her, then across at the plain so smothered with people it was like an ant heap. 'I will find him, mistress,' he said.

'Don't take long!' she said, and tried not to sound as fearful as she felt. 'Bring him back quickly, please!'

*

Fulk and Odo joined Sir Walter's party, Odo glaring about him suspiciously as they moved about among the men, as if he was expecting to see vice on all sides.

For his part, Fulk was struck by the size of the army. Walking here from Sens he had been aware of the swelling numbers, but as they marched he was not aware of the sprawling mass of people. Men, women and children of all nations and positions were there at the river's banks. Fulk had never seen so many people; it looked to him as though the whole of Christendom had been emptied, and it was shocking to see them milling about. For the first time he began to appreciate the enormity of the undertaking in which he was involved.

Sir Walter's men were different from the men-at-arms he had seen before, who had been mercenaries and always on the brink of violence. These men were from a very different mould. They were organised and disciplined.

They were a mixture: some younger, some older; Fulk saw many with fair hair who wore body-mail only, men of Lotharingia and Francia and Bavaria, who looked as fierce as Viking berserkers; near them was a collection of heavier-set men who spoke in the guttural tones of the men of the mountains. Unconsciously, Odo and he walked closer together.

'Are you sure he said we would be welcome?' Odo whispered.

Fulk said nothing. Towards the middle of the men he could see flags fluttering, and bent his feet towards them. There, in a pavilion, he found the knight he sought.

'You did come,' Sir Walter said. 'Good! Find yourselves somewhere to rest, for it will take us time to negotiate.'

There was a clerk with him, who looked like a harassed older uncle. He shook his head perpetually with a worried frown on his face. 'I do not think you comprehend the situation, Sir Walter. If we don't get passage, we will soon have problems.'

'*We* will not. The governor of the city will. If he wishes to delay us here and prevent us crossing the river, there will be consequences.'

'Yes. We won't get access to his markets and will starve,' the clerk said.

'John, my friend, we are here on God's business, but we were asked to come here by the governor's own master. The Emperor of Byzantium sent a message to the Pope and asked for the aid of the Christians to expel the heretics from Jerusalem. If he wishes to hold us here, that will redound to his discredit. And because I will not see so many good Christians suffer hunger, we will be forced to lay waste to the lands all about here. Now, do you go and tell him that I am adamant in this. We need ships and we need food, and for that I demand access to his markets in the city.'

Fulk had heard from others already that the army must pass over this great river to the city on the other side, Belgrade. With such an expanse of water to cross, and with so many pilgrims, they would need an entire fleet of ships. He was daunted to hear that there were difficulties. Apparently the people of Zemun wanted nothing to do with the pilgrimage, and the governor of Belgrade had already declared that he would not allow access to his food stocks or markets. Fulk had a strange feeling of despondency as he and Odo bowed their way from the knight's presence and sought a place where they might put their belongings and rest as Sir Walter had commanded them.

Fulk found a space where he could lie down, but Odo scorned his wish for sleep. Instead he investigated what he could find. Although the town's markets were barred to the pilgrims, occasional traders were appearing to offer food. Odo could see some carters setting out a variety of vegetables and dried fish on blankets laid on the ground.

He ambled towards the traders. More and more pilgrims were making their way there, and he eyed his roadside companions with distaste. Most of the men looked like the dregs of every tavern and low wineshop of Christendom, while the women looked like beggars and worse, and all about them ran the brats, bare-footed and ill-kempt. They had the fire of God's will in their bellies, and that should count for something, but to him these people looked like scoundrels.

Into his mind, suddenly, flashed a picture of a battle. He saw bodies, limbs, blood, entrails lying in misshapen piles on the sand, with flags and banners fluttering. Carrion birds hopped and pecked, gorging themselves. He saw Fulk's body, his eyes full of distress, and at Fulk's side, that woman, his whore, with an expression of satisfaction.

Odo shook his head. The woman may be a prostitute, but he could not think that she was an agent of the Devil, here to tempt Fulk from the path chosen for him. And yet, who could tell? Perhaps some of these females who had professed their correct desire to join with the pilgrimage were, in truth, agents of Satan, come here to bring about the failure of this holy march?

No. Such thoughts were the meanderings of the unconvinced. Odo knew that the pilgrimage was desired by God, because the Pope himself had declared it so. The only matter Odo should concern himself with was that of how he would acquit himself, and that did worry him greatly. He feared that the first clash of arms would unman him. He had never been engaged in anything more deadly than a drunken brawl with a clerk in an alehouse. Never had he seen a man slain in anger, let alone killed one himself. The thought of standing in a battle and wielding weapons was terrifying.

He must do his best.

The picture of the battle returned to his mind's eye, and he felt a flash of jealousy at the thought that Fulk would have a woman beside him even in death. With a loyal, loving woman at his side, Odo felt he would achieve so much. One like that young female who was walking with Guillemette: Jeanne. She would calm him, and allow him to fight for God without fear.

A man barged into him, and his maudlin mood was gone, replaced by irritation.

There was a wonderful array of foods set out on trays or sacking now, with dark-skinned locals shouting in an unintelligible confusion of noises. The pilgrims stood thickly about it, the men and women barging each other out of the way, so great was their desperation for food. Odo frowned to see a man place his hand on a woman's breast and shove her from his path. It was tempting to remonstrate with him, but Odo could tell that it would be foolish. These men may wear pilgrims' crosses, but they were tired and hungry. Tempers were frayed and the lack of language between the people of Zemun and the pilgrims was exacerbating a bad situation.

A man cried out and the mob was unleashed. Later, Odo heard that one pilgrim had punched another, but in the febrile atmosphere, none stopped to think. Pilgrims stormed forward, grabbing the men of Zemun and beating them. In moments Odo was caught up in the middle of a riot. He was struck on the back and almost fell to the ground, then a blow aimed at another man bounced off his shoulder, and he was shoved sideways. A fist was aimed at his face, and he tried to jerk his head away, but it caught him a glancing blow on the cheek and he fell against a man behind him.

Pushing and shoving, he made his way through the press, trying to get back to the safety of the camp, but even as he found himself in a clearer space, he heard shouted orders and the clash of weapons. There was a sudden panic, and men began to pull back as soldiers from Zemun appeared. They had been watching from the shelter of a small wood near the camp and at the first sight of violence they unsheathed their weapons and rushed forward. They pushed the mob back, trampling the food that had been spread out so appealingly. All was crushed underfoot as the soldiers began to wield clubs and other weapons against the pilgrims. As they were forced to retreat, the merchants of Zemun began to jeer and make obscene gestures, and Odo felt a loathing for them growing like a worm in his bowels.

These were supposed to be Christians. They should be glad to support the people's pilgrimage. Instead they were determined to thwart the people marching to save the Holy Land. Odo longed to punish them.

They were doing the work of the Devil!

Sybille sat cross-legged on the ground, her daughter in her lap, and patted Richalda's forehead with a dampened cloth. Panic was starting to rise in her breast. The muscles of her back tightened and her neck was tense. Her little girl was muttering to herself about aches in her joints and muscles. She felt so hot, and had clammy, sweaty skin, for all that she kept complaining about the cold. Sybille had never seen such an illness in her own child, and the sight was utterly crippling. In the face of Richalda's illness, Sybille was incapable of logical thought. She sat and rocked her daughter, her mind empty of all but the thought that kept circling her head: 'My daughter is dying and I can do nothing to help her.'

She was only dimly aware that a voice was speaking to her. Looking up she saw an older woman. Through the haze of tears, she saw only a woman clad in black, and felt an instinctive trust, perhaps thinking that it was a nun. She wiped her eyes as the woman spoke to her, and realised that this was no nun. She was as scruffy and unwashed as all the rest of the pilgrims here, but her face was kind. 'My name is Mathena. My little girl over there, Esperte, once had a similar fever. We had to bleed her to let out the bad humours. She recovered well, and your child will too.'

Sybille nodded, but she had no words. Looking down at her daughter, she thought how thin Richalda looked, how deeply shadowed were her eyes.

'Mistress, you are tired out. My friends and I can look after your girl. You rest.'

'I don't know what to do!'

'Let us worry about that. You won't help her by exhausting yourself,' Mathena said firmly. She sat down beside Sybille and held out her hands. Sybille passed her child to the stranger in a daze, not quite sure that she was doing the right thing, but as Guillemette and Jeanne joined them, she felt an overwhelming sense of gratitude, as if these women were going to make all well for her.

The first cries came on the cooling early evening air. Fulk had been dozing, his back to a tree, his chin on his breast, when he heard the bellow of outrage. He clambered to his feet, still muzzy, fumbling for his sword.

'What is going on?' he asked.

Odo was standing nearby, tense and alert. He had returned and told Fulk of the fight and how the pilgrims had been beaten. Three men were killed. Now he stood watching Sir Walter at his pavilion.

'I told you what happened,' Odo said.

'This isn't the same thing, surely?' Fulk asked.

Odo shook his head slowly. 'No. Other pilgrims didn't hear what happened to us. They were enticed away before the riots. Some twenty of them wandered off towards Zemun because they have no weapons and wanted to buy some. But they were tricked.

The people of the town beat them, robbed them, stripped them and sent them packing, as a message to all who seek to enter their town without permission, I suppose.'

Fulk looked at his brother. He had keen hearing, and just now he could hear stifled rage in Odo's voice. 'Odo, there's nothing for us to get upset about here.'

'Nothing for us to get upset about?' Odo spat. 'We're here to *help* these people and all Christians. They have the temerity, the vicious, wicked desire to prevent us! I told you how shamefully they treated us at the market? They stand not only against us, not only in the way of men who want to cross this river, Fulk! They set their faces against God Himself!'

Fulk was alarmed to see Odo grasp his sword. 'Odo, what are you doing?'

'We came here in peace, didn't we? I'm going to show them what happens when they try to stop a pilgrimage in support of Christ and His city!'

Fulk caught his arm. 'Odo, don't be a fool! We have to stay here with the men! You can't just run out and fight all the men of the town.'

'I won't stand here and listen to them jeering us!' Odo said.

Fulk heard the incomprehension and frustration in his tones. When he was a child, Odo would rage against what he saw as injustice, confused and angry at cruelty or unfairness. Hearing those tones in his voice now made Fulk smile to himself. 'Odo, brother, they aren't trying to upset you. They don't even know who *you* are. They're just protecting their own, that's all.'

'They robbed Christian men; they killed some of us!'

'This is the border between two lands. It's where Hungary ends and the Empire begins. There are always likely to be problems buying things. Maybe one of the pilgrims tried it on with a man's wife or daughter? It's easy to make enemies of people when you don't understand their language or customs as well as you might.'

'They robbed them. They stripped them naked and took their money, Fulk. That's an insult to all of us!'

'And an insult we'll have to swallow. We have a long way to go. What, would you have us fight every city where an insult was hurled at us?'

He could see his words were not working. Odo was childlike in his response to an insult, and this, for him, was profound. To his mind, it showed that the people of the city did not respect God. It was an appalling slight, and the reaction had to be proportionate.

'No! This must leave our pilgrimage in disgrace if we swallow such an offence.'

Fulk would have remonstrated further, but to his relief he heard the horns blaring. Soon they had their orders.

At dawn they would cross the river and continue on their way, whether the men of Zemun wanted it or not.

Josse was back before nightfall, and with him he had a shamefaced, anxious Benet, wrapped in a thick, coarse blanket that smelled of horse. Benet walked to the fire and sat at its edge, while Josse bowed to Sybille and walked away to help with the packing of their goods, ready for the morning's river crossing.

'What happened?' Sybille said. She sat on the ground with Mathena still cradling Richalda. Jeanne and Guillemette had shared a small pottage with Sybille, and the women had managed to get some food into Richalda. She was still very pale, her eyes sunken, and with small, high spots of colour on her cheeks, but the cooled pottage with shreds of chicken meat had made her more comfortable.

Benet's voice was tremulous, his hands shaking like a man

suffering from a fever. His eyes were wide with horror, and he grabbed Sybille's arm as though it was a lifeline in a swelling sea. She felt his shock, and drew him away so that his words could not be heard by Richalda, but he blurted it all out as they walked away.

'They set upon us, Sybille! They set upon us as though we were no more than thieves and brigands. We went to buy arms and some mail, and the merchants we spoke to promised much, telling us to join them. They took us to the suburbs of the city, to a dwelling where they said they kept their goods, but as soon as we entered, they caught us and bound us. They beat us, and laughed the whole while, Sybille! They *laughed*. They stripped us naked, and took everything!' Benet said. 'Clothes, knives, armour – everything! – before throwing us from their door and jeering at us.'

Sybille stopped and stared at him. 'What do you mean, "everything"? Husband! Your belt has gone – did they take your scrip? Your purse? Husband, tell me they didn't take *all* our money?'

He looked away, shame and humiliation battling within him. 'They took everything. We have nothing.'

Sybille stared, appalled. All their money, all the savings from Sens, had been tied about his belly, the coins enclosed in a roll of leather. It was the money they would need to travel to Jerusalem, the money they would need for food and drink.

It was all gone.

CHAPTER 12

Zemun, Wednesday 4th June, 1096

Fulk woke from a pleasant dream that involved a pot of ale and a pair of friendly maids.

'Leave me in peace!' he groaned as he saw the half-light before dawn.

'We're to make a move soon,' Odo said. 'We're to cross the river before the men of that town can think about preventing us.'

'They'll be happy to be rid of us, won't they?'

'Probably, but the folk over the river might decide to try to stop us.'

'Why would they do that?'

'Because the governor in Belgrade has said we may not use any of his markets. I don't know what he expects us to do.'

'Stay on this side of the river, I suppose.'

Odo pulled a face. 'How could any man with half a mind think that he could order knights like Sir Walter to remain when they are on a journey for God's glory? No knight who cared about his honour could obey an order like that, let alone a knight determined to fight for the Lord. What, would the governor expect the entire following of pilgrims to meekly accept his command and turn for home?'

'Perhaps he just thought that we would take the easier option, since to argue would be to incur the displeasure of his Emperor.'

'Then he's a fool,' Odo said. 'Now, get up! We're to break camp. We are to cross on ships Sir Walter has commandeered.'

He pulled the blanket from his complaining brother and packed his own effects quickly before standing and staring over the grey, sullen waters towards the city on the far bank. Behind the city lay broad plains and the shadows of great trees.

Odo felt a tingling in his belly. He thought it was God sending him the courage to continue.

Belgrade

Crossing the river had been difficult, but the people of Zemun appeared to be thrilled to be rid of them, willingly helping sail the army across to the other side of the river. Fulk had to distract Odo from others who were gleefully expressing their contempt for the pilgrims, some pulling down their hosen and baring their arses, others pointing with delight at the walls of the town. When Fulk stared, he was unsure at first what dangled there, until one of the other warriors in Sir Walter's company told him that they were clothes and armour taken from the pilgrims who had been robbed and beaten the day before. Fortunately Odo did not hear. Fulk feared that his brother might succumb to outrage, were he to hear that.

About a hundred boats were gathered, and the men were gradually transported. Sir Walter sent a strong contingent of men-at-arms with the van, while he waited with the rest of the army, using his own company as the rearguard. There was little trust for the men of Zemun, and Sir Walter had a similar shrewd suspicion of those who lived on the other bank of the river.

Fulk and Odo crossed with the vanguard, Fulk glad to be leaving the Zemun banks of the river. As the fleet of boats disembarked, men on horseback could be seen riding from Belgrade. Fulk and Odo watched them anxiously, but as the pilgrims began to march, Fulk became aware that they were being organised into a solid phalanx many men abreast, with the wagons and women towards the rear. Fulk worried about that. 'They will be at risk.'

'What sort of risk?' Odo asked.

'Any riders from the city can ride in among them. The women and children wouldn't stand a hope of escape against armoured men,' Fulk said.

Odo shrugged. 'There's little we can do about that.'

Fulk was less sure. He and Odo alone could do little, but surely a protective screen could be thrown around the more vulnerable?

He was about to go and suggest such a manoeuvre when he saw Sir Walter's horse wheel, closely followed by a number of his men-at-arms. They rode back, one force breaking away and cantering in the direction of the city horse, while the rest joined up with the rearmost sections, riding in a column between the wagons and the city. The riders from the city changed their direction and began to move away from the columns, seeing their easy prey barred by a fence of steel. The column continued on their way, but even as Fulk started to think that their path might be safe, he saw a fresh force form.

It was a shining army. Banners flew high overhead, and there was the glitter of steel through the heat haze and dust. Odo nudged him.

'Fulk, I really think they don't want us here,' he said.

*

The thought that they might be embroiled in a real battle was enough to make Odo break out in a sweat. He clenched his fists tightly and stared at the balls of muscle and bone. It seemed odd to think that soon these fingers, which had until now only ever kneaded dough to feed people, might soon be busy trying to kill other men.

He could see that Fulk was anxious. At least Odo had the conviction that this was God's own march. Fulk was less certain, and so he felt more nervousness. Odo only hoped he would have the strength of character to lead Fulk by his own example. For now, all they need do was keep stolidly plodding on, while the riders trotted in a course that took them parallel to their line of march.

'What are they doing?' Fulk said.

'I don't know,' Odo said.

An older man to the left of Fulk glanced across. 'Isn't it obvious?'

'What?'

The man had the look of an experienced fighter, and said his name was Peter of Auxerre. He had greying hair and a face that was as weather-beaten as an old mariner's. Faded blue eyes the colour of steel gauged the distance between the pilgrims and the horsemen, and he nodded to himself. 'Aye, they'll be here soon. They don't want us to escape after crossing when we were told not to, and with the raiding Sir Walter has organised they will want to punish us. While he sends his knights to raid the countryside, the people in that city, especially the governor, will expect to see us all pay the price. And they'll want it to be a high price, I'll wager.'

'What will they do?' Odo asked. There was a flatness in his voice that told Fulk he was worried.

'Do? They'll attack us as soon as they might, when they feel certain that they are safe, when they feel that we are unprotected. Aye, that's what I'd do.'

'You have experience?' Fulk asked. His own voice was not so flat. It sounded high and fearful even to his own ear.

Peter grinned. 'Don't worry, youngster. Sir Walter isn't dead yet. He's a good lord, and a better warrior. These bastards haven't ground him into the dust, and nor will they.'

'Fulk and I aren't worried. These men won't stop us. We're serving God,' Odo said. 'With Him on our side, we cannot fail.'

'Good. But I think God will help most those who know how to help themselves. So you trust to God, if you wish, but I'll put my trust in Sir Walter and Wolf-biter.'

'Eh?' Odo said blankly.

Slapping the sword at his side, Peter said, 'This! When I was a lad, my father was attacked in the woods, and this was the sword he bore to fight off the wolves.'

'So it saved his life?'

The man looked at him blankly. 'No: he died, which is how I got his sword. Still, the wolf died too. Have you two fought before?'

'In taverns,' Fulk said, his eyes turned towards the horsemen. Were they nearer now? It looked as though they might be converging on the marching men.

'A tavern, eh?' Peter looked at him more closely. 'Well, the main thing today will be to stand up to the horses. Throw stones at the beast's heads, hit their eyes, if you can. And hold your shields up.'

'We don't have shields,' Fulk admitted.

The man rolled his eyes. 'Then stand back and keep out of the way. I've been here before. They will try to ambush us, or tempt us into chasing them. The main thing is, keep in the ranks and do not leave them for any reason. If we start to chase after them, our column will collapse and they will pick us off one by one. It's how they're trained.'

149

'How can they hope to ambush us here?' Odo said, staring about them. There was a patchwork of fields here, with a series of channels dug into the soil to irrigate them. The road itself was solid, but the dust was choking.

'They know this land, boy. Don't think that because they wear shiny metal that they're only keen to look pretty. Those bastards are good fighters, and they win often because they make sure they know the territory where they fight. Here, it's all their own turf, so you can be sure that they'll know it like the hairs on their hands.'

The crossing of the river was terrifying for Sybille. All the way she clung to a rope for fear that she must be thrown from the craft. She had been quite certain that the shipmen knew nothing about sailing, for all their loud confidence, because every time the wind caught the little vessel, it heeled over, convincing Sybille that it must surely capsize, and she could not swim. If it were to turn over, she would die, and Richalda too. So she gripped her daughter tightly as the craft wallowed and bucked, and the waters slapped against the hull, and the wind blew gently, and the sun shone down. Mathena at her side felt like a rock of confidence compared to her.

While she endured the crossing, Benet lost little of his fretfulness. His eyes were fixed on the approaching shore, and she could see he was terribly anxious. He chewed at his lip until it bled, and he could not keep his fingers from playing with a loose thread on his tunic. He was fully aware of the disaster that losing their money represented, and he was ashamed.

Not that the money was uppermost in her mind just now. She was more concerned about her daughter.

Overnight Richalda had been sick, and then suffered from diarrhoea. Disembarking, Sybille watched over her with increasing concern. The child was pale, and as they waited for their pony, she began to sleep once more. She was over the worst of the fever, Sybille felt, but was still very weak, as was Sybille after staying up all night with her. She had no energy. A man at her side offered to carry the child a distance, but he himself looked so old and decrepit that Sybille could not trust him to bear her any distance without dropping her. As the horns blew again, Sybille began to plod on without thinking, stumbling when her weary feet struck rocks and rubbish left in the roadway, her eyes half-closed, her mind empty. Josse had to touch her shoulder to attract her attention when Benet hurried up with the pony, and helped her swing her leg over the saddle, passing Richalda to her when she was seated.

Horns blared, brazen and alarming, up and down the marching line, as Sybille bound her daughter to her. She had a long loop of material and wrapped it about them both, as she had when Richalda was only a babe. After all the privations of the last weeks, Richalda seemed little heavier than when she had been a baby. When Sybille touched her brow, the child did not seem to be burning, but Sybille was anxious that she was not drinking enough.

Richalda moaned and mumbled, her eyes shut, her forehead creased with whatever nightmares were intruding. Sybille smiled down at her, but she was constantly aware of the tears threatening. No child should have to endure the risks associated with such an appalling journey, especially one who was unwell. And now they did not even have money to buy her herbs or a medicinal draught.

'Dear God, please, don't take her!' she murmured, looking down at Richalda's face again. The child's eyelids fluttered, but she didn't wake. 'Please, take me in her place. Punish me however you want, but don't take my little girl!'

Josse looked up at her as though he had heard her words, and she said defensively, 'God wouldn't want to take her, would he?'

'Mistress, God will seek to protect her, I'm sure,' he said. 'But we must hurry.'

She looked about them. They were at the rear of the column with the other camp-followers, the old, frail, unwell, the women and the children, and the marching men were drawing away, leaving a space between the followers and the main body of men. Suddenly she saw a cloud of dust rise from towards the city. 'What is that?'

The man who had offered to help was still near them. Now he glanced back at the rising dust. 'They follow us. I expect they wish to ensure we do not steal from them. The governor has denounced us for defending ourselves against his henchmen yesterday. Now he wants to make sure we go away for good – or perhaps he wants our baggage?'

'He is a good Christian,' Josse said with heavy sarcasm.

'Why don't they help us?' Sybille said despairingly.

'We will be safe, wife,' Benet said. 'They will not hurt us. They know we—'

'Husband, be still!' she snapped. The memory of their lost wealth lent poison to her tone. 'They are not behaving like friends, are they? Do you think they'll wait until we are many miles from them, and then send for us to return and use their market? And then beat and steal from us, just as they did from you?'

'This is different,' he protested.

'How so? We starve because they will not let us into their market! Now they chase us away!'

'They are fearful, that's all.'

'They are *fearful*? What, of us?'

'We have nothing to fear, woman! Here, we are in the Empire.

152

The Emperor will hear if we are mistreated, and surely he will punish those who dare—'

'I would prefer that we weren't mistreated in the first place,' Sybille said. She looked down at Richalda again. 'Oh, God, please hear my prayers. Don't take my little child. Take another,' she said, deep in the protection of her heart.

There was a shout from in front, and she peered forward urgently.

'What is it, wife?' Benet demanded. 'You can see better than us!'

'It looks like a herd of cattle,' she said, and her mouth watered at the sight. It seemed to her that God had answered her prayers. 'Perhaps they have taken pity on us!'

Her husband exchanged a glance with the man in the cap.

The older man said, 'We should hurry to keep up. I doubt those beasts were willingly given. Sir Walter has captured them for our food, and the Bulgarians will want them back.'

On they trudged. Seeing others do so, Fulk had wound a strip of linen about his mouth and nose against the horrible dust that rose on all sides. It got everywhere. His eyes were gritty, his lips sore and dry, and he blinked as he marched, trying to clear his eyes of the tiny particles of grit in the air. Even clenching his teeth made them grate and crunch, as though he was chewing on a cheap maslin bread crust. It was horrible.

'How much longer?' he asked of no one in particular. He felt as though his entire body was shaking with fear.

'We'll soon rest,' their companion Peter said. He had experience of many battles in his life. 'We will need a camp where the cattle can be butchered.'

'At least we have food now,' Odo said.

The appearance of the first herds had been a surprise, but it made sense. Since the Bulgarians would not allow Sir Walter's men to buy food, he had taken the initiative and seized what he wanted. Raiding parties of men-at-arms had scoured the countryside nearby in search of cattle, sheep, anything that could be used to feed his host. Now Sir Walter's men were marching to the tune of lowing cattle, which promised a meal later on. There was a more cheerful atmosphere among the men, and some sang as they passed by the city and on beyond.

'What is that?' Fulk said.

Odo peered forward. 'It looks like a dust cloud.'

Peter hawked and spat. 'Aye, well – perhaps the men of Belgrade want their cattle back.'

At the rear of the column, Sybille rode on with mindless mechanical repetition. Her head was empty of any thought but concern for her daughter, and she hugged Richalda to her as they jogged along. Sybille hoped that soon the army would halt, and she would have an opportunity to feed her. Richalda was waking periodically, but she felt horribly hot again, and when Sybille felt her brow, it was burning.

There was a shout, and she saw a man a little further ahead suddenly plunge face-first to the road, where he writhed and wriggled like a dog with a broken back. She watched him with dull incomprehension, until she saw the shaft jutting from his shoulder.

Sybille heard a low, growling moan. It came from her own throat, she realised. Josse looked up at her, startled. Benet was at the far side of her pony, unaware of the danger until, all at once, the arrows began to strike all about, the vicious missiles bouncing from stones with sharp metallic clicks, or striking people with sad little soggy slaps. Benet's eyes opened wide, and he was about to shout, when an arrow plummeted down and pierced the pony, hitting just in front of the withers. There was a jerk that Sybille felt through her thighs, and then the pony began to stumble and walk around to the right.

'My God! No!' Benet shouted, staring with horrified fascination at the arrow's fletchings protruding from the beast, even as Sybille shrieked, fearing it had struck Richalda, but her child was safe.

All about there was sudden mayhem. Men and women screamed and wailed, running in wild confusion, some this way, some that. No one knew where the arrows came from. When some saw horsemen riding quickly towards them, a few ran to meet these newcomers, thinking it was a force of pilgrims, friends who could protect them.

But it was not; it was the enemy.

'Husband!' Sybille wailed, but Benet could do nothing.

He stood unmoving, gaping at the sight of men and women being slaughtered as the arrows flew, striking at random. His mouth moved, but he was slow and befuddled like a man intoxicated. 'No, no, they cannot mean to hurt us,' he muttered.

Josse ran to Sybille, but before he could reach her Guillemette was already there and took Richalda, muttering, 'Quickly!' Josse daringly threw an arm about Sybille's waist, pulling her from the saddle. The pony wandered on a few paces, but the arrow had found its mark. The pony collapsed, tumbling to the ground, hoofs kicking. If Sybille had been in the saddle, she would have been crushed.

Men were falling all about, but there was a wagon a short distance away and Guillemette was already pelting towards it. Josse pushed Sybille, and they ran to it. Sybille saw Esperte standing and screeching as the men rode towards her; Sybille grabbed her arm and pulled her along too. Seeing Sybille running, Mathena and Jeanne hared off after her. Benet at last came to his senses and, with a little whimper of terror, joined in the mad rush as more arrows dropped in among the column from the fast-approaching horsemen. Sybille reached a wagon and flung Esperte beneath before hurling herself after, scarcely aware of the stones that ripped the skin from her knees and hands. She crawled further under the wagon until she was nearer Richalda, who lay still in Guillemette's arms. Her elbows flayed by the sand and gravel, Sybille held out her hands and took her daughter, sheltering her head in her hands, arching her body over her daughter's and looking about her.

Already several men and two women were dead. One old man was crawling towards her, an expression of desperate determination on his face. She could see the arrow in his back, but then another hit him, high on the spine, and she saw his eyes register utter hopelessness. He still attempted to drag himself forward, but to no avail. It seemed to take an age for him to die. His head dropped to rest on his arm as though he was resting. His eyes held hers as the life seeped from them and his body slumped.

Richalda was whimpering, and Sybille rocked her and shushed her, as if the child had been woken by a bad dream. Except this was no bad dream, it was a horror. She saw Josse run to a fallen man. There was an axe near him, and Josse grabbed this and crouched near the wagon. Meanwhile, she felt a hand on her foot, and saw Benet trying to scramble beneath with her. He crawled up beside her and put his hand on Sybille's shoulder. She shrugged it away. His eyes were wide with horror and terror, but even as she thought of telling her husband to join Josse, Richalda's eyes opened, and Sybille found the tears welling. While the arrows sleeted down and the cries and screams rose to the heavens, she sat rocking gently, tears running freely down her cheeks.

There were shouts, a rumble of hoofs that was like thunder

drumming on the ground, and a long-drawn-out shriek as a woman was speared in the belly and pinned to the wagon behind her. She stood, her hands on the shaft almost as though she was holding it there, her face white and strained with the agony, and Sybille wanted to tear her eyes from her, but she could not. As she watched, the woman began to choke, and blood dribbled from the side of her mouth. Her cries became a long, low wail of pain and grief, and then the sight of her was blocked as another body appeared. Sybille saw a child flung into the air, then a woman was cut down and fell in front of the wagon, her dying eyes staring into Sybille's. Sybille was fleetingly grateful that the woman's body would hide her and the others from the riders; self-disgust followed swiftly on the heels of her gratitude.

She heard a shout, and suddenly the woman's body was stabbed by a long lance and thrown up into the air. A thunder of hoofs went past, a thick cloud of dust rising from them, and she could feel the ground trembling as though rejecting the horses riding to battle. The noise and the reverberation increased, and she closed her eyes, putting her hands on Richalda's head, waiting for the spear-thrust that would end both their lives. This was the end.

CHAPTER 13

Belgrade, Wednesday 4th June, 1096

The horsemen were trained in their manoeuvres. Fulk saw a number start to ride in at the column. 'They're attacking! They're attacking!'

'No, boy, these are just skirmishers. They'll loose a few arrows to soften us up, see how we respond,' Peter said.

He was standing at Fulk's right, and nodded with professional approval as he watched the Belgrade cavalry. 'They'll send in bowmen first, to sting and irritate us. Then, if they can, they'll hope to get some of the marching men to give chase. Those few will be tempted away from the main column so they can be cut to pieces in safety by the main force of horsemen.'

'What do you think the pilgrims will do?'

Peter shrugged at the man's question. 'So long as there are enough like us, the lines will hold. Besides, I think the average pilgrim won't want to break from the line. Not many have seen battle before. This will be their first experience. And few have horses. The knights and men-at-arms in our forces will be trained to keep back, so there will be less chance of the ploy working.'

Fulk was reassured by his air of quiet confidence, but he eyed the approaching horsemen with anxiety verging on panic. They were coming at such a speed!

'Here they come, then,' Peter said. 'Keep your heads down.'

Obediently, Fulk ducked, thinking Peter meant that the horsemen were close with their lances, but he did not. It was the arrows he was talking about.

They flew so fast, they seemed to strike in an instant without warning. Many came in among them, but only a few men were struck. The Belgrade men rode in furiously and, at the last moment, drew and sent arrows flying into their midst before reining in, whirling and riding away. Five waves of these attacks were endured, and Fulk was sure that the majority of their arrows were aimed behind them, at the baggage train where the women and elderly were. He frowned and stared back, and as he did so, he saw the flurry of arrows sleeting down. 'They're trying to steal the baggage.'

'It's the food and supplies they'll want,' Peter said knowledgeably. He peered back the way they had come. 'We have to hope they won't succeed.'

'Hope?' Fulk said. 'We can't let them take all our food!'

'Don't even think of returning, boy. These horsemen know their work. You go back, and you'll end up with a lance through your gut.'

Fulk thought of the wagons. He knew that the women and children were all back there, too. Staring back now, he could see only people scattering as arrows fell among them, and screaming women, and men who dropped all their goods and were now fleeing towards the middle of the column. In the middle he could see one child, only young, standing in terror, petrified, shrieking as the deadly storm sheeted down around her. For an instant he had a vision of the young girl Esperte with Mathena. He had a clear picture in his mind of Jeanne and Guillemette as a rider cantered at them, his lance piercing Guillemette's torso, the blood erupting from her breast. 'No!' he said, 'I have to go back. The women need us!'

'Don't be stupid!' Peter said. Odo caught hold of his arm and tried to remonstrate, but Fulk snatched himself free and, before Odo could stop him, began to hurry back. The arrows were diminishing in number, but even as he felt a quick relief, he saw the horses begin to charge the wagons.

Fulk ran. He could see that some of the carts and wagons had their oxen or mules dead in their traces. A few sumpter beasts and donkeys had gone mad, one rearing, maddened with pain from a shaft that was embedded deep in its back. Fulk was soon one of only some thirty men standing among the wagons, and as the horsemen approached, he gripped his sword with the determination of a man who knew his action was ridiculously foolhardy. He could see the cavalry charging as a wall of men and horseflesh, straight at him. It was a daunting sight, and he saw some of the other men begin to pull back, staring at the advancing enemy with terror. As well they might.

There was a shout, and Peter appeared. He cuffed one retreating old man over the pate, shouting, 'Run and they'll skewer you faster'n a hog! Stay and face them and you may just live!'

'This was your idea, brother,' Odo said from his side. 'So what do we do now? Stand here and get a lance in the guts?'

'You too, brother?' Fulk said.

'There cannot be many men so stupid as to follow where you would go,' Odo said. He gripped his sword, and the patterned blade flashed in the sun. 'Shit! What now?'

'Let's get behind a cart. At least then they can't pin us to the timbers so easily,' Fulk said. He felt a silken heaviness at his belly. It was, he felt sure, the onset of a belly-rot that would show the world how fleeting had been his courage. But then he thought to himself that no matter how fearful he was, he was here on pilgrimage. These men of Belgrade had no right to stop those in the service of God.

He heard Odo begin to murmur the Paternoster and the sound strengthened him. He joined in, the familiar words giving him strength so that he stood more straight, preparing for the moment when a lance should come too close, and he clenched his belly muscles as he bent his back slightly, lifting the sword, unsure where to hold it for maximum safety, staring down its length at the nearer of the riders, feeling the fear dissipate as his life came to focus on this one, terrifying moment . . .

And then, just as both Fulk and Odo thought they were to die together here in the plains outside Belgrade, they heard the blast of a horn and saw the charge of Sir Walter and his men bearing down on their enemies.

The first crash sent the Bulgarian riders reeling.

Sir Walter and his kinsman, Sir Walter of Poissy, were at the head of more than forty men-at-arms. The men rode together in a solid formation of steel, iron, blood and bone, and they punched a hole through the Belgrade cavalry. There was a vast crunching sound, a rattling of steel and splintering of wood as heavy lances punched through shields and mail and flesh. The horses of Sir Walter's men slammed into the flanks of the enemy. Fulk saw one man, who had not recognised his danger, suddenly crushed. Sir Walter's squire rode into the man at full tilt, and Fulk was sure he heard the man's leg shatter, crushed by the squire's mount. Many men were broken in a similar manner, the great warhorses charging into them, their breasts smashing into men and horses alike.

Others were speared by the lances. Sir Walter himself had to let go of his own lance when it penetrated two riders side by side.

Bulgarian horses were thrown sideways in mid-gallop, their riders dying as weapons tore through them, and the mounts turned away from the terrifying charge, but turning brought them into the path of succeeding pilgrim knights, knocking them aside so that horses and riders alike fell into the carnage. The uniformity of the charge was destroyed in an instant as riders tumbled to the ground. Fulk saw a man take a lance-point under his chin, the wooden shaft ripping through his throat and all but removing his head. Another was caught beneath his armpit, and he was thrown over the cantle of his saddle to slam on the ground. He disappeared as the waves of men behind Sir Walter rode over him.

From his position, Fulk saw the enemy falter, men scattering. Sir Walter's men swept on, and past, but not in time to halt the whole of the cavalry. Some who had been at the rear of the charge were now advancing, their mounts taking them around and behind Sir Walter's men. Fulk saw a group of six swerve around the rear of the reinforcements, and pound on towards him. They were deliberately aiming at him alone, he was sure, and his belly lurched again at the thought. Their lances were pointing at his breast. To stand would be to die. Odo was beside him. Fulk turned and shoved him down, under the wagon behind them, and he dropped and rolled beneath it, even as the first lance crashed into the timbers above him. A spear was hurled at him and Odo, but the two rolled away.

As he struck the wheel at the far side of the wagon, Fulk found his eyes meeting those of Guillemette. She was under the fourth wagon along, her eyes wide with terror, and beside her were other huddled figures. Fulk was sure he could see the child, Esperte, and the other women. Behind them was a man, he thought, his arms over his head. It gave Fulk a spur of rage. In front of him, he saw the legs of one of the Bulgarian horses. Without thinking, he rolled out, swept his sword around in an ungainly curve, and heard the sharp crack of the beast's hind tendon shearing. With a squeal, the beast crashed to the ground, the knight dropped his lance and fell with one leg trapped beneath his thrashing mount.

Fulk shot a look all around, then quickly thrust at the Bulgarian. His blade snagged on some cloth at the man's throat and missed his mark. The man realised his danger and reached for his own weapon, but Fulk chopped down with his sword. The edge of the blade hit the man in the face. He cried out, and Fulk thrust, desperate only to kill, to stop the fellow's pain. His blow struck just below the man's ear, and Fulk felt a sickening friction transmitted from the blade to the grip as the edge slipped through the fellow's throat.

He pulled his sword free and turned away, a sob threatening to choke him as the man shook in his death throes. Fulk could not watch, but he could hear every sound. He looked down at his hand. It was shaking. He could not even focus on the blade itself.

There was a bellow, and he turned to see another Bulgarian riding at him. The dropped lance was nearby. Without thinking, Fulk snatched it up and held it angled at the rider's horse. As the knight rode at him, Fulk's spear was thrust into the horse's breast. Fulk was suddenly thrown backwards, knocked from his feet and slammed to the ground. The mount was dead before the rider could bring his own spear to bear on Fulk, and he was thrown as his beast collapsed. Fulk let go of the spear and rolled onto all fours, gasping. His right arm felt as though it had been wrenched from his body, but he took his sword in his left hand, determined not to give his life cheaply. The knight was on his feet, and thrust at Fulk, but he was winded and his first blow missed its mark, and then Odo was behind the man, and his blade took the knight's life.

There were still four more, but now Sir Walter's men were returning, and the remaining Bulgarians chose life and safety. They took off, and were soon raising a cloud of dust on the way to their city.

Fulk fell to his knees, coughing. 'Odo, are you well?'

'Yes, but if you ever, ever jump out to attack two horsemen like that again, I'll leave you to it. You madman!' Odo said, and gave a feeble chuckle.

Fulk rose with difficulty, for his knees seemed to be astonishingly weak, and made his way to the other wagon like an old man.

'Mistress, you are safe now,' he said. He could not hold out his hand to her. It still shook profoundly.

He saw the relief in Guillemette's eyes. Hers was the most beautiful smile he had ever seen. 'You might get one for free for that,' she murmured as she crawled out. Then she suddenly enfolded him in a great hug, kissing him on the lips, before drawing away to help the others from beneath their refuge.

Lying behind Sybille as she made her way from the wagon, he saw Benet. The man gazed at Fulk with the loathing that only the true coward could feel, and then he rolled to the far side and climbed to his feet.

She had seen it. Sybille saw him.

Josse had stood alone as the horsemen appeared and thundered in among the remaining, screaming people. Why? He could have lain with them, safe from the lances of the riders. He turned as the riders approached, glancing at her briefly. She saw then the fierce devotion gleaming in his eyes. It was a love so intense, it took her breath away.

The moment was gone. He hefted his axe and cut at the first horseman, but misjudged his strike, and his blow went wide.

The second rider spurred at him, and although Josse swung his blade with full strength, he only managed a glancing blow on the man's mail. Even as he tried to aim again, the rider's blade slashed down and hacked into Josse's shoulder. His arm was almost severed, and his hand opened to let the axe fall from his fist. He stared down as though astonished, and Sybille met his eyes for the last time. She was unable to speak or move, but she thought he tried to say something. Whether he spoke or not, he had no time to repeat his words. The sword flashed again, and this time Josse's eyes rolled up and he collapsed.

It was possible, she realised afterwards, that he saved their lives by falling dead there at the side of the wagon. His body shielded Sybille and the others from the eyes of other Bulgarians. They rode about, and one or two she saw dismount as though to search for spoil amid the stores, but then there were more horn blasts and bellowed commands, and the men remounted and departed.

Guillemette and Jeanne were already standing beside the wagon. While Sybille dusted herself down, she smiled weakly in gratitude at Fulk, but then her eyes went to Josse's body. He lay near one of the wheels, and she felt a sob convulse her body at the sight. 'He was defending us,' she said.

Fulk looked down at the body. 'He died bravely.'

Behind him, Odo had joined them. 'Your husband?'

'No, my servant. My loyal servant.'

Odo nodded. 'Mistress, you can be sure that he will receive his reward in Heaven. To have given up his life for Christians while on a pilgrimage, that is a wonderful act.'

She stared down at Richalda's face. The child was silent, and Sybille felt a pang of terror that after all this they might lose their daughter as well. Then Richalda opened her eyes and smiled thinly.

Her husband stood at the far side of the wagon, staring at the Belgrade horsemen riding away.

She could not look at him. In that moment she knew only complete contempt for him. Josse's last glances to her told her that he had known what he was doing. He was deliberately fighting, willingly giving his life to protect Sybille and Richalda – while her husband cowered behind her. The memory came back to her of the day so many weeks ago, when Josse told her he would protect her. Her heart lurched with the memory, as if Josse had foreseen that he would die guarding her.

If only he were still alive!

Benet muttered, 'Poor man! Poor Josse! He didn't deserve to be cut to pieces out here in this horrible country! Why did we come here? We should have taken ship, rather than march all over these plains where the people are such barbarians they rob pilgrims while professing to be Christians!'

Sybille shrieked. 'Benet! It was *your* choice to come here, not mine, not *his*! If you seek someone to accuse, blame yourself for his death, and in all likelihood, for Richalda's too! Look at her! The poor child is feverish still, and you complain about being here, as though it is the responsibility of someone else? *You* made the choice, husband! No one else!'

'Wife, be calm! I know you are upset to lose Josse, but—'

Sybille passed her daughter to Jeanne and stalked to Benet. 'No, *husband*, I am upset because my own husband lay hiding while his servant tried to defend us. Josse saved our lives, but you did nothing!' Sybille took a step forward and hissed into his face, 'You should have helped him, not concealed yourself like a cur!'

His eyes narrowed, and she saw his hand move, but the slap, when it connected with her cheek, came as a surprise. Her head was turned violently by the force of the blow, and she stood without moving for a long time, while Fulk and his brother watched.

Benet said with forced calmness, 'My dear, we've had a terrible shock, I know, but you must keep yourself composed for Richalda. We cannot have you growing hysterical. Think of your daughter.'

'Don't speak to me of keeping *calm*, husband! You crawled in there behind me to protect yourself. You would use your wife and daughter to protect yourself, and now you will beat your wife because you dare not protect us against the enemy.'

She flinched as he lifted his hand again, but Fulk had rounded the wagon, and he caught Benet by the wrist. 'Master, you should not hit her again.'

'Let me go! A husband should chastise his wife when she is making villeinous comments.'

Odo looked at Fulk, then over at Benet. 'My brother is right. We have to get this army moving. We can't keep the pilgrims waiting while you dispute what happened here. Better that you send your wife to go and help see to the injured, while you bury your servant. After all, he did protect you and your family.'

Sybille rejoined Mathena and Guillemette to help the injured.

She was grateful for Fulk's intervention. Her cheek still felt warm to the touch, much as did Richalda's brow and, when she put a hand to her face, it stung. He had never hit her before. Mathena put her arms about her, glaring at Benet as she did so. Guillemette and Jeanne stood a little way away, both watching Benet too, as though they were ready to spring to Sybille's defence were Benet to try to hit her again. Sybille felt that she did not need their help. The blow had made her feel stronger.

She would never forgive Benet that smack. She could not, any more than she could forgive his cowardice in leaving Josse to fight alone.

And then she remembered: when she had feared Richalda

might die, she had prayed that God might take someone rather than her daughter.

The guilt struck her so hard, she almost collapsed. *She* had killed poor Josse!

CHAPTER 14

Belgrade, Thursday 5th June, 1096

'Help me, Sybille!'

Sybille ignored his calls for as long as she could, but finally his patience was fraying, and she set her jaw and went to assist him. Since their pony's death, it was clear that they would have to make an effort to carry more themselves, but much of their property would have to remain here. Without Josse to help carry things as well, their burdens would have to grow.

'Well, husband?'

'Pass me that,' he said shortly. She took up the pack he indicated. It was a flask of wine. 'This? What will you do with it? I won't carry it for you. If you want to carry this, you can carry it in your belly.'

'Woman, will you stop your complaining!'

'Why? Else you will beat me like a dog? You enjoyed slapping me yesterday, did you? Did you find it served to bring back a little of your manhood after seeing Josse die?' she asked cruelly.

'You would prefer that it had been me who died, would you?'

'I would prefer that you had done *something* rather than lying on the ground and hoping that one man could avert all danger.'

'I will do what I can in the battles to come, wife. For now, though, I have secured some space on a wagon, and if we are quick, we may be able to stow some of our belongings. But if you prefer to expend your bile on me, we can easily leave it all here to rot.'

He turned away, and was about to stalk off when the sound of a multitude of horns being blown drifted over on the cool morning air.

'What was that?' Sybille asked. She felt a cold, leaden certainty in her stomach at the sound.

'I think you know what it is,' Benet said. He hesitated, and then began to march towards the sound.

'Where are you going?'

He paused, then, without turning to meet her gaze, he said over his shoulder, 'I am going to try to retrieve my honour and your love, wife,' he said, and walked on towards the sounds of battle.

Fulk woke from a pleasant dream in which Guillemette and Sybille had been sponging his injuries after a brave battle, to find that the whole camp was already packing and preparing to march again. This time the women and wagons were brought up closer, so that they were better protected from attack.

'The men from Belgrade are there,' Peter said, pointing ahead as Fulk wrapped his belongings into a neat bundle and rolled them up in his cloak. 'They will want to stop us raiding further, I suppose. Perhaps they just want to kill us for daring to come here. Well, they can try, but I for one will not agree to return. I've come this far, I will go on, unless they cut my arms and legs from my body!'

There was a large force of men from Belgrade blocking their path as the pilgrims gathered together into a column to march. Fulk walked to join Odo and Peter. They were in the forefront of the pilgrim force, and Fulk looked about him with interest. He was concerned that there might be more Belgrade fighters concealed in the countryside about. Odo had the same idea and, pushing past Fulk, strode on a few paces ahead.

'Odo, be careful!' Fulk cried, but he might have held his breath for the impact it made on his brother. Odo kept on walking. Fulk muttered to himself, and then trotted after him. Odo was standing on a small hillock a short distance from the river, and there he studied the land all about for a while. Fulk pointed. 'There they are.'

'I can see them!' Odo said. He felt enormously calm, as though God Himself held him safe in His arms, and Odo felt a great welling of love and joy in his breast at the thought of the battle to come. For battle, he was sure, there must be.

A long column of men and horses had ridden from the city and now covered a small area of rising ground in the path of the pilgrim army. While Odo and Fulk stood staring, Sir Walter appeared before them on his horse. At his side were two knights who glanced at the brothers while they surveyed the land. One of the knights ordered them to return to the main pilgrim army, and the two scurried back down to where Peter stood waiting. When they reached their ranks, a priest was already there celebrating Mass and joyfully informing all the pilgrims that those who died in God's battles would dine that evening with His saints.

Odo listened raptly, but Fulk could not help but think he would prefer a good meal of stew and bread with Guillemette and Sybille.

Before long, Sir Walter appeared before them all, a lance in his hand. He had seven other knights with him now, and they sat on

171

their mounts staring at the army. Fulk saw Sir Walter point, and two of the knights wheeled and rode away. Fulk had no idea who they were, but Peter said that one was Sir Walter's kinsman, his uncle Walter de Poissy. The two knights took their men-at-arms to the right flank, and Fulk was just wondering why when the brazen call of horns came from before them.

He muttered a swift prayer, wondering what was to become of him. It was evident that they were about to engage in a fresh battle, and he did not like the thought. He had not enjoyed being attacked yesterday, and was not ready to be thrown into another fight so soon. Fleetingly he wondered about the women, but then his thoughts were fixed on his own life and the risks he faced again.

'Pilgrims!' It was Sir Walter. He shouted now at all the men as they marched, riding his great destrier from side to side, head up so that all the men could hear him clearly enough. 'Pilgrims, we are here on a sacred journey. Our Pope told you all that this was a holy mission. We are travelling in peace so that we can rescue Jerusalem from the barbarians who enslaved the Christians in that city. We are not here for self-aggrandisement or reward, only to fight a blow for God. Yet some would prevent us from our mission. Some here say that we are too destructive, that we steal and kill. The governor of this city says we are to be denied the use of his markets, that we must flee this land and depart back to our homes and give up our holy cause. I say, no! *No!* I will not halt until I have reached Jerusalem, and have liberated that city to the glory of God. But to reach the city we must continue on our road through here. And the governor's army stands in our path. They are determined to contest our way. What should we do, my Christian friends? Submit? Turn our mounts to the west and return to our homes? What should we say when we reach our homes? That we tried, but a man thwarted us; thwarted *God*!

For that is the issue here! It is not that we want to cross this land. We are here because we are on our way to rescue God's city. Those who would prevent us are God's enemies. These men of Belgrade, these are enemies of God, for all that they call themselves Christian!'

He paused and his horse stood still. Then Sir Walter spoke again. 'I will not tolerate a man standing in the path of God's own people trying to do His will. I will fight this day, and I will fight with the knowledge that God stands at my side. These men cannot stop us, for God is with us. I will fight for God. What do you say? Are you with me? Are you with God? Are you?'

The response came back clearly from the thousands. *'Yes!'*

Sir Walter drew his sword and roared his battle cry: *'Dieu le veut!'*

'Dieu le veut!' Fulk shouted. 'God wills it!'

And he found that all the men about him were moving forward. He marched with them and soon the battle began.

Fulk felt empty of emotion. There was a strange thickness in his throat, and his hands were sweaty and slippery, but there was an absence of the bowel-emptying terror he had known the day before, although it was a good thing that his sword's grip had leather and wire to hold it in place, for it must have turned in his hand else. There came a bellow, then a series of blasts on horns from the front rank, and shouted orders, and suddenly all the men about him were trotting, and he was obliged to increase his own speed to keep up. Whatever happened, he was determined to remain not far from Odo. He didn't want to lose sight of his brother, for to him that would seem like desertion, as though were he to lose visual contact, Odo could instantly be cut down. But soon he found he had little time to worry about Odo.

He was some thirty men from the front line. Where he was,

he could see nothing of the enemy, only the hair or bald pates of the men before him. He could see metal caps on some of the men in the ranks in front, and he could see the shoulders of men at either side, but that was all. The feet of the first men were raising a thick, clogging dust once more, and his vision was clouded as his eyes became filled with grit and uncomfortable. The sun was out fully now, and the heat was horrible in the padded jackets that most pilgrims wore. It was a great deal cheaper than mail for a poor man, but it was appallingly hot in the sun. Fulk wished he had taken a throatful of water before they set off, but it was too late now.

'*Dieu le veut!*' he heard Odo roar, repeating the words like the chanted prayers in church. Fulk muttered them in his turn.

They were picking up speed now, the ground flashing past. Fulk saw a man tumble, not struck by an arrow, but tripping on a rock. None of them could see the ground now, for it was hidden by the men in front. Another man fell, and he screamed as he was trampled. There was no space to move to the side to avoid him, no space to place a boot carefully at his side, no space to stop and let him rise. To fall was to be crushed, and Fulk stared down, trying to make sure he missed rocks and holes to avoid a similar fate. He tried to allow a little more distance between himself and the man in front, but the press behind was too great. His scalp was tingling, tight, like leather stretched across a drum, and his back muscles were taut as a ship's hawsers. He wondered at that, but then all thought of muscles and fear was driven from his mind.

They met the men of Belgrade in a clash of weapons that was deafening, and suddenly the soldiers before him stopped. As the two forces collided, the onward march was halted. Fulk saw men roar incoherent curses and challenges, some flinging rocks they had picked up earlier, some few throwing spears. At the same time the enemy were hurling their own weapons. Beside Fulk a man was hit full in the face by a stone from a sling; he collapsed so suddenly it was as though a demon had gripped his ankles and yanked him down.

It felt as though time was held in check. Fulk could see men shouting, screaming, laying about them with swords and spears, some falling with sudden wounds that gaped, bodies sprawled underfoot, and Fulk was aware of an overwhelming confusion. He found himself staring about him, gaping, as though he was a spectator safe from all danger.

But the Belgrade men were loosing more than stones at them. Fulk saw one man hit on his bald scalp by a javelin and he fell instantly; another took an arrow in his shoulder, and turned round and around in his panic, lost, witlessly trying to see where to go for safety, his hand holding the barbed shaft to pull it free, and a man's throat was opened, spraying blood widely, covering Fulk and forcing him to return to his senses.

Already the men fighting were gathering like a clot at the front. The lines about Fulk were thinning, and he could see that he was close to the line of Belgrade men. Suddenly he saw Odo, who was grasping an enemy's spear in one hand and hacking with his sword at the man who held it. He saw Odo stab suddenly, and there was a gout of blood, and the spear was free. Odo sheathed his sword and held the spear overhand, jabbing it viciously at the men before him.

'Be careful!' Fulk shouted, and shoved through the throng, ignoring the men underfoot who cried piteously as he stamped on them, hurrying to Odo's side just as a man leaned forward from the Belgrade line to stab at Odo's bare armpit. Fulk's sword knocked the lance away, gouging a great chip of wood from it, and the shock almost tore the sword from his hand, but he managed to keep his grip and stumbled as he thrust forward. He saw a gaping wound open in the man's cheek, and the fellow dropped

175

his lance and put his hand to his face with dismay. Fulk realised that the man was younger than him. This was probably his first battle too, but then he heard a screamed warning, and ducked as another spear came at his head. It ripped a slash in his scalp, and gave him a headache, but he found to his surprise that he could still wield his weapon. Another spear was thrust at him, narrowly missing, and he saw that it nearly took Odo's eye, and that was when the real raw, red rage took him over. He bellowed something, he didn't know what, and fought.

There was no time to think of the enemy, no time to care for a man who might be only a boy, there was only the next stab and slash, cutting at men as best he may. He took the spear in his hand and yanked it, then turned it to stab at another man, the leaf-shaped blade slicing through the man's shoulder, and Fulk shoved hard, and tried to recover it, but it was jammed in the man's side now, and Fulk let it go, hacking at a forearm with his sword and seeing the blood mist the air, but then men behind were pushing, and in the press there was no space even to hack, and it was a case of battering with his hilt at a head, bringing the pommel onto a pate, punching with the cross-guard, dragging his sword's blade across a face, head-butting another, and all the while he was aware of the deep, all-consuming fury, the desire to kill, to maim, to injure, to *punish* those who tried to stand against him and his brother.

Fulk hacked, stabbed, slashed and buffeted the men before him, determined to kill and keep on killing until these men withdrew. When there was a momentary lull, he glanced about him, searching for Odo, but he was nowhere to be seen.

Odo was punched in the face and saw bright blue and red sparks even as the teeth were loosened in his jaw. He swayed, and stumbled backwards. A youngster, perhaps only fourteen or fifteen years old, was with him, and helped Odo take a few steps away from the fray.

'Master? Master? Are you all right?' he asked.

Odo could barely hear him. There was a ringing and a hissing in his ears. He shook his head and closed his eyes, feeling waves of nausea crashing through his body, but then the lad's urgent call got through to him, and he looked up with a smile. The boy was a man's height, but had the build of a ferret, thin and scrawny. His eyes were too close together, and Odo thought he looked like a boy he had once known back in his home village. It gave him a fleeting nostalgia to remember him, and he had a sudden memory of a walk along the riverbank, the two of them talking under the willows and beeches about the girls in the village. Odo recalled he had been embarrassed, for he knew that he had a calling to go to work with the Church, but still he was aware of the attraction of women. It was not long afterwards that he and Fulk had left the village to be apprenticed in Sens.

This boy nodded to Odo as though confirming he was recovered, then turned and ran to the front again. Odo's eyes followed him. He wanted to display his gratitude, but even as he opened his mouth to call his thanks, he saw the boy jerk, suddenly taking a pace back. When he turned to face Odo there was confusion on his face, and he looked down to his breast. With horror Odo realised there was a bloom of crimson on his tunic. The boy looked at Odo with alarm creasing his brow, and he opened his mouth, but no words came, only a stuttering. He suddenly gave an inarticulate cry and his face shattered like a broken jug before he fell to the ground.

'No! *No!*' Odo bellowed, and the anger slid into his body like a blade of ice, cold enough to chill, hard enough to kill. It froze his pain and he leapt to his feet, scrabbling for his sword. He gave a roar, lifted his weapon, and ran at the enemy.

*

Fulk saw him.

Odo ran full tilt into the front rank, hacking and slashing wildly, his blade catching one man under the jaw and knocking his head back, a great gash opening from chin to eye, then he brought the blade down onto another's head; deflected by a cap of steel, it bounced into another man's neck and he went down. In his fury he was fighting without skill or science, but his emotions lent strength to his arms and he knew no fear. Those before him began to melt away, injured or in terror at his lunatic onslaught. He beat at shields, and when a pair of men in mail and capped with strong helmets stood in his path, he knocked aside their weapons and got so close, he could draw his dagger and stab at their faces until they too fled from his anger.

A man rushed at Odo from his side. It was a heavy-set youth, whose initial attack almost brushed Odo aside, but then Fulk's brother sprang back, grappling like a wrestler. His sword was gone, and he had only his dagger, but although the youth tried to disembowel Odo with a wide cut, Odo let the blade pass him and closed with him, trying to stab. The youth grabbed his knife hand, but Odo managed to slice into his sword arm and the weapon fell to the ground.

The two were struggling together now, and Fulk realised that both were gripping Odo's knife between them, each attempting to stab the other. Odo had his teeth bared, and his face was white and sweating as the knife's point moved this way and that, now under the youth's chin, now curving back to Odo's throat. They swayed with the effort, and all the while the two stared into each other's eyes in an obscene parody of sex.

Fulk shouted and started to move to them to help his brother, but even as he did, Odo's face suddenly changed. His expression grew feral, almost inhuman. It wasn't Odo in that moment. He leaned forward and screamed abuse at his opponent, then opened his mouth and clenched his teeth on the man's nose, twisting and pulling like a terrier at a rat, until he could jerk his head away with a gout of blood. His enemy roared in pain, and Odo bent his legs and thrust upwards, legs and arms together. The dagger slid into the youth's breast, even as Odo spat the bloody lump into his face, and he bared his teeth, now red and befouled, as the youth stiffened, twisted and slowly weakened, the dagger deep in his heart.

It was good to see that Odo was safe, but even as Fulk felt the relief flood him, it was tempered with a cold disgust. Odo had never fought with such ferocious determination. It was good that Odo had won, but Fulk was simultaneously chilled by the expression he had seen on Odo's face. It was almost demonic.

The pilgrims were pulling back, and Fulk could not see why. Then all thought of Odo was driven from his mind as he heard another noise, a terrifying sound like thunder, and felt a pounding concussion at his feet. At first he had no idea what could have caused it, but then, over the heads of those nearest him, he saw the knights again. Sir Walter and his men-at-arms were charging into the Belgrade flank at full gallop, and he heard their battle cries and bellows as they came, saw a knight's pot-helm struck from his head in the first crash as a spear caught it, saw the eruptions of blood as spears pierced the bodies of the men standing before them, and he felt simultaneously joyous and horrified to see such slaughter.

He cheered, he could not help it. His horror was overwhelmed by the delight to see how a force of Christian knights could tear a bloody hole in an enemy's line, but even as he did so, he caught sight of Odo. Odo had grabbed the hair of another man lying on the ground. He pulled the man's head up, and looked deep into his eyes. Then Odo laughed, rested his sword's edge across the man's throat and, even as the fellow begged for sanctuary, drew it slowly across his neck.

The sight was enough to freeze Fulk's bowels.

Sybille heard the blaring of horns and saw the mad rush of men to join the battle. The terror of another attack like that of the day before held her in its grip, but she busied herself looking after her daughter. She had made sure that she was close to the wagons, and now she rested her back against a wheel, holding Richalda in her arms. The men rushing to and fro paid her little heed, and it was only when an older man strode past with two sheaves of arrows in his arms and a spear held under his armpit that she began to look up and pay attention. She could see that the fight was continuing, and looked up to see the sudden charge of the horsemen. She carefully set Richalda on the ground, climbing onto the wagon for a better view, and could dimly see through the roiling cloud of dust how the horses slammed into the men of Belgrade, rolling up their flank and carving a bloody wedge through them. Sir Walter de Poissy and his men had destroyed the Belgrade left flank before the battle had been fully joined.

The enemy were pouring away from the field. It was a great relief to see, but she felt little joy. She knew that somewhere in that struggling mass was her husband. She stood as though petrified, staring. Even as the pilgrims pressed forward, she saw the aftermath lying on the earth. A mess of entangled men lying moaning or weeping, many already dead. Blood lay thick and clotting on the ground making the grass slick, and she could smell it even from here, the steely odour assailing her nostrils, mingling with the garderobe stench of bowels opened. She heard a man calling desperately for water, and she went to fetch a flask, but then she stood and gazed. There were too many men here, far too many for her to assist.

'Come, let us help,' Guillemette said. 'Mathena can see to your daughter.'

She had appeared behind Sybille and carried three leather flasks. Her words woke Sybille from her horrified daze, and she hurried to join in giving some succour to the wounded.

Many were too badly injured. The first was a man with a horrible wound in his belly. He smiled weakly, muttered, 'I'll see God now,' and died. A second lay on his back with a hideous maul-blow to the left of his forehead. He stared at her with an expression of terror in the remaining eye. He was younger than Benet, she was sure. He sipped water and lay back with a grunt. Another man, and another and another, all with dreadful wounds that seemed destined to kill them, and she dispensed sympathy and water, hurrying to the river as her *botelle* ran dry.

It was much later that Benet came back. He appeared from the direction of the main battle carrying a sword and tramped heavily towards her, slumping to the ground nearby. She was dealing with another man, dabbing at the wound on his scalp with a damp cloth. She felt drained as though all the life had been sucked from her this day.

'Yes, wife. I am alive, I thank you.'

She rested a hand on the man's brow, and turned to look at her husband. His face was thinner, with lines etched more deeply into his brow and at the sides of his mouth. He looked like a man who had pulled aside a curtain and peered into Hell itself.

'This man is injured. I must care for him.' She didn't know what else to say.

'And not me?'

She caught her breath. His linen shirt was stained with clots of blood. 'My husband! What has happened?'

'This? This isn't mine. Another man had his head broken, and this is his blood.' He leaned back against a pack and closed his eyes. 'I killed a man down there, Sybille. I knocked him to the ground and stabbed him in the face until he stopped moving. It took a long time for him to die. A long time.'

'Are you wounded?' she asked, staring at his shirt.

'I don't know. I don't think I care,' he said. 'It was not easy to kill that man.'

'Benet, I am sorry! I didn't mean you to go and suffer. I was just upset when—'

'You thought me a coward, and ... and I was. But Sybille, don't ...' His voice caught, and she could hear he was so close, so very close, to sobbing. 'Don't ever make light of my courage again. I don't think I could cope with it. Fighting in that mêlée was ... it was hideous, wife. I fell because I put my foot on an arm. A man's arm, just left there on the ground as though a man's body was nothing. And I stepped on it.'

She fetched the wineskin from the cart, and drew the stopper for him, tipping a little down his throat. He looked up at her, and she was reminded of the look she had received from Richalda when she had been young, and used to look up at Sybille while suckling. It held the same innocent, trusting, vulnerable quality. In Richalda it had been endearing, and life-affirming for her; in her husband, it was oddly shocking. He was the man she wanted to look up to, the man who she expected would guide, guard and protect her.

To find him so dependent upon her was repugnant.

Fulk stumbled about the battlefield and stared at the dead.

Pilgrims were milling about and helping their injured comrades to their feet, or carrying them away. Kindly hands brought them water and eased the passing of those who were dying, but Fulk could see his brother bringing a different solace to the injured.

He felt as though he was watching a different person, a

stranger. Odo went from one to another of the enemy's fallen, lifting their heads, staring into their faces, and then cutting their throats, each time watching the eyes of his victims as though savouring their final moments.

'Odo! Leave them!' he said.

His brother turned to face him and gave a brittle smile. 'This is the butcher's duty at the end of a battle, Fulk. Didn't you know? It is the job of the soldier to make sure that the wounded are given a speedy release.'

'You don't have to do this, Odo. Others can do it.'

'You want to take over?' Odo said. He stared at Fulk for a long moment, his eyes searching Fulk's for any sign of weakness, before his eyes fell to the blade in his hand. The beautifully wrought steel looked dull and befouled by the blood it had drunk. 'Perhaps I have done enough,' he added, and he sounded weary, but then he pushed with his boot at another body, rolling it and peering down before stabbing.

There were still shouts and cries, the clash and clatter of weapons striking steel, the screams of the wounded and bellows of commands being given. Some thirty yards away, the battle still raged, and as Odo cast his eye over the fallen, Fulk found his attention taken by the last few men standing against the pilgrims. There was a last contingent fighting about a flag, and he felt his shoulders sag at the sight of it.

'Stop! *Stop!* Can't you see they're Christians?' he cried. 'They fight under the cross too!'

Odo grabbed his arm as he made to rush past. 'Of course they are, but they're still enemies of God. Otherwise, why would they try to stop us from continuing on our way?'

'Odo, they're—'

'They're fighting to prevent us, Fulk. That means they're enemies to us and to God. They will die.'

Fulk could do nothing to stop the onslaught. He watched as the last men were hacked to pieces, and the flag slowly toppled, the great cross flapping like a bird captured on a limed branch, and then fell.

He was chilled. Instinctively he felt as though that was a premonition of what must surely happen to the pilgrimage itself. This was no pilgrimage, this was savagery.

Odo was at his side, but when Fulk glanced at him, it was as if his brother had been replaced with an inflexible man of iron will and no compassion.

For the first time in his life, Fulk felt truly alone.

CHAPTER 15

Plains outside Belgrade, Thursday 5th June, 1096

Sybille and Benet had returned to the wagon and to Richalda, releasing Mathena from her duties. Now, hearing a sudden cry and the clash of weapons, Sybille turned her head, seeking the source of the noise. Guillemette and Jeanne were nearby, and they sprang to their feet at the sounds. Esperte was with them, and gave a scream. Sybille stood and saw a group of Belgradian men. They had erupted from a copse farther down the line of the pilgrims, and now their swords flashed in the sun as they attacked men and women indiscriminately. A party of pilgrims was gathering, and launched themselves at the enemy.

'More work for the poor coward, I suppose,' Benet said. He hefted his sword in his hand. 'When I return, think better of me, wife. I do my best.'

She nodded, but not coldly. 'Be careful, husband.'

She settled down beside the wagon again, staring down at Richalda's beautiful young face, and prayed that Richalda would be healed soon. Her breathing was quickening again, and Sybille was worried for her.

Sybille suddenly had a sharp pang of fear. With Josse gone, Benet was her only protection. If he were to be lost, she would be alone in the world, and responsible for Richalda all on her own. Richalda was breathing harshly, and Sybille stared after Benet. She could see men struggling and hear the clashing of weapons. She stood on tiptoes, as though it could help her see further, and she was sure that she saw Benet hurtle into the midst of the fighting. It made her heart miss a beat, to see him throw himself into the fight. It was not like him. Perhaps he had discovered some new wellspring of courage, she thought. Then the mass of men were moving away, the pilgrims pushing and shoving, the Belgradians retreating into the copse and out of sight.

Sybille was glad to see that the fight was moving away. If the pilgrims were forcing them back, the Belgradians would not be able to come and threaten the camp or the stores.

'Come back,' she said quietly. 'Be careful!' Richalda muttered and moaned, and Sybille went to her, wiping her face and brow. When Richalda was calm, Sybille stood once more, her eyes going back to the copse, wondering how much longer the pilgrims would be. 'Come back, husband,' she said.

'He'll be back,' Guillemette said. 'He won't want to leave you.'

She was collecting firewood. Sybille eyed her for a few moments. In the little time she had known this woman, she had noted her dress, her confident manner with men, and her cynical, caustic manner when talking about life. It was no great guess to form a conclusion about her own position in life. So many women had joined the pilgrimage to win absolution for lives of sinfulness, but one profession was over-represented, because those who sold their bodies were marked with their sin.

'You,' she began hesitantly, 'you are—'

'I'm a whore, yes,' Guillemette said. She straightened her back, raising a querying eyebrow. 'I'm hoping that I need whore no longer, but sometimes a body must do what she can to live.'

'I do not judge,' Sybille said.

'Yes you do. Whether you mean to or not. You look at me and think, how can she cope with the dishonour, how can she live by opening her legs to every foul man who will pay her, how can she live with herself? You think all this and comfort yourself by thinking that you would not. Yet you marry a man and open your legs for him, you will do as he asks whether you have a headache, backache, or the flux, because otherwise he might beat you.'

Sybille's hand went to her cheek where Benet had slapped her. It was still raw.

'Yes, we are not so different,' Guillemette said. 'But I chose my life, just as you did. I don't enjoy it, just as many wives don't enjoy theirs, but it is the life I chose. Now I hope to get to Jerusalem and beg God's forgiveness, and then I will start afresh.'

'How?'

'I don't know. Perhaps I can take a market stall? No matter what, it will be better than living as the chattel of a whoremonger in Sens.'

Sybille nodded. 'What of the others?'

'I don't know Esperte and Mathena very well. We met them on the road. Mathena also made her living on her back, and Esperte is her adopted child. Jeanne was a poor woman sold by her husband. Then he gave her away to his drinking friends and she learned how much she was valued by him. She wants freedom from him.' Guillemette eyed her more closely. 'You are anxious? He will return.'

'It is not for him. We were robbed. Everything we had was taken,' Sybille said.

'Everything? Perhaps I can help.'

'I don't think I could . . .'

'I'm not talking about selling you,' Guillemette said. 'But I can earn a few mouthfuls. There are some who will pay me with food. I won't see you starve.'

'I . . . I don't know that—'

'If you feel food from a whore would dishonour you, I won't force you,' Guillemette said tartly. 'But your daughter needs food. Do you have the right to force her to starve?'

Sybille glanced down at the child in her arms. 'I don't know.' Richalda whimpered slightly, but then opened her eyes. They focused. Her fever seemed to have abated. Did Sybille have the right to deprive her of food? 'Thank you. Yes, I would be honoured if you would help.'

Odo moved slowly about the bodies of the enemy. There was nothing in his mind as he kicked a man's body, looking for signs of life. There was a dull ache at the back of his skull that stopped any sympathy for the figures at his feet. He had no compassion. These were only simulacrums of humans, not true beings at all. They had fought against the pilgrims, and that showed they were no better than heretics.

He picked up a body by the collar of his mail shirt and peered into the eyes. Was there a small flicker? He thrust his dagger's blade into the man's throat, and there was a sudden flaring in the depths of the fellow's eyes. Odo ripped the knife sideways, cutting the vein at the side of his neck, and dropped the body, moving on to the next one.

The picture of the youth running back to the line and dying so swiftly was in his mind constantly. That courageous young man had shown Odo how the pilgrims must fight. It was all or nothing. Kill or be killed. The enemy were so numerous that the pilgrims must be more brutal even than them. In battle the pilgrims must be more determined. They must give no quarter: in a fight against heretics there could be no compunction about ending lives. This sort of being deserved a quick ending, no more.

He kicked another figure. It moved. He stabbed.

Sybille helped Guillemette gather sticks and set about making a fire. She would heat some water with leaves and a little of their dried meat, she thought. It would make a broth for Richalda, and Benet would want some food when he returned. He was bound to be hungry. Guillemette left her to it, saying she would soon be back, and Sybille dared not ask where she was going. The answer could be embarrassing, although not for Guillemette, she suspected.

She struck with her steel at her flint, but could not coax a spark. She struck again and again, desperate to make a fire, but after many attempts she had to restrain the urge to fling the steel and flint together as far from her as possible. Taking a deep breath, she tried a last time, and this time a spark landed on her tinder. She picked it up quickly, blowing on it, her eyes flitting back to the copse as she did so. When a flame suddenly erupted, she set the tinder on the ground and placed small sticks over it until she had a good blaze, and then put a pot of water beside it.

There was still no sign of the men.

'Where are you!' she muttered, torn between anger and fear, hoping against hope that Benet would soon return.

A man was hurrying past, heading in the direction of the copse.

'What is happening?' she asked.

'I don't know, mistress, but you should get ready to leave here,' he said. 'We've been attacked up ahead, and it's said that there're more attacking our rear. We've had a number of our people murdered and robbed. It's dangerous. You need to get back with the main body, if you want to be safe.'

'My husband, he was up there,' she said.

'There? With luck he'll be back soon, but don't delay. Prepare to leave so you can go as soon as he's back.'

Sybille watched him hurry away with a great emptiness opening up in her belly. She stood, staring after him, and then down at her daughter. Richalda needed her, but perhaps Benet did too. He could have been struck down and left for dead somewhere out there. Where was Benet? He should be back by now. He had only been going to stop the Belgradians from assailing the camp's stores. What, was he chasing them all the way back to their city? She wanted to go and find him, but she could not leave her daughter here alone and unprotected. She felt tears begin to spring, tears of despair and confusion, but she knew that she must remain here. Richalda could not be left alone, and Sybille did not want to move her.

Richalda gave a soft moan, and Sybille cast one last look towards the place where the men were all hastening, and then knelt at her daughter's side and rested her palm on her brow.

'Benet, hurry back! Please!'

At the time Benet was leaning with his back to a tree.

He had come here into the woods to find that the first fierce little battle was almost done.

When the small force from Belgrade had erupted from the trees, the nearest pilgrims had grabbed whatever weapons came to hand and flown at them. Belaboured with sticks, rocks and some lances, the enemy had been held back, and then the pilgrims had closed the gap and began to fight with their bills and knives. Although they were not so well armed as their enemy, the pilgrims fought with desperation born of the distance they had come from their hearths. Theirs was an uncertain future, and they attacked with the fervour of the dispossessed.

Benet ran up to find that the majority of the men of Belgrade had already taken to their heels. He rested at his tree watching them run away, a number of pilgrims pelting after them, occasionally pulling down a less swift man.

He could return to Sybille, but his blade had not drunk blood. To go back meekly now would only encourage her to believe him a coward, and he could not bear the contempt in her eyes again. The shame he felt from hiding beneath the wagon while Josse was killed was there in his heart. It always would be. He had let down his servant, and Sybille could not trust him until he proved himself to her. He was not so devoid of courage that he could endure her contempt.

A sob racked his breast and he put his hand to his face. He should never have brought his family on this pilgrimage. Richalda could die, and how could he look his wife in the face again if that were to happen? No, he would follow the men and kill at least one of the enemy. Then Sybille could see that he was a man still.

With that determination, he pushed himself away from the tree and trotted after the others. The woods closed in about him, but there was a defined path leading between the trunks, and overhead it grew darker as branches met and obscured the sky. He heard shouting somewhere up ahead, and forced himself to a greater effort, lurching along as fast as his legs would allow.

Suddenly he came to a roughly rectangular clearing. There was a little chapel ahead and on his left, more trees beyond, and in the middle, a mêlée of pilgrims and Belgrade soldiers.

Benet felt his legs slow at the sight. It looked as though the fight would go to the locals, and he had a premonition of danger and death, but even as the icy chill of fear assailed him, he lifted his weapon, gave a cry, and launched himself into the fray.

*

Fulk pulled Odo away from the figures at the battle site.

'What is it?' Odo said irritably.

'I didn't like to see you doing that,' Fulk said.

'It's the reality of war, Fulk. Men will die. Men *must* die.'

'I know. But I don't expect to see you *enjoy* killing them!'

Odo stared at him. 'Killing the enemies of God and our enemies isn't cause for celebration? What is the matter with you?'

Fulk let go of his brother's tunic. 'Odo, I don't understand . . . This isn't you! You're no killer, you're not bloodthirsty, man!'

Odo pulled his tunic straight and glanced back at Fulk. There was a look in his eyes that made Fulk recoil.

'This is holy war, Fulk. If you don't want to do God's will, you should go back home to Sens. What did you think this would be? A pleasant walk in the sun, two Paternosters, a Hail Mary, and all would be done? This is *war*, Fulk. War! I will do all I can to destroy the scum that stole Jerusalem from us.'

'Odo, these aren't scum, these are Christians!'

'They cannot be. They are trying to stop us.' Odo turned his back and walked back to the bodies, but Fulk could not watch.

He turned away blindly, filled with revulsion. It was Odo who would usually remain calm and prevent a fight. When people squabbled, it was Odo who went to stop them. Fulk had always been the one to ignite passions, but Odo was the brother who smoothed things over again. To see him, Odo, his own dear brother, blithely executing wounded men shocked Fulk profoundly. His legs shivered, but it felt as though the ground under his feet was itself trembling with horror.

He stumbled on, away from the battle, back down the line of the pilgrim army.

A voice stopped him. 'Hello, Fulk,' Guillemette said.

He turned to her.

'Fulk, what is it?'

'I . . . Odo, he's . . .' Fulk could not find the words, and stammered to a halt.

Guillemette walked to him, and as he bent his head and began to weep, she put her arms about him and gently placed a hand on his scalp, pressing his face onto her shoulder, stroking his hair until she felt his sobbing abate. 'This pilgrimage must change all of us,' she said.

'He's killing all the injured. I suppose it could be that he's saving them from further pain, but . . .'

'It is the effect of the battle, I expect. Fighting can make men behave oddly.'

'I never would have thought to see it,' Fulk said.

'Go back and find the woman Sybille,' Guillemette said. 'She is trying to cook. Her daughter needs food.'

'How is she?' Fulk said, embarrassed by his sudden outburst. He sniffed and cleared his throat.

'Richalda is not well. I have said I'll do what I can to get more food,' Guillemette said, and put her head to one side.

'Ah, you want some from me, then?' he said.

'I can pay you.'

'There's no need. I have some to spare,' he said, and reaching into his scrip he pulled out his last pieces of sausage. They were blackened where they had been dried.

She took them from him. 'I will repay you when you want.'

'Thank you, but you need not. You shouldn't be offering yourself while on pilgrimage.'

'If I need food, I would rather pay than be in any man's debt,' she said.

'You don't need to with me,' he said.

'I must return to Sybille,' Guillemette said.

*

Sybille heard the roar and started to her feet, peering in the direction of the noise. She could see little, only groups of pilgrims walking towards her in dribs and drabs, some limping, others clutching their own bloody wounds, or helping along those who were more cruelly injured.

'Did we lose the battle?' she asked of one man.

He had grizzled hair and a cap with a tassel dangling. She recognised him as the man with the bill on the march who said he had been on pilgrimage before. Now he gave her a wolfish grin that for an instant drove away the weariness from his eyes. 'No, mistress, we killed them all!'

Sybille was watching the other men and thinking, *So this is what a victory looks like,* but the thought was soon driven from her mind. She saw the man with the grizzled hair begin to totter. He coughed, his throat sore from shouting, inhaling dust, and the effort of breathing in the fumes of death, and she realised he was desperate for water. She hurriedly picked up her flask and ran to him, setting the bottle to his lips and pouring. He choked a little, and opened his eyes to look at her a moment with a small frown. Then a grin twitched his lips. 'Is this Heaven?'

She smiled. 'No. Your struggles are not yet over.'

'In that case, I thank you, mistress,' he said. He tried to rise, but coughed again. 'My head feels like sixteen smiths have used it for their anvil,' he muttered.

'Lie here and rest,' she said. 'Are you wounded?' There was no sign of blood that she could see.

'No. It is only my pride that is injured. I thought I was young enough to join the youths in the front line, but when the fighting grew more ferocious, I learned that an old man's arm quickly loses its vitality. I'm exhausted, but only because I am ancient.'

'You are not ancient,' she said with a smile, and left him to return to Richalda.

Sybille's daughter was not improved. Her eyes moved beneath her lids, and she was shivering, although her brow was hot to the touch. When Sybille tried to speak to her, she got no response at all. The girl moved and groaned, but Sybille could get no other reaction, no matter how much she prodded and whispered with increasing agitation. 'Richalda? Richalda, wake up!'

'Can I help?'

It was the old man. He had managed to clamber to his feet, and now stood over them, staring down with a frown of concern on his brow.

'My daughter. She has a fever, and I cannot get her to wake,' Sybille said.

'She looks deeply asleep,' the man said.

'She always wakes usually when I prod her. She never sleeps this deeply.'

'Do you want to find help? I'll stay here with her,' the old man said.

Sybille ran her fingers through the stray hair that had escaped Richalda's coif, and felt her chest heave with sobs. 'I can't leave her, but I need my husband. He went over there because of Belgradians who came to rob us, and I want to go to find him, but I can't leave Richalda here alone!'

'Then you go find him, and I'll sit here with the maid and make sure no harm comes to her, mistress. I swear, no one will come close to her while I'm here,' the man said.

Sybille gave him a grateful smile, cast an anxious look down at her daughter, and then fled.

CHAPTER 16

Plains outside Belgrade, Thursday 5th June, 1096

Benet brought his sword down on the bald pate of a Belgrade man, and it sheared through the bone, the sensation jarring his hand like the blow from a cudgel. He pulled the blade free, all the while giving a high, keening sound. It was terror.

All about him, it seemed, there were men with weapons crowding in on him. He had been mad to attack like that, rather than waiting and trying to join the other pilgrims. Now he was all alone at the rear of a great line of Belgradians, and they were turning to him. Two ran at him on his left, and he wildly flailed with his sword. He was lucky; one tripped over a body on the ground, and the other held back, less enthusiastic to join the fray on his own.

'Pilgrims! To me!' Benet cried, and saw another man at his right, a sword rising; he blocked it as best he could, and the clash when the blades met was enough to make something snap in his shoulder. He took the sword in both hands, trying to swing it around to defend himself, but a man ran into him from behind, taking his feet out from under him. A boot stamped onto his sword's blade, and then a cudgel caught him on the back of the head, knocking his face into the dirt.

Benet felt his front teeth snap in the moment before blessed unconsciousness overwhelmed him.

When Fulk reached the edge of the baggage train, he continued on, as though the act of walking could eradicate the images of Odo slaughtering the wounded. But it did not. He was exhausted, mentally and physically, and his legs moved like those of an automaton. Once past the army, he carried on, walking to the copse of trees. In front of it there were the bodies of fifteen men, all cut about and beaten, sprawled in the undignified postures of death. Fulk set his hand to his sword, but there was no sound of murder, no fresh clamour of weapons. Near the copse was a wood, and he peered inside as he walked. He was also moving further from the camp and closer to the town beside the river, for the river curved here.

Fulk walked into the cool shadows beneath the trees, barely aware of anything but his misery. There, he grew aware of a noise: shouting and taunting cries. He frowned to himself and pressed on, his eyes moving about. There was a thicker barrier of trunks, but then a sudden clearing.

There was movement. He stopped, sliding sideways in among the trees at the side of the path. He approached, watching and listening carefully.

He saw the chapel with the struggling men before it. Perhaps a hundred pilgrims assailed by three or four times their number. Soon most were lying and whimpering on the ground, while the few remaining on their feet were beaten into submission. A number of men from Belgrade stood with amusement as others beat the pilgrims with their spear-butts, pushing them towards the chapel.

Some tried to escape. Fulk saw one man who drew back and screamed for help. He ducked and darted from the line of Belgrade soldiers, trying to run to freedom. He managed only five paces before a spear penetrated his back, and he tumbled to the ground squealing like an injured rabbit. A Belgrade soldier walked to him and pressed the spear down with both hands, twisting it while his victim struggled.

Benet felt himself being dragged over the ground. His head hurt like the Devil, and he felt sick. When he opened his eyes, the light was blinding and he had to narrow them urgently. He groaned and tried to kick his feet to free them, and he was dropped unceremoniously, then kicked in the flank. He rolled over. 'What's going on?'

Pilgrims were all about him. He clambered to his feet, but even as he gazed around he saw the man bolt, darting between the Belgradians until the spear brought him down.

To stay was to die. Benet saw a gap and threw himself forward, running swiftly, slipping between two Belgradians, darting around another, then entering an open space. The path was in front of him. It was only a short way to the pilgrims' camp, and there he would find Sybille, and she would love him again, knowing he was brave, that he had fought for her.

Fulk saw a second man bolt from the line of pilgrims and try to flee, and recognised him, but the soldier with the spear swung it like an axe as he passed, and Fulk heard the shin bone snap. The man went down, the spear stabbed, and Fulk heard a horrible scream.

His attention moved back to the chapel. The others were forced inside, to the jeers and taunts of the Belgradians, and then the doors were slammed and wedged closed. Then Fulk saw the soldiers light a fire. As soon as the flames were well lighted, they grabbed torches. They must have had oil on them, because they ignited with a ferocity that mere bundles of twigs would not have had. Hurling them in through the windows, the soldiers laughed to hear screams. The pilgrims were pleading for help, for mercy, as the chapel began to burn, but to no avail. Fulk felt sick. The Belgrade soldiers mocked their victims as the building caught fire. Flames licked from the broken windows and began to curl up from the roof as the timbers caught, and the shrieks from inside rose in intensity as a thudding grew. Fulk realised they were beating at the doors in a vain attempt to escape.

There was a sudden shout, and the Belgrade fighters turned as one. A force of pilgrim knights was riding towards them at the canter, lances held aloft. In a moment many of the Belgrade men had set off for their own mounts, clambering aloft with desperate urgency, while others without horses formed a square with a bristle of spears jutting like an angry hedgehog. While the riders were soon disappearing in the direction of their city, the pilgrim knights charged the men on the ground. They hurtled past Fulk and their lances speared twelve men in the first pass, and then the knights were hacking down at the men with their great swords and axes. It was all quickly over. The Belgrade men lay sprawled on the ground in the undignified postures of death.

Fulk pushed his way through the last of the trees and undergrowth as the pilgrim knights paused. One saw him and lowered his spear as though to attack, but Fulk raised his hands and shouted quickly in French, 'I'm a pilgrim!'

The knight lifted his pot helm and peered at him. 'Very well. What is happening here?'

'They shut captured pilgrims in the chapel and set light to it! We have to release them!'

There was a roaring from the conflagration, and the heat was obscene. Fulk could feel it like the searing of a smith's forge at his cheek and brow as he ran to the doors. Shrieks and cries came from inside, and although Fulk tried to remove the wedges, they were distorted by the heat and would not budge. The fire was so intense that he could not touch them. He resorted to kicking them away, and then tried the door handle. It was so hot it scorched his fingers, and he snatched his hand away, the searing pain driving out all thoughts for a moment. Then he snatched a spear from one of the riders, shoved the end into the metal ring of the lock and pulled with it as a lever. Gradually, he felt the lock move, and at last the door opened.

The gust of heat that emanated from within was like the exhalation of the Devil. Inside Fulk could see some men moving about, but they were flaming, like living torches. Even as he stared, they fell.

The party of horsemen eyed the building one last time, and then trotted off in the direction of the city, seeking someone to punish for this latest horror. Fulk said nothing, but crouched at a tree and watched as the chapel burned and collapsed in on itself. The roof gave way, and then the end wall collapsed, throwing a shower of sparks high into the sky.

Fulk slumped at a tree trunk near the chapel and covered his face in his hands. He had done all he could to help the pilgrims inside, but it was not enough, and he wept for the poor men who had burned to death.

Sybille hunted about the entrance to the woods where the initial fight had been, desperate for news of her husband, but he was not among the dead there. She was certain that Benet must have gone into the woods with the other pilgrim fighters. Perhaps the fight had not gone so well? It was likely that he would be somewhere in among those trees, she thought. Perhaps he had been beaten, and even now lay in there, injured and desperate for help.

She ran on towards the trees, and as she went she saw a column of smoke rising. It was enough to make her hesitate. She felt a clutching in her breast, as though an iron fist had gripped her heart and was squeezing it tight, until she must slow and pause, panting. The thought of Benet drove her on, but her legs were reluctant, and seemed to turn to lead. She feared what she might discover in among the trees. There was a rattle of harnesses and steel, and a troop of men on horseback burst at the gallop from a track that led through the little wood. It made her cringe and throw herself in among the trees, but the men turned their beasts to the city and were swiftly off, their hoofs thundering on the heavy soil.

Once the noise of their passage was gone, all was still. Not a bird sang, and all she could hear was a crackling and high keening noise.

She entered the woods, fearful and cautious. No one knew what might lurk in the deep darkness of a forest, whether it was the danger of a vicious boar, a bear, or wolf, or the still more terrifying threat of a witch or spirits.

Today Sybille forced all thoughts of such superstition to the back of her mind. She pressed on through the trees, all the while aware of the reek of burning; not the fresh smell of clean, well-cured wood, but the sour tang of old and rotten timbers. The smoke was thinner now, and she could discern the odour of burning meats, as though there was a campfire ahead of her and someone had set the spit too close to the flames.

She sidled about the track, wary of meeting more men here in the trees where no one could see her and protect her, terrified of what she might find, but more scared of leaving, never to find her husband again. Her eyes hunted among the tree trunks and bushes, searching for a body that could be her man's, but there was nothing to be seen. Not until she approached a wide clearing.

The crackling of flames was louder, and she saw, dimly through the trees, the burning chapel. She hurried forward, her mind empty of everything but the need to get to the building. The dangers of the forest fell from her mind as she hurried onwards, and she stopped at the clearing just as the roof finally collapsed with a shower of sparks. A gust of air, hot and foul, wafted past her, and she held up her forearm to shield herself, before peering at the building again.

That was when she saw Benet at the side of the path.

He was on his back, and she ran to him. 'Benet! Oh, God in Heaven, no!'

There was blood at his mouth, mingling with the blood on his breast. He had a wound in his throat that bubbled as he breathed out, he had lost three fingers of his right hand, and there was a cut over his eye that was as long as her forefinger, but there was also a black hole in the side of his skull. Even as she fell to her knees at his side, his body was racked and he gave one last gasp as he died.

'Mistress, go back!'

She looked up to see Fulk. At first words failed her, and then she felt a fire of rage engulf her and blazed, 'I won't leave him! He's my husband! My husband! My love! Oh, God, what can we do now?'

Odo stood, stretching his back, peering about him dumbly. Other men were engaged in a similar fashion, strolling about the battle-field, taking choice pieces of mail, gauntlets, boots or weapons. Many were searching for the easier items: bangles or rings. Many found swollen fingers hard to manipulate, and snipped off the offending dead finger. Odo paid the ghouls no attention. The dead had no need of their wealth.

Carrion birds alighted on bodies near him, and Odo watched as they set about their task with gusto. It reminded him of his vision earlier, when he had seen Fulk injured. He felt no horror here, nothing for the bodies being desecrated any more than he felt anything for the birds. To feel sorry for the enemies of God would be heretical, and he was no heretic. No, he was God's own man. He could feel that now. He hoped that Fulk too would soon come to realise the truly divine nature of their pilgrimage and stop his fornicating and complaining when Odo carried out God's will. God wanted this. *Dieu le veut.*

For this was not a mere walk to the Holy Land: this was a *cleansing.* God's lands had to be purified and purged of the heretics who infested it.

Fulk had seen her as she came around the bend in the road, and hurried to her side as she found Benet.

He could not have mistaken her. Since that first day when he saw her in the market square, he had been aware of her, even when she had been out of sight. Her smile, her calm eyes, both had been much in his mind, especially since helping her from beneath the wagon. Now he saw her again with her face fixed into a mask of horror. He wanted to console her, but there was nothing he could do as she bent over the body of her dead husband with a grown woman's desperate sobbing. There were not sufficient tears in the world for her misery.

As he watched her he felt his heart tear at her grief.

BOOK FIVE

The
Eastern Empire

CHAPTER 17

Constantinople, Thursday 5th June, 1096

The thunderous knocking was enough to jerk Alwyn awake in an instant and he sighed as Sara began berating the man for waking the household so early. He climbed from his bed and stretched, pulled on a long tunic and walked to the door.

He was a cocky one, this. Armed and gleaming like all the palace guards, and he held Alwyn's gaze as he spoke as though to save himself the indignity of meeting Sara's furious eyes. 'You are to come with me. The Vestes has need of you.'

'I will be with you shortly.'

'He said to come now!'

'And I will. As soon as I have dressed,' Alwyn said mildly.

The man opened his mouth, but Sara stepped in front of him. 'You think you can command a man who served the Emperor before you were born? He was killing the Emperor's enemies while you had snot on your face!'

Alwyn grinned to himself. While she tore the man off a strip, Alwyn returned to his bedchamber and dressed.

A call to the palace was a cause more for irritation than concern. Others would fear such a summons, but Alwyn was fortunate in that he had the measure of the Vestes.

When he returned, Sara was watching the messenger with her dark eyes full of suspicion. She was Alwyn's woman, a slave he had been given years before, and now his constant companion, more loyal even than his old hound. Three years ago he had offered her her freedom, thinking that she would appreciate the gift, but she had refused with an angry expression in her eyes that said she thought it an insult. He didn't understand, but he was relieved when she chose to remain. She might have left him, and that would be intolerable.

He marched to the palace with the guard. They did not speak on the way. Alwyn was known to him, of course; all the guards knew of the Saxon. His life had been one of constant service to the Emperor, and his position in the Varangian Guard had sealed his honour in the eyes of the Byzantines, even if his survival was, for him, a source of shame.

The way to the great palace of Blachernae took him through the city from the rougher area near the coast where he lived, up to the rarefied atmosphere of the northwestern tip of the city. At the main gates Alwyn could not help but stare up at the gatehouse. It soared so high overhead it always seemed to him to float on the air. He was taken around the main buildings and out to the administrative chambers at the east. Finally he was taken to the room on the eastern upper circle of the building, with views over the Golden Horn and beyond.

'Ah! Alwyn, you are most welcome. I thank you for coming to me so – ah – swiftly,' the man at the table said.

He was taller than Alwyn, a slimly built man with an easy smile that never touched his eyes. His beard was long and gleamed in the morning light, with red and golden tints gleaming.

'Your messenger made it plain I was needed urgently,' Alwyn said. He glanced about the room. It was richly furnished, with all the trappings to show that this was one of the Empire's most powerful men. John was the Vestes, the head of the imperial wardrobe, and as such second only to the Emperor Alexius himself, in charge of all aspects of spying and control within the Empire.

He was said to be almost as rich as the Emperor himself, and although Alwyn doubted that, the man had money. His riches came from the knowledge that he owned. When a ship arrived in port, it was John who received the most important cargoes: the messages from spies all over the Mediterranean and beyond. When a foreign city was attacked, John was first to know, and could advise his friends which investments to retain, which to discard; when plague ravaged a nation that was important on the spice routes, John knew to buy up stocks of the goods that would soon be in short supply; and he knew when an army was marching and it would be a good time to invest in arms manufacture. John held all the tendrils of information at his fingertips and, like the professional lyre players he admired, he was adept at playing them.

'Ah, well, I thought it would be useful to have a talk with you,' John said. He waved to a slave, who approached and bowed low, holding up a tray with wine and goblets already filled. John took one and sniffed the bouquet, indicating that Alwyn should also. 'Some months ago the Emperor, may his reign never cease, heard of manoeuvres across the sea. Our lands in Rum are taken, as you know. We have lost Nicaea and land from the Black Sea to the Mediterranean. So the Emperor decided to write to the head of the – ah – Catholic church to ask for some knights to help us in our struggle to protect our city. He anticipated a few mercenaries who could be used to stiffen the Varangian Guard. It was a good idea,' he added, sipping at his wine. 'But the Pope, perhaps accidentally, misunderstood. He preached a new war against the Turks and Seljuks. And the – ah – *common people*,' the words were spat like poison tasted on his tongue, 'these peasants, decided to march. There are many armies of them, both at the borders with Hungary, and waiting, so we hear, at Bari and other ports, waiting to cross into our Empire.'

'What will you do?'

'Me? I will advise his Imperial Majesty to the best of my ability. Perhaps bring them here, feed them, entertain them, make them feel valued, and – ah – if they are true barbarians, we can send them across the straits to see how they fare. However, at all costs we ensure that all take an oath to return to the Emperor any lands they capture. We do not wish to have scoundrels appear and detach attractive lands from the Empire, after all. But a strengthening of the blood of some of our people may be useful. From all we have seen, there are some enormously vigorous men in the west.'

'What of it? I cannot stop them.'

'No, but you can – um – assess them. Who better? You can watch them, take a view on their strength and likely ability. We need to know whether they come to aid us, or to storm us. You were born among them, fought with them twice, and showed your valour against them. There are few indeed who can have the same appreciation of their strength and skills.'

Alwyn said nothing to that. He felt only a coldness in his heart that John could ask this. John knew it was a Norman army that had shattered the shield wall at Hastings; Normans who had destroyed the Varangian Guard at Dyrrhachium. He had lost everything to them.

'You have safer men to do this, Vestes. Don't ask this of me.'

'I need you to speak with these fellows and report back.' His tone had hardened.

'You know that they stole my country. They killed my King and all my family. If I meet with a Norman, I am likely to kill him,' Alwyn said softly.

The Vestes eyed him. 'You must not. That could exacerbate … difficulties for us.'

'What if I meet the man who slew my father and uncle? The man who killed my comrades at Dyrrhachium? I would not be able to hold back my rage. Send someone else.'

The Vestes' voice grew silky smooth. 'I do not like to threaten, Alwyn. However, consider. Think on Sara and Jibril. Their fates depend on you.'

'You threaten my woman and my boy?' Alwyn said bitterly.

'You think I want to?' John slammed his goblet onto his table with an uncharacteristic display of anger. 'There is no one else I can send! You are the only man I can trust in this. So control yourself. If you hurt any of them, you may as well not return; you will be banished from the city and the Empire. Return to your own land, if you can!'

'You know I cannot.'

'So go and see them. Use this seal. It will ensure that your reports are brought back as swiftly as may be.'

He looked away, down at the papers on his desk, and then out to the window and the view over the Golden Horn. At first Alwyn thought it was the natural cavalier rudeness of an aristocrat, a hint that Alwyn was dismissed. But then he realised that there was no intentional slight. It was just that the Vestes was at a loss.

John was one of the most powerful men in Constantinople, and yet in the face of the armies heading towards his city, he was as anxious as a penniless peasant faced with an imperial command.

Alwyn returned home and sat on his stool. Seeing his mood, Jibril was nervous and moved quietly about the room, bringing wine and bread and olives, but Alwyn paid him no heed. He was seeing in his mind's eye those he had lost: Eadnoth, Godwyn, his father, his uncle ... and he saw the flames of his hall leaping up to the skies again.

John was a spider, sitting in the middle of his web and waiting for news. But was the news to be of rescue or of disaster? Normans were coming: the same men who had stolen Alwyn's lands and killed his King before coming here to the Empire. Now more of the northern devils were approaching the Empire, and who could tell what havoc they would wreak when they arrived? Alwyn felt sure John feared these northerners more than he did the Muslims.

The Empire was so vast, so strong and so impregnable in every way that the populace believed it to be inviolate, but Alwyn had stood against the Normans in the shield wall of the Varangian Guard, and he knew that the border between strength and submission was thin. Just as the barbarians had entered and broken Rome, so too could these new savages destroy the Eastern Empire by mauling the city that controlled it. It would take only a little for the safety and security of life in Constantinople to be overthrown. He loved this, his adopted city. If it was to be in peril, he wanted to help serve it and protect it as best he may.

He would go and look at the different men coming to the city, he decided. But if there were any Normans there whom he recognised, he would risk banishment and exile from the city for revenge.

CHAPTER 18

Belgrade, Thursday 5th June, 1096

Sybille was distraught when Fulk tried to pry her from her dead husband's body.

She screamed, clinging to Benet, wailing and sobbing, her desolation too great to endure, her entire body racked with grief. It felt as though she was floating outside her body, as if this horror was so profound that her soul was itself breaking free of her heart and rising in the still air, up among the branches. She was dizzy, and she could almost allow herself to believe that this was all a foul dream, a vision placed into her mind by an evil mare. But the moment passed, and she returned to her body with her anguish renewed and strengthened. It was soul-destroying, impossible to accept. Her husband could not have died!

All recriminations – for his cowardice, blame for bringing his family here, for the death of Josse – left her. In her mind's eye she saw her husband's gentle smile; she remembered his soft strength as he held her in his embrace, and she recalled how they had separated earlier that day. The pain of that parting wrenched at her breast as if her soul was being ripped from her, and it was almost a relief to slide once more into mindless sobbing, her face at Benet's breast.

She was scarcely aware of Fulk as he pulled her free. He put one arm about her back, another under her rump, and lifted her to his chest. She clung to his neck like a child as he unsteadily rose to his feet. Although she weighed little, he was unused to bearing such a load.

When they reached Walter's men, Fulk set her down. There was a pot set over a fire, and he took a little of the broth from it, trying to feed Sybille, but she would take none of it. After a while, one of Walter's men passed him a small, flat loaf. Fulk broke it and tried to push it between Sybille's lips, but she pushed his hand away and stared about her wildly.

'Richalda! Richalda!' she cried, and sprang to her feet.

'Mistress, wait!' Fulk said, but she was already gone. She had to get to Richalda, to protect her. Sybille had to make sure that she was not alone in the world. She shoved men and women from her path, running as hard as though she were being chased by the Devil and all his demons.

Fulk sighed and took some of the bread for himself. He almost ran off after her, but there was little point, he knew. She would be going to her daughter and her friends. The women would comfort her better than he could. He felt desolate to see her so distressed and to be incapable of helping her.

Peter was watching him with a hard expression on his face. 'What was that about? Have you—'

'She's just seen her husband die.'

'She won't be alone in that today,' Peter said.

'No.'

Fulk returned to his camp. On the way he met Sir Walter's priest and told him about the atrocity committed at the chapel.

The man was shocked. He was ten years older than Fulk, balding, with a shock of grizzled hair about his tonsure, and he muttered a short prayer as he absorbed Fulk's words. His tale of Benet and Sybille made the cleric grimace sadly.

'The poor woman!'

'She would not leave her husband. He was dead, but she was most devoted. I wish I could have consoled her.'

'You did your best, and now you should take some men and, when it is possible, retrieve the bodies. A sad business.'

'Where is Sir Walter?'

'They are burning the land all about to punish the city for their attacks. We shall be here for another day or two,' the priest said. He passed a hand over his face as though to wash away the memories of the last hours. 'It is a terrible thing, war against other Christians. A matter of great sadness. But what else could we do?'

Fulk had no answer. He left Sir Walter's pavilion and made his way back to where he and Odo had left their gear that morning. His brother was there already, and looked up.

'Fulk? Are you well? When you ran off like that, I didn't know . . .'

Fulk gave him a faint smile. 'I am well enough. No serious injuries, I thank God. Only this,' he added, touching the cut on his scalp.

Odo thought he looked like a man who had endured a hideous ordeal and barely survived. His face was strained and pale, his eyes a little bloodshot. Odo went to his side and put an arm about his shoulders, leading him nearer the fire. 'Sit.'

'How about you?' Fulk said.

Odo ruefully lifted his left arm. 'A little scratch.' It was more than a scratch. A long, raking tear in his underarm's flesh had been bleeding profusely. 'It was one of the little shits who pretended to be dead. I missed him, and he suddenly did this when I was over him. He won't do it to anyone else.'

Fulk eyed it. 'You should have it washed and have a poultice put on it. You don't want it to go rotten.'

'I will. Where are you going?'

Explaining about the chapel, Fulk didn't mention Sybille. She didn't seem relevant just then.

Odo heard the reticence in his tone but didn't want to question him. There was no need to reignite the embers of their earlier row. Instead Odo sat with his back to a wagon's wheel and tried to close his eyes for a while. He was satisfied with his actions that day. God would be pleased, he thought. His mouth stretched into a smile of contentment. Yes, He would surely be pleased and want to reward Odo.

Just as he was sinking into a doze, female voices stirred him.

He opened his eyes, and instantly recognised Guillemette, but he had eyes only for Jeanne.

'Is your brother here?' Guillemette asked.

'No. He has gone to perform some service for our knight,' Odo said. He wanted to turn away from Guillemette; he didn't like to be in the presence of a prostitute, but Jeanne was entrancing.

'I was hoping he might be able to help. A friend is in sore need of assistance.'

'A friend?' Odo said. He shot her a look. 'You mean another of your intolerable craft?'

'No. A friend, who has been widowed. A good, Christian woman,' Guillemette snapped. 'Her husband is dead, her servant too, and her daughter is prostrated with a fever. She has lost everything to serve God, and yet you would condemn her because she is my friend! What a true, Christian attitude you have!'

Odo scowled and would have spoken, but Guillemette had already spun on her heel and was stalking away, back towards the main wagon park. Well, if she did not want to wait and hear his apology, so much the better.

Seeing Jeanne, who had remained, he said, 'I am sorry. I did not mean to embarrass you.'

She nodded. 'You dislike her?'

'I just think that for her to ply her trade here jeopardises the whole venture. How would it be if God looked down on the pilgrimage and saw whores and their gulls disporting themselves?' He winced and glanced down at his wound. 'He might even decide to halt us or deprive us of our goal: the Holy City.'

Jeanne said no more about Guillemette, but insisted on looking at his arm. 'I have two brothers, and would often bind their wounds,' she said, crouching beside him, taking his arm and resting it in her lap. 'It's a nasty cut,' she said, studying the puckered skin, 'but it's clean enough.' She took his knife and cut a strip of material from her hem. She used it to bind his arm, and tied it off carefully. 'Try to keep it from bad odours and keep it clean. If we had honey, I'd have covered it in some. That always helps.'

'You are a midwife? You are an excellent nurse,' Odo said warmly. He would not confess to the renewed pain that she had stirred in his arm, and he didn't care. Her lap felt soft, and he felt a flush at his cheeks at her innocence in letting him put his hand there, in the warmth of her upper thighs. He wanted to leave it there, to stay sitting like that. It felt like Heaven, even though his heart was thumping as though trying to escape his chest.

'I have been many things,' she said, standing again. 'I must go back.'

'Do not go back with the whore,' Odo said. 'I have seen her with other men, even my brother. She would sell her body for a cup of wine. Do not go with her, in case you become tainted yourself.'

'I have no fear of that.'

'I do.'

His words stilled her. She studied his face as though seeking an ulterior motive. 'Why?'

'Maid, you are so young and the world can be cruel to beauty. I would not see you hurt or at threat.'

She nodded, with a small smile that put his heart at ease.

Fulk made his way back to the chapel.

It was after dark when the flames died, and with the heat it would be the following morning before they could look through the ruins.

Fulk had much to think about.

His participation in the battle had left him torn. His confusion had dissipated, but it was replaced by a sense of profound loss. Odo was a different creature from the careless baker's apprentice with whom Fulk had set off from Sens, and Fulk suspected that the old brother would never return. The battle had changed both of them; neither could be unaffected.

It was not only the sight of Odo cutting the throats of injured men. It was an act of mercy to slay them gently. Yet still the picture of the men lying all about the field, and his brother drawing his blade across their necks as though he enjoyed watching the light of life dim in their eyes, intruded. It made him feel unclean. Worse, it made him uncomfortable in the presence of Odo. He would grow used to it, he told himself, he would get over it. They were brothers.

As night came, he rested with his back against a tree trunk, although he slept little. The little ticks and clicks from the cooling walls were enough to keep him from sleep, and the noise as one of the walls fell in startled him from a doze in the middle of the night. He could not rest too close, for the heat was brutal.

He fell asleep at some time around dawn, but something woke him, and he glanced around anxiously in case the men of Belgrade had returned. Instead, he found himself looking up at Guillemette.

'I brought you bread,' she said.

He took it gratefully, realising how hungry he was.

'Your brother is a pig,' she said.

'What has he done?'

'He looked down his nose at me and made me know how unwelcome I was,' she said.

'He has a very long nose,' Fulk admitted.

'He almost accused me of fornication with the whole army.'

'He thinks you have stamina,' he said, and was relieved to see her expression lighten.

'He knows nothing of lovemaking, I suppose. Not many women would want to sleep with a supercilious fellow like him.'

'It is a cross he has to bear,' Fulk said. 'I got the good looks and personality in our family.'

'You got something, certainly,' she said, and bent to kiss his brow.

'Is that all?'

She looked at the chapel. 'It doesn't feel right. Not with all the men who died in there.'

'I know.' He shivered.

'Besides, he did say something that makes sense,' she said. 'How can we hope for God's support if we behave as badly as any others? Perhaps fornicating will only lead us to failure.'

'What, you and me?'

'I've been giving you sex in exchange for food. I think I can't continue,' she agreed.

'So this is the end?'

'I don't know. I have a lot to think about,' she said. She put her hand on his shoulder and leaned to him, kissing him on the mouth. 'That's not farewell,' she said. 'Only goodbye for now.'

Belgrade, Friday 6th June

The bodies were mostly unrecognisable. Many were blackened balls, foetal figures that looked scarcely human, their faces scorched and swollen, all hair and most of their clothing gone. After the roof collapsed, many had been crushed together. It meant that the fires had burned less fiercely, but the effects of their appalling deaths choked by smoke, crushed by the timbers of the roof and burned as well, meant that each was a mass of bones in scorched sacking. There was little that a relative would be able to spot as representing a husband or brother.

Fulk enlisted the help of some men from Walter's household, and they began picking their way through the rubble. It took much of the morning. One man pulled at a fallen stone, not realising it was still appallingly hot, and burned his hands so badly he had to be taken away, weeping, to a physician. Another man burst out laughing, and held up his boot, smouldering, but with the use of iron bars and baulks of timber they began to clear away the stones and expose the bodies.

It was not pleasant. Fulk found the first when he moved some rubble aside. He had carefully covered his hands with thick strips of cloth wetted with water, after seeing the other burn his hands so badly. He found scorched timbers, and pulled them away, and then there was a large rock, which he levered away with the help of a fellow from the south of Tuscany, who had an accent as thick as the mud that pooled beside the river. Underneath was a panel of wood, and he lifted it away, only to give a short gasp of horror. Underneath, white with stone dust and ash, was a face from Hell, screaming into eternity.

Fulk helped pull away more wreckage and the bodies were dragged and carried away.

He helped the others to dig a broad pit, and they carefully

placed the bodies inside. Fulk had men help him fetch Benet and the other who lay nearby, and set them with their companions. The bodies were covered with soil and stones from the chapel's walls and Sir Walter's priest held a short service over the grave. Fulk hoped they would find peace. In his heart, he wondered whether they could. After seeing the gaping, screaming mouths of the dead, it was hard to imagine that they could find peace even in Heaven. At least, the priest reminded them, all these fellows were innocent of any sin for, by taking up the symbol of the cross on this pilgrimage, they were freed from the burden of the sins they had earned through their lives. They had achieved remission. That was good.

But as Fulk passed the last of the rocks to the man standing on top of the mound they had erected over the bodies, he was struck by the thought that the men who had killed these were also Christians. Would they be forgiven for killing others of His faith?

Fulk hoped not.

Sybille had slept fitfully. The recollection of the burning chapel was always in her mind, whether she was wide awake or dozing. The only difference was that the flames seemed more real, more appallingly scorching, when she was not quite fully awake. When she awoke, it seemed for an instant that the battle, Benet's disappearance, his death, were all mere imaginings, that they were the hideous proof of a mare's visit during the night. Everyone knew that the horrible little fairies would sit on a nodding person's breast and introduce the most hideous dreams to the sleeping mind. That was how this seemed: a fiction designed to cause her horror.

But as consciousness returned to her, with it came grief. She rocked back and forth, tears welling, and it was only the appreciation of the desperate exhaustion of all those around her that made her put her hands over her mouth and stop her agony from wailing forth.

Benet had been so good a man, attentive and kind, but it was not only that which made her eyes widen. It was the realisation that she and her daughter were now lost in a sea of men, many miles from their home. Richalda and she were all alone, with no one to defend them.

As the light arrived, she set her hand out to her daughter, and felt the chill of her face, and a sob choked her as she stared down, thinking only that she could not cope with another death. It was an unbearable relief to see her daughter's breast rising and falling, and to realise that her coldness was proof that her fever had left her, not a sign that she had joined her father.

Richalda was alive. So Sybille had a duty to live. She could not give herself up to her grief. She must live and survive for her daughter.

'How are you now?' Odo asked.

Fulk hadn't noticed him. He was still musing over the dead whom he had buried, and was startled by his brother's sudden appearance.

Odo had the look that he had so often worn when they were children, when Odo had stolen a cake or apples and denied his crime. All too often, their father would assume that his eldest son would not lie, and beat Fulk instead. Afterwards, Odo would plead forgiveness with this same look in his eye, a sort of nervous trepidation, like a dog desperate to appease his master's righteous ire. It always worked.

'I'm well enough, Odo,' he said.

Odo inclined his head in a shamefaced fashion. 'I am sorry about yesterday.'

'Me too.'

Fulk knew Odo had changed in the last days, but so had he. Neither was entirely comfortable in the other's company. Perhaps partly it was Guillemette's comment. Fulk had set out thinking that this would be almost a holiday, like the brief pilgrimages to local towns or Paris back home. This would take longer, but he had thought it would be a similar journey. And because they were going to the Holy Land, God would protect them when they attacked the unbelievers who had taken Jerusalem. *Dieu le veut*, as they had all said on leaving. But now he was confronted with the fact that, on the way, they themselves would be the targets of every governor who felt he had cause to fear their massed strength. They would be fighting all the way themselves.

Now he knew that this was a stern undertaking, as unlike a walk to Nôtre Dame or St Denis as it could be. Here there was every chance of death before they had even reached the Holy City. Even if they did survive the weary leagues to Jerusalem, there was very little chance indeed that either he or Odo would ever make it home again.

'What's got into you?' Odo cried, as Fulk turned and threw his arms around Odo's neck.

'Nothing, brother. It's only that . . . nothing. You're all I've got.'

CHAPTER 19

Bulgarian Plains, Tuesday 17th June, 1096

Alwyn had a clear sight of the pilgrim army on the march, and it was a scene that filled him with surprise, but little dread.

An army on the march is a terrible sight, but it was obvious to his eye that this was no disciplined force that could threaten a city like Constantinople with destruction. There were few ranks of marching soldiers such as the Byzantine Empire could field, but for all that there was a cohesiveness and power in the quantity of people there. He could not count the total from vanguard to the sprawl of wagons, but it was plain to him that there were many tens of thousands. They stretched across the plains like locusts, destroying and consuming all in their path.

Alwyn turned to his companion, a dour man with skin burned dark by the sun. He was chewing on a strip of dried meat, his arms crossed, his elbows resting on the pommel of his saddle as he peered at the horde. 'What do you think?' Alwyn said.

'The sooner they're away from our plains, the better. They're devastating the crops, as you can see. What will they do next?'

'I have to report to the Imperial court,' Alwyn said. 'Do you think that they pose a significant threat?'

'These are not so bad. They got into fights at Zemun and Belgrade, but they have been more controlled since then. But there are stronger forces gathering on the border already, and they are said to be more military in outlook. If they are similar in size, but better armed and arrayed, we will have trouble. These appear to be peasants and their women. I've heard that many are whores who are seeking salvation.'

'Salvation?'

Alwyn had not heard of the Pope's dispensation to all those who took part in this grand *iter*, and he listened to the other's explanation with interest. 'If that is the case, it is hardly surprising that so many are marching.'

'More will come.'

'Even if these are kicked back with their tails between their legs?' Alwyn said.

'Especially then. If they believe that by fighting for the Holy Land they can win a place in Heaven, all the felons in Christendom will want to try their fortune. If they succeed, more and more will come as pilgrims; if they fail, others will take up weapons to show their dedication to God.'

Alwyn stared out over the plains again. He was thinking how awesome this great army was; truly, it was a terrible sight. If it troubled him so deeply, it must surely appal even the Saracen hordes in Rum and beyond. Perhaps, at last, this was proof that Christians could unite and win back Jerusalem.

It was an idea that both thrilled and alarmed him, proof that the existing world order was about to change. No matter whether a man wished for the reconquest of Jerusalem or not, this army would ensure change.

Alwyn sighed once more, and set off to return to Constantinople. He would bear this message himself.

Philippopolis, Sunday 22nd June

For the next two weeks Odo was content.

Fulk and he marched together with Peter of Auxerre in Sir Walter's company and, as they tramped onwards, Odo was never given cause to be concerned about Fulk's behaviour with women. His brother was behaving impeccably.

When there was a break in the constant marching, they tended to train with Peter, learning how better to block and parry, how to use strength and guile, how to kill with little effort. Although both were exhausted after their long marching, they were not so foolish as to reject his instruction. They would train with their own swords, repeating manoeuvres without pause until Peter felt they had learned the basics of defence and attack, and declared them safe enough to join him in the line when there was a fresh battle. Peter appeared to have taken to them, as a father might adopt a pair of children.

The pilgrim host had many adventures. Local warlords took umbrage at seeing their crops destroyed or stolen, and attacks were common, although the heavily armoured knights and men-at-arms were able to beat off all. When they reached the city called Nish, the army was buoyed to hear after a day or two that the governor had promised them not only both food and weapons, but also letters of safe passage.

'Aye, well, they want to be rid of us,' Peter said.

'Why would they want that?' Odo asked uncomprehendingly.

'Look at us! We are a city compared with the majority of the little towns about here. If we were to grow angry, we could take this place in two days. If we wanted to march to Constantinople and lay waste the lands between here and there, we could. With this army, we could burn a swathe four miles wide for a thousand miles, and nothing would grow there for a year. The governor here isn't stupid enough to want to have to deal with us. He'll have heard what happened to Belgrade's men, and those of Zemun, so he's going to send us on our way with as much speed and little fuss as possible. If it costs him some money, so be it; if it costs him some food, he has enough and to spare. But if we stay, his women are at risk, as well as his food stores. No governor would want an army like this outside their walls.'

The mood of joy and relief was not to last long. The army welcomed the wagons of food and equipment (Peter stole two mail shirts, helmets and shields for Odo and Fulk before anyone else got to see them) from the governor of Nish before they set off again. When they had passed halfway to Constantinople, news came of a disaster in the army's ranks. The uncle of Sir Walter de Boissy-Sans-Avoir, Sir Walter de Poissy, fell ill as they approached the town of Philippopolis. Many of the pilgrims had been succumbing to diseases, often caused by simple exhaustion or malnourishment, and a few to fevers, but Sir Walter's ailment was more speedy than most. He lingered for two days, and then was gone.

Fulk had scarcely known the man, even to recognise him, but Peter was sad. 'He'll be missed, boy. You mark my words. He had a good head on his shoulders, God love him.'

Odo nodded, and crossed himself. 'Yes, but he will make a swift entry to Heaven for having died on this march,' he said.

'Aye,' Peter said, but there was an edge to his voice that Fulk had begun to notice.

227

Later, while Fulk was whetting his sword's edge, Peter came and watched approvingly. He sat beside Fulk and was for a while quiet, apart from correcting Fulk, taking the whetstone from about his neck and demonstrating the long, firm sweeps that would keep the edge keen.

'Your brother Odo, he is very religious, isn't he?' he said at last.

'Yes, and I've seen that it alarms you,' Fulk said.

'It's not his religion that worries me, it's his conviction. It's almost as if he thinks he can do no wrong. He's keen to judge others, but he doesn't consider himself bound by the same rules.'

'But we're all religious here,' Fulk said.

'Some are, some less so. There are a few here who have committed crimes you can barely imagine, and who hope to be forgiven when they knock on the gates of Heaven and beg to be allowed in, as well as those who believe that they have a simple right to enter, no matter what. Some think no matter how badly they behave the saints will welcome them, just because they've joined in slaughtering the Saracens.'

'You don't agree with that?'

'I don't think the idea of taking Jerusalem is bad, just as I don't think that the angels would be upset if we do. But I just have this idea, of me appearing at the gates, smothered all in blood, and Jesus Christ Himself waiting. What would He say about the blood, do you think?'

'If it's all the blood of unbelievers and heretics, surely He would be content,' Fulk said.

'You think so? I wonder. But your brother there, he's one of those who would think that the more blood he's covered in, the more keenly he'll be welcomed to Heaven. You see, I don't know that they would think like that. I reckon they'd like to see some-one who hasn't tried to wade through the blood of his enemies, because if there's one thing I know, it's that old blood soon starts to smell, and there's not much you can do to get rid of that odour. It stays in your nostrils once you have wallowed in it.'

Fulk pulled a face at the thought. 'In Heaven all is made anew, I think. Your clothes are as clean as new material.'

'You think so? I think the reek of blood would stay on a man even in Heaven. And I don't know if the angels would want that smell near them.'

Peter wandered away to see if he could find a pot or two of wine, leaving Fulk unsettled.

Odo was definitely enthusiastic for glory. He had declared as much often enough. He wanted to get to the Holy Land and begin the slaughter of the heretics there. Yet Fulk did not believe him to be overkeen on glory for glory's sake. It was more that he was determined to bring about the end of the cruel regime that had conquered Jerusalem, and destroy those who sought to enslave Christians under a brutal, uncivilised government that would leave them as little better than cattle to be farmed. Stories of Saracen cruelty were rife, from the determination to force men and women to recant their religion and become Muslim, to the tales of Christian babies being spitted on swords, mothers raped, men slaughtered. The stories of the evil behaviour of these god-less men were legion. Odo was not the only man who sought an apocalyptic end to his enemies. The priests had been foretelling the end of the world for some years now, ever since the schism in the Papacy and the calculations that the Bible meant this to be the time of Armageddon.

Not that Fulk desired that. If the world was to end, then he would endure the last days with as much fortitude and equanimity as he could manage, but he would prefer to think that the world was to survive a few years. Still, that was in the hands of God.

Peter was clearly concerned with the way that Odo was behaving, but that was ridiculous. Odo was a religious man, but in that he was like so many others who were here on pilgrimage. It did not make him odd. Since receiving the wound on his arm he had been much more his old self, although there were times when he appeared to be a little secretive. As he was now. He had disappeared before Peter came, and Fulk was not sure where he had gone. He must speak to his brother and find out.

Philippopolis, Monday 23rd June

The cries of delight were heard early next morning. Fulk woke to a clashing of cymbals and the blaring of trumpets. Groggily he rose from his sleep, rubbing his hip where the skin had become sore overnight, and took up his belt. He peered towards the source of the noise, and realised it came from near Sir Walter's tent.

'What is it?' he asked Peter.

The older man was standing with a knife in his hand, cutting slices from a piece of dried meat. He held out a piece to Fulk. 'By all that's holy! Haven't you heard?'

'I heard the row.'

As he spoke, the city's bells began to ring. Fulk glanced up at the spire of the cathedral, whose own bell was tolling sonorously. 'Is it war?'

Peter stopped chewing, stared at him, and then began to laugh, wiping his eyes with the back of his hand as the tears fell. 'You poor fool! Have you never heard all the bells ringing like this? It's a miracle, boy! A miracle! A cross has appeared on Sir Walter de Poissy's body. They're all declaring a great miracle, and it looks like we'll get all the help we need, now that the sanctity of our pilgrimage is confirmed.'

'Miracle?' Fulk repeated, dazed. 'What do you mean, a cross on his body?'

'A great, painted cross.'

Fulk felt his mouth fall open. 'So an angel came down and painted him last night?'

Odo was walking towards them. He had been to the tent in which the body was being displayed. 'Have you seen it?'

His excitement was infectious. Fulk peered round him towards the tent. 'Is he still there?'

'Yes, the bishop from the city is on his way to view the body, but there is a firm belief that it is genuine. He has the mark of the cross, Fulk. It's all over his torso, a great pilgrimage cross. It's astonishing.'

Peter coughed and held his hand over his mouth as he bent. Fulk patted his back while he choked. Odo had already departed.

'Are you well?'

'Oh, aye. I'm well. Godspeed to your brother, though.'

'What do you mean?'

'Boy, have you learned nothing? Look, the bells are ringing, yes? The bishop is coming, yes? But shouldn't the bishop view the miracle, hear the evidence such as it may be, and then declare that the bells should ring?'

'I don't know.'

'Well, take it as the truth. Yet today we have the bells rung and then the bishop comes to view the miracle.'

'Who declared it, then?'

'Who can tell? But a painted cross on a dead man's body could have been performed as much by a man with a pot of paint as an angel.'

'You mean it is a fraud?'

Peter glanced around to make sure that no one was listening. 'All I'll say is, Sir Walter de Boissy-Sans-Avoir is a shrewd

231

man. We've had soldiers trailing after us for days, we've endured attacks from outlaws, we've been refused access to markets and the chance to buy food on the way here. A miracle sealing the importance of our journey would not go amiss, would it? Aye, Sir Walter is a shrewd old man,' he added, chuckling softly as he carved a fresh slice of meat and began to chew.

Sybille and Richalda had survived. It was over two weeks since Benet's death, and yet still Sybille could not believe that he was gone. She plodded, with her eyes on the man in front of her or on the wagon. Although a few people had noticed her, and looked at her askance, many thinking that she was nothing more than a waste of food now that she had no husband, some men had taken her defence in hand. Roul, the man who had looked after Richalda on the day she went to find Benet, had recovered well from the wound in his arm, and was now often by her side to protect her from unwelcome advances.

He was a good, kindly man, she felt sure, with blue-grey eyes under his grizzled hair, and he smiled often. His tasselled cap was faded and dirty, but it added a jaunty air to his square face.

'Why are you here?' she asked him once.

'I was born to a life of comfort, and I just felt that once, before I died, I would like to do something that was not purely for my own pleasure,' he said. 'I am three-and-fifty years old now, and my wife is long dead, and I considered it right that I should ride and join this great venture, like a knight errant of old. Of course, they were younger.'

'You are young enough. An old man would not manage to make this journey,' she said.

'That's better, mistress,' he said.

'What?'

'You almost smiled!'

She had allowed his teasing to bring a smile to her lips then, but it was only for outward display. In her heart, she was constantly aware of the hole left by Benet, and her guilt that he had felt the need to go and prove his courage. Her cruelty had sent him to his death.

'Almost,' she said.

Richalda was still weak and rode on the wagons to rest during the day, but she did not appear to strengthen. It was making Sybille anxious, for she felt she must go mad, were she to lose her daughter as well as her husband.

At Philippopolis they could rest for a few days, and at last Sybille saw Richalda was healing. Soon they would be moving again, but for now she was glad to see her daughter grin after eating a bowl of pottage and a crust or two of bread. It felt as though the sun shone in her heart to see that little smile on her daughter's face.

On the Monday, when the bells began to ring, there was a different atmosphere in the camp. Although the market had been made open to the people under Sir Walter, the citizens themselves had made it clear that they wanted nothing to do with the individuals of the pilgrim host. Now all was to change. The people wanted to retain the body of Sir Walter de Poissy and bury him in their cathedral, for a man who had received a notable miracle was pleasing to God, and would thus bring good fortune to the city. They arranged a great celebration and feasting to celebrate the miracle of Sir Walter's cross, and the pilgrims were not only permitted entry, they were given to know that they would be welcome.

More than that, they would be protected all the way from the city to the great imperial capital, Constantinople. At last they might be in sight of the end of all their journeying. And

Sybille would have to decide where her future lay; on the road to Jerusalem, or on the weary way home to Sens.

Except she had nothing there, she reminded herself. All their money was lost, their house was sold, they had no goods, and she had no family to fall back on.

She was all alone in the world with her daughter.

Bulgarian Plains, Tuesday 24th June

When they were next marching, Fulk saw his brother's gaze hunting along the lines of men and women on the march.

There had been a shower overnight; for once they were not choking in thick dust and could see for hundreds of yards in all directions. A column of wagons and camp followers was marching parallel to the army. At first Fulk had assumed that Odo was searching for any signs of enemy forces opposing them, but there were none to be seen.

Fulk tramped on, all thought of enemies far from his mind. He found his own mind was dwelling on the pretty widow Sybille. Even the memory of her face brought a smile to his. He would like to . . . but she was only recently widowed. He could not conceive of spending time with her. It was impossible. In any case, there was no need to worry about enemies here, surely. They were inside the Byzantine Empire, and any governor who tried to delay them must surely be held to account by the Emperor – and they had been promised protection all the way to Constantinople.

His brother's gaze swept along the camp followers again, but Fulk paid him no attention. He was falling into the trance-like state that all soldiers marching day after day will reach: when every conversation has been drained of all merit, when the jokes have been heard too often, and even the rivalries and disputes have lost their savour, each man would retreat into the bastion of his mind and memories. Fulk was settling into a semi-stupor, as if he had taken a strong soporific. His eyes saw the horizon over the shoulders of the men before him, his feet registered the thud, thud, thud of his steps, his shoulder registered soreness where his spear rested – he had acquired it after the battles on the plain at Belgrade, but it was heavy – while his back spoke of the weight of the shield and his pack, but none of them intruded on his dazed mind.

Peter had said to him once that the secret of being a soldier was coping with the tedium. 'It's not all death or glory, boy.'

'But to fight for your lord or for God, that's exciting!' he had said.

Peter had looked at him with a pitying smile. 'You only spend one hundredth or one thousandth of your time actually fighting. Most of the life of a soldier revolves around marching for mile after weary mile or worrying about when the next meal will arrive.'

This was the marching boredom, then. Fulk trudged on. His feet plodded onward, seemingly without any need of intervention from Fulk himself. If asked, he could not have brought back to mind any aspect of the last five leagues. His world was bounded by the horizon and the future. Nothing before *now* had ever been. The lands he had passed through were irrelevant. They might not have existed.

Into this waking dream-state, Odo's behaviour intruded. He was walking along with his head locked on the camp followers, but now, rather than looking up and down the line of people, he was staring fixedly, and when Fulk turned to follow his gaze, he saw Guillemette.

'You like her?'

Odo coloured instantly. 'Who? Why, what do you—?'

'That woman, Guillemette. She is pretty enough, I'll agree.'

'The whore you had? I was not looking at her,' Odo said contemptuously. 'I was just observing the followers, that is all.'

'I see,' Fulk said. His eye followed the line of people, but then Guillemette moved aside slightly and he gasped. 'It's Jeanne? The younger woman?'

'It's none of your business, brother,' Odo said, but although he turned his head to the front with resolution, yet Fulk could see that he was blushing beneath his sun-bronzed face, and he could not help but glance towards Jeanne every so often.

Fulk smiled to himself. The woman had ensnared Odo, he was sure. Odo was now thinking more of her than of slitting the throats of wounded Saracens. So be it! If the woman would persuade Odo to lose his bloodthirsty streak, so much the better. Odo would surely be happier for a roll with a wench, and God would forgive him, Fulk felt sure.

He only hoped the woman wouldn't charge him too much, because it was as plain as the sword in his scabbard that she was a friend with Guillemette because she came from the same profession.

Bulgarian Plains, Wednesday 25th June

It was the second day after they left the city of Philippopolis that it happened.

Richalda was suffering because of this journey. Not that matters would have been improved if they had stayed behind at Sens, and Benet had left them to go with the pilgrims.

There was no telling how long it would have been before they learned Benet was dead. Most likely, Sybille would have had to wait and hope, until hope itself had died, and she was forced to beg the priest to declare her widowed. He might have done, but there was no guarantee. Meanwhile she and Richalda would suffer for want of money. Sybille would have been too old to attract a good man, and she and her daughter would be consigned to a life of misery and starvation. She had seen it happen to others.

There was no benefit in these thoughts. She must go and fetch water from the river and see to Richalda, without all this self-pity.

She went to the riverbank and filled her leather flask before making her way back to the camp. A number of fires were burning, and she eyed the men sitting about them. Some were drinking wine. One party was dancing, while a man played the tambour and pipe. The reedy tune came to her on the cool air, and she heard a couple of men singing along. It reminded her of happier days, and brought a reflective smile to her lips as she set off to get back to Richalda.

'Ho! Woman, you are a sight to please a king!' a man called, and Sybille set her chin a little higher and tried to ignore him. He was fair-haired, with a pointed face like a hatchet, and close-set eyes.

Another man rose from a hearth in front of her and she could see by the flickering flames that he was leering, a grin twisting his square, dark features. His eyes were cold, like a hog's, and she felt a sudden icy certainty of danger in her belly.

'Join me. Have some wine,' he said.

'No,' she answered, but suddenly the blond had gripped her biceps and held her close. She felt his rough stubble on the back of her neck, scratching, when he kissed her neck, and she caught her breath with horror as the second man in front of her approached, licking his lips.

'Go on, mistress! We can have some fun, we three!' he said.

'Leave me! Let me free!'

The man behind her whispered, 'Now, mistress, don't go making too much noise. You wouldn't want all the rest to join us, would you?'

The idea that more men could join these two in ravishing her had not occurred to her. She froze with horror. The man behind her began to fondle her breasts through her thin tunic, and she felt the hands of the other stroking her thighs and reaching round to her buttocks. She shuddered with revulsion as a hand probed between her legs, and would have tried to escape, but the two had her in their grip.

'Let me go!' she whispered. 'Please!'

She had no control. She felt that the situation had sucked away all energy, all ability. Her terror was such that even drawing breath to scream made her sob, and only a murmur of despair escaped her lips. She dare not scream and bring others to join these two.

'You think you'd satisfy her? You two?'

Sybille felt the man before her step away. The hand at her groin was gone, and she saw that Guillemette was a short distance away, hands on hips, head to one side.

'Go on,' Guillemette said. 'Show me what you've got!'

The man holding Sybille had both hands on her breasts, and she angrily broke free, lifting both her arms and spinning to slap his cheek. 'You think me fit for your paws?' she shouted, heedless of the men all about.

Guillemette was laughing. 'You think that would satisfy a woman? Fie! Such a big man, you need to go find a mouse, with a pizzle that small!'

'You bitch!' the man said, and lurched to grab her, but Guillemette danced lightly to one side, laughing. 'You're a big man now, aren't you? So strong you can hurt a woman like me, eh?'

'I'll break your pate for you, you—'

'You carry a heavier weapon, then?' she laughed.

He was furious now, and ran at her. She moved aside, but as she did, the man with Sybille sprang forward and caught her arm. The second man had slipped, but now he ran at her and, clubbing his fist, swung at her. Sybille saw Guillemette's face as he clenched, and screamed. It was a piercing shriek. Men all over the camp jerked upright, reaching for weapons and staring wildly all about, thinking that there was an attack. Sybille saw three men nearby who stood with spears or swords, and pointed at Guillemette.

The whore stood on legs that wobbled. The man had punched her on the side of the face even as Sybille screamed, and now the man holding her let go of her arm hurriedly as other men approached. Sybille wanted to see that Guillemette was not badly hurt, and ran to her side as she began to collapse.

'I did that well, didn't I?' Guillemette said, and her eyes rolled as she lost consciousness.

CHAPTER 20

Rome, Thursday 26th June, 1096

Lothar walked the narrow streets of the city with a sullen glower on his face.

It was bustling and manic, with trade at all hours of the day and night. Men bellowing commands at the port, hawkers at the market, fishermen shouting about their latest catches, and preachers at every street corner added to the cacophony, in Lothar's embittered view. All the business of the town was conducted at such a volume, he was astonished that the inhabitants were not mute from overuse of their throats.

Sir Roger and his men had been as good as their word, and not only helped Lothar to join them on their march, they acquired a spare mount for him too. All was well enough, although at one small town north of Rome the men were forced to cross a bridge that had suffered such a deplorable lack of maintenance over the years that the way was dangerous. The rotten timbers were full of holes. Sir Roger's man Gilles studied it carefully and then instructed the men to cover the worst with their shields, and in that way they crossed slowly but safely.

That, so Lothar had hoped, would be the worst they would suffer, for the populace of Rome must surely be glad to see so many religious travellers. They should be keen to throw wide the doors of the basilica, and bless this holy campaign. After all, the Pope himself had spurred them on to travel to Jerusalem. At Lucca, Lothar had seen Pope Urban II for the first time; a small, shrewd-looking man, keen-witted, but with thin lips and the look of a money-lender. He had given the army his blessing, and Roger and his men were convinced that the people of Rome must want to demonstrate their religious enthusiasm, and give what support they could.

That was Lothar's impression as they marched down the coast from Lucca towards the city of Rome, but their welcome was a rude shock.

They were ridiculed and insulted.

Soon they were to learn why. The Holy Roman Emperor, Henry IV, had been disputing Pope Gregory VII's right to install his own prelates over those selected by Henry himself. The Pope sought to punish Henry, and excommunicated him, which led to Henry besieging Rome, sending Gregory into exile and nominating his own Pope – first the frail Victor III, and more recently Urban II. Now Lothar and the men with Roger were to learn that the Romans disapproved of Henry's presumption – and the pilgrims too.

Gilles had selected an inn where they could stable the horses, and the men were sitting outside in the warmth when the sound of wailing and running feet came to them. Lothar stood with his hand on his sword's grip, Gilles at his side. Lothar was content to have Gilles with him. The man exuded confidence and competence.

241

Lothar eyed the way ahead. The street was little wider than an alley; there was no space here for even a cart to pass. Upper storeys had open windows, the shutters thrown wide, and he cast a glance or two up when he saw movement. It would be a good place for an ambush. The sunlight gleamed from pale-coloured rocks and tiles. There were many cloths dangling from upper windows, tunics and chemises drying in the lacklustre wind, which served to obscure their view. Then Gilles drew his sword as a clattering and shouting mob ran towards them.

'To us!' Gilles shouted, and the rest of Sir Roger's men scrambled to join them. The panicked people hurtled down the street towards them even as the other men formed a defensive line, weapons unsheathed.

One, a little ahead of the others, cried out piteously to be allowed to pass.

'What are you running for?' Roger called.

'We are pilgrims joining the Pope's *iter* to Jerusalem, and we went to visit the Vatican to pray, all of us unarmed,' he said. 'But on our way, supporters of Clement attacked and robbed us. Those of us who made it inside to pray were beaten as we knelt! Men above us dropped stones on our heads. One man was knocked unconscious, and a boy was grievously injured when a rock struck his pate! They were not Christian, those people. They defiled the holy church!'

Sir Roger de Toni was despondent to hear such news. Lothar heard him discussing the affair with Gilles.

'It was surely nonsense. The people of the city must wish to help support us and all pilgrims,' Sir Roger said.

Gilles was less sanguine. 'You may not believe the pilgrims, sir, but for my part I will watch every doorway and window as we pass. Not all Christians are keen to see our Pope succeed.'

They were soon to learn that the pilgrims had been telling

the truth. After their experience, many declared that they could not be certain that they were working to the glory of God. God would not allow men to injure them while praying in His church. Some hundreds decided to leave Rome and the pilgrimage. They would make their way home.

Rome, Friday 27th June

The next day, Lothar saw Gilles checking the equipment for each of the men. He would not let any man mount until he had tested buckles and belts and swords, and confirmed all were as warrior-like as he could wish.

'Do you truly believe we need be so careful?' Sir Roger asked with a chuckle, but the humour died in his throat.

'Two pilgrims were murdered last night,' Gilles said. 'A mob found them and beat them to death.'

They mounted to cross the city. Lothar was riding at the back, and as they passed further and further into the middle of the great city, he began to doubt whether Gilles's caution was justified. He rode forward to Gilles's side. 'Where were the two pilgrims killed?'

'I am not aware of any dying,' Gilles hissed back. 'But Sir Roger believes this is little more than a stroll in a deer park. I want him aware that there are dangers in foreign lands.'

Lothar gave a low laugh, but then, as they crossed one road and entered another, broader way, the first missiles began to strike.

There was a rattle at first, and a number of lighter stones struck the party from behind. Lothar sprang from his pony and grasped his sword, keen to fight. He slid along the wall of a house while the others fought to calm their mounts.

Behind them were some fifteen or more youths, mostly clad in loose-fitting linen, who jeered and bit their thumbs at the little force. Glancing about him, Lothar saw that Gilles had already positioned himself before his knight, while the other men-at-arms spread into a circle about the two. They appeared to be considering the best manner of responding. However, Sir Roger was not willing to be kept from the fray. As Lothar watched, he pulled out his sword and spurred towards the youths. It took Gilles by surprise, for he had clearly been thinking of evading conflict. Instead he found himself atop a horse that was startled, angry and uncontrollable, and he bawled at it until he could set it to ride after Sir Roger.

Lothar did not hesitate. On seeing Sir Roger's attack, he sprang forward, running swiftly along the wall of the building at the side of the road. One man saw him and hurled some rocks, but they all missed, and as Lothar came closer, the youths already had the furious Sir Roger to contend with. He slashed down once, and his sword cut into a man's shoulder and collar-bone, making the fellow howl, but Lothar saw that the blow had been an error. His blade was entrapped by the victim's bones, and Sir Roger was forced to try to recover it, jerking it this way and that, each movement making the unfortunate youth scream in agony, until a blessed swoon overtook him. As he slumped, the blade was released, and Sir Roger hefted it only to find that he was surrounded. He cast about him for an escape and at that moment Lothar, with a bull-like roar, exploded from the side of the roadway.

The youths were so certain of their victory, they had not glanced in his direction. He ran like a berserker into their midst. Surprise lent him wings, and he slammed into the first two men, belabouring them about the head with his pommel before lowering his blade and slicing a man's arm to the bone, whirling and stabbing a fool who left his belly wide to attack, and punching a youth who was trying to throw a rock at him, knocking him senseless. While he assailed the men on the left of the knight, Sir Roger kept up a vicious assault on the other youths.

Lothar swung his sword at one of them, still roaring, but his blow missed and he was left standing alone as the wounded lay at his feet, staring up with terror in their eyes.

After that their way was unchecked.

Later that evening, Sir Roger took him to a small chapel and there filled a cup with wine. 'You saved me today. Gilles told me I was rash and foolish to ride into the midst of such a force. He said that discretion is as much a part of a knight's duty as rash courage. What do you think?'

Lothar considered. 'I think that the proof of a man is what he succeeds in doing. All else is unimportant. You were insulted, and you avenged your honour.'

'Would you call me rash or foolish?'

'I call you my protector,' Lothar said. 'You saved me when I was on the road. I will serve you as I may.'

'Would you swear fealty to me?'

'If you would have me.'

So Sir Roger called to the priest, and in the presence of his copy of the Gospels, Lothar knelt and held up his hands, fingers and palms together. Sir Roger placed his own hands about them.

Lothar repeated the priest's words: 'In the name of God, and in His presence, here in this chapel, I swear to serve you faithfully, to guard you, never to do you any harm, to speak to your defence, and to serve you always in good faith and without deceit, to take your orders, and to serve your interests at all times. I swear this by my faith.'

Sir Roger squeezed Lothar's hands together, and stared at him closely. 'I accept your oath, and I will swear here, in the presence of God, that I will honour you, feed you, clothe you, and share any largesse that comes our way. This I swear.'

It was a moment of great pride. Lothar had been given a new belt, a tunic with Sir Roger's emblem on the breast, and the gift of a new dagger. Then he, his master, and Gilles had taken a tavern by storm and by the middle of the next morning, all were finished spewing enough to take heed when the message came that they were to pack and depart for Bari, there to take ship to Durazzo.

Durazzo. It was a place he had never heard of. Others knew it as Dyrrhachium: the gateway to the great Eastern Empire of Constantinople.

Constantinople

Alwyn reached the city late in the afternoon.

The Vestes had been grateful for news of the pilgrims crossing the plains from the north, but he believed that there were more to cross the seas from the old western empire.

'Go to Illyria, and see what the merchants there are saying,' he said. 'They will have their own resources at Bari and elsewhere. Find all you can about the numbers of pilgrims who intend to cross into our lands.'

'I haven't been to Illyria since the disaster.'

'Perhaps it is time you went to see the lands again. Dyrrhachium was many years ago.'

'Not to me.'

John peered at him. 'I need you to listen to those who know about the pilgrims. I want to hear all that can be learned about them. Where are they from, how many are there, whether they form a threat to the Empire.'

'How can I learn all this?'

'There is one merchant in particular, a Levantine. I will give you instructions on how to find him. He has a finger in every pie that crosses the Adriatic. He lives in Dyrrhachium.'

'I never want to see that place again!' Alwyn said.

'I need information! I don't care where you have to go to get it, but I need facts!' John had shouted.

It was the first time Alwyn had heard him shout; it was the first time he had seen the Vestes so completely confused. Dyrrhachium had been the scene of Emperor Alexius's greatest defeat. The Normans had tried to take the city from the Empire, and Alexius had sent his strongest army to oppose them as they laid siege.

Alwyn had been there. He could remember it to this day. He and Eadnoth and Godwyn and the others, all the dispossessed of England. They had entered the battle full of fervour, eager to kill the Normans who had taken their lands and killed Harold, their rightful King. But their attempt had failed. The Normans had been routed early on, but rallied, and the Varangian Guards, who had pursued them so enthusiastically, were encircled and slaughtered almost to a man. Alwyn had been lucky to escape with his scars. At least he had his life.

Even at that time John had been resolute. There were failings when the Normans slaughtered the Varangians, but John had remained confident that given time the Empire would recover, as it had. Yet now, with pilgrims arriving to help the Empire, he was seriously concerned. It was enough to give Alwyn pause.

Bari, Tuesday 8th July

They were in Bari in the second week of July, riding with Sir Roger's uncle.

They had met Sir Stephen of Blois south of Rome on the second day after the attack, and Gilles was wearing himself out, searching constantly for any signs of other men who might try to attack them. He felt he could relax a little when they met Sir Stephen, for with the nobleman was a strong force of knights and men-at-arms.

Bari was not a huge port. The town was set about a wide, natural harbour. Ships were run up the beach and lay there at low tide, leaning forlornly like birds waiting to feel the wind under their wings, while some few were moored at the harbour wall that had been built out into the sea, extending the spit of land that seemed to point towards their destination.

As he rode along the road towards the centre of the town, Gilles found the view much to his taste. If this was to be the last sight he would have of a Christian shore, he would be content. Small houses were closely compacted along all the streets, and looking out to the promontory he saw the lines of their roofs, with a church standing over them like a shepherd in the midst of his flock. Houses were coloured in the ochre of the area, with some few painted with lime-wash. It was a sight to gladden the heart after the last few weeks, and although the weather was cooler, still it was warm enough for a man on horseback.

Gilles decided that here he would relax. He would need all the strength of his spirit and mind when he came to land on the shores of the Holy Land.

They found a tavern where they could rest, and Gilles and Lothar were content to sit and enjoy a flagon of wine together when Sir Roger went off to speak with his uncle that night. He did not return until late.

'Did you know that there have been two armies already?' Sir Roger told them.

Gilles nodded. He had heard as much from the tavern-keeper. 'They have already set sail.'

'Yes,' Sir Roger said. He pursed his lips for a few moments, and then added, 'It could mean we'll be the last to arrive. That we shall miss the fight for Jerusalem.'

'Sir Roger, there will still be heretics to attack. They won't reach Jerusalem by Christmas.'

'You cannot know that. The armies are enormous, it is said. And more have marched by land and not bothered with ships. They could be there already.'

He looked out over the sea. 'I will miss it all!'

Dyrrhachium, Wednesday 9th July

Passing the church of St Michael the Archangel, Alwyn found the memories rising and threatening to engulf him again: memories of dust and heat, and death. He saw again Godwyn's smile, Eadnoth's self-deprecating grin – and he saw their bodies on the ground. He saw the last desperate fights, and the slaughter.

It was here at the church that the worst of the battle had raged for him. Already his companions were dead, but then the last Varangians were caught, shut up in the church. They had seen it as a place they could fortify, but it was a trap. They did all they could to repel the enemy, but the Normans set it afire, and the remaining Varangians were burned to death. Alwyn had been fortunate. He had been injured with a blow to his left hand that took off two fingers, and then another sliced down his brow and cheek. Unconscious, he had been left for dead amid the piles of dead Byzantines while Emperor Alexius rode away to lick his wounds. Alwyn was only glad he had not seen the destruction of his comrades in the fires.

He had come to with a hideous pain in his injured hand, and when he roused himself, he found carrion birds. As he moved, seven or eight nearby moved sluggishly to escape him, but they did not need his flesh. They had already gorged themselves. The memory made his stomach rebel, and he had acid in his throat and in his mouth. He had to spit it away.

The church had been rebuilt, it appeared, and as Alwyn rode past, he saw groups of laughing people at the doorway. It struck a strange note. Alwyn knew this place as a scene of death. People should not be happy here. He turned his horse away from the church and towards the town itself, a small provincial place with a strong wall.

He would spend no more time here than he must.

Dyrrhachium, Friday 11th July

Lothar had taken the news without emotion when Sir Roger came back from his meeting on that last day in Bari.

'We are to take this message to the Emperor of Byzantium,' Sir Roger said. He had been to meet his uncle that morning, and after breaking his fast he was as excited as a young knight on his first quest. 'We hold the success of the whole journey in our hands.'

'The Emperor asked for us to come to him,' Lothar pointed out.

'Yes, but he may be reluctant to allow so large a force as this inside his borders. After all, he will never have seen so glorious a sight as our army.'

'You think so?' Lothar said.

Sir Roger glanced at him. 'Yes,' he said firmly. After all, he was a knight, and he had seen the full glory of England's knights under the command of the Sheriff of Devon, but the army that his uncle had gathered was vastly larger and more impressive.

They had embarked and were soon sailing from Bari. It was not a long journey, but it was made longer by a sudden squall that drove them from their course, and then the wind ceased and they were left spewing as the vessel bucked and spun on the sea, but in the morning of the second day they were making head-way again and reached the harbour of Dyrrhachium. There, Sir Roger's men were glad to leave the ship and regain dry land. For Lothar, who had never travelled across any waters larger than a lake, the experience was hideous, and even when he was able to walk on the land once more, it still felt as though the ground was bucking and weaving underfoot. His knees were weak and feeble and he was forced to sit at the foot of a little wall while his belly and legs calmed themselves.

Later he made his way to a tavern, paying no heed to the small boy who watched him walk unsteadily to the bar, and who then ran from the port and into the town itself.

It was a while later that a large, fair, hunched man entered the tavern and stood looking about him. Seeing Lothar, he crossed the floor to him.

Lothar had managed to indicate that he wanted a large pot of drink, and was now staring into a cup of wine that tasted of sour horse-piss.

'You are Frank?' the fair man asked.

Lothar looked up, oddly gratified to hear a familiar tongue. He took in the scarred man's injured hand. So, he had been a warrior. 'No, I am a Rhinelander. You?'

Rhinelander, Alwyn thought. So, a man from the Holy Roman Empire. That was a relief. Alwyn had feared meeting a Norman and being forced to hold his hatred and anger at bay. 'My name is Alwyn. I am from Wessex.'

251

Lothar nodded. That explained his strange accent. 'Are you a shipman?'

'Me? With this?' Alwyn said, and held up his left hand with the missing fingers. 'I wouldn't be much use hauling on a rope with this. No, I was a Varangian Guard, but now I live in the city and trade.'

'In what?'

'Mostly whatever other people want,' Alwyn said. 'Where are you from, do you bring goods to sell?'

'Me?' Lothar laughed aloud. 'I am a warrior, master. I live to fight. I am with the pilgrims who are coming to help your Emperor and to regain the Holy City of Jerusalem for God.'

'A noble cause, if it be successful,' Alwyn said. 'How many are you?'

Lothar shrugged. 'Coming from Bari, we are some thousands, but our compatriots are marching over land, and they number the tens of thousands. It must be the biggest force ever gathered together to support our God.'

'That will be a magnificent sight,' Alwyn said. 'When will they arrive?'

'We have to take messages to the Emperor and wait for his response.'

'I can help you to get them delivered.'

'How?'

'I have been sent to report on you and your companions.'

Lothar looked at him. The man did not inspire confidence. He had no gold at his fingers, and the tunic he wore had seen better days. He did not look the sort of man who would have the ear of the innkeeper, let alone the Emperor. Which made Lothar wonder who this earnest-looking man was. Perhaps nothing more than a felon seeking to reach inside Lothar's purse, he wondered. There were felons all over the Empire, so he had heard. They were a strange folk, full of trickery and deviousness, who had raised lying and deceit to an art form, people said. 'Why?'

'The Emperor is astute. He wants to know that your commanders will keep the men in his entourage under control, he wants to know that the people with him will obey the laws of the Empire, and that he is not allowing a dangerous army to enter his lands, but a willing comrade-in-arms. You have many thousands in your armies,' Alwyn said.

Lothar nodded. 'I will introduce you to my master, then. He will be glad of your help, I am sure.'

'Good.'

Lothar knocked at the door of the inn where his master had taken rooms, and stood aside to let Alwyn enter first. 'Sir Roger, this man says he can help us.'

Sir Roger was pulling a chicken carcass apart, and he sat back on his bench and peered at the man in the doorway. 'You can help us? How?' then a thought struck him, and he glanced at Lothar. 'He can speak French, I assume?'

'I speak it a little,' Alwyn said. His hackles had already risen at the accent of the man in the room. He walked in and bowed his head slightly with the respect due to an equal, no more.

Sir Roger looked at Lothar again. 'You are sure of his credentials? He doesn't look like a sheriff's messenger, let alone a king's or emperor's.'

'For all that, I am your contact. I have the Emperor's seal and can have your messages taken to him at the speed of the imperial messengers.'

'Show me this seal.'

Alwyn slowly pulled a thong about his neck and withdrew a heavy golden ring. A disk had been carved into the upper surface.

He held it up momentarily, then dropped it back down his collar. 'It is sufficient to get your messages to the Emperor as swiftly as it is possible.'

'It is good! I will allow you to take the messages, then. I and my guards will go with you and witness the message being sent. Is that fair?'

'Yes.'

'Your speech reminds me much of home. Are you from England?'

'I am from Wessex.'

'Quaint! I had forgotten the old names. Of course, our lamented king, William, changed the names, did he not? Whereabouts were you in Wessex?'

'I come from the lands of Devonshire, from a town called Lydford. It was a thriving burgh.'

'It is no longer. The rebellions over the years—'

Alwyn was peering at Sir Roger closely. 'You are Norman?'

'My father is Sir Radulph de Toni. I am his son. We live in the manor of South Tawton.'

Alwyn took a deep breath. There was a sickening pounding in his belly, and a roaring and hissing in his ears. For an instant he felt dizzy, and his vision clouded as if a black veil had dropped over his eyes. He felt stunned, as though a man had broken his pate with a maul, and could scarcely think. He wanted to grab his knife or a sword and hack this man to pieces, but even as he felt his muscles tensing, he heard the Vestes words in his mind again: *Think on Sara and Jibril, Alwyn. Their fates depend on you.* 'I know it.'

Sir Roger shot him a curious look, then motioned to his men. 'Lothar, tell Gilles we will soon be leaving. We shall go with this fellow and be the first of the pilgrims to see Constantinople!'

'Yes, Sir Roger,' Lothar said. He was surprised to see that

Alwyn had already left the room, and hurried out, calling to Eudes as he went.

He need not have worried. Alwyn was outside, breathing deeply, a hand resting on the wall.

'Are you all right, fellow?' Lothar asked.

'I just felt a little sick,' Alwyn lied. 'Something I ate.'

It was nothing to do with his stomach, it was the effect of meeting the son of the man they called 'The Butcher of Crediton'. And he had not tried to kill him. Yet.

CHAPTER 21

Constantinople, Thursday 31st July, 1096

It was a relief for Alwyn to return to the city. He left Sir Roger's party at the area designated for their encampment, and rode up to the gates and into Constantinople, slouched after riding many miles in the heat. His mount was exhausted too, and he dismounted and left the horse at the barracks' stables near the gate before walking on to the palace with Sir Roger's man, the fellow called Eudes. He seemed to take all in his stride, like a bumpkin who visits a city for the first time and refuses to be overwhelmed.

Alwyn took him to the Vestes' chamber and made a show of handing the document to John. John opened it and read, then instructed slaves to take Eudes to eat and drink while he discussed affairs with Alwyn. Soon they were alone with slaves bringing them drinks and platters of fruit.

'I am glad to see you once more, safe and well,' the Vestes said, and looked him over with apparent compassion. 'Your journey has been difficult, I see. You are weary. Please, be seated. Take refreshments.'

Alwyn took the cup of iced water and drained it thankfully. He could feel the chill liquid pass down his gullet, and sighed with gratitude as it settled in his stomach. It seemed to ease all the strains of the journey. A slave refilled his cup but Alwyn pointed to the jug of wine instead.

'And now, to business,' the Vestes said.

Alwyn sipped. 'The letters you received will have explained much about these barbarians.'

'Yes,' John said. He gave a laugh. 'They actually *demand* the assistance of the Emperor, and said they want access to the city's markets, and ships to transport them to Anatolia, and, and, and . . . They had a most impressive list of demands.'

'I am not surprised,' Alwyn said. 'These are the same Norman bastards who beat us at Dyrrhachium. The same men who stole my land from me and my kin. Their arrogance is legendary.'

'Are they trustworthy?'

Alwyn curled his lip. 'I would rather trust a rabid dog.'

'They have no redeeming features?'

'I don't know. They look like barbarians, and steal other men's lands.'

'That is politics, and as for how they look, well, others have learned the benefits of silks and comfort.'

'You want to know, are they a threat? Yes, they are. If you can, I would have them pushed off imperial soil as quickly as you may.'

'I lean towards the same view. Did you see the army on the plains?'

Alwyn nodded. 'They are probably the fellows I saw before.'

'Possibly. The first to arrive was a strong force led by Sir Walter de Boissy-Sans-Avoir. There is another group not far behind which has caused no end of trouble. It is a mob, an army of malcontents, peasants and felons, from all accounts. They're led by a scruffy preacher they call "the Hermit". He has the dregs of all the cities in his company: thieves, beggars, whores, all the most sinful and disgraceful dregs of northern cities; and he has told them that they will achieve salvation by coming here and killing Saracens. I suppose they may be good enough for that: killing or dying. They caused dreadful problems on their march. They robbed granaries, stole wives and daughters and raped them, and killed people even when they were offered supplies at low cost. It seems they expected to be fed for free! The first army was at least led by a knight, and had a modicum of discipline.'

'Why did you send them on, if they were better than this rabble?'

'You think I wanted to have the two armies merge on our doorstep? No, those already arrived here we will send on their way as quickly as we may. Those approaching our walls now, under the command of this "Hermit", sacked Zemun and slaughtered all those inside. Thousands are dead, I am told. I heard this morning from Nish, where the King of the Hungarians has destroyed another army, putting all to the sword or introducing them to the benefits of culture by enslaving them. No, I want them gone as soon as may be. Our aim must be to have them all pass over the border as quickly as they may. If they achieve victories in the Sultanate of Rum we can capitalise on their gains, but otherwise we are best served by pushing them onwards.'

'How many are there in the armies?'

'Who can tell? Enough to take Zemun by storm, and to fight a pitched battle with the Governor at Nish. These are dangerous men, Alwyn.' He picked up a paper and studied it, then peered over it at Alwyn. 'Now, this messenger with you. What would you have me do with him?'

'Send him back with a message to his lord,' Alwyn said. 'Tell them your terms and that you will help them on their way. You do not wish them to encamp here and become prey to ideas of taking the Empire.'

'No.' John was thoughtful. 'Such an army, if disciplined and with sufficient numbers, could pose a threat even to the city.'

'Especially with the Normans among their number,' Alwyn said bitterly.

'There are many of them? Yet you didn't attack any of them?'

'One is the son of the man who butchered my people,' Alwyn glowered. 'If I had the opportunity he would be dead.'

'Perhaps. Yet I think they should be allowed to escape your wrath – for now. The Emperor has promised them safe passage. If you were to fight them, that would not serve his aims. No, I think we should let them join the army that has already landed on the shores of Rum, don't you?'

'I will claim my right to kill him. I will seek trial by combat, if necessary.'

'Later,' the Vestes said sharply, 'when the man is of no further use to me. If you move before that, Sara's existence will become more difficult. I will take her back, and Jibril too. Sara would be welcomed in the brothels at the port, and Jibril would fetch a good price. Perhaps in the same place. Do not forget, Alwyn, your position here depends upon my goodwill and the Emperor's favour.'

Alwyn lowered his head. 'In return, if I am injured, swear to me that you will look after the interests of both. If I am killed, you will seek to give them a pension. Send Sara to a good house and look after Jibril.'

The Vestes looked at him, but nodded. 'I so swear. But destroy my faith in you, and everything you value will be taken from you.'

'Then keep the Norman from me,' Alwyn growled, adding under his breath, 'Because if you harm my Sara, I will kill you.'

Outside Constantinople, Tuesday 12th August

Fulk stared out at the sea and threw a pebble into the waters. It was a warm day, and he was bored of inactivity. He craved *action*. He wanted to get to Jerusalem, fight and win it, and return home with Odo.

When they had set out, all had seemed so easy. They would take back the city, and return home with stirring tales of their battles and conquests. There was no expectation that the people of the Empire would show such distaste, even contempt, for the army that had set off to help them.

They reached the great city full of joy. The sight of the massive walls was an inspiration to all. It looked impregnable. The walls were whitewashed with red tiles at the castellations, and could have been new. They ran for almost four miles, a great sweep of triple defences, with a moat, low outer wall, and then double inner walls to trap the unwary besieger. Villas and shanty towns spread in a suburban mess at the moat's side, but all about was greenery, with gardens fed from carefully designed irrigation systems. Even from a distance the city inspired awe.

'I had expected a more enthusiastic welcome from Emperor Alexius,' Odo said.

'He did promise food and supplies.'

'But at the same time he refused permission for any of us to enter the city.'

Odo stared blankly over the waters. Fulk knew his brother had felt the ban keenly; he wanted to pray at the great churches in the city where relics like the head of St John the Baptist were held. Praying for the intercession of such saints would be bound to help the pilgrims.

'Odo? Are you all right?'

'We should have been entitled to enter the city.'

'Yes.' Fulk was as enthusiastic to see the city as his brother, but for different delights. Peter of Auxerre had waxed lyrical about the Greek women in the Constantinople brothels. Fulk had heard so much about the earthly delights that eastern women could bring that it grieved him not to visit one. With the blanket prohibition on visits to the city, the only offers he received came from the broken women who were permitted to ply their trade outside the city walls. They were not what Fulk had envisaged, either in age or quality, and he had hoped that the order refusing permission to enter the city would be rescinded. Instead they had been bundled here, outside the city walls, while ships were readied to carry them on the next stage of their journey.

Fulk glanced over his shoulder. Here he was near the first gate of the city, the so-called Golden Gate. It was built of huge slabs of marble, and had one vast entrance and a smaller way at either side. This main one in the middle was only rarely opened. It was the city's most important gate, Fulk had heard, the ceremonial portal through which the Emperor would enter after a victory, or foreign potentates who deserved special honour. Sir Walter had not been allowed to enter through this gate, which showed much of the attitude of the people here to the pilgrims.

As he stared at it, a horseman burst through a side gate and cantered down the roadway. Fulk watched apathetically as the man, clad in fine Constantinople mail, rode along the road from the city towards the pilgrim camp.

He was not the first messenger to Sir Walter. Usually they brought complaints: apathy and indolence had led to disturbances. There were fights between pilgrims and city folk; some pilgrims took to breaking into houses. It was even said that some robbed people in the suburbs outside the wall, leading to much bad feeling. But it was all this inactivity. That was what caused the problems.

It was the Emperor's own fault. He had enjoined Peter the

Hermit and Sir Walter to remain here at the coast outside the city. There were many more armies marching now, he said, and their reinforcements would be needed if the pilgrims were to meet with Kilij-Arslan's armies. Kilij-Arslan was the ruler of the Sultanate of Rum, as the Saracens named the territory of Anatolia, and he was reputed to have an army that was the equal even of the men of Constantinople. But, as Peter the Hermit told his followers, even such a powerful unbeliever would be forced to suffer the realisation that for all his vaunted wealth and authority, the God of the Christians was superior. The pilgrim army would destroy that of the Saracens.

All Fulk knew was, he wanted to get moving. He felt lonely and distracted here in this strange land, and without the comfort of Guillemette he was desperate and confused.

Odo glanced over his shoulder at the rider clattering along the road. 'Perhaps we will be moving on again soon.'

It was good to sit with Odo, although Fulk dared not broach the subject that tormented him. He had a suspicion that his brother was carrying on an affair with Jeanne, the youngest of the whores, but he wasn't sure. It could have been just that Odo was bored with Fulk and Peter's company. Certainly he spent a lot of time away.

There was no hiding the fact that the army was growing fractious. In a real army, discipline could hold groups together, but here, with so many ordinary folk lumped together, natural rivalries abounded. Not that Fulk had any argument with Odo . . . but Odo had already ordered Fulk to keep away from the women, and now, Fulk thought with a grin, he had discovered the same delights of feminine company himself.

Fulk wanted to move on and win back Jerusalem. That was the whole point of their pilgrimage, and he was keen to march on, not kick his heels at the seashore here.

The army of Peter the Hermit was ready. It had reached this land of unbelievers, and now they were going to march to the Holy Land and take it back for God, surely.

His wish was soon to be granted. Soon they would be transported over the sea to the coast of the Sultanate of Rum. There they would be able to continue their long march to Jerusalem.

Moson, Friday 15th August

It had been a long march, but for many it was to end at Moson.

Heinnie watched as the massive catapults were pushed forward, the men forcing the wheels over the rough ground until they were within reach of the city's walls. Wagons with rocks hewn from the quarry lumbered along behind the ox teams. Here the ground was more or less stable, while behind the city there was a maze of swamps and mires that could swallow a man in less time than it took to drink a quart of ale. The army was avoiding that.

After Lothar's departure, it had taken Heinnie two weeks to recover. He had a scar now that ran from his destroyed right eye all the way to his chin, and he longed to meet Lothar and thank him personally for it.

There had been little enough time to worry about Lothar in the last weeks. Count Emicho had taken every opportunity to hunt down Jews, and now he had a bulging war chest, and over ten thousand men. With warriors like Drogo of Nesle and William of Melun to lead them, Heinnie had no doubt that they would soon defeat all the Saracens who had dared to try to take Jerusalem.

But before that, Emicho and his army must defeat King Coloman of Hungary.

It was as they marched that Heinnie and the men had come

across the little parties of pilgrims limping along. Some had terrible injuries, but for the most part their wounds were mental, and their story touched all Count Emicho's men.

They soon heard the cause. The Hungarians had tried to close their border to the Frankish armies, and in the days before Emicho's arrival, not only had Peter the Hermit brought his men through here, but another pilgrim army under a priest called Gottschalk had tried to pass as well. King Coloman had decided to stop them when pilgrims had a dispute with a merchant over a debt for food, and killed the man.

Coloman had drawn up his army southeast of Moson, but persuaded the pilgrims that he would escort them to his border and let them continue on their way. However, he asked that they surrender their weapons first so they would not murder any more of his people. When Gottschalk agreed, the royal army fell on them and slaughtered them almost to a man, leaving only a few men to escape and speak of the bad faith of this false king.

Emicho was nothing loath to punish Coloman and his people, especially when his army reached Moson itself and came across fields filled with the stinking corpses of Gottschalk's army. It was a sight to fill any devout Christian full of righteous anger.

Heinnie had been involved in many of the attempts to climb the walls and break into the city of Moson, but had not succeeded. They had constructed bridges to try to attack from the farther side of the city, but the marshes there prevented this, so the Count had ordered them to build catapults, and now these two were slamming their missiles into the walls.

It was a sight to bring joy to any soldier's heart, Heinnie felt. He giggled at the sight of the catapult's arm rising, suddenly halting and flinging its massive missile into the air. The stone rose, slow as a duck from the water, until it reached the top of its arc, and then fell, suddenly. Heinnie could see the explosion of dust where the rock struck the walls of the city. The first few rocks had made a cloud of dust at the immediate point of impact, but now he saw it was rising from further along the wall, each strike causing more and more dust from yards away as the mortar and stonework were shivered to pieces under the thunderous attack.

The end, when it came, was almost an anticlimax.

A last rock had been thrown, and when it hit the wall, there was a trembling, as though God was striking it with His own hammers, then a sudden flash of smoke rose and, faintly over the air, Heinnie could hear the rumble of falling masonry. Already the catapult was being wound back, the men on the windlass groaning and complaining as they sweated, pushing the wooden bars around, but even as the arm was slowly hauled down, there was a bellow of satisfaction from the soldiers nearer the city, and Heinnie saw that there was a huge breach where the walls had collapsed. And not only one: the second catapult had also brought down a section.

Heinnie giggled at the thought of the women and the plunder in the city. He pulled his sword from its scabbard, and with a grin contorting his scarred features, he lifted the blade high and shouted to his men. Soon they were rushing forward over the rough ground.

There was a clatter and rattle of arrows striking the ground, but he was a hard target. Most of the arrows were aimed at the mass of men behind him. He pelted along until he came to the splinters of rock and rubble at the wall itself. He clambered up, slipping and sliding in the looser spoil, before reaching larger rocks where he was more stable. Men were coming out from the city, a few high on the remaining sections of wall hurling rocks and loosing arrows, but Heinnie knew he was blessed. There was a tug at his tunic as an arrow narrowly missed his body, and then he was not alone again. His men had caught up with him, and he and they were slithering down the far side, into the city itself.

A shrieked order, and a mass of Hungarian pikemen ran at them. Heinnie's men lifted their shields and knocked aside the long weapons. Three were too late, or were unprepared for the suddenness of the attack, and were speared, but then Heinnie's men were in close with the Hungarians, and more of the Count's army was pouring into the breach, their appearance forcing Heinnie and the others further into the city, pressing the Hungarians back along the streets.

Rocks slammed into the roadway. It was a vicious mêlée, with men shrieking war cries or shrill screams of agony, and Heinnie concentrated on the men before him, ignoring those with him who fell, ignoring the possibility of danger, just stabbing and slashing for all his worth, counting on God to protect him from the many dangers.

They pushed onward, onward, and came to a wide square where people were milling about in terror, and the men began to attack the townspeople. Heinnie thrust and sank his sword into a young man's body and smiled as the fellow's mouth moved helplessly. And then he saw her: a young girl, her head covered by a great hood.

She was over to his left, and he ran from his men with a thrilling in his blood at the thought of her slim body. His men were already gorging themselves on death, and Heinnie chuckled to himself as he chased her. She moved like a deer, fleet and sure-footed, darting around to a narrow alley, and Heinnie ran after her, his grin broadening.

'Hoi! This is good, I like to work up an appetite for my women!' he shouted, and laughed again.

As he did so, he saw that she had stopped. He laughed louder at the thought that she was willing to have him come and take her, and quickly took hold of her shoulder.

A quickening chill touched his spine, as if a sudden wind had blown along the alley, making the sweat chill on his body. Her shoulder was too thin, like that of a child who had been starved for a month. She began to turn, and he felt the hairs on his neck and head rising as he found himself peering into the blackness under the hood.

He dared not look at her face. He backed away, averting his eyes. 'No!'

In his mind, he saw again the girl, the one he had slain at Rudesheim with her brother. She had died badly; when they broke into the house, they had found the fat woman who owned the place trying to tell them there was no one there, but they had shoved her from their path. They were soldiers of God. Heinnie and the others knew they were doing His work. They found a locked door and smashed it with hammers, and in there they had found the cowering girl with her brother. They were only Jews, though, and Heinnie had let his men have their fun. The boy they slew on the spot, but then there was the girl and the woman who had tried to hide her.

Afterwards they had torched the building with the bodies inside. They had all died. It was impossible that the girl could have escaped that pyre.

It could not be her. He told himself that, but he still refused to meet her gaze.

'No!' he said again. But more weakly and, as he said it, he saw the shape of a boy entering the alley behind her, and Heinnie felt his legs become weak. It was as if the energy had been sucked from him. He almost fell, and as he did, the girl lifted her hands to her hood.

'*No!*' he screamed, and fled.

Civitot, Thursday 21st August

There was a cooling breeze, and Odo revelled in it, feeling the wind ruffle at his hair. Behind him, flags and banners fluttered loudly. Each proclaimed the ancestry of the knights and men-at-arms who were camped here. Sir Walter de Boissy-Sans-Avoir's was the most magnificent. It flew high over his pavilion, the bright colours fading in the bright sunshine.

In recent days Odo had been called to help Sir Walter's clerk because Odo's ability to read had endeared him to the over-worked cleric. Now Odo was comfortably assured that he was essential to the smooth running of Sir Walter's household. It was a great honour.

They had been here for three days already. At Constantinople, they had kicked their heels for five days while the Emperor decided what to do with them, and the laziness of the citizens of the city did not inspire confidence. The Greeks seemed to have no energy, no desire to get on with things. This was God's greatest adventure, and the people of Constantinople seemed to care more about forms of address and the correct display of manners than actually going to Jerusalem and fighting. It was incomprehensible. And then, when they had been transported, it was said that Sir Walter was told that he should wait here for more armies to arrive. They were large, he was told; they were *professional* – as if that mattered.

Odo felt his anger grow at the thought. God would prefer a legion of his own faithful followers than a collection of merce-naries and displaced men-at-arms whose only claim to faith came from their need for salvation after a life of rape and murder. Odo would not wait, he determined. He would go and make his way to Jerusalem alone, if need be.

Others were of a similar mind, he knew. Peter the Hermit's

army had joined with Sir Walter's at last, and now there were Lotharingians, Rhinelanders, Bavarians, Flemings and people of all the nations under the cross, who were equally inspired to make haste to reach Jerusalem. Many had endured hard battles to reach here, Odo knew. He had met one with an appalling scar down his face, who had been with a later force attacked by the Hungarians, and so cruelly beaten that many had turned back for home.

He was walking about the beach in a foul temper, wondering how much longer they would be sitting here at the sea's shore, and investigating a large, part-ruined tower, when he almost tripped over her: Jeanne.

'Hello,' she said.

He instantly forgot his bad mood when she grinned at him. Suddenly the people who had been irritating him, the slowness of progress, the dismay at sitting here at the coast while the Emperor and others decided what the pilgrims should do, all faded away and in their place Odo knew only a melting happiness because she had noticed him.

The wind whipped at the skirts of her tunic, and the thin material did little to conceal the lines of her body. Sparkles of gold showed where her hair was pulled free from her coif, and Odo felt a tugging at his heart to see her. She was in every way perfect. Intelligent, astute, and so beautiful: he was convinced that she would make him a perfect wife. Not that he had broached that subject yet, of course.

In the last days they had met, always here at the seashore, far from prying eyes and wagging tongues. She had said to him, quite correctly, that she did not intend that other people should see them together; she did not want to earn herself a reputation as a flirtatious woman, after all.

'You know how men and women gossip. There is little else for them to talk about while we remain here,' she had said, looking up at him with those delectable eyes.

Who was he to argue with her? He quite understood her concern. After all, it was the way that he looked at Fulk's woman too. A woman should be chaste and careful in her dealings with men. It was a part of her attraction to him that she was so careful of her good name.

She was calm, resilient and beautiful, he thought, and then gave a wry grin. Besotted was entirely too mild a word for his feelings towards her. He adored her.

'Where have you been?' she called.

'I ... er ...' he said, and felt his face colour.

'Walk with me,' she said shyly. 'I don't want to be alone. This land scares me.'

She was shorter than him, and as she asked, she stepped closer to him, her face appealingly tilted up towards his. He could not help but smile with happiness. She was most attractive, he told himself. When he looked down at her, he reflected that this was more the kind of woman whom Fulk should be seeking, rather than the whores and slatterns he had been consorting with.

'I love the sea,' she smiled. 'I would like to live by the sea. Once, I thought I would marry at the seaside and live with the sound of the waves for all the rest of my life. It was a happy dream,' she added sadly, staring out over the water.

Yes, he swore. *I will marry you here, by the seashore, and we will live with this glorious sound all our days. I swear it.*

That morning he spent with her, and afterwards, he was still more convinced that this was a woman whom he could admire and respect. That she liked him he never doubted. There was a sparkle in her eyes whenever she looked at him, and a smile was never far from her lips.

He resolved that he would marry her, and they would live

together in Jerusalem and raise a large family that would become a dynasty. Their lives would be happy and contented for all their days.

Mountains over Trieste, Saturday 23rd August

Heinnie leaned on his staff and stared down the valley. There, just on the horizon, he could see the silvery shimmer. He recognised that sight: the sea, at last. There, with luck, they would be able to find a shipman to take them further on their journey, away from this accursed land.

A priest came and stood at his side quietly. 'So there it is,' Father Albrecht said. 'We are a little closer.'

Nodding, Heinnie kept his eyes fixed on the distant gleam. He had not lost the terror he had experienced at Moson. Even now, in the broad sunlight on this hill many leagues from the Hungarian city, he knew the same dread. When he slept, he saw her in his mind's eye, and again chased her down the alley until she stopped and started to lift her hood as the shade of her brother appeared behind her, accusing; always accusing.

Each night he had that dream, and each time it ended there, with her about to reveal her face, like a demon about to drag him down to Hell. Always he woke, sweating and shivering and petrified with horror.

Now they were staring down towards the sea at last. He was here with some few hundreds of men. After he had run from the alley, panicked and irrational, out to the walls and beyond, the other men had seen his terror, and it had been communicated to them. Those in the square heard his screams, and the entire force began to waver, thinking that there was a great army chasing towards them. As it was, he did enough damage. The

Hungarians had rallied and, while the army of Emicho hesitated, they scented imminent victory. Soon their men were pushing forward, and as more and more of the Count's men faltered, the townspeople eagerly sprang to the pursuit, cutting down the soldiers as they fled.

It was a catastrophe.

Many thousands had died that day. Count Emicho took one look at his retreating force and rode away, leaving them to their fate. All his proud ambitions to be the next – and last – Emperor of Jerusalem were ground into the dust as his men ran, and he rode back homewards with as many men as he could rally. Only some few priests stood their ground, trying to persuade the terrified army to stand its ground, but soon they too had to submit to the all-pervading panic, or be trampled in the rout. Father Albrecht had been one of the few to join in a fighting retreat, dealing death with a ferocity Heinnie had never before seen in a priest. Heinnie had seen him and hurried to his side, and the two fought a strong rearguard action as they made their way into a stand of trees where the Hungarians were less keen to follow them.

After that, many decided to follow Emicho, to their shame and the contempt of their comrades. Others were less willing to give up the pilgrimage. Heinnie found William of Melun and several others who were all for seeking another pilgrim army and joining that.

William of Melun said that a force under Sir Hugh de Vermandois, the brother of King Philippe of France, was marching to Bari to take ship for Jerusalem. That seemed preferable to making further attempts to cross Hungary to reach Constantinople.

Now, when Heinnie glanced at Albrecht, the priest was staring at him. 'We have to get down there,' Heinnie said.

'Yes. And then we can sail for Jerusalem,' the priest said.

Heinnie nodded.

'There we will be granted absolution for all our sins,' the priest said softly. 'You will be renewed.'

'Pray for me, Father,' Heinnie said.

He was convinced of one thing: he needed God's forgiveness. Even now, at the edge of his hearing, he thought he could hear her screams, the sound of her pattering feet. If he was ever to lose this foul horror, he must make his way to Jerusalem, because else the spirit of the girl and her brother whom he had killed in Rudesheim would remain and haunt him every day for the rest of his life.

Civitot

Lothar and Sir Roger were deposited at the harbour of Civitot, while their horses, complaining wildly, were led from the hold and helped from the ship, and the shipmen unloaded the food and goods which merchants had brought for the pilgrims to buy.

Watching the horses, Lothar winced with every whinny. It was not a task in which Lothar would have wanted to take part. The destrier of Sir Roger was not as much of a man-killer as some he had known, but handling a brute as big as him, and trying to avoid the slashing hoofs and his bites, was more than Lothar would have wanted.

When all their belongings were piled on the wooden boards of the harbour, Lothar and the other men began to saddle their mounts and load their goods onto the packhorses and mules, while Sir Roger petted his beast and looked about the place with interest.

The town had the small, whitewashed buildings that seemed

to suit all the peoples of the Empire, but beyond the town's walls and a large tower that looked as though it was partly ruined, Sir Roger could see the pilgrim encampment. It sprawled over a large area, and he could see many pavilions with fluttering banners, but between them were the hovels of the majority of the pilgrims. Some little better than a cloak thrown over sticks, others more substantial, this was where the army of Peter the Hermit had been left. Already Sir Roger could smell the stench of unwashed bodies, of woodsmoke, and the stink of latrines.

'There is little organisation here,' he said.

'They are mostly peasants,' Gilles said. 'What organisation would you expect?'

Sir Roger nodded. It was unreasonable to think that such men would know how to set up a camp. Still, after marching all the way here, he would have thought that someone would have set their mind to it.

They made their way down through the streets and out to the camp itself, avoiding the beggars, slapping the hands of the urchins who demanded alms, and making their way to the largest pavilion of them all.

A pair of men-at-arms stood with pole-arms held lazily in their hands, although they stiffened when they saw the party approaching.

Sir Roger walked to them, studying the banner that flapped overhead. 'I am Sir Roger de Toni. Inform Sir Walter that I would speak with him.'

'There is no need!' a voice boomed from inside the tent, and Sir Walter came to the flap. 'I thought I recognised you, Sir Roger! Come, enter, and take a little refreshment!'

Inside the pavilion was austere, but comfortable. Sir Walter's armour was standing on a wooden former, and nearby was an open chest, displaying his weapons. A youth was sitting on the sand beside it, polishing the knight's helmet. A trestle table had been set up, and a bowl of fruit was attracting the attention of flies, while thick rugs had been placed on the floor where his chair stood. It had the appearance of a room that had been well used.

Sir Walter waved a hand and bowed. 'You are most welcome, Sir Roger.'

'I am honoured,' Sir Roger said, bowing in his turn. It was four years since he had met Sir Walter while travelling to his ancestral home. Sir Walter had been kindly and generous to him then. Now he gazed about him with interest. 'You have been waiting here for long?'

'We came to Constantinople about ten days ago, and have been advised to remain here until more men arrive.'

Sir Roger accepted the cup of wine that Sir Walter's bottler passed to him, and sipped. 'Are the pilgrims all happy to remain here and wait? I had imagined they would be all afire to kill Saracens.'

'They are, but when you are given advice, it is worth listening to it,' Sir Walter said. 'It is always as well to be prepared when entering an enemy's lands.'

'Perhaps,' Sir Roger said.

The older knight looked at him sharply. 'You disagree?'

'No, Sir Walter. You are much more experienced in such matters than I. I am only keen to get to test my sword on a Saracen neck!'

'I feel sure you will have your opportunity soon!'

The quiet voice came from behind Sir Roger, and he turned even as he saw Sir Walter bowing low.

That was how he first met the Hermit.

BOOK SIX

Invasion
and War

CHAPTER 22

Civitot, Monday 25th August, 1096

Peter the Hermit was not an impressive figure. He was not above middle height, was as emaciated as a fasting monk, and had a long, unhandsome face. Sir Roger could easily see why others had named him a 'donkey', for his features were curiously similar. He had large, brown eyes, and his brow was surmounted by a shock of mousy-coloured hair. But for all that he was unprepossessing in appearance, and stank like a tomcat, there was an unmistakable aura about him. When he entered a room, humble though he might be, others would stop and listen to him.

'Sir Roger, this is Peter, the man who leads us.'

'No, Sir Walter, I lead no one. I speak the words that the Lord God has generously given me, and His words touch the hearts of those who want to see His Kingdom here on earth. It is not me. God gives us our direction and our inspiration.'

'I am eager to follow His commands,' Sir Roger said, bowing and taking Peter's hand. There was a large ring on his finger, and Sir Roger kissed it as he might the episcopal ring of a bishop.

'I am glad to hear it, my son,' Peter murmured. 'I am sure you will satisfy Him. Remember, all you need do is follow His will.'

'How soon shall we leave?'

'You see, Sir Walter? The energy and enthusiasm of youth. This young knight is as keen to be off as your destrier when he hears the trump of war. He is made of fire and energy!'

'We have been advised to wait for the other armies,' Sir Walter reminded him.

'That is good. We should always take the advice of those who have our interests at heart,' the Hermit said.

Sir Roger could feel the tension between the two men. It was plain that Peter was keen to continue, while the knight wanted to remain here and wait for more men.

'So long as waiting is not to be misconstrued as cowardice,' he added mildly.

Sir Walter looked at him. 'What do you mean?' he said quietly.

'Nothing! Except ... if our enemies begin to think that we are lying here idly, their confidence will grow. They can prepare better defences against us. The surprise of our attack will be diminished. I wonder why the Emperor would want us to remain here longer than necessary.'

'What makes you say that it could be longer than needed?'

'Only that we have no idea how long it will take for other armies to reach us here. There are the men under Hugh de Vermandois, more from Lorraine and Normandy. They will try to reach Constantinople in the next two months, but I don't know whether they will succeed. And in the meantime we will be stuck here for the winter.'

There was no need to say more. The frown on the Hermit's

face was all too eloquent. Armies died in the winter, even without an enemy.

'We would be foolish to leave the coast until we have replenished our forces,' Sir Walter said, with the tone of a man repeating an oft-articulated argument.

'But our enemy will improve their forces and defences. They will know to recruit more men, to look at their walls, to prepare.'

'If we launch ourselves at them now, they will assuredly have the upper hand.'

'But we have the Lord God on our side,' Peter said.

'And surprise,' Sir Roger added. He could feel Peter gaining in confidence.

'At the very least we must wait until we know what has happened to the other armies,' Sir Walter said. 'It would be foolish to march when we have no idea how long it will be before we have more soldiers. They will be with us, perhaps, very soon. Why do we not send someone to find out whether there is any more information about the armies before we make a decision?'

Peter the Hermit nodded slowly. 'I suppose that would seem sensible.'

Roger agreed, but in his heart he was cheering. He was sure that his words had helped tip the Hermit over the brink. Much though Sir Walter would be infuriated, Roger was sure that he had the same reticence as so many older warriors. His natural inclination was to wait until he had at least twice the number of men as his enemy to ensure success, but Roger had no such inhibition.

A Christian knight was worth three or four of the men in a heathen army. There was no need to be diffident. They would sweep away their enemies with the wrath of God's vengeance.

Civitot, Wednesday 3rd September

They had been at the coast in Anatolia almost two weeks when matters came to a head.

'It's not fair! How dare you, you thieving coxcomb!'

'Master, this is less than the prices charged in the city!'

'It's a liberty!'

A small crowd had already gathered about the merchant and his servants when Fulk heard them. There was a sharp cry as a stone was flung, and the people would have launched themselves at the trader and beaten him to death, had Fulk not shoved his way between them.

'Good friends, wait! What is this? A dispute about prices, and you would slay a man for the price of a loaf?'

'These bastard dealers reckon we're all thick as a castle's wall!'

The trader was waving his hands urgently. 'No! It's not true! We are charging less than we would in the city, for our Emperor has told us to be . . .'

'You're lying!' the man said, and threw a punch. The trader was thrown to the ground, and the man who had hit him hurled himself forward. Others joined in, and it was only as Fulk's sword flashed and ended near the first man's neck that a sudden stillness fell over the men there.

Afterwards Fulk could not say why he had done it. There was something about seeing the whole crowd moving forward as though to tear apart a man who was, when all was done, only trying to bring them food. But just at that moment he felt only the raw, fierce injustice, and he was close to killing the man who had broken the trader's nose. 'Get up! If you so much as touch him or his food, I swear you will die here and now!'

'You can't—'

'Speak again and I'll have your head!' Fulk snarled, and

his blade wavered close to the man's throat. He stepped back urgently, and Fulk looked at the rest of the men in the crowd. 'This man is only here to trade. If you don't like his produce, if you don't like his prices, if you just dislike his face, you can leave here now, but in the name of God, anyone who attempts to hurt him or any of the other traders here will answer to *me*!'

There came another voice to his left. 'And to me. I am Sir Roger de Toni, and any man who attempts to steal from honest traders will suffer the penalty. These are not Saracens! Gilles, Lothar, help him.'

'I am glad to see you, sir,' Fulk said, ducking his head in a brief bow, while keeping his eyes on the crowd. Sir Roger's men were already pushing through the people to his side. Some had already slipped away, and while the ringleader stood eyeing Fulk warily as though trying to memorise Fulk's face, his support was dwindling rapidly. He realised this soon enough and backed away, his face black as a thundercloud.

Fulk turned to help the merchant, who was effusive in his gratitude, and pressed a large loaf of bread on him.

'You were brave to leap into the fray like that,' Sir Roger said.

'No, it was foolhardiness! I could have been pulled to pieces.'

'But you were not. You had the correct amount of courage and anger to cow even the bull at their head,' Sir Roger laughed. 'Who are you?'

Fulk had seen Sir Roger many times about the camp, usually close to Sir Walter's pavilion or talking to the Hermit, but he was not surprised that the man had not noticed him. How many knights remembered the faces of their own vassals, let alone a man-at-arms from another man's retinue?

He explained his position with Sir Walter, and that his brother was with him.

'That is good,' Sir Roger said. 'We will have need of men like you very soon, I am sure. Can you handle your sword well?'

'I suppose I shall only learn when I use it in earnest in battle,' Fulk said.

'I shall look forward to seeing you, then.'

Fulk continued on his way, but then he caught a fleeting glimpse of a woman at the well near the town's walls. With a lifting in his heart, he set off towards her. Surely it was Sybille?

Sybille carried the jug of water back to Richalda and Roul, her mind empty.

She spent much of her time with a blankness in her heart and head. There was little enough to think about. Only finding food for Richalda, and hoping that God would protect them in His mercy.

'Mistress! Please!'

She heard the calling, but for some time it did not occur to her that it was she who was being hailed. Only when Fulk appeared before her, red-faced from running in the heat, and gasping, did she realise he had been calling her. 'Master,' she said, and waited for him to speak.

·'You remember me, I hope?'

'Of course.'

'I wanted to know you were well, and your daughter?'

'She is well enough, I thank you. Her fever broke, but she is still rather weak. I hope she will ...' she felt tears flood her eyes and did not finish the sentence: ... *she will survive to see Jerusalem.*

He could guess her thoughts. 'At Jerusalem she will be healed.'

'You think so?'

Her tone was dull, weary and defeated. He leaned down a little, until she looked up into his eyes. 'I am certain of it, mistress. She will be fully healed as a child touching the Madonna's skirts. Believe me!'

She gave a thin smile, but it was at least a lightening of her previous mood. 'Come with me, sir, and meet her. Since you are so convincing about her health.'

He followed her to where the wagons all stood in a rough circle. Many people had formed a tented community there, protected from the wind by the wagons themselves. She led him past the wagons and out to a quieter area to the north. Here there was a smaller encampment, and she took him past little groups and families sitting by their fires.

'Why are these people all out here?'

'In there,' she said, nodding back to the wagons, 'no woman is safe. There are gangs of men who get drunk and decide to fornicate with any woman who has no man.' She held his gaze for a moment, then continued walking. 'I have a friend who defended me against men who tried to take me, but it was too dangerous to remain there. We came out here to be safe, just as have these others.' Safe. Yes, she had felt more safe out here.

'It could be dangerous. If the camp were to be attacked,' Fulk said. 'You would be at risk, this far from the camp.'

'At risk?' Her mind went back to the night outside Philippopolis, when Guillemette had saved her. Ever since then she had been intensely aware of the way that men watched her. She could feel their eyes on her body, imagined their rough hands on her breasts and buttocks again, imagined the stubble of their beards on her neck and throat ... it was disgusting: a nightmare. Out here, away from their lascivious attentions, she was happier. But she could not tell him that. Not here, with so many others about.

She had been lucky. While she ministered to Guillemette that evening, the men who had sought to rape her had been persuaded to leave her by the others whom they had woken. But Sybille knew how close it had been. She could have been raped and murdered and no one would have known. What then would have happened to Richalda? That was the thought that tormented her every day now: that Richalda could be left orphan here on the road.

Her daughter was sitting under a blanket, with a man standing by. Seeing Fulk, he scrambled to his feet, but Sybille raised her hand and shook her head. 'He is a friend, Roul.'

Fulk nodded to Roul, and peered down at Richalda. 'You look a lot better,' he said.

She gave him a smile, and he was glad to see that she was in truth more healthy than when he had seen her outside Belgrade when her father died, but she was still very weak-looking. He recalled why he had been in the market, and unwrapped the loaf from its kerchief. 'I have bread. Would you like to share it?'

Their delight made his gift worthwhile. While they ate, Fulk eyed Sybille. 'Do you have much food?' he asked.

'No. We live as best we can while begging for scraps,' she said with a kind of desperate forlornness about her as she continued, 'It's impossible! My husband was robbed, and everything we had was taken before he was murdered, so now we have nothing. No food, no shelter: nothing! He was planning to make a business out there, and without him, I can see no life for us in Jerusalem, but neither can we afford to return home. The cost of the food here is ruinous, but the cost of the walk back to Sens would be beyond our means. My only course is to marry another man with money, or . . .'

She did not have to voice the thought in her mind. A single tear ran down her cheek as she stared down at the bread in her hands. Her voice held only wretchedness and futility.

Fulk puffed out his cheeks. 'I would offer myself and—'

'No, I need no man's offers from sympathy,' she said, and now she bustled about as though regretting a momentary lapse into dejection. 'We will survive, and, as you say, the Lord God will provide for us. We were lucky to meet Roul after my husband and servant were both killed. Master, I am grateful for your gift of food and your company, but I am sure you have many other calls on your time.'

'So this is time for me to leave,' he said. He grinned. 'Never mind, mistress. I will return, and I hope to find you in better spirits when I do.'

'You may wish for it,' she said. 'I only pray that we leave this place soon and make our way onwards. How much longer must we wait here?'

Constantinople, Friday 12th September

Alwyn's summons came sooner than he had expected.

As he entered the Vestes' office, he found another man there, a man-at-arms, he reckoned, taller and more thickset than most. 'You wished for me, my lord?' he said to John.

'We are to have more armies arriving soon,' the Vestes said. 'But the people who have already crossed the Horn are growing restless, apparently. They are concerned that they are depleting their resources too swiftly.'

'They are poor folk, and they're paying too much here,' the man said. He was wearing a thick leather jerkin, and a sleeved shirt of linen. At his belt was a short sword that looked as though it had seen service in several battles. Alwyn noticed that the cross was notched and scratched, while the hilt had been stained over time. The man had the look of a religious fanatic about him, more than an ascetic.

'What of it?'

'This man, Odo of Sens, is a captain in the pilgrim army. He has come to ask when they might leave the coast. I wanted to persuade him that it would be best to remain there,' John said. 'What would be your opinion?'

Alwyn glanced out through the eastward window. 'If the pilgrims march east now, they will be annihilated. The armies of Kilij-Arslan will easily overwhelm them.'

'You say that, but we are determined, and we have many knights,' Odo said angrily. 'God will protect us on our journey, just as he will defend us in battle. It is God's will that places us here! We go to free His city.'

'God would prefer you to wait a little longer until your reinforcements have arrived,' Alwyn said. 'You would be better served sitting in a church and praying for His help than rushing off with inadequate men.'

'If we were permitted to visit a church, we would do so. As to reinforcements, we have tens of thousands. More than enough.'

'Enough for what?' Alwyn said. 'Enough to topple Kilij-Arslan? Perhaps so. Enough to capture the whole of his Sultanate of Rum? Yes, possibly. But then you still have hundreds of miles of dry, mountainous lands and deserts to cross before you reach the Holy City. Do you have any who have made the journey before among your company? No? Do you have trusted guides whom you can hire? Do you know which languages you will pass? Do you know where the markets are so you can buy food and drink? No? Then why are you not planning these details, rather than pestering the Vestes?'

'You seem keen to prevent us.'

Alwyn stared down at his broken hand. 'You think so? I have fought in battle, and I have experienced the joys of victory and

288

the deep humiliation of defeat. Am I keen to slow you from making a rash decision? Yes. Would I stop you from winning back the Holy City? No. I would happily lay down my own life in that endeavour.'

'You speak as though you know the lands.'

'I have seen some of them.'

'And you speak the languages.'

'Only poorly,' Alwyn said with a frown.

He felt John move, and there was a new atmosphere in the chamber. Alwyn glanced at him. 'What are you planning?'

'If you were to go with the pilgrims, that would indeed be a great relief to the Emperor. You could guide the armies.'

Yes, guide them to the enemies the Emperor wishes to see destroyed and protect those whom he seeks to protect, Alwyn thought to himself. He said, 'I do not think I am fit enough to take on so onerous a journey. For this you will need a much younger man, and one who is proficient in the languages to be met on the way.'

The Vestes waved a hand. 'There are few who have the skills of a warrior and who understand the terrain so well.'

Odo looked at him. 'This is so?'

'I have not travelled over there in many years,' Alwyn snapped. 'Besides, you know how I feel about Normans. Do you want me to—'

'You will of course have to smother any feelings of anger. The Emperor would be displeased to learn that you had helped foster bad feeling between the Empire and the pilgrims who are to fight so valiantly in the defence of Christendom. He would be very grateful for your help. Whereas a refusal to do this little thing might result in the loss of the imperial favour.'

Alwyn could understand that. It was the threat: *Do as I ask, or be cast from your little shop, from the city, and make your life somewhere else. And see your woman and slave sold into intolerable servitude.* He had no choice.

'Very well,' Alwyn said. He knew he was defeated. Walking to a stool, he slumped into it. 'What do you want me to do?'

CHAPTER 23

Civitot, Friday 12th September, 1096

Unknown to Alwyn or Odo, events were already overtaking the best intentions of the Vestes.

Even as Alwyn made his way to the office in the palace, over the water Sir Roger was giving voice to his rising frustration. The same warlike spirit was enveloping much of the pilgrim army.

'We are held here like the lions in the Emperor's bestiary,' he fumed. 'He has us caged nicely, doesn't he? Stuck on this side of the water, subject to his whim. If we misbehave or upset him he can tell his traders to stop supplying us; if we don't obey his orders, he can deny us our food. Yet what we want is only to go and obey God's commands. Surely His will should trounce the ambition of some bloated, earthly potentate?'

Gilles said nothing.

'I think we should go ahead. We ought to go and attack the unbelievers in their own lands, take their food and money. Our way lies before us, yet we sit here pacing up and down and waiting.'

'Go ahead where?'

'At least to the nearest villages and towns.'

Gilles was not on pilgrimage to hold back his master, but to defend him. He had the rest of Sir Roger's men gathered together, and before the end of the morning, they were mounted and riding briskly to the east.

They rode only a matter of two or three leagues before they came across a large flock of sheep. Two shepherds shouted at them, but both were cut down by good Norman steel, their bodies left beside a small fire. They had been cooking unleavened bread, and Sir Roger tried a piece. It tasted good, he thought, as they returned to the camp, driving their plunder before them.

Civitot

Alwyn stepped ashore and stared about him with disgust.

The camp here was a cancer on the landscape. It stretched foul and noisome in all directions from the port, encompassing the little town. Flags and banners hung listless at pavilions to show where the men of note had their lodgings, but beyond was a mess of canvas or felted wool where others took their rest or hid from the sun. Few appeared to be warriors. Most were peasants and opportunists, to Alwyn's embittered eye.

Odo strode on ahead, and Alwyn walked after him. 'Who commands here?'

'Peter the Hermit,' Odo called back.

'A *hermit*?' Alwyn muttered to himself. He stared about him as they marched over the sands towards a large pavilion in the middle of the camp. There a man was conducting a service to several peasants while other religious men prostrated themselves before the cross nearby, piously emulating Christ's pain with their arms outstretched. Alwyn found himself led to a tent nearby. In this he was introduced to Sir Walter de Boissy-Sans-Avoir.

'I am glad to meet you,' Sir Walter said. He eyed Alwyn's hand. 'You were a warrior?'

'I was one of the Emperor's Varangian Guard,' Alwyn said. 'You are the commander here? That man told me a hermit leads these people.'

'Peter is our leader, but I am responsible for our fighting skills; he gives us our spiritual guidance, I the discipline,' replied Sir Walter.

Alwyn turned and gazed over the encampment. 'Have you many fighting men?'

Odo interrupted. 'We have no need of such fellows. We have God on our side.'

'Even so, training the men in how to hold a sword could be useful,' Alwyn said.

'Do you mean to blaspheme?' Odo said.

Alwyn nodded, and then whipped out his sword. Before Odo could place his hand on his hilt, Alwyn's blade was resting on his throat and he moved closer, speaking through his clenched jaw. 'I could have killed you then. I could kill you now. I had two good reasons to do so: one, because I will not have any snot-nosed runt like you accusing me of blasphemy when I am trying to help God's cause here; two, because it would demonstrate that having skills with weapons can only serve to aid God in the struggles to come. You are fortunate indeed that I have another reason to leave you alive.'

'What is that?' Sir Walter enquired. He had not moved, but watched Alwyn with an approving smile on his face.

'I have been ordered to help you all by my Emperor. I would not seek to fail him because that would have consequences for people who rely on me. But if this prickle decides he can accuse me of blasphemy, I may just decide the consequences are worth it!'

Sultanate of Rum, Tuesday 16th September

In the next days Sir Roger and Gilles rode further and further afield, seeking ever more livestock and grain for the pilgrims. It was easy enough, for none of the flocks were guarded, and more knights and their men took to this lucrative trade, riding far and wide and selling their winnings to other pilgrims on their return. Sir Roger was delighted with his ventures, and persuaded Gilles and his men to look to the lands further away, where they found that all the lands were empty of men-at-arms or even castles to protect the lands.

It was on the fourth day, when they returned to the camp, that Sir Walter de Boissy-Sans-Avoir met them.

Sir Roger dropped from his horse and bowed slightly to the older man. 'Sir Walter.'

'You have been given success,' Sir Walter said, eyeing the flocks as Gilles and the others drove them towards the slaughtermen. A series of fenced paddocks had been erected, in which the animals could be contained until the butchers could come to them. Sir Roger looked on as the animals were driven in and the bars pulled across to keep them contained. 'How far did you travel for these?'

'Some five leagues, I suppose,' Sir Roger said. 'And there was no fortification in all that way. I begin to wonder if the stories of the dangers posed by heathens here have not been entirely blown up out of all proportion.'

'The people here are growing more restless as they see you riding away each day,' Sir Walter said.

'Then let us all ride together! This is a ridiculous situation. We have all travelled hundreds and hundreds of miles to go to Jerusalem, but here we sit . . .'

'Yes, you have said it all before. And now it appears that there are more malcontents who seek to ride away with you.'

'That is good!'

'No! We need to keep them here. The Emperor has said, we should wait until the other pilgrims arrive!'

'We could wait for another three months before they're all here! I want glory and honour, not a rest in the sun by the sea!' Sir Roger said. 'I will ride to the next town tomorrow, and any who wish to join me will be welcome to ride at my side.'

'You will ride without my approval,' Sir Walter said, and turned on his heel.

'So be it!'

Alwyn watched as the two broke apart, leaning against a pavilion's pole and listening impassively.

The knight's face spoke volumes. Seeing Alwyn, he stared hard at him. 'What more would you have had me say?'

'Nothing. He wants to put his life into jeopardy, but that is no reason for the rest of the army to do the same.'

Sir Walter turned and surveyed the camp. When they had arrived he had immediately taken this small promontory as the location for his pavilion because it gave him a good view over the camp, while also allowing all the pilgrims to see his flag in the wind. 'You know, I took this place here because I thought it was important that all the folk should be able to see that I was with them. Now they think me weak and cowardly for remaining instead of riding out with the young rascals like Sir Roger.'

'He is a danger. Let him go.'

'Danger? How?'

'You and I have fought in our battles, Sir Walter. We both know that it takes more than courage and determination to win. If a captain has a small force that is battle-hardened, he will win against far greater odds. It is a simple fact that a man who has been trained will fight better than one who has been brought fresh from the fields. We have an army that is large, but it isn't disciplined or effective, whereas Kilij-Arslan has men better drilled and equipped. But your peasants down there think that they are a match for him because they have courage and God on their side.'

'You doubt the righteousness of our cause?'

'I make no comment on any matter other than the quality of the men down there,' Alwyn said. 'I think each of them has confidence in God, each has the bravery to match any man, but they need training. They need discipline.'

'They have little enough of either.'

'No. Because they think that God will give them the strength to endure any battle. It is His arm they think will fight, not their own. But you and I know that it is the men and their abilities and fortitude that will win through. Kilij-Arslan has many men with him. He will find Sir Roger sooner or later, and when he does, the men down there will discover that they need to learn much for their own safety.'

'If we wait until then, we give the initiative to the Saracens.'

'Yes. But when the men here learn how the Saracens can defeat them, they will become more amenable to suggestions from others. Such as you.'

'Perhaps Sir Roger will meet Kilij-Arslan and defeat him?'

Alwyn smiled thinly. 'That would be a miracle indeed. No. Kilij-Arslan will meet that ignorant pup and destroy him. So be it.'

Civitot, Wednesday 17th September

Odo woke Fulk in the early pre-dawn coolness. 'I am going, Fulk. Will you come with me?'

'Eh?' Fulk was slow to wake. He rubbed his head and stared at Odo. 'Going where?'

'Many of us are disappointed with the slowness of the march. We will go and begin the reconquest of the Holy Land today. There are many of all nationalities who will come with us.'

'Don't be ridiculous!' Fulk was suddenly wide awake. 'All the men have said that it would be folly to ride to the east without the rest of the pilgrims. They will only be a little while, and then we can all march together.'

'These people of Constantinople!' Odo said. 'They want us to wait, sit on our arses and give the Saracens as much time as they need to prepare. We are here, we should strike while we can! Come with me, Fulk! I'm going to go with the Normans. Sir Roger and his companions have asked me to join them. Will you too?'

'I cannot! Not yet! Peter the Hermit is in Constantinople right now, petitioning for more resources so that we can remain here safely – at least wait until he is returned.'

'It is not because of the woman, then?'

'What?' Fulk said.

'The pretty widow. You've been making moon-eyes at her every time you see her.'

'Not like you, then!'

It was Odo's turn to be surprised. 'What?'

'I've seen you with Jeanne.'

He flushed. 'She is a sweet and kindly woman.'

Fulk grinned, to Odo's increased discomfort. 'Stay here, brother. Don't go riding off into danger like this. Should I ask Jeanne to plead with you?'

'No!'

His emphatic response made Fulk grin irritatingly, as only a brother could. Odo could not be persuaded to stay, and a little later the two stood with the raiding party as the horses puffed and blew, stamping their feet to be off. Odo and the other men mounted in a jingle of chainmail. Odo bent down, and Fulk and he clasped hands.

'Go with God,' Fulk said, and buried his face in his brother's thigh. 'I would not lose you, Odo.'

'And Godspeed you too,' Odo responded. 'I will look for you when I reach Jerusalem, brother.'

Fulk playfully punched his leg. 'Sir Walter will lead me there faster than you!'

'In a pig's eye! Go safely in God's care, brother.'

Odo smiled down at Fulk. Then, as the knight and his party blew horns and began to ride off in a long column, Odo joined the rear, one of a column of men-at-arms from the Holy Roman Empire, and men of Lombardy, Turin and Milan. He was certain that this was the right thing to do. He had tried to reconcile the long wait at the coast with his desire to reconquer the Holy Land, but he could not. Sir Roger and the others were, like him, weary of the prevarications and arguments of the French. It was time for action; it was time to fight! His heart swelled to be part of this force. They would bring God's justice to this land. On the way from the camp, he glanced towards Sir Walter's pavilion. There he saw the knight standing and, a little distance from him, Alwyn. They looked stern and grim. Odo looked away.

Yet, as Odo trotted off, he dared not look back at his brother. Fulk was his last tie to the world they had left, and he felt a superstitious fear that, if he were to look back now, he would never see Fulk again.

Civitot

Sybille saw them while walking to fetch water.

The blond with the close-set eyes, the dark man at his side, were walking through the crowds; the same two men who had tried to rape her. Even as she saw them, the fair-haired man caught her eye. Immediately he nudged his companion, and the two stared at her. She began to move more quickly, feeling a tightness in her breast that left her feeling breathless. There were people all about her here, but that left her with no sense of security. She had a feeling of certainty that the two wanted to continue where they had left off.

With relief she saw Roul and hurried to him. 'Help me!'

'What?'

He was with an older man, who stood leaning on an old staff. 'What is it, maid?'

Roul nodded. 'This man is a friend of mine. His name is Gidie, and he lived on the Yonne. You can speak in front of him.'

'Two men want to rape me,' Sybille gasped. 'They tried to before, just after we left Philippopolis, and they're following me now!'

Gidie glanced over her shoulder and saw two men edging through the main encampment towards them. 'I've seen their like before often enough,' he said. 'Thieving scrotes. You'll be safe, madame. Stay with us.'

'But they—'

'Roul, you take her back to the camp with the girls,' Gidie said. 'I won't be long.'

Sybille shook her head. 'You mustn't try to take them on alone, Master Gidie! These men are violent, and they will fight.'

'Don't you worry about me,' Gidie said with a smile. He liked the woman. She looked so desperate, and yet she was still keen

299

to protect *him* from any innate rashness. He watched her walk away with Roul, occasionally glancing over her shoulder at him, until her figure and that of Roul were almost hidden between the wagons and carts that were dotted about between the tents of the encampment. Then he turned and, leaning heavily on his staff, hobbled forward.

The two men paid him no heed. The fair one glanced at him, but an old pilgrim with a limp was of little interest. He was seeking better prey. Gidie turned as soon as they were past him, and straightened. He hefted his staff and walked after them.

Roul and Sybille were with Guillemette and Jeanne already when the men moved forward. The darker one pulled a knife and was about to dart in to grab Sybille when Gidie's staff cracked on his forearm. He dropped his knife with a thin cry of pain. His blond friend heard him and whipped out his sword, but when he turned to defend himself, Gidie was already holding his weapon quarterstaff, his left hand halfway along the shaft, his right at the butt, and he crouched with the point near the man's throat.

'What are you doing?' the man demanded, his sword-point up in defence.

'You were following this lady. She's a friend of ours, and we want her safe and unmolested. You will leave her alone,' Gidie said.

'And you'll stop us, will you, old man?' the fellow said, and suddenly lunged at Gidie.

The point of his blade moved forward, but before the man could threaten the old tranter, Gidie snapped his staff left, smashing the man's forearm, then whipped it right, across his jaw. He pulled his staff back, and then thrust hard into the man's belly. He collapsed with a loud gasp, and as he fell Roul stepped on his sword. His comrade had picked up his knife in his left hand, and as Gidie shifted his grip on his staff, he stepped forward to stab.

Before he could, Gidie had grasped his staff halfstaff, and jabbed the butt-end into his face. There was a crack as the iron-shod tip opened a wound from the bridge of his nose clear along his cheek. He was jerked backwards, and as he did so Guillemette brought a griddle down on his head with full force. He fell like an axed tree.

Gidie walked to the still-conscious blond man and leaned over him. 'You try anything with these ladies, boy, and I'll feed your liver to the crows. If you are seen near her again, you will die. The Hermit dislikes men who succumb to their natural desires on a pilgrimage. Now take this other piece of shit and *fuck off*!'

CHAPTER 24

Nicaea, Saturday 20th September, 1096

'There it is!' Sir Roger breathed.

It was not a huge town, but it was a daunting sight. They had ridden south and west from Nicomedia, until they found themselves alongside a vast area of water, which Odo realised now was probably a lake rather than a sea, and turned east and south. Now they were confronted with the first town they had encountered. It had a wall about it in the Byzantine style, but the pilgrims all knew that this entire territory had been taken by the heretics some years ago.

Odo watched, feeling his excitement mount, while Sir Roger and other knights discussed the attack to come. This was to be a war of destruction. The Pope himself had enjoined the pilgrims to go and drive out the 'heinous' people who had stolen the land from Jesus's own. Now the Christians proposed to do so.

They rode in from the north, keeping their approach as quiet as they could, and came across a scene of pastoral peacefulness. At the front near the water, Odo could see women in the waters of the lake washing clothes, and a raucous market was in full swing over towards the town's walls, with men bellowing their wares, women laughing and singing, and children shrieking. Many were running along a small wooden jetty and leaping or plunging into the water of the lake. Others had a mud-slide on the lakeside, and slid down to squeals of delight. Some men were walking about the town with slaves or servants behind them.

Odo took in all this at a glance, and then his blood surged to hear the trumpets blow, and the flags were raised, and suddenly they were all riding at the canter, and men were whooping and howling, and the horses sped along at the gallop, and Odo had to crouch low over his mount's neck. He dared not draw his sword; his entire attention was focused on remaining in the saddle as his horse thundered along with the others.

In his ears the wind was deafening, but he could still hear the screams of terror as the little army plunged into the middle of the crowds. He felt his own horse stumble as it blundered into a woman, and he saw her lying shocked on the ground, her face eradicated forever as a hoof stamped on it. Then his own horse was stopped by the press, and he saw Sir Roger and Gilles pushing on forwards, their swords rising and falling; and with each blow, another person fell.

The women in the market were crazed with terror, but he felt no pity. These were heretics. They deserved no sympathy, no compassion. He pulled his own sword free of the scabbard. There was no joy in it, but as others continued to cut and hack, so he too began to strike at the people. He slashed at a man and saw the thin line of red suddenly explode into a hideous wound; a woman ran past, and he aimed a strike at her head. It cut through her coif and swept down into her skull. She fell instantly like a puppet whose strings are cut. A child, a girl with long hair, was spattered with blood from his blow and when he had wrested his blade free, it seemed to stab her breast almost without effort on his part.

303

He had a thick, pulsing lump in his throat, and a roaring in his ears as he felt his arm moving. He saw, as if in a dream, how his blade flicked right and took a man's throat, then up and down to brain another. He felt all his emotion deadened. He had no feelings for these people. They were deniers of God. How could a Christian man feel anything for them, any more than for cattle slaughtered for food? He rode on through the crush, moving with the men in Sir Roger's company, watching as Gilles dropped from his horse, took up a spiked war-hammer and began to use it on the people at their feet, ensuring that they were dead.

Odo sat and watched. His ears still had that deafening roar in them as he looked about at the bodies. Farther away, there was a fire burning, and he saw a Bavarian knight who had spitted a baby on his lance trying to remove it, while others threw children onto the flames and laughed to see their agonies. He saw women being chased and raped by entire groups of men, and other men forcing victims to kneel, then trying to remove their heads with their swords, laughing at their failed attempts at butchery. All about him there was the pitiable sound of men, women and children being tortured or dying.

His horse was cooling after the heat of the battle, and now it sidestepped and pranced, revolted by the metallic stench of blood which ran in thick rivulets, the reek rising to the heavens. Odo took the reins and persuaded it to move away from the main market. He had no idea how much time he had spent there; it felt like half the morning, but it could only be minutes, surely. Yet hundreds had died here.

He told himself: God gave us the victory! *Dieu le veut!*

And then he saw the figures: a woman and a child, one wearing a crucifix, the other bearing a rosary. They were Christian.

Civitot

Fulk felt lonely without Odo. It was as if his brother had become a stranger to him. His religious fervour had grown every day during their march, and Fulk was alarmed. He did not like this new brother, who went to find dying warriors and cut their throats like a butcher in a slaughterhouse, or who was grown so entirely careless towards the feelings of others. Odo was not the same man with whom Fulk had grown. He was unrecognisable.

Walking mournfully back to his own little pavilion, Fulk saw a familiar face.

'I hope God comforts you?' he said.

'He has not sought to punish me yet,' Guillemette said.

She was carrying a large bucket, from which the water slopped with every step. Fulk took it from her, and joined her walking back to her camp.

'I am grateful to have seen you,' Guillemette said. She gave him a very direct look. 'But that does not mean I will pay you in our agreed manner. We are too close to the Holy Land here. I can feel God watching and judging.'

'I'm not seeking it. Consider this a last gift to you.'

She looked at him with a suspicious tilt to her head. 'What does that mean? Have you suddenly decided to stop whoring?'

'I ...' He reddened. This was not how he had anticipated the conversation.

'Ah!' Guillemette said. She felt a sudden shock, as if the breath had been stopped in her breast. No matter what she had said about God watching, she had felt Fulk was an admirer who could be counted on. She fitted a teasing grin to her face to cover her discomfort. 'So you have found another woman, then. And about time. Who is it? Can it be anyone I know?'

Fulk walked on a short way in silence. 'It is Sybille.'

Guillemette's face froze. 'You know what you are saying? She has only recently been widowed.'

'I know that,' Fulk said. He looked at her. 'I am sorry, Guillemette. If I could guide my heart, I would have fixed it on you alone. I know that you are—'

'I need no man's sympathy,' Guillemette said, but then she softened her tone with a smile. 'I am grateful for your help and food in the last few weeks, but I am content with my place in the world. I may find a man when we get to Jerusalem, if I am fortunate, and if God wills it, but otherwise I will continue with Jeanne. But it was not for me that I was concerned. You must be cautious if you are keen to win Sybille. She is still in mourning for her man.'

'So, what should I do?'

'You must give her time. Time to get to know you better, time to heal from the death of her husband. Benet was a weakly, foolish man, but she knew him in better times, when he was less of a fool. Perhaps he was a good man before he took up the cross? She must have had good times.'

'Why do you say that?'

'She weeps often enough. She remembers him fondly, as a woman should. Benet gave her the little girl, as well as all else. You must give her time to come to terms with her loss.'

'I shall.'

She saw his small, sad smile and put her hand on his forearm. 'You are a good man, Fulk. You're too keen on women, but with hope you will soon find that you love Sybille, and can win her love in return.'

Nicaea

Odo's joy and confidence did not last.

When they left the town, he was glad to be away. The horror of the error would not leave him, even as he rode from the town.

Gilles saw his mood as they left, the smoke from the fires they had set rising high into the sky and hanging like a pall over the town in the still air. He left Sir Roger and joined Odo. 'Was that your first battle? You fought well.'

'All those people,' Odo said.

'They were unfortunate. We won.'

Odo was shivering. His belly roiled, the acid burning his throat as he tried to keep the bile at bay. 'Yes, we won, but—'

'Of course we did! God wills the capture of His lands and the slaughter or eviction of the heretics who have taken it. What else could God want?'

'*Dieu le veut*,' Odo said. 'Yet they weren't.'

'Weren't what?'

Odo faced him. 'They weren't *heretics*! We killed Christians today! I saw crucifixes on two bodies there! Those people we slew were no more heretic than you or I!'

'Then we have helped them on their path to Heaven.'

'But we killed the very people we should be helping!'

Gilles looked at him steadily. 'What we did was leave a message to the heretics who live here. It says, "If you remain here, we will slaughter every last one of you." It says, "We are here to take back what is God's." What else could we do, try to work out which was a Saracen or Christian? It would be impossible. We have to kill some of our own if we are to clear this land of the pestilence of the heretics. And then, if we have killed some Christians, we can pray for their souls and beg God to take them to his heart.'

Odo nodded. He wanted to be convinced. After all, he was expecting to kill many people on this journey. Perhaps it was impossible to tell who came from which religion. Certainly in the market square at Nicaea, it was impossible to see what faith a person had. Perhaps when they had returned to Civitot he could find a chapel and pray for those he had killed, if they were Christian.

More, he wanted to see his brother. Perhaps he should feel guilty at that. He wanted to get back just to see Fulk. He wanted someone to talk to about this horror, someone who would sympathise.

But more, he realised, he wanted to see Jeanne. She would soothe his soul.

CHAPTER 25

Civitot, Wednesday 24th September, 1096

Their return to the port was clamorous, with pilgrims and local Greeks demanding to take a look at the plunder from Nicaea. Odo was jostled and pushed as he walked his horse into the middle of the camp. He was keen still to find a chapel in which to pray for the Christians he had killed, but the main thought in his mind as he shoved his way through the press was that he wanted to find Fulk. He needed to know that his brother was safe. The sight of all the men lying dead in the streets about the market at Nicaea had brought home to him how hazardous was their journey.

Once he had left his horse with Sir Walter's grooms, he hurried to the camp to where Fulk and he had shared a space with Peter of Auxerre.

'Peter, it is good to see you again,' he said when he saw his friend.

'You look like a man who has managed to get some experience of fighting in a short time,' Peter said, looking him up and down.

His measuring gaze gave Odo a sense of pride. He was now surely a real warrior for God, he thought. 'Where is my brother?'

Peter smiled. 'He's with his wench again.'

Odo frowned at that. 'He's back with the whores?' He did not want to think that his brother had ignored all his words. If he was womanising once more, he would be threatening the entire pilgrimage. Odo could feel a hot, angry disbelief rising.

'Don't worry, it's not the whores,' Peter said, seeing his expression.

'He has grown serious about a woman, you think?' Odo said. 'If you believe that, you will be disappointed. He is only ever interested in the easier women, those who are more available.'

'I don't think so. He's trying to help others,' Peter said, disapproval at Odo's assumption lending sourness to his voice.

Taking directions from Peter, Odo made his way along the camp until he reached the edge where he had been told that Fulk could be found. There, he stood and glowered around, trying to see his brother. At last he caught sight of the familiar figure ambling along carrying a skin of water. At his side was a woman, but it was not Guillemette, Odo realised. She was small and held herself like a lady, with a decorous manner, not laughing or giggling like so many silly women would nowadays, and was clad in sober black cloth to indicate widowhood, but she was walking too close to his brother, that much was clear to him. Others did not appear to notice, or at least paid them no heed, but he could see that she was within arm's reach of Fulk, and such flagrant behaviour was not becoming.

'Fulk!' he called, and his heart was lifted to see how his brother's face lifted to see him.

'Odo, you're back! How was it?'

It was good to see how Fulk's eyes flew over him as though seeking proof of his freedom from injury.

Odo smiled. 'I'm fine! We took a deal of plunder, and we're selling it now. It was remarkably easy. The Saracens will think again before trying to stand in the way of God's pilgrims!'

The woman's face had paled as he spoke, and Odo was fleetingly irritated, because any Christian woman should have registered pride to hear about the glorious attack by the army of God, but then he reflected that it was impossible to know what went on in a woman's brain. Besides, whether she knew it or not, she was correct: they had mostly killed Christians. He turned his attention back to Fulk.

'I'm glad you got back safely,' Fulk said. There was a smile on his face, although it had faded a little. 'We hope that there are soon to be more armies here. There is talk of a great army from France that is about to arrive.'

'We shall ride out again soon,' Odo said, unyieldingly. 'The whole of this land is wide open for us. It would be an act of huge folly to rest on our laurels after one easy victory. We need all the men we can gather to begin the great reconquest.'

'Soon we shall have all the men you could wish for,' Fulk said.

'We already do! We must hurry. The Holy City is waiting for us, Fulk. The people of the city are suffering under the Saracen yoke.'

'Odo, I don't think that waiting a few weeks will make such a huge difference.'

'Do you mean you refuse to join us? That would be to foreswear your oath, man! God would never forgive you!'

'I am not foresworn! But others with more strategic experience than me say we should wait until the rest of the army is here so that we can mount our most effective effort. It makes sense. I hear Sir Walter himself prefers to wait for additional forces. Otherwise, if we throw our men in small packets, they will be cut to pieces with ease. We need an army, not small raiding companies.'

Odo narrowed his eyes. 'We need to maintain the initiative, brother, and show these heretics that they cannot stand in the path of the one true God!'

'They will learn that soon enough, when we have our strength mustered, Odo; can't you see that? If we throw away our men in small combats, we will lose the war.'

'What do you know of war?'

Fulk met his glare with a degree of defiance. 'While I have been here, I have been talking to as many of the seasoned warriors as I can find, Odo. I have learned much about fighting.'

'You would learn more about fighting by going and joining in a battle, brother!'

'Perhaps I would learn how to handle a sword, but I think it is as best to understand how to command a battle as well.'

'It's not just a way to evade the danger of the fight, then?' Odo said. There was a sneer in his tone.

Fulk's face changed. His cheeks became pale, and his head thrust forward. 'You think me a coward?'

'You don't like to kill, do you, brother? You did nothing to help when we fought the various battles. You were always happier with the company of women – of any grade – weren't you?' he added.

'Are you commenting on this lady's honour, Odo?' Fulk said, his voice low and angry.

Odo looked at him. He knew he was being unreasonable, but he was angry. This woman appeared respectable enough, but Fulk's history spoke loudly. 'You know more about her than me, brother.' He could not help adding, 'Just as you have known other sluts along the way.'

Fulk punched at him. The effort was wild and ill-judged, and caught Odo a glancing blow on the cheek. Odo knocked his arm away, clubbed his fist, and was about to strike when Fulk's second swing connected with the side of his jaw.

There was a crunch as a tooth snapped, and Odo felt a sudden excruciating pain in his cheek and jaw together. His hand went to it and he staggered back, even as Fulk aimed another strike. But now Sybille had his arm in her hand, and begged him to stop. Fulk stood with his fists bunched, but under her gentle remonstrations, he gradually calmed and unclenched his hands. He let them drop and glared at his brother.

'You insult a good woman, Odo. Men tried to rape her a little while ago. Pilgrims!' he spat. 'I am here to walk her to the market and protect her. Nothing more. She is an innocent widow and I will not hear you speak to her or of her in that vein.'

'But you won't defend yourself against accusations of cowardice?'

'I see no need to defend myself. But as a Christian, I will not listen to your villeiny-saying about this woman or any other. You do not know her. She lost her husband back at Belgrade, and—'

'I say you are a coward, then. You should leave her behind and join in the attempt to win back the Holy Land from the invaders, but you prefer to sit here and pet your latest lover. It is a disgrace that you should want to keep away from the fight, and worse that you would inflict yourself on a woman who should be mourning a dead husband, not flirting with you, brother. Your behaviour with her is likely to cause people to view her with contempt. Especially if they think you a coward too!'

'Odo, I am no coward, but I won't fight with my own brother. If you want to go and flail about, fighting peasants and robbing the odd shepherd boy, go ahead, but do not expect my approval. I will wait for a real army and I will fight with that.'

'You will not join me?'

'No.'

Odo nodded. 'You are no brother of mine.'

Fulk ignored him, and returned to Sybille. 'I'm sorry about him, mistress.'

'Go to the devil!' Odo snapped.

Alwyn had stood in the shade of the pavilion as the riders appeared, and he remained there, glowering at the man who carried the pennant of the family of the de Tonis. He could see the man now, laughing with his companions, no doubt telling stories of how brave he and his men were while fighting shepherds and mothers. It made Alwyn feel nauseous.

'My son, you are unhappy?'

'Peter, Father, I am sorry. I did not see you there.'

The older man stood at his side. There was an unwholesome odour about the Hermit. Alwyn had heard that he ate only fish, and drank nothing but wine, and it smelled as if his skin was impregnated with both: it gave off a sourness and smell of decay that was quite overpowering. But there was no denying his charisma. Alwyn had known some men who had the ability to silence a room by merely entering. His uncle had been one such man, and he had always heard that King Harold had been the same. Certainly the Emperor had that effect on people. But this shabby, shambolic old man had the same effect. If he stepped into a large gathering of people, they would grow quiet almost on the instant. It was the same when he came to the pavilion. Knights and men-at-arms would all give way to him, respecting him as a man, more than his position. He demanded their esteem by the force of his personality, even though he was himself so mild and humble.

'I'm sorry, my son. I didn't mean to surprise you. I saw you standing there, and wondered what was making you sad.'

'It's nothing.' Alwyn glanced over his shoulder. Three of the Hermit's companions were with him. They rarely left his side now. All were thickset young men who had devoted themselves to his protection. They would guard his body from the masses when pilgrims grew overenthusiastic in their proofs of devotion to him: touching his robes, kissing his hands. In battle these three would protect him. He inspired their loyalty and devotion.

Peter stood watching the Saxon, a little smile curling the edges of his mouth up, as though listening to Alwyn's soul. The silence grew unbearable.

Alwyn said, 'It is the man de Toni. I know of his family. They killed my father and uncle and helped take our manors. Even now I expect his father is raping and murdering my people. When he came to the shire first, he burned the great church at Crediton and killed many of the people. For that reason they call him the Butcher of Crediton. The church was a canonical church,' he added. While Peter listened to a man, it was difficult not to fill in the empty silence: the Hermit's own stillness demanded that a man fill the void.

Peter nodded after a few moments more. He retained the little smile. 'Yes, I can only imagine the horror of such events. But be at ease, my son. Here, you will achieve much more than you could at home. The people here need your help. Yet you must control your warlike spirit. Save your violence and anger for the heretics you must kill. Sir Roger does God's will. Look! There he is, riding on his great destrier. He will earn renown! Mayhap you will too.'

'I do not seek renown.'

'What do you seek, then, my son?'

Alwyn looked up and felt the sun on his face. 'Justice would satisfy me. But I can have none. I am doomed.' In his heart, he added, *Doomed to serve those whom I should kill to honour my family and my King.*

'You will find peace with the great *iter*,' the Hermit declared comfortably.

'There is much distress. The men here grow restless,' Alwyn said.

The Hermit sighed. 'I know. I must soon go to beg more food. The army is hungry, and that makes for disputes. I shall arrange to visit the Emperor again and plead with him for help.'

He walked away then, serene amid the clamour of the people, followed by the three guards.

Alwyn shook his head and watched the Normans ride away. They had gathered about them a significant number of other warriors, and as Alwyn followed the thick cloud of dust that followed after them, he saw Sir Walter striding towards him.

'I did my best, but they wouldn't listen,' Sir Walter said. He dropped into his chair with a grunt and bellowed for his steward. 'The fools don't have the brains they were born with. Well, if they ride into danger, I will not send more after them to be destroyed.'

'Where are they going?'

'They have heard of a flock of sheep a couple of days from here. They'll raid it and steal all they can, and then sell it off back here, I suppose. It's hard to tell with men like them. Those Lombards and Rhinelanders don't ride for the glory of God, but for the joy of battle and plunder,' he added sourly.

Alwyn nodded.

'What would you do?' Sir Walter said. 'I have asked you often enough, and you always look like a man who has bitten into an apple to see half the maggot remaining. Why are you here?'

'I was sent to serve you and the pilgrims. I didn't come of my own free will,' Alwyn said.

'No? You were forced to join us here?'

'My woman and servant are held captive against my good behaviour.'

Sir Walter gave a fleeting frown. 'That is not the act of a friend. These two are held hostage?'

'Yes, but now I'm here, I will do what I can to help you.'

'Will you? Against the threat of death to those closest to you? Would that mean I could trust your judgement? I need men I can trust just now,' he added bitterly. His steward hurried to him with a cup of wine and Sir Walter drank it off quickly. 'More!' Turning to Alwyn again, he shook his head. 'Are you content that they remain there?'

'No.'

'Very good. I will see what may be done. Now, the Hermit is determined to press on. All those who stood against him on the way here were destroyed by his peasants and whoremongers, and he expects to do the same with the Saracen armies.'

'He'll have a rude awakening,' Alwyn said. 'The Saracens are lusty fighters, and they have vast resources of men to support them.'

'Then give me something – *anything* – to help me! I need to persuade Peter that it will be best for us to wait for the arrival of more men, and better trained and armed men than this,' he said, waving a hand vaguely that encompassed the whole of the peasant camp. 'Because unless you do so, and I get a delay, we shall see the army break into small portions with the Holy Roman Empire's men riding in one direction while the Franks ride in another, and the remaining pilgrims will get slaughtered by the first Saracen skirmishing party they meet. Give me something to stop this army collapsing!'

CHAPTER 26

Bari, Monday 29th September, 1096

Heinnie paused as Bari came into view. He was marching ahead of the main body of men as was his wont. Occasionally Father Albrecht would join him, but others tended to avoid him, uneasy in his presence, as though there was some emanation about him, a hint of a ghostly presence. Heinnie had become a solitary man – walking, eating and sleeping away from the rest. None guessed that he was haunted, and he must keep it that way, for superstitious soldiers would sooner end his life than keep him near if they learned of his burden; but it meant he must walk on ahead, with only the one companion – whom he dreaded.

There was no peace, no comfort. He was always aware of the horror nearby, and when he slept it was a fractious, unrestful sleep, with the dream tormenting him.

They had met with other remnants of the Count's army. William of Melun, who since Moson had been affectionately nicknamed 'The Carpenter' by his men because he hewed down his enemies like wood, had a force of five hundred with him. But so many men tended to straggle, and the marching column was spread over almost a half-mile as Heinnie broke through a small wood and into the sun at the other side. To the brigands who stood waiting, he appeared to be on his own and easy prey.

There was no warning, only a sudden whistle, and Heinnie found himself surrounded on all sides. These were not warriors but peasants, men attempting to steal from pilgrims. Their leader was a heavyset man with a barrel chest and a square head sitting on a thick neck that was so short, Heinnie could imagine his neck had been cut away and his head replaced. There were three others, two of whom looked as though they would gut a man for the fun of it, and a third who it seemed would barely know which end of a knife to hold.

Heinnie could have negotiated, but these men would not bother to discuss their demands. They would kill first and investigate his wallet later. Besides, he was already on edge. A fight came as a relief.

He looked at the foolish one, who smiled back at him, and then he swept out his sword and slashed it across the fellow's belly. The man had no time to escape, and he shrieked, clutching at his stomach as his flesh parted.

Heinnie did not bother to watch and wait. He had already darted to the side, leaving the heavyset man while he attacked the first of the peasants, driving forward hard with his sword. The man foolishly tried to block his sword, and Heinnie turned the blade, using all his body's weight to drive it into the man's breast. He coughed, retching as both felt the metal saw past a bone and slip on deeper, and then Heinnie had pulled it free and was facing the last two – but it was already too late for them. They were about to leap on Heinnie when the main column saw them and a shout went up.

While the idiot alternately wept and begged for help, some twenty of the men hared after the felons, and soon the two were brought back to stand shivering with their companion. His belly had been opened by Heinnie's blade, and he was in a grievous way. He sobbed with his hands over his belly as though holding himself together.

When Father Albrecht reached them, he had the brigands trussed in short order, then ropes were slung over a couple of branches and the men were lifted by their necks until their choking dancing ceased. Their dead companion was hanged beside them as a retort to those who sought to take up the same trade.

All the men stood about and watched as the three clung to life while they could, and jeered when the idiot's wound began to widen and coils of intestine shook free. But Heinnie was not watching. His eyes were fixed on the road behind him.

She was there still. A shape like a column of dark smoke in the roadway. He knew it. No one else could see her, but Heinnie could, and the sight of her chilled his soul.

He had to get to Jerusalem to escape her. He *must* reach the city and find peace.

Civitot

Five days after Sir Walter's plea for help, Alwyn watched Peter the Hermit make his way along the road to the harbour, his three guards following him, for all the world like a trio of cubs hopefully trotting after their vixen.

He was uncomfortable to see the hermit leave the camp. Sir Walter was finding it ever more difficult to persuade the pilgrims to remain at the camp. Every day little groups of men would come and demand that they be permitted to leave, to take a large force and raid to the south and east, both to find food and to harass the enemy, and every day Walter grew more wan and angry at the constant demands.

'Soon I will have a riot on my hands,' he said to Alwyn, 'and what do I do then?'

'You prevent it, Sir Walter.'

He threw a look at Alwyn. 'You are a most composed man. Does this not alarm you?'

Alwyn turned to him and smiled. 'Sir Walter, I was never a commander. It was always my duty to remain in the line and obey orders. I used to crave action and battle, if only to relieve the boredom of lengthy marches and endless nights about the campfire listening to the same tales told by my friends. Now, they are all dead and I am here. If the men decide to go, you must let them go. Better that they ride out and use up their energies in raids, than that you should fight them and lose some of your men as well as them. We should not seek fighting between Christians.'

'True enough,' Sir Walter grunted. 'Although it grieves me to admit it. We shall be likely to lose a large number of men, if we are not fortunate.'

Civitot, Tuesday 30th September

Sir Walter's prediction was soon proved to be accurate.

A small raiding party under the leadership of a French knight had ridden south and captured some men. From one they heard of a castle further to the south that was filled with wine and food, all there for the taking. Only a few days' march, so the captive said, and so full of stores of all kinds that the army could be fed for a month.

321

It took only a short time for news of this to spread like fire on the moors. All the pilgrims heard of the castle, and Alwyn and Sir Walter soon had a delegation.

'We should ride now.'

This was Sir Rainald, a one-eyed warrior from Bavaria, who was already jealous of the successes of other raiding parties and wanted his own fun.

'We have been advised to leave the people of Rum alone until our other armies join us,' Sir Walter said.

'Although there is not enough food for us as it is!' Sir Rainald snapped. 'How will our situation improve with even more mouths to feed? No, I say we should ride, today, and bring back these stores. We have our prisoner as our guide, he can help us find the place.'

'Peter the Hermit gave us instructions to wait here,' Sir Walter said. 'Wait until he returns from Constantinople, and then—'

'How much longer? Suppose he says the others will be here in a month, in two months – what of it? We can begin this campaign now. I say we go. God wills it!'

Alwyn turned away. Sir Walter saw him, and their conversation of the day before must have returned to him. 'Very well. If you are so disposed, you may go. But only with a small force.'

'I will take those who seek adventure and honour,' Sir Rainald said.

Sir Walter did not respond. Inwardly, he was seething at the implied insult, but he closed his mouth and said nothing as Sir Rainald and his companions left the pavilion, bellowing commands to their servants and men-at-arms.

'You were right,' he said to Alwyn.

'I hope so.'

Xerigordos, Saturday 4th October

This was a larger force than that which Odo had ridden with before. There were many in the pilgrim camp who had been jealous of the success of the first raid, and who wanted to join in this latest escapade.

Sir Rainald had formed a force of some five thousand men, with priests and even two bishops joining in for the ride. He organised them into a raiding party, which Sir Roger was invited to join, and Sir Roger offered a place to Odo. Odo, his broken tooth sparking and flaring like a hot coal in his jaw, was nothing loath, and they had left at noon that day.

Now, four days later, the dust rose and dried his nostrils, and no matter how he wrapped a cloth about his face, the grittiness of sand seared his throat.

They were on their way to the place that the captured man had spoken of, a castle called Xerigordos, which was said to hold a large storehouse. They had brought their prisoner with them and, although he claimed to be a Christian, Odo suspected that the Lombards who held him would soon remove his head once they had reached the castle.

Their captive was true to his word. After only four days they reached an unprepossessing little fortress on top of a rocky hill. Sir Roger and two other knights led their forces to its foot and surveyed the walls for a long while. There were shouts and jeers from the walls, but the knights ignored the jibes and made a methodical study. Soon they were back and calling a council.

The castle was little more than a large keep, with walls that had been added later. Clearly it was never intended as a major defensive work. Even where the walls met the keep at the rear of the castle, the builders had not fully incorporated them into the tower's stonework, but had allowed many of the rocks to butt against the tower's squared sides. It had been a shoddy job. Perhaps the builders intended this to be only a watchtower to guard food stocks and protect the flocks in times of trouble against ruffians. The castle was enough to keep out raiders, but not adequate to defend it against determined men like Sir Roger.

At the rear of the men, Odo listened as the knights discussed what they had learned. It was thought that there was a route to the top of the walls, if they could keep the defenders' heads down. One of the Bavarian knights had a company of archers with him, and he promised that they would keep a withering assault on the castle while the walls were scaled. In short order the plan was agreed, and the men went to put it into operation. There were no ladders, but a pair of grapnels were found and attached to ropes, while a pair of carpenters took apart a wagon and fashioned a makeshift ladder. It would only have to work for a short while, because the men of the assault force would hope to be up and over the walls and opening the gates in no time.

Odo was fearful of the coming struggle. He had been nervous riding into the town's market with Sir Roger's men, but this was different. He had no horse to sit on, only the expectation of climbing a ladder while men tried to burn him, stab him or fill him full of arrows. It was not a prospect to gladden the heart, and his stomach had that heavy sensation, as if a lump of clay was forming, but he reassured himself that God would be at his side. He was safe in God's hands, he reflected.

He looked at the walls and saw some of the garrison. A man suddenly jumped up onto the castellations, lifted his mail and pissed towards the Christians in a bold display of contempt.

At the sight, Odo froze. This was not mere bravado. To him it looked like a deliberate insult to God Himself. His fear abated. For a man to show such disdain for God was shameful. The man must be punished. And then Odo realised that God had given him a sign. It was that the garrison deserved to be put to the sword. Destroyed. They were heretics.

Odo strode to Sir Roger and stood before him. 'Let me be first on the ladders. I will go with the storming party.'

Sir Roger looked him up and down approvingly. 'That's good, Odo. We'll go in and take the place quickly.'

'Be quick and Godspeed,' Sir Rainald said.

Sir Roger was to lead the attack, and he took his command, which was swollen by volunteers to over sixty men, towards the lower slopes of the rocks. There they waited, Odo fingering the edge of his sword and wondering whether he should sharpen it now. He saw one of Sir Roger's men, Lothar, muttering over his crucifix and kissing it, making the sign of the cross, while others stood staring into the distance. Only Gilles and Sir Roger himself seemed at ease with themselves. Gilles stood staring up at the walls as though gauging the best place to erect the ladder, while Sir Roger gazed back at the main force, watching as the archers strung their bows and stood testing the pull, feeling the tension in the wood and glancing every so often at the walls.

Before long the archers were ready. As their officer began to give commands, and the arrows began to fly, Sir Roger shouted encouragement to his men and set off up the hill like a greyhound after its prey.

Odo was at the middle of the ladder. It was rough and splintery, and with each step he felt a new fragment of wood stabbing his palms. It would be a relief to set the ladder down. There was a shout from above, and a rock fell with a heavy crunch. Stone splinters burst from it, slashing at Odo's legs. A second rock, and a man fell screaming with a broken foot, but then the rocks stopped falling as the arrows began to take their toll. Now, as soon as a man appeared over the parapet, he was the target of twenty arrows. Two men fell screaming with three or more shafts in their faces or bodies, and the rest were content to roll rocks over the walls without aiming. One snapped the leg of a pilgrim, but that was the only injury.

They were at the wall. The men at the front set the feet at the wall's base, and the men carrying it at the rear began to walk forwards, pushing the treads upwards as they came. Gradually the ladder rose higher and higher, and more men ran to push the side rails towards the walls. Then, with a sigh from the men, the ladder tipped past the vertical and crashed against the wall. Odo stared at it with a sense of achievement, but even as he felt the relief of a task fulfilled, men were leaping onto the rungs and climbing quickly, Sir Roger and Gilles just behind them. The first to reach the top was stabbed in the throat by a lance, and he lost his grip, falling and taking the second man with him, and Odo watched them fall with a horrible fascination. Odo was already on the ladder, and he hurried up it as fast as he could, springing over the wall at the top.

Sir Roger was working his way along the walkway, stabbing and lunging with his sword, and as Odo watched, the man fighting him took Sir Roger's point in his thigh, and was soon grown lethargic. He slipped and fell from the wall. Sir Roger pressed on, attacking the next man, and Gilles rushed to his side in support. Odo landed on the planks and slashed at a man who appeared before him. His sword rang on his opponent's, and Odo felt the blow shivering in his broken tooth. The man shrieked and raised his weapon again, but a Norman soldier pushed past Odo and slipped his blade into the man's flank, under his armpit. Behind him, Odo saw the door in the tower on his left had opened. Suddenly it was thrown wide, and a number of sentries came hurtling out, screaming and waving their weapons.

It was time to show these heretics God's divine wrath!

Odo was not alone. Eudes and three others were with him

already, and he ran with them at the castle's garrison, their weapons cutting and causing terrible carnage. The blood flowed freely, and Odo felt his boots slide and skitter even as his heart sang in joy. Once he almost fell into the castle's court, but a hand grabbed him and saved him, and then he was stabbing at another dark face before he was rammed against the wall. He felt his face hit the stonework, and the scrape as the skin was rasped away. He saw bright pinpoints of light glittering before his eyes. He fell to his knees, shaking his head, and when he could look up again, the battle was over.

The castle was theirs.

Civitot

Even before the clash between Odo and Fulk, Sybille had been growing more aware of Fulk in recent days. She rather liked his serious expression, his dark eyes with their long lashes, and the evident signs of respect which he gave her.

At first, she had been suspicious. The men who had tried to rape her, and the lascivious glances of others, had made her fully aware of the less than honourable intentions of many of the men in the army. She was aware of Guillemette's and Jeanne's trade, and she tended to assume that any man coming to their encampment must be interested in availing themselves of the prostitutes – many must assume that she was of the same profession. While she had no desire to be associated with them, especially with her Richalda at her side, they had proved themselves supportive and kind.

More, she knew that she might have no choice. In the months to come it was eminently possible that she would be forced to resort to the same means of supporting herself and her daughter. It was a prospect that filled her with dread, but she could not in all conscience deny the possibility that this might become the sole means of maintaining themselves. If that were the case, it would be better to have their friendship and support still more.

'He is a good man,' Guillemette said to her, seeing how her eyes strayed every so often towards Fulk.

'You think so?'

'You can trust my judgement when it comes to men. I know those who are good, bad and indifferent. Fulk of Sens is a kindly, amiable fellow.'

Sybille chuckled without humour. 'You mean he pays well for services?'

Guillemette's face hardened. 'Yes. He paid me in food when I was hungry.'

'And that makes him a good man?'

'No. But he is kind with me, and he would make a good husband. If I had not been as I am, he might have wedded me. He would have made me happy. He would make any woman proud, I think.'

'It is too soon for me. You should snap him up.'

'You should. It is you he has eyes for, not me.'

'What would people think of me, if I were to throw myself at another man so soon after Benet's death?'

'Sybille, they will be glad for you. Those who have known you will know that you are a lady of honour and sensibility. But how can any woman survive long here in the midst of an army, without a man to protect her? All here will understand and appreciate your reasons for allying yourself to him. Necessity is a harsh master.'

Sybille nodded slowly. She thought again about Fulk's long eyelashes, his lazy way of smiling, his easy laughter and . . .

'No,' she said. 'Now is not the time for me. It would be . . .
wrong. It is too soon after dear Benet's death.'

Alwyn had spent a half-day thinking about the message he must
send, and then sealed it and gave it to a shipmaster to take to
John. It would arrive. No mere sailor would dare to hold back a
message for the Vestes. Now he had received his reply.

He had indicated Sir Walter's concerns, but the response
had been scarcely more than a line: *You must keep the pilgrims
together and wait until they receive reinforcements.* He cogitated
over it for a long time before coming to the conclusion that there
was nothing to be gained from staring at it any longer. He rose
and walked from his little tent and stared out. The pavilion of
Sir Walter moved in the wind, and his flags and banners waved.
There was a gathering in the pavilion, and Alwyn rubbed at his
rough cheeks where the stubble was softening as it grew longer.
He grunted to himself and set off up the incline towards Sir
Walter and the others.

As he approached there was the sound of raised voices.

'I say we should ride out. Those Bavarians will take
everything if we leave them to it!'

'We are not here for plunder alone!' Sir Walter grated.

'But if they win all, we shall be forced to buy food from them,
and that will be intolerable!'

'You worry about the price of food, Godfrey?' Sir Walter said.

The man he spoke to was shorter, very thickset, and had a
bushy brown beard shot through with grey. 'I and my companions worry about the heathens, and nothing else,' he said.

'Friends, *friends*!'

Alwyn stopped. It was Peter the Hermit, who held up his
hands and strode in among the bickering men. His guards shoved
people from his path and formed a close cordon around him,

329

their hands gripping clubs, or resting with dangerous calm near their sword hilts.

'My friends, there is no need for dispute! Be calm, I beg of you! You are concerned, my friends, I know, but there is no need to be alarmed, and no need for bitterness. All of us here, we are here to do God's bidding, and if we adhere to His will, and His purpose, all will be well for us. For we will have His approval, and there is nothing more guaranteed to bless us, each and every one, than that. So please, let us pray now, and ask for His advice. God will guide our path!'

All the men there bent their heads, Alwyn too, while Peter prayed loudly for God's intervention and aid.

When he was done, he looked around brightly. 'My friends, what is the cause of this dispute?'

'Some wish to ride out and advance,' Sir Walter said. 'And I know that you feel the same, my friend. But I feel sure that the best course of action for now is to wait for supplies. An army without food entering lands we do not know, will be in peril. We have to know we have supplies.'

'I say we should move on!' said Godfrey. 'God will provide!'

'We know God will provide for us. But we have many more people arriving almost every day, and they need to be fed,' Sir Walter grated.

'My friends, please, let us be calm,' Peter said. 'I have already heard from the Emperor that supplies are on their way even as we speak here.'

'Good! Let us receive them, and then march,' said Sir Walter, glaring at Godfrey.

'And then,' Peter said, smiling brightly at the men all around, 'then we may continue on our historic journey. We shall be in Jerusalem before Christmas, God permitting!'

Alwyn remained at the back of the crowd, but he saw Sir

Walter's eyes light upon him. Later, when the men were breaking away and walking to their own groups, Sir Walter strode down to meet him. 'Well? You heard the Hermit's view. What would you advise?'

'The same as before. If we do not receive more experienced fighting men, to press on would be foolhardy.'

'Then you say we should stay here. Is that the word of your heart, or the instruction of your Emperor?' Sir Walter asked shrewdly.

Alwyn looked out over the camp. Men stood chatting, or fiddled with weapons and equipment, while women trudged about with buckets or yokes with baskets of food. Children hurtled about as children would. There was an air of calm satisfaction such as a man might sense on a market day. It was as if the people had reached this place, and here they were content to wait until they could wander the last leagues to the Holy City.

'This is not an army; it is a gathering of pilgrims, and few have handled anything bigger or more dangerous than a knife. You have to meld them together so that they become a collection of fighting men. I can train some, but only a few. You need many more. These,' he added bleakly, 'will not last above a few minutes against Saracens in battle.'

'I see.' Sir Walter nodded. 'Could you fight better with an incentive?'

'What do you mean?'

Sir Walter's face eased into a grin. 'I dislike the idea of a man being with me because of a hostage held elsewhere. And why would I want to provide you with a servant when you have one of your own?' He pointed behind Alwyn, who turned and saw Sara and Jibril. Sara raised her hand tentatively, like a woman waving farewell, but then she smiled, and Alwyn felt his heart swell.

'I had to bribe a gatekeeper, but I considered it a worthwhile expense. Go to them! Go on, go!' Sir Walter said. 'Rest a while, and then we shall discuss how to train this mob of feckless peasants. Go!'

Xerigordos, Monday 6th October

They were there for two days before any effort was made to consolidate their position. It drove Odo to distraction.

It was clear that Nicaea was a plum that they should pick as soon as possible, and after the ease of their raid into the market, and subsequent capture of this castle of Xerigordos, the pilgrims had their confidence boosted. They were excited and eager to join battle with another group, and since they had won the stores of grain, wine and even meat at this castle, they had enough food for a considerable time.

The pilgrims met in the court of the castle, and initially Odo sat on the ground among them with a sense of fulfilment. This was the life he had been born for, he thought.

He was thirsty, and walked outside to the well. It stood a few yards from the entrance to the castle, while there was a spring below in the valley. Even in the heat of summer, the spring and the well seemed to be full of water. It would make this place a good fortress, Odo thought. He stood at the gates and stared about him. He could see why those who built this little castle had chosen the location. It stood on a little hill, and the views all around were excellent, with the softly undulating land rippling away in all directions like a green sea, with only an occasional tree to mar the smooth perfection. Yet although there was so much greenery, the ground was parched. Every step raised a small cloud of dust. It was not so verdant as his own home at Sens.

He returned to the meeting.

When they had entered the castle, he had been glad to see that the whole fortress was taken swiftly, and he had been among those who enjoined the pilgrims not to kill all who lived inside. Rather, those who were Christians were to be allowed to live and join the pilgrim army. Some were angry and reluctant, but they were more than overweighed by the numbers who agreed. Only the heretics were slain, taken out through the castle gates, there to have their throats cut. Odo had joined in, finding the task to his liking. Releasing the souls of those who were enemies of Christ was God's work. It was good to feel his blade cut into the soft tissues and sweep it across swiftly.

Thinking it may be quicker, he had tried to decapitate two. The first attempt was almost enough to put him off trying it again: the man had screamed at the first strike, and it took him three more attempts to remove his head. The second was easier, perhaps because the fellow was younger, Odo thought. The sword had swept across with barely a dragging sensation as it clove through the man's spine, and his head span slightly, so that it ended up facing him on the dirt, eyes blinking, while his body sagged to the right and toppled over. It was a great confirmation of the quality of the steel, he thought. It made him feel a swelling pride to be executing God's enemies. He hoped that Fulk would also soon be able to test his blade too.

Fulk should be here. He should discover the pleasure of destroying God's enemies, of seeing the shame in their eyes as they felt their lives end. Surely at that moment they were aware of God's greatness and the foolishness of their own heretical perversions.

Odo was called back to the present by the voice of a tall, dark-haired knight with one eye, who stood and held up his hands for silence as Odo took his seat once more.

'Who is he?' Odo asked Lothar.

The Bavarian shrugged, but Gilles leaned forward. 'I think he is called Sir Rainald. I believe he's from Tuscany, Lombardy – somewhere like that.'

'We are here to decide on our future arrangements,' Sir Rainald said. He stood in the middle of the pilgrims and spoke loudly. He had a strong accent that showed he came from the Holy Roman Empire, as did so many of the other men-at-arms, but fortunately all spoke moderate French. 'We have captured this castle. Do we move on and see where else we may conquer, or do we return to Civitot to tell the others how easily this fortress fell? We should perhaps tell them how easy is the path of glory!'

There was a lot of debate. Like Odo, many of the Lombard knights were all for pressing on. As one said, 'If we continue, we can cause more devastation for our enemies, and the armies which follow will consolidate our initial successes. We don't have to go back.'

Sir Rainald disagreed. 'If we continue, we do not know when we will find food. If we have any difficulties, it may mean that the Saracens could come behind us, cut off our supplies, and use Nicaea as a base from which to raid against us. I think it would be prudent to prevent that.'

Odo shook his head vigorously at that. He was keen to march on further into the Holy Land itself. Delay was not to be tolerated. They must all surely see the need to carry on with their journey?

'You do not wish to delay?'

Odo glanced over his shoulder. Lothar was there, watching the crowd with a bland disinterest.

'I would certainly prefer to be riding.'

'You were not happy in the town.'

'I saw that we had killed Christians. I'm not here for that. I came to kill the heretics,' Odo said.

'Yes, I am too. I want to help Christians. It is difficult to see how slaughtering our own will aid our cause. We must go further if we are to find the enemy.'

Odo nodded. 'I have no interest in remaining here.'

Lothar nodded, and then held out his hand and clasped that of Odo. 'We shall do our best for God.'

The deliberations continued on into the afternoon. It was noticeable that the majority of the older knights thought they should first protect their lines of supply, while the younger men and most of the pilgrims wanted to ignore that and continue on their march. In the end the consensus was that the pilgrims should initially make a fresh attempt to take Nicaea. However, while the wine still flowed, many of the men there were unenthusiastic about setting off immediately. Rather, they thought that they should take a rest.

Odo was frustrated. He did not want to remain here or turn back to Nicaea, and was reluctant to now sit about and wait while they all drank their way through the wine in the undercrofts. Making that choice, he felt torn.

It was plain to him that Lothar was not alone in being keen on the idea of moving on, for Sir Roger was also enthusiastic. But it would be hazardous in the extreme to try to ride far with only Sir Roger's company. Odo knew that a larger force would be needed

As the men evacuated the courtyard, he walked to Sir Roger.

'Sir Roger, am I right to think that you were less keen on the idea of waiting, as was I?'

'I would much prefer action to all this sitting about and waiting,' Sir Roger said. 'I despise this laziness with all my heart.'

'Could we not persuade others to join us?'

'To what end? We may be able to waylay some travellers, but that will hardly suffice.'

Lothar joined them. 'There is another way, Sir Roger. All the men here are relying on the fact that there is no force nearby. Were we to scout about the lands all around here, maybe we could find other opportunities. At the least we could ride towards Nicaea and see that the road remains open.'

'Yes.'

'And some may think that we seek plunder. They may choose to join us, if they fear that we will take much wealth and keep it for ourselves.'

'If it achieves nothing else, it will stop me from boredom,' Sir Roger said. 'Very well. We will ride tomorrow at first light.'

CHAPTER 27

Xerigordos, Tuesday 7th October, 1096

Odo woke next morning in the darkness before dawn and smiled to himself at the thought that he would be doing something again. He checked his sword was secure in its scabbard, bound his belt about his belly, took his scrip and a flask of water, and was at his horse outside the main gates as the dawn's light spread over the lands before him.

It was a beautiful country, he thought. Green, rolling hills with darker green trees and bushes, and pale-coloured, scrubby grasses covered much of the land about here.

'You are keen, Odo,' Sir Roger said as he and his men left the gate.

'Who would want to remain in a building when there is a glorious view like this?' Odo replied.

Gilles looked over the land and shrugged.

'I suppose you would prefer to see the hills of Dartmoor shrouded in mist and rain?' Sir Roger teased.

'I would be happier to know that I was in a land where there was not a great army gathering.'

Odo peered at him. 'What mighty army?'

'If you think that the King of Rum will tolerate us kicking the shit from the people of Nicaea, and then capturing this fortress, I think you have a lot to learn about rulers,' Gilles said.

'Ignore him,' Sir Roger said. 'He likes to look on the worst of all possible eventualities. He has grown more and more gloomy as we've travelled. I think that he is never happy unless there is a dire warning ready to be given.'

Odo nodded, but he kept an eye on the older soldier. Gilles rode with his spear in his hand like a man prepared for an ambush. It was, Odo thought, an eminently sensible attitude. Not because of fear, but as a matter of precaution. He rested his hand on his sword hilt once more, for comfort, and there was excitement, too, at the thought that he might soon be able to use his sword again. In his mind's eye he saw the young man's neck before him again, his blade slicing down and through, the head falling.

It was a thrilling memory. He wanted to repeat it.

They had already stopped to break their fast and rest the horses, when Odo heard a strange noise. It sounded like a number of rocks were being rolled over and over at great distance, or perhaps the sound of a thunderstorm far away. He stopped and listened with a frown on his face, and turned to Sir Roger. The knight had not heard it, and gazed at Odo with incomprehension, but Gilles had already jumped from his horse and lay at full stretch on the ground. 'A long way off, perhaps a league or so, but it's big.'

'What is?' Odo said.

'The army that's coming to take back the castle,' Gilles said shortly. 'Sir Roger, we have to ride back and warn them.'

'Yes, of course. Is it a mighty army, do you think?'

'If I can hear it that distinctly from so far away, yes, it is a huge army,' Gilles said. 'We need to get back now.'

Their horses were already tired, but the men pushed them on, and by the middle of the afternoon they could see the castle on its hill directly ahead of them.

At the sight, Gilles pulled up and stared about them. Odo saw him fix his gaze on a valley some two miles from them, and bent his own attention in that direction, but could see nothing. 'What is it?'

For answer, Gilles said, 'The dust. Can't you see it?'

Sir Roger was with them now, and he too peered into the distance. 'All I can see is a darkness in the sky.'

Gilles put his foot in the stirrup and hoisted himself into the saddle, taking the reins. 'It's the dust of many thousands of horses and men. *Many* thousands,' he said with emphasis. 'They are marching to take the castle, I would guess. We must get back and warn them!'

Civitot

Guillemette was sorry to see that Fulk spent little time near Sybille and her, but her time was taken up with other matters. Jeanne was upset and fractious, and Richalda appeared to have a return of her fever, although this time not so strong or debilitating. Still, it kept Sybille and Mathena busy, trying to keep her comfortable.

Recently Fulk was rarely to be seen. Guillemette did make a point of looking for him when she crossed into the main camp, searching for food or water, but he was usually engaged with others, either learning new fighting skills or teaching them to others. She was proud to see that Sir Walter was making use of him. It gave her a little flaring in her breast to see him working patiently with the other men, sharing with them the skills that he had himself only recently learned.

It was pathetic, she would tell herself at those moments. He had been a useful client on the way here, nothing more. She had taken his food, and given him her body in return. In all her years of whoring, she had never become that sad, jaded creature, the wench who fell for her client. That was invariably a sorry maid.

But there was no denying her feelings. When she saw him and watched, a slight flush would colour her breast, and she was forced to hurry away before it could rise, blotching her throat or making her cheeks redden. If she heard others praise him, her heart would thrill; if they were unflattering about him, she would round on them like an alewife whose brew was derided.

And the worst of it was, he had set his face on Sybille. There was nothing Guillemette could do about that. She knew as well as any draggle-tail that the men who would pay for her to lie with them were the sort who would think her beneath their status. A whore was a diversion, not a wife. Who could trust a wife who had been content to relieve an army of men? She must seek either a man who knew nothing of her past, or be content to die a spinster.

It was painful, though, to see how Fulk would make sheep's eyes at Sybille. Guillemette liked Sybille, but to know that she had lost Fulk to her, that was hard. Very hard.

Xerigordos

They rode as fast as they could, keeping to the valleys and avoiding any places where they might be seen and ambushed. The threat of the army behind them was constantly in their minds, and the thought of the army was enough to make Odo feel a panic, as he had just before the battle at Belgrade when they first entered Hungary. It seemed that he could any moment expect the horror of an arrow shaft in his back, and he crouched low over the horse's neck as he rode.

When they were close enough to hail the castle, Gilles began to roar his warning, but the gatekeepers did not appear to understand. There were two men sitting on a bench and drinking from pots of wine, belching grossly as they enjoyed the sun. Guards lounged at the open gates, and beyond them Odo saw a party of pilgrims watching a dogfight. All was peaceful and calm, and it was hard to imagine that they were bringing tidings of such fury. Then Lothar cantered past him and into the court.

The company rode in past the two drinkers and after Lothar. Men shouted angrily as the dogs drew apart, one yelping as a horse drew too near.

Sir Roger bellowed at the men. 'There is a huge army on the way here! Man the defences and bolt the gates.'

'Who are—?' one of the drinkers began tipsily, but Lothar's sword was at his throat and he stopped speaking as he felt the cold steel.

'You heard Sir Roger. Bar the gates and sober up, man! There is an army coming, and when they reach us, they will rip out your liver to feed the pigs!'

There was a snigger from the second drinker, and a bellow from the keep: 'What is all this row?' Sir Rainald appeared, his sword-scabbard and war belt in his hand. He peered at Sir Roger. 'What is this?'

Before Sir Roger could answer, there came a cry from the topmost tower. 'There is a force approaching from the east! I can see a great cloud of dust, as though there is an army!'

Sir Rainald gaped, but only for a moment. He bellowed for a horse. 'I want scouts to ride east and south to confirm their line of march, and whether there is a place to form and hold them back. We may be able to ambush them.'

Sir Roger glanced up at the tower. 'How far are they?'

'Two miles at most. They approach at some speed.'

'We have no time to scout extensively, Sir Rainald. The enemy is almost upon us. We have to ride now to deny them this castle.'

'Then ride! We will mount our beasts and join you as best we may!'

There was one pass that Sir Roger had seen on their ride: a pair of hills that blocked the path of the Saracens. There was one valley between them, and it was to that pass that Sir Roger rode now, his numbers swollen by knights and men-at-arms from the castle. Sir Rainald was to gather more men and join them shortly.

Lothar was content to be ordered by his knight, but as he looked about them he could not help thinking how desolate was this place. Even if they were to hold back this initial attack, there was little in the way of local plunder to restock their supplies at the castle, and little chance of a rescue column arriving. The dust in the air was choking as they rode, and he hawked and spat to clear some of the grit from his throat. It did little good, and as they slowed and came to a halt, Sir Roger holding up his arm, he took the opportunity to swill his mouth with a little water.

'We will wait here,' Sir Roger said. 'As soon as they come about the bend in the road there, we can attack. I need a man on top of the higher hill there to keep a close watch.'

While a volunteer hurried to the hill, Sir Roger took charge of the men in the valley. His plan was simple, and to most of the men it appealed in its simplicity. Odo listened as he outlined it. The Christians would remain in one block on the slope of the left-hand hill, and as the Saracens came though the pass, the Christians would ride down the slope and take them in flank. It would cause mayhem, being unexpected, and would throw the Saracens into disarray in an instant, so that even though the Christian numbers were tiny, they should still be able to score a great victory.

'Don't forget, the worst error is to let yourself get overtired in the first rush!' Sir Roger called to the men, tying the laces of his padded coif. He exhorted them to deeds of valour. 'We are here for Christ and the Lord our God. These heathens have no idea of religion, and they will be dismayed when we break their ranks with our charge, so it is likely they will turn tail as soon as we appear. If so, we must enjoy the fruits of our assault and follow them. There will be a great carnage here, God willing! We are here on God's service; do not forget that! God wills it! We cannot fail!'

Odo listened, and he felt almost ashamed to acknowledge his excitement at being on the brink of a battle again. His scalp seemed to contract, and he rubbed his brow with one hand, his other clutching at the spear he had been given. All about him was the squeaking of leather saddles and harnesses, the chinking of mail byrnies. Hoofs stamped and mounts blew and whinnied, but all the noises seemed dulled. Instead he could hear the thunder of his heart, the hiss of the breath in his throat, the subtle churr of the blood in his veins.

He looked over at Gilles, who was eyeing the sentry on the hill and appeared to be listening with only half an ear; Lothar was sitting on his horse and idly swinging his sword about his side and over his left shoulder, limbering up his wrist and forearm. He caught sight of Odo's stare and met it without blinking. There was no fear in his eyes, Odo thought, but neither was there any apparent confidence.

Spurring his mount, Odo went to Lothar's side. 'God be with you,' he said.

'Let us hope He is with all of us today.'

'He is!' Odo declared fervently.

'Good. Because we are going to be a pinprick in the side of an army the size of this.'

'What do you mean?'

'Think of the cloud of dust that they threw up. Only a large force would cause that. We will be facing many thousands of men. And we have a matter of a few hundreds? It is not enough. Prepare for one good charge, and then do not become embroiled further in the battle, but make your way back to the castle. Here we can become overwhelmed.'

Odo was shocked and disgusted to hear such talk, but he curbed the barbed response that sprang to his lips. God would show the faithless; He would give them a great victory! In Odo's mind he saw a great field of dead heretics. And God was there: He stood over them, over the rent and tattered flags and shattered bodies. There would be a great victory here.

God willed it!

He sat restlessly as the company waited, and as he did, the scene took on an unrealistic nature. It seemed strange to be here in the heat of the sun, waiting for an enemy to arrive and be cut to pieces. God would see such a battle here as had not been seen in many times a hundred years. The Christians would wield their weapons with such mastery. But meanwhile, the sun was hot, the air breathless and dry. He felt his throat hoarse and uncomfortable, and pulled the stopper on his water flask, drinking sips to clear it. Lethargy crawled over him, and he closed his eyes, nodding.

'There!'

Gilles's shout startled him into wakefulness. The sentry on the hill was waving frantically.

'Soon, my friends,' Sir Roger said. He had a gleam in his eye, Odo thought, like a boy who has seen an opportunity to scrump from a neighbour's orchard. Sir Roger gripped his lance and glanced from side to side at his men with a wolfish grin fixed to his face. 'Are you ready? Ready to strike a blow for God against His enemies? Are you ready to fight for Him and for your place in Heaven?'

The noise of approaching men was growing. It was less a thrumming of hoofs on the sandy paths, and more a solid sound, as if a leaden maul had struck an echoing stone, a dull, relentless, reverberation that was intriguing and appalling at the same time.

Odo watched the sentry scramble and slide down the hillside until he reached the more shallow incline where he had left his mount. In an instant he was in the saddle and riding for the rest of the force.

Sir Roger smiled as he came level. 'Well?'

'There are thousands of them! It is like watching bees inside a hive!' the man panted. He wore a look of fixed horror. 'There are too many!'

As he spoke Sir Rainald arrived, riding along the same roadway. He saw Sir Roger and his men, but before either could speak, the vanguard of the Saracen army arrived.

Odo had never seen such a force before. Flags and banners fluttered from a thousand lances, and rank upon rank of men on horses advanced along the roadway, their polished helmets gleaming in the sun, their mail shining like cloth made of thousands of diamonds. It was a sight to take a man's breath away.

Sir Roger lifted his hand, and was about to give the order to attack when there came a sharp trumpet blast, and the first ranks of the Saracens suddenly spurred at Sir Rainald's men. Sir Rainald himself roared and lowered his lance and he began to charge, his company following suit. Sir Roger bellowed his own command, and Odo found his horse plunging down the hill towards the growing army. At his side Lothar allowed his lance-point to drop until it was pointing at his enemy, and then Odo felt a fierce exultation, as though God Himself had blown vitality and courage into his veins. Odo saw dismay on the faces of the leading Saracens, and he felt God's power surging through him. He felt *invulnerable*.

Their sudden assault on the flank of the leading columns was a complete surprise. The Saracens had only seen Rainald's force, and the crash of armour striking at their side was enough to shatter their march. It slowed and stopped, the leading men panicked by the unexpected ambush. To Odo, the charge was a series of rippling crashes as succeeding ranks of Christians pounded into the Saracens, their lances stabbing through mail, leather, flesh and bone, crashing into the men and horses with the strength of a thousand hammers. A great concussion seemed to punch through his own arm as his lance struck a man's torso, and the lance's shaft seemed to come alive, thumping him hard under the armpit, then jolting sideways, almost breaking his wrist, and he tried for an instant to snatch hold of it again, before realising that his target had fallen from his horse and the lance was embedded so deeply in his body that it would be impossible to catch it again.

Instead, he grabbed his sword and drew it, waving it at another man, and somehow blocking a blow that was aimed at his head. It sent a painful reaction down his arm to his shoulder, and he hacked at his opponent's face, but already the two were driven apart by the mêlée, and another man was ramming into him, all but crushing his left leg against his horse's body. The blood sang in his heart, and he fought on, secure in the knowledge that God was with him. A heavyset Saracen with beard and white teeth struck at him with a gauntleted fist, and he had to duck, wondering why the man didn't use a sword. He heard a scream, and Lothar rode into the fellow, his sword whipping round and cutting deeply into the Saracen's neck. At once he fell without making a sound.

Lothar punched his shoulder. 'Get back, you fool! Ride for the castle!'

Odo could make no sense of his words. They had ridden into the side of the Saracen horde, and surely they had slowed their advance. With their attack, and that of Rainald, the Saracens would be retreating soon. He glanced to where Rainald's attack had started, and realised there was no sign of the knight and his men. Only some bodies on the ground showed where they had been. Then, he looked to the left, and saw advancing towards him the full might of Kilij-Arslan. Thousands of spears, thousands of archers, thousands of fierce warriors, and at last he realised the danger they were all in.

He snapped his horse's head around and set spurs to his flanks, riding as fast as he could, aware all the while of the loud noise of Lothar's horse. A zipping sound in the air came to him, and he looked over to see a black-shafted arrow flying past him. Looking behind him, he saw others from Sir Roger's party following and, behind them, archers on horseback, casually drawing their strings back and taking care to aim before letting fly into the backs of Sir Roger's men. But for all his panic, it felt as though his horse was little better than ambling, no matter how hard he raked its flanks with his spurs.

Then they were around a curve and riding hard, and Odo felt his beast lengthen his stride and he had to cling on for dear life, praying that he would not fall, and he saw another pair of men tumble from their horses with arrows in their backs, but he felt the alarm start to leave him, because when he looked over his shoulder, the pursuit was not keeping up. Their horses had travelled too far already that day. Sir Roger held up his hand when

347

they saw the enemy was returning to their comrades. All the men gathered, most of them breathing heavily, while their mounts stood with heads held low, desperate to gather their breath. After a few moments to rest, they continued back to the castle, each of them counting the cost.

From Sir Roger's own company Odo thought four men had disappeared. That meant he had lost half the men who had accompanied him from Tawton already on this pilgrimage, a shocking number. Lothar and Gilles were still with him, as was Eudes, but when Odo looked at Sir Roger, the shock was clear in his eyes. He had brought his men here thinking that he would win honour and glory, and instead he had thrown away his men needlessly.

'Sir Roger,' Odo said firmly, 'you must not weary yourself with feeling blame for this. God will reward those who died with a place in Heaven, and He will send you a still greater victory.'

'They responded faster than I would have imagined,' Sir Roger said quietly. He shook his head as though to clear it. 'In God's name, we must have reinforcements to fight these. We are not so numerous as to be able to defend ourselves.'

'But we have a castle,' Odo said. 'They will not be able to winkle us from that so easily, will they! We are Christians, after all!'

He spoke with confidence, but when he looked at Lothar, he saw an expression of resigned hopelessness in his eyes. Lothar was less convinced of the protection offered by the castle.

Lothar looked as though he thought it would be a trap.

As they clattered into the castle's court, it was obvious that only a few of the Christians had managed to escape the slaughter. Sir Rainald was already sitting on a bench outside the hall, bellowing commands while a surgeon pulled at the arrow in his shoulder. The barbs were hideously elongated, and the surgeon was inserting a knife to hold back the flesh while he wriggled the barbs loose with pliers. A bishop was intoning a prayer nearby, his face as white as marble as he eyed Sir Rainald, who was rapidly losing blood.

It did not affect his voice. 'Is that the last of them? Close the gates and bar them! The bastard Saracens will be all over us like lice on a peasant in a moment! Sir Roger, do you have many archers? Have them all posted on the walls. We need all the archers we can get. Have the rest of the men hunt down every last arrow in the castle. I want every archer to have sheaves of arrows. Where are the boys? Ah, there!' Three lads who had been used to serve as grooms on the ride to the castle scurried forward. 'When the arrows start to fly, boys, you will collect all those you can find from the enemy, you'll gather them up and take them to the archers. As soon as you have enough for an armful, take them to the men who need them. And we'll need someone to bring water to the archers, too. Who can do that?'

Lothar walked to Sir Roger. Odo was near, and went to listen, wondering what could be so urgent that Lothar would think it worth interrupting the preparations. He had a suspicion it was something to do with the expression he had seen on the man's face earlier.

'Water. What is there here?'

'We have the cistern.'

'How full is it?'

Sir Roger shrugged. 'I don't know.'

'How many men are there here?'

'What is your point?' Sir Roger said.

'Just this: we have enough water in the cistern for a matter of three or four days, with all the men here. This little castle was designed for a garrison of perhaps two hundred. With so many, the cistern would keep them in water for a few weeks. With as many men as we have, there is not enough to survive a siege.'

'What of it?'

'We have no fresh water, Sir Roger. Only the cistern. Our enemies outside will have access to as much water as they wish. There is the well outside the castle walls, and the spring down in the valley. They will keep the Saracens well supplied. At the same time, we will suffer the torments of thirst.'

'Then we should fetch water to fill the cistern.'

'To what end? To increase our ability to live here for another two days? Three? Sir Roger, we should ride from here. Now!'

Odo interjected, 'Ride away? We are soldiers of Christ, in God's name! You would have us flee from these Saracen butchers?'

'Yes,' Lothar said. 'To remain here is to fail. My cause is to fight Saracens and protect Christians, not to pick fights which I cannot win, but to fight the battles I can, to the glory of God.'

Odo was looking over his shoulder to the nearer valley. 'I think you are too late, Lothar. They're here.'

Civitot

Fulk was weary after a day of training a score of youths and three ancient men. Trying to explain to them how to block an enemy's blow, and retaliate immediately, with men who had never held a sword in their lives before, was exhausting. Most would do better to grasp a club or polearm.

He had avoided Sybille since the day he had quarrelled with Odo. It was unseemly for him to try to speak with her. Others would see him and come to the wrong conclusions, and that could reflect on her. He wouldn't put her through that kind of torment. No, he must leave her. It was a relief that his duties occupied his mind and time so much. Not that they pushed her from his mind; that was too much to hope for.

The sun was moving to the west as he reached the main camp. It was growing. Every day more dribs and drabs of pilgrims arrived, and the encampment grew further to the north and east. Now it took time to walk from the harbour out to the farther edges.

A wind had picked up, and it was raising dust and sand and throwing it into people's eyes as he passed by the market area. As he walked, he heard a familiar voice. Looking past a huddle of men and women near a stall, he saw Sybille and Guillemette talking to the proprietor. He was holding up a glistening, slimy mess that, Fulk realised as a tentacle drooped free, was an octopus. Fulk turned his head and bent his feet to walk away from the women, but he could not. He found he had stopped in the roadway, and he chewed his lip, thinking, 'No, I have to leave her alone. I cannot speak with her. She's only been widowed a little while ... I must leave her alone.' But his feet refused to walk on, and soon he heard Guillemette call him for his advice. He would have seen, if he had looked, a look of delight to see him pass over Guillemette's face, but that it was quickly wiped away and replaced with a look of calm indifference as Sybille caught sight of him.

'You want?' the Greek trader was asking as Fulk drew nearer. He allowed it to dangle temptingly.

'How much?' Guillemette asked, and on hearing the man's response her face fell. She glanced at Sybille, and the two shook their heads in unison.

The trader permitted a slight frown to cross his brow. He suggested a lower price. Sybille shook her head more vehemently and Guillemette rolled her eyes in disgust. 'That is twice its worth!'

'You may go and buy one from another trader if you think you can win one as plump and tender as this,' the merchant declared.

Fulk leaned on the counter and peered at his wares. 'You call that fresh? It's been in the sun all day. You won't sell that to anyone else. You're trying to catch these ladies because they're alone in a strange land.'

'No, it is perfect!'

Fulk turned his back decisively and glanced at both women. 'There is a man on the harbour selling fresh fish. We would do better—'

'Wait!' the merchant called quickly.

'Do not waste any more of these ladies' time,' Fulk said.

Soon the octopus had passed into Guillemette's ownership for a fair price, and the three walked back towards the camp. Fulk escorted them to the outer fringes, near to their own tent. There he took his leave.

'He was brief,' Guillemette observed.

'He knows he cannot hope for anything from me. He has avoided me since his fight with his brother.'

Guillemette nodded. Sybille had told her of that. 'You give him no encouragement?'

'How can I? It will be months before the anniversary of Benet's death. I cannot fling myself at him. If I did, he would respect me as little as . . .'

She broke off before mentioning Guillemette's profession.

'I think you are being ridiculous,' Guillemette said. There was a tension between them, but Sybille was wrong to think it was her faux pas.

Guillemette was deeply jealous.

BOOK SEVEN

Disaster

CHAPTER 28

Xerigordos, Tuesday 7th October, 1096

They arrived like a plague of locusts, Odo thought, swarming over the plain before the castle, destroying everything in their path.

He stood on the walls as the first outriders appeared, and he had thought that they would make perfect prey and took a bow, nocking an arrow to the string before drawing it back as he had seen others do. The riders remained at the far edge of the plain, but he felt sure that he could hit them. He let the missile fly and simultaneously let out a sharp cry of pain. The string had raked down his bare forearm, scraping the flesh from elbow to wrist, and the arrow hurtled off harmlessly to the left.

'Do not loose any more,' Lothar grunted beside him. 'You won't reach them there, and you'll do yourself more injury if you're not used to loosing arrows. We don't have enough arrows to waste.'

'I thought I could hit one of them,' Odo muttered, gripping his forearm and holding back the words that wanted to fly.

'At that range? Have you ever used a bow before?'

Odo didn't answer that. He had not, as it happened, but he had seen others, and it did not look difficult.

'Those men are there only to test us, and count our heads,' Lothar said. 'Do not do their work for them.'

'What will they do?'

'The same as us, I expect. Launch a ferocious assault on the walls, see if they can fight their way to the causeway here, and then, if they can't, build siege engines to batter the walls, or send engineers to mine beneath and force their collapse. Either way, we will be here for days, and we don't have water for that.'

'So ...'

'So we shall have to ration the water, sharpen our weapons, and pray,' Lothar said uncompromisingly.

Civitot

Alwyn was lying on his back and meditatively wiping his whetstone along his sword's blade when he heard the shout and a scream. He rolled from his palliasse and hurried out.

He saw Sara with two other women, both cowering from a pair of men who were attacking an older fellow with a staff. The older man was being forced back, and he would surely die unless something was done. He ran to the fighting men just as the older fellow stumbled. One of his assailants was a fair-haired man who gripped his sword two-handed. He was about to deal the death blow when Alwyn grabbed his elbow and pulled, kicking his leg away. The fellow was overbalanced, and tumbled to the ground. Alwyn did not wait, but thrust his sword at the other man. 'What is happening here?'

Sara ran to him, but he thrust her aside. She would be in

danger if she stood there. He kept his eyes fixed on the assailant's face. 'Well?'

The old man spoke first. 'I am called Gidie. These two tried to molest this lady, Sybille,' Gidie said. 'They have tried before to take her honour.'

'Is this true?' Alwyn asked Sybille.

She nodded, her face a mask of shock. Jeanne was with her, and she put her arms about the older woman while glaring at the man still standing.

As if he suddenly realised his danger, the man struck. His sword rose and he would have slashed Alwyn's arm from his body had Alwyn not anticipated his attack; stepping forward, he blocked the man's sword with his own and punched him in the face with his damaged hand. The man fell, but as he did Alwyn heard Sara scream. Turning, he saw that the other fellow had climbed to his feet again, and had his sword in his hand.

Alwyn stepped away and tested the weight of his sword once more. He swung it loosely about his wrist, waiting while the other man caught his breath. He snapped a blow to Alwyn's left, which Alwyn could easily ward, and then moved in closer, his left hand clenched to punch Alwyn's face. Alwyn had to duck his head below his shoulder, and the blow caught him on the top of his skull, making him see stars for a moment, but then he slammed his right hand and his sword's pommel into the man's face. The steel hit the man on the cheek and scraped up to his temple, tearing a gash in his skin and sending him flying backwards.

He heard a crack as Gidie's staff rapped sharply on the other man's head, and then Alwyn was standing, panting, the victor.

While other pilgrims came and bound the two, trussing them ready for judgement and a short jig at the end of a rope, Jeanne and Sybille went to Gidie, and while Sybille took his arm and held it to her cheek, Jeanne flung her arms around him and clung on like a lost child.

Sara ran to Alwyn and clutched his arm. 'You must be careful! I thought he would kill you!'

Alwyn gruffly tried to speak, but no words would come to him. Instead he hugged her. 'When you see men fighting, don't come to me, Sara. You have to run and hide until it's safe.'

'No. I won't leave you. I will be with you – always.'

Xerigordos

The Saracens were still arriving. Their men filled the lower plains now, and their flags could be seen all about the castle, fluttering gaily in the breeze. More were arriving, and the sound of tent pegs being driven into the ground could be heard as a constant timpani. There were shouted commands in the strange tongue of the Saracens, and Odo could see groups of men rushing backwards and forwards, bringing weapons and materiel to set positions. Then Lothar gave a short prayer. 'There.'

Odo followed his pointing finger. 'What?'

'They are coming!' He leaned down and bellowed into the main court, 'They're forming ranks! To the walls!'

'What is it?' Odo asked. He felt foolish, not understanding what was going on, but still filled with the thrill of imminent action. As he stared over the plain, he saw men forming into columns. Some had tall ladders, others carried bows and axes, and all appeared to be waiting for a command; even as more and more Christians came rushing up the stairs and took up their positions on the walls, Odo could see the Saracen leaders before their men, riding up and down on their horses and urging them to great feats of courage.

And then his mind seemed to go into a strange stillness. He watched, and his ears could hear noises, but he could make no sense of either. Odo peered down at the men milling about, and saw archers send their missiles up at him, but he could not so much as flinch from their passage. He gazed about him at the men on the walls. In their faces he saw resolution, defiance, courage or fear, but in all he saw determination. Yet he felt none of it. He was a spectator, not a participant. He was a straw in the wind, a man who had joined the pilgrimage without knowing what it might involve. When they set off, he had thought it would be a glorious effort, an easy opportunity to come and fight the weak, cowardly Saracens who waged war only on the poor Christian population. He had thought it would be an easy task to assail these godless people and throw them from God's lands. But now he was confronted by them, and the sight emasculated him.

A clump about the back of his head made him turn. He found himself facing Lothar, who glowered at him. 'Are you asleep? You think to stand here and watch while they attack? You are only a watcher at this battle? No! Prepare yourself, and listen to the orders. When the men place their ladders against the walls, you must push them away. Yes? Then, if men succeed in climbing the walls, you must kill them and knock them down, yes? Keep your head down from the arrows, and pray to God that none of them manages to hit you with an axe or sword. Do you hear me?'

Odo nodded, but his head felt as though he had drunk too much wine. There was a rushing, whistling noise in his ears, and he was dizzy. It seemed that the wall was spinning slowly beneath his feet. As he stared at the enemy, he felt he was viewing the scene through the smoke of a fire: it swirled and danced, and he could make little sense of it.

A man barged into him, swearing volubly, and a second stumbled, shoving Odo into the stonework of the castellations, and suddenly his senses returned to him. He heard a swish, and realised that it was the sound of an arrow passing close by. He ducked as another flew past, but it was wide and struck the stonework of a nearby tower.

At his side a youth turned and faced him, and in his eyes Odo saw the certainty of death and agony.

'Do not worry, my son! We are here on God's business, and He will guard you.'

The youth did not look comforted, but he nodded. Another arrow hurtled past them, only a matter of inches over their heads, and Odo did not flinch this time. If it was his time to die, God would take him, he knew. And he smiled.

'They come! Prepare to repel ladders! We have God with us and they will die! *Dieu le veut!*'

Odo and the youth stood at the wall while arrows hurtled past as though the air sizzled in their wake, but they held no fear for Odo. He was reciting the Paternoster as he drew his sword, and then he smiled broadly as he watched the men below.

They had brought massive scaling ladders, and now men ran forward bearing them to the foot of the walls, setting the wide-spread feet of the ladder on the ground some distance from the walls, and then thrusting the ladders upright until they could slam against the wall of castle, just as Odo and the others had done only a few days ago. So soon as they had thudded into position, the first men were already climbing up.

Odo saw others were grabbing rocks, and he took one from a nearby pile and gazed over the wall, dropping it on a man halfway up the nearest ladder. The Saracen was looking up as he dropped it, and Odo saw it smash into his face, turning the brown features to a red, bloody mess in an instant. The man said nothing, and did not scream, but let go his grip and plummeted, sweeping a second man from the ladder. Odo felt only a glorious sense of achievement. An arrow struck the wall by his head with a loud *tock* as the steel bounced from the stone, but Odo barely noticed it. He bent and took another rock. This time he hurled it with full might at a man who was clambering up gripping a shield that he held over his head. The rock struck the shield and there was a great cracking sound, but then the man gave a wail, his shield dropping, and Odo realised his arm was broken. He took up another rock and flung that, and the man was struck on his shoulder, and Odo heard the bones crack under its onslaught. The man fell tumbling from his perch and Odo gave a whoop of joy. He offered up a prayer of thanks to God, and reached for another stone. An arrow hit his mailed shoulder but flew off without piercing the steel rings, and Odo hurled his rock at the next ladder. It missed the men, but the rock crashed through two rungs, tearing them apart and making climbing that section all but impossible. A fresh rock removed a climber's hand from the ladder; he screamed, flailing his bloody limb, while the men on the walls jeered, but although more and more were hit and killed or knocked from their ladders, still more men came and mounted behind them. And all the while the arrows were spat up at the defenders. Many missed their mark, and bounced uselessly on the stone walls, but some succeeded in finding a target, and every so often a man would give a shriek, a moan or a cough. Beside Odo was a grizzled old veteran of a hundred fights, but an arrow lanced into his eye, and partway out through the back of his skull, and he slowly toppled to his knees and then slid sideways, almost tripping Odo as he tried to drop a rock on another assailant. He missed that one, but although his aim was sent wild, he did have the pleasure of seeing it strike a captain of the enemy full on the point of his helmet. The man was killed instantly.

And that appeared to be the end of it. There was the sound

of horns being blown and rapid drumming could be heard, and suddenly the men were fleeing the walls, running back to their ranks, leaving a bloody pile of bodies, some feebly moving, at the feet of the scaling ladders.

Odo turned to the youth at his side. 'You see? God will not leave us to die!'

Lothar heard him and glared. 'Keep your mouth shut until we see the enemy has given up. Do not tempt God to try us further.'

Odo watched as the Saracens erected more pavilions and tents. When evening came, there were thousands of small campfires all about the castle. It was like looking into the sky in midsummer, seeing all those tiny little specks on the ground before the walls.

Lothar joined him and stared out. 'You fought well today, boy. I was thinking you would be panicked, but you stood your ground like a warrior.'

'The enemy fell like the corn before the scythes of the Lord,' Odo said.

Lothar eyed him. 'They fell like men hit on the head with rocks, but they fell. That is all we need worry about.'

'We cannot fail,' Odo said.

'I hope you are right. There are many of them out there.'

'It will make our victory all the more glorious,' Odo said with confidence.

'Or our defeat all the more certain.'

'You should not speak in such a manner.'

'Perhaps. But we are surrounded by a force many times the size of our own, and we have no hope of rescue. And while we sit here and wait, we are cursed with the sight of our well out there, in the hands of the enemy.'

'God will provide for us.'

'We will die before He can do anything to save us.'

362

Odo was irritated to listen to such defeatist comments. To him it was so certain that they would live, that to hear Lothar talk of failure was like hearing a heretic preach against God Himself. 'You should pray more. God will help you to see your errors in a clearer light.'

'You think so? I have eyes and a brain, Odo, and I know what I see before me,' Lothar said, staring out over the uncountable fires.

Odo left him there and went down to the courtyard. There were enough men on the walls already. There was no need for him too. He watched the men huddled about the Christian fires. Outside the walls, he heard a sudden chattering and then drums beating as the Saracen soldiers danced and clapped. Here inside the walls the soldiers were anxious and fretful. They sat in small groups, every so often a man looking up at the walls as though fearing that the enemy was preparing an onslaught. Odo wanted to go among them and reassure them all. He had an absolute conviction that they would pull through this. It was one battle on the way to Jerusalem, that was all.

He went to the little chapel at the left of the gates and crossed himself with holy water from the stoup at the door, genuflecting and bowing his head to the altar. This had been built when the Greeks from the Eastern Empire constructed the castle and although the Saracens had used it for their own heretical devotions, it took little time to clear their artefacts. There were three priests and a bishop in there already, each prostrated on the floor before the altar, arms outstretched in imitation of Christ's crucifixion. Odo went to join them, lying down and extending his own arms, praying and seeking forgiveness for any sins he might have committed. The sound of cheap candles hissing, the wind outside, all brought an atmosphere of calmness and peace. He felt himself soothed as he lay there.

And then ... There was something wrong. The pain in his jaw had largely subsided. Now it was a constant ache, but it lay at the back of his mind, behind the sting of soreness where blisters had burst and rubbed raw, behind the bruises and scratches and cuts. There was something amiss. Perhaps it was his guilt speaking to him? He had committed a sin of some form, he was sure. There was a muttering in his head, although he was unsure what his offence could have been. He had striven hard to get here. The journey had been hazardous, and the fights had been very dangerous. He had struggled and fought all the way, with the elements, with the distance, with men ... and then he realised.

It was the way that he had spoken to Fulk. His brother was not so religious as he. Fulk was a more secular fellow. He liked women too much. It was the difference in their apprenticeships. Odo had spent his baking bread and speaking with the wise men of the church, while Fulk had spent his in the company of a drunken smith. Was it any surprise that Fulk had more earthy tastes? He had no real understanding of the importance of their cause. He had not been given the same insights as Odo.

That was when Odo realised the implications of his thoughts. He had been chosen! God had *selected* him. He understood the seriousness of the cause. It was more than merely the winning of the *land*, he saw. It was a battle for what was good and what was evil. It was the beginning of the final war between angels and devils. The churches all had their own depiction of the end of all time, when the Devil would be overthrown and God would rule over all from Heaven.

And that was when he felt the flaring of pride and certainty in his breast, for now he knew that he was not meant to die here.

Odo smiled. Yes, God had selected *him* to be a leader of men, and He would not permit Odo to be harmed.

CHAPTER 29

Xerigordos, Friday 10th October, 1096

The attacks on the castle continued all that week.

Lothar had been correct. He had estimated that the water would last a matter of days, and it was after only four when the green, brackish water in the cistern had been drained, and men started to search for liquid. The stores of wine had already been plundered and consumed. Now the horses were bled, with men sucking the blood from their throats, and other men started to scrabble in the soil in a vain search, not that any had enough energy to dig a well by the fifth day. Men drank urine even, so desperate were they for a little moisture. But nothing they did would help save them. Their thirst grew and grew, and few would listen to the priests promising eternal life to all who fought and died in the castle.

Xerigordos, Monday 13th October

'It will not be long now,' Lothar said on the seventh day. He was squatting beside Odo, who lay on the timbers of the castle's walkway near the gates.

Odo's lips had cracked and his face was burned from overexposure to the sun. He could hear Lothar, but he was unsure of the meaning. He found that he could understand little that was spoken by men like Lothar. The heat had dissipated his strength so severely that making sense of a foreign accent grew harder and harder. For now he merely nodded.

'You must be ready,' Lothar urged him. 'You have to rally your strength.'

'Yes, yes,' Odo said. 'God will not allow me to die. I am His servant.'

He could see that Lothar was eyeing him oddly, but that was normal. It must be hard for those who were not selected by God to understand what a man like him was privileged to feel. He was thirsty, but God's love welled in him and could extinguish even the most terrible deprivation. He knew that God would not allow him to die here. Odo was destined for greater things.

Lothar was gone. Odo did not feel lonely, not with God at his side. He peered up at the clear, blue sky and blinked at the sight of great birds whirling in the sky. He heard shouts and cries, but they made no sense to him. Then the birds were almost hidden by a cloud, and he blinked, thinking that it was a film forming over his dried eyeballs, but then he could see that it was not his imagination or sight playing tricks. There was a dark cloud, and it seemed to be rising from the gates.

'Fire!' he heard a man shout, and suddenly the castle was all activity. The Saracens must have lit a fire at the gates, and the dry timbers were at risk. There was no water with which to dowse the flames, and Odo peered about him, his eyes narrowed against the sun's glare.

A hand gripped his shoulder. 'Come! We must be away!'

He looked up into the face of Lothar, Sir Roger behind him. Both looked weary and blackened. Three surviving members of Sir Roger's company were with them: Gilles, Eudes and a man called Guarin.

'You must join us,' Sir Roger said. 'We have to go, now, and tell the other pilgrims of the risks here.'

'How?' Odo managed.

'Come with us,' Sir Roger said, and this time he smiled.

Civitot

There was much work to be done about the camp, and the pilgrims had begun to organise themselves into parties. Guillemette and her companions grouped together with some forty or more pilgrims and shared cooking and washing between them.

That morning Sybille joined Mathena and Guillemette working at the bread ovens. It was hard work, rolling out the dough on flat stones and slapping them into the hot clay pots to cook. With the sun high overhead, the women wiped their brows and sweltered. Sybille herself panted like a dog as the heat soaked into her body. She could feel it like a thick blanket lying across her shoulders as she rolled out another loaf.

Sybille threw down a fresh lump of dough and rolled it out. It felt good to be involved in productive efforts. It kept her mind from other matters. Matters like the two brothers.

Odo's outburst had shocked her, but no less surprising had been Fulk's response. To see him strike his brother and knock him down had been gratifying – and dreadful. After all, it seemed to show that she might be the cause of a separation between the two. She had no wish to be the cause of a rift between them.

She liked Fulk. He was a welcome companion. But there was a thread of fear that ran through her at the thought that he might become more than that. Already she had seen so much death on this journey. To give her heart to another man, and see him die too, was an appalling thought. She wanted the support and aid that a man could give her, but she was terrified of accepting it. To take a man's help meant to make a responsibility to him, and she was unable to consider that just now.

The ideas kept circling around and around in her skull: she wanted help but could not accept it. She noticed a headache forming, but tried to ignore it.

She worked as though in a dream; initially, it was the repetitive nature of the effort that made her feel as though her head was swimming. While performing such duties at home, she would usually slip into a thoughtless, mindless trance-like state, but today was different. Thoughts of Fulk, added to the heat and the dryness of the air, made her feel dizzy, and then nausea began to assail her. It was hard to concentrate. So much had happened to her already, with the death of Josse, then of Benet, and the constant worry about the health of her daughter, that she considered she was growing hysterical, although she felt more as though she was in a daze.

'What of the army, sister?' the woman at her side asked. She had a face the colour of an ancient acorn, and white hair that wisped about her face from beneath her wimple like feather down, but her features were entirely amiable, unless someone mentioned the Saracens. Then she would spit and curse like a woman possessed.

'The army?'

'Yes. It must be ready to move soon. Will you continue on?

I will be going to Jerusalem. I had a son who came here. He walked all the way to the Holy City, can you imagine it? But then we heard that a boy like him had died . . .' Her eyes peered into the distance for a moment, and then she smiled again. 'But he was probably wrong. My little lad is in Jerusalem now, I hope, and when I get there, I expect he'll be a rich man. So long as those murdering, butchering Saracen sons of devils haven't done for him!'

Sybille smiled vacantly. Her movements were automatic, but suddenly her hands were in the wrong place. They weren't functioning as they should. She had a roaring in her ears, and she had to frown to try to roll out the present loaf, but when she raised her hands they were shaking like leaves in a storm. Guillemette was nearby, and she glanced over to see Sybille squatting on her heels, holding her hands up to her face as though disbelieving what she saw.

'Sybille?' Guillemette called, but Sybille could not hear her. The noise had turned into a deafening thunder, and she felt as though it was waves, as if the ocean was slamming into her. She was weak, and she toppled to lie with her cheek on the sandy soil, shuddering, then suddenly she burst into tears, although she could not have said why.

'Are you feeling well?' Guillemette asked. Sybille blinked as she peered up at her, but said nothing.

'She's got sun-mazed,' Mathena said. She put her hand to Sybille's brow and felt it. 'She's burning up!'

For the rest of the morning both of the women worked fetching cool water and spreading damp cloths over Sybille's forehead, hoping to cool her down. They had found a blanket, and Sybille lay on that, an old sheet of canvas spread over her to keep her shaded. Sybille sipped the watered wine that Guillemette held up to her mouth every few moments. Guillemette knew as well as Mathena that when someone became affected by the sun, the best cure was plenty of water and liquids. Sybille looked dreadful at first. Her lips were chapped and dry, her eyes sunken, and she languished like a woman Guillemette remembered who had been struck by a racing horse in a street in Sens. Outwardly there had been no sign of injury, but her head had been dealt a dreadful blow, and she had faded away like a wilting flower.

Guillemette hated herself, but she could not help but think that were Sybille to die, then Fulk might look on her again. It was a terrible thought, but the idea that he might return to her was captivating. Even while she wrung out the cloth to spread over Sybille's brow, she could imagine the scene in her mind's eye: the shallow grave dug for Sybille's body, the weeping form of Mathena and Jeanne beside her, and then she saw poor Fulk, and she had to leave Mathena to go to him and comfort him.

She shook her head and the scene fled from her mind. Frowning now, she dabbed at Sybille's brow with perhaps more force than was necessary. After all, Sybille was to blame for much of Guillemette's current distraction and distress. It was frustrating to know that the man for whom she had developed more affection than any other was so infatuated with this widow, who showed him little if any regard.

Men were fools at the best of times, she considered. But still her thoughts would turn to him.

Xerigordos

Lothar stumbled with the men to the staircase, and from there made their way to a storeroom beside the main tower, where there was an undercroft. Sir Roger opened the door and led the way inside. Outside all was mayhem as the pilgrims fought to escape the heat of the burning gates, but in here the air was cool and refreshing. A man could almost imagine he was no longer thirsty. Odo felt the wall and was certain there was a faint moisture there. He longed to suck at it, and had closed his eyes and begun to press his lips to the rock when he was startled by a shaft of light. There was a rumble of tumbling stone, and when he opened his eyes, through the mortar dust and dancing motes he saw that there was a hole, through which he could see a portion of the sky.

'Listen!' Sir Roger said. He eyed Odo doubtfully, licking his dry lips. 'We can escape, if we are lucky. This hole is at the foot of the northern wall where the curtain meets the old keep. It was not built as strongly as a castle at home and where the two meet, the curtain butts against the keep's wall, without being fixed into it. We've pulled out some of the rocks to give an escape. We can flee from here. We will run the gauntlet of all the Saracens in the area, but they will not expect to see us. I am willing to guess that they will all be at the front of the castle, ready to capture and slay all the men within. As soon as we hear the noise of their attack and the beginning of the slaughter, we must run. We have to find horses, and we need water, so we shall run for the horse lines. It is not far. We shall ride from there and make our way to the camp at Civitot. But when we run from here, be under no illusions. If we are caught, we shall die. Is there any noise yet, Guarin?'

Guarin, who was nearest the hole, shook his head. 'It is all quiet out here,' he said.

They stood and listened. The noise from the courtyard was all of men shouting to build up their confidence for the battle to come, while from outside the gates they could hear trumpets and the sounds of jeering as the Saracens built their own courage. Then there was a rumble, like a distant roll of thunder, and Lothar said quietly, 'That will be the gate. The timbers are falling, and perhaps the gatehouse above it too.'

There came shrieks and the low, growling bellows of the pilgrims, and Odo felt his scalp moving as though there were a hundred lice beneath his skin, all marching as one. It was a hideous feeling. All at once he felt dizzy, light-headed and slightly sick. He saw the bright patch of light darken, and he saw Guarin's legs as he climbed out. Gilles followed him, then Eudes and Lothar, before Sir Roger slipped out and hissed to Odo to hurry.

He shoved his head through the gap, staring all about. Sir Roger was fleeing across the narrow plain after the others, who were already crouched in the shadow of rocks. Odo wriggled himself out of the hole and stood, jolting forward uncomfortably on legs weak from lack of drink and exercise. All the while he could hear the screams of the pilgrims as the Saracens loosed arrows through the open gates.

Lothar and Gilles were not with the others when Odo reached them. A short cry could be heard, but it was nothing compared with the gleeful shouting that emanated from before the castle. Then Lothar returned, crouching low. 'There are some soldiers, but very few.' He had found a skin of water with the sentinels, and he passed it to Sir Roger. 'Drink, all of you. We can take horses and ride when your thirst is slaked.'

The water in the skin could have been bear's piss for all they cared. It wouldn't have mattered. It would still have tasted as fresh as a mountain stream, and Odo let the wonderful liquid into his mouth and down his throat. Swallowing was joyous. He felt as though this drink had come to him straight from Heaven. It brought life, energy and renewal. He could feel the strength returning to his legs, and as the strength came, so too did the ability to think. The muzziness left him, the sense that the earth was reeling beneath his feet dissipated. It felt as though he was returning to the world from a dark, grim tunnel of deprivation into the light of a summer's day. He was more aware of the world about him, of the men, and of the joy of escape.

At the horse lines they found two boys with their throats cut. These two were the sentries Gilles and Lothar had killed before bridling the horses. The men mounted beasts which felt fresh and eager as newly broken colts. Sir Roger made no signal, but as soon as he saw all the men were ready, he turned his face to the north. They avoided roads, making their way up a steep hill that lay beyond the castle; when they were almost at the top, Odo turned and stared back.

From here he could see over the walls and across to the gate. The timbers had collapsed, and the fires formed a hellish maw, through which arrows were exchanged. Already inside the court-yard he could see a number of bodies. A storming party had been formed, and now Odo saw them plunge through the flames. They would soon be slaughtered out in the space before the gates. Even as he watched, a party hurtled through the burning gateway and into the court, and there began to lay about them with sword and spear. Captives were being led out to the space before the castle and made to kneel.

Odo had seen enough. He kicked his beast and rode off after the others.

As night fell they made camp in an open space between some hills. There were some scrubby trees, and they made a fire from broken branches against the chill.

Odo was collecting firewood, and when he began to make his way back to their campsite, he saw that Sir Roger was distraught. The man had aged during their time under siege in Xerigordos, and he was withdrawn, like a man contemplating his own execu-tion. When the men began to settle, Sir Roger sat apart, staring into the flames.

'He looks like a man who has learned his lord has died. Is he ailing?' Odo said to Gilles.

'He's learning the challenge of leadership: how to live with the death of your comrades,' Gilles said. He looked at his charge. 'I was sent here with men enough to protect him in a battle, men to guard him and serve him, but he has seen them die on the journey here, and now he is struck by the cost of his adventure. He didn't expect to see his men slain about him. It is a strange thing,' Gilles said meditatively, 'that a man can decide to go to war, assuming that he will deal death and destruction on all sides, and not consider that the enemy might have weapons and strong arms to wield them. Perhaps men would be more reluctant to go and fight if they realised that simple truth.'

'But he must realise that his men have gone to Heaven. It was promised by the Pope.'

'Yes, the Pope promised it. Yet Sir Roger has the guilt of bringing men to their deaths. Whether or not the Pope has promised them Heaven, Sir Roger has seen them die.'

Odo looked over at the young knight. Sir Roger's eyes glistened in the light from the flames as he stared, unseeing. He looked like a man who had given up, who had decided to submit to Fate and accept whatever might be hurled at him.

This was the man who should be leading them. Odo could not allow him to surrender to his misery. He walked to the knight's side. Sir Roger looked up briefly and smiled, but it did not touch his eyes.

'We should be back soon, Sir Roger,' Odo said. 'We must ensure that the men of the pilgrimage rouse themselves and prepare.'

'Prepare? Did you not see the army? It was vast, Odo. *Vast.* How could we hope to defeat so magnificent a—'

'We have no need of *hope*. God is on our side.'

'Yes. God is with us. But why then did he allow so many to die? You know, when I close my eyes all I can see are the men who were trapped with us at Xerigordos. They are all dead now.'

'What of them?' Odo said, and injected a little sharpness into his voice. 'They are gone, but today they dine with Christ in Heaven. Would you see their efforts and their sacrifice wasted?'

'Who are you to speak to me of their sacrifice?' Sir Roger snapped. 'They came here with me, and I led them to their deaths.'

'And God requires you to avenge them.'

'You know this?'

Odo stared at him unblinkingly. 'God speaks through me. I have been chosen by Him. And I choose *you* to help Him in His cause, to rid the Holy Land of heretics. Would you deny Him?'

'You say He has chosen *you*?' Sir Roger said doubtfully.

'Look at me! I am here because God chose me. If I lie, let Him strike me down here, where I stand! I swear it on my mother's soul; I swear it by the Gospels. I am His servant and I will bring about the conquest of the Holy Land in His name! Now, kneel and pray with me. Through God's grace, we will prevail!'

CHAPTER 30

Civitot, Tuesday 14th October, 1096

Alwyn was at the pavilion with Sir Walter when the news spread through the camp. It ran from man to man like a hissing, spitting wildfire in a forest, while behind it was left only a silent horror, and he saw men turning towards the pavilion with mingled hope and fear.

Sir Walter heard the noise too, and he and Alwyn walked to the pavilion's open doorflap. There they saw an astonishing sight: a straggling party was making its way towards them. In recent days Fulk was often at the pavilion, for Sir Walter valued his judgement, and now Alwyn heard him give a gasp of joy. At the front were three men: Odo, Sir Roger and Lothar. Alwyn felt none of the same joy at seeing them. He stepped away from the Normans, feeling that familiar churning in his belly, the same hatred and loathing that chewed at his stomach like a rat. If he could, he would kill them, but that would leave Sara and Jibril to fend for themselves. He could not do that to them.

'Odo, my brother!' Fulk pushed past Alwyn, his face radiating delight at seeing Odo again. 'I had thought you—'

'Wait!' Odo said. He spoke as one who demands authority and respect. Fulk's face fell to be so peremptorily dismissed. Turning to Sir Walter, Odo said, 'My lord, I carry news of terrible importance. All the men who rode with us have been slaughtered or enslaved by the Saracens after they besieged the castle we had captured.' He went on to explain all about their battle and the eventual annihilation of the Christians. 'We are all who survived.'

'How did you escape?'

This was a short, ginger-bearded man-at-arms who stood at the side of Sir Walter. Alwyn recognised him as Godfrey Burel, the commander of a group of Hungarian foot soldiers, but just now it was his tone of voice that caught his attention. It contained no jeering, but he sounded suspicious.

Odo appeared not to notice his tone. 'It was fortunate that we found an escape at the rear of the castle.'

'Although an entire Saracen army surrounded the place?'

Sir Roger's face darkened, and he made to step forward, but Odo placed a restraining hand on his forearm. It made Sir Roger grit his teeth, but Odo's intention was clearly to prevent a fight here between Christians, and Sir Roger subsided, averting his face slightly.

'Yes. We were very careful, and the Saracens were inefficient. What would you expect from heretics? They knew that the castle's garrison was dying of thirst, so they chose to assault it in a hurry.'

'You say all died?' Sir Walter said.

'Yes. Our comrades fought with courage for days, but there was no water. I am sure all were slain. When the Saracens launched their final assault they had no chance.'

377

Alwyn shook his head. 'They will have been offered the opportunity to convert to Islam. Those who agreed will be enslaved, the rest beheaded.'

Godfrey shook his head. There was a sneer on his face. 'But you and your friends here got away.'

'You think we ran like cowards?' Sir Roger blurted.

'Master Godfrey, we were lucky. I say God allowed us to escape to come here and warn the army to prepare for battle,' Odo said.

'You think so? I say this stinks of a deliberate act. The Saracens allowed you to get away. They think we will leave the shore here if we learn of their army. They think us cowards.'

'No,' Alwyn said. 'That is not how the Saracens think.'

'No?' Sir Walter said. 'You have more experience of the Saracens. What do you think they would want?'

'They will want us to meet them in pitched battle.'

'What would be wrong with that?' Odo said. 'It is why we came here.'

'Yes,' Godfrey said. 'We should march to meet them now.'

Alwyn spoke urgently. 'Sir Walter, it would be an act of folly to go after Kilij-Arslan with the army here. There are not sufficient men trained in arms to take on the Saracen forces. They will capture or destroy all of us.'

There was a muttering in the watching crowds at that. Alwyn heard the word 'coward' from several lips. He saw Odo's flash of contempt and glared about him. 'I have fought these men – you can see my scars. Recognising weakness is not cowardice, it's—'

'If God is with us, it is heresy to suggest He would let us be defeated. Besides, what would you have us do?' Odo asked, and faced Alwyn. 'Run to the shore and hope ships will come to take us back to Constantinople? We have ridden hard to bring this terrible news. It was a hard-fought battle at the castle, and our companions were slaughtered, but we escaped to warn you. We could remain here and build defences, but they will be prepared for that. There is little here which could be made defensible in the time we have. But if we march, we can attack them before they expect us. We can turn the tables on them. In their pride and arrogance they will think us cowed, but if we take the battle to them, we can swiftly succeed.'

'Charge a Saracen army?' Alwyn scoffed. He could not imagine that others would agree with Odo. 'Do you have any experience of battle? Do you know nothing about your enemy? You've seen how they fight. They are professional, terrible – and numerous! Better by far to wait here until reinforcements arrive.'

'If we take the fight to them it will show how Christians with God on their side can defeat even this great enemy host. Think how that will add to God's glory! Where is Peter the Hermit? We should consult with him.'

'He is gone to the city to discuss food with the Emperor,' Sir Walter said.

'When will he be back?'

'In a day or two.'

'He may be too late.'

Looking at the people who ringed their discussion, Odo felt satisfaction that most of the pilgrims understood the need to engage the enemy. It was clear that the same was not true of Alwyn. The Saxon registered stark horror to see that they were agreeing with Odo.

Now Alwyn spoke more loudly, trying to persuade the audience. 'You want to be glorious? Defeat is not glorious! Running back here with your tail between your legs, and all your comrades dead or enslaved behind you, is not glorious! It would be folly to risk so much when all you need do is wait a little until more men – trained men – can lend their aid.'

'God willed us to come here and fight,' Odo said.

'Yes. Not to throw away your lives needlessly, but to win back His city.'

'Then what would you do? Sit here and wait? For how long, master?' Odo asked, flinging an arm towards the east. 'Until winter comes? Or until the Saracens appear over the horizon? Soon, I have no doubt, the Saracen army will turn its attention to us. Perhaps you would prefer that they should arrive unannounced? There was no quarter given at our castle. I expect none here. We came to bring you news of this disaster and prevent one still greater. We can only win if we march to meet them, not by sitting on our arses here and waiting for them to sweep down on us!'

'Enough!' Sir Walter eyed Odo and the others. Sir Roger had been silent all this while, although he watched and listened keenly as Fulk's brother spoke. Fulk was surprised to see how the knight deferred to Odo. 'There is nothing to suggest that any of these men behaved in a manner that was anything other than honourable, and it is good to have their warnings. However, if they are right, we could have the Saracen army riding to us at any moment.'

'All the more reason why we should ride to fight them,' Godfrey said.

'We shall do nothing until we have the agreement of all the commanders here,' Sir Walter snapped. 'These men rode from here without the approval of their leaders. If they had taken a more commanding force, perhaps they would not have been slain. As it is, they were wiped out, if the evidence of these men is to be believed. So, first, I want scouts to take to horse and search the land for any sign of the enemy. We need a message to go to Peter too. When we know the force against us, and where it is, we can plan our campaign.'

'Plan our campaign? Wait to be caught between them and the sea, is more likely,' Godfrey muttered.

Sir Roger had held his tongue until now, but he could not remain silent any longer. 'I doubted him too, but I believe Odo when he says that he has been given this task by God. How else could we have escaped from the castle where we were held? How could we have made our way here safely? God's Grace saved us. I believe that it must be Odo's influence. God wants us to follow him.'

'You think God speaks through him?' Godfrey said.

'There have been less likely prophets,' Sir Roger said. 'But it is not my place to question His authority or His choice. God wills it! *Dieu le veut!*'

'Odo, it is good to see you again!' Fulk said effusively as the two walked from Sir Walter's pavilion.

'And you. I hope I see you well?'

'God has protected us.'

'Where is Peter the Hermit? Sir Walter said he was gone?'

'He has gone to Constantinople to ask for more and cheaper food. There have been fights with pilgrims convinced that the Greeks are trying to rob them. We hope Peter can persuade the Emperor to supply us more generously.'

'Good.' Odo looked at the ground.

His tone was cool, Fulk thought, but at least his brother was talking to him. He could not forget that Odo had cursed him on the last occasion that they met.

'Would you have a cup of wine?'

'Yes, although . . .' Odo was hesitant.

Fulk held out his hands. 'Come, we are brothers.'

'You know, you broke my tooth?'

'I am sorry, Odo, but you insulted my friend.'

'I see.' Odo was silent a moment, but then said, 'Are you still seeing her?'

Fulk felt his words like a physical blow. 'I see her occasionally. There's nothing more to it than that, brother. She's still in mourning. But men have tried to rape her. Would you have me leave her to that? She has nothing in this world to feed herself or her child.'

'You should be concentrating on the pilgrimage, Fulk, not on her.'

Fulk made to move away, but Odo grabbed his arm. 'I am sorry, Fulk. It is just . . . You should have seen the town of Nicaea when we took it! There were silks and riches of all kinds there!'

'That's not the point of the pilgrimage,' Fulk protested.

'The point is, to take back the land for Christ. To do that we must remove God's enemies. Whether that means killing them or driving them away, it must mean that there will be things left behind. If we can take it and sell it to help provision ourselves or find weapons, that is all to the glory of God.'

'Odo, I didn't mean to accuse you!'

'Good, brother, because I have already risked my life, and I can tell you this: God approves! I *know* it. He looked after me when it seemed inevitable that I should die, and even on the long ride back here, He was with me the whole way. I prayed to Him, and He answered me. He is with me.'

'That is good.'

'I feel honoured – touched by His grace.'

Fulk grinned. 'You don't claim much!'

'Are you laughing?'

'Odo, you have only been away a scant fortnight, and now you think you're God's chosen war leader?' Fulk said with a grin.

Odo was coldly angry in an instant. 'I don't need to question that fact. I went to war for Him, while you were here, *chastely* preserving that widow's honour!'

'I do not want to fight with you,' Fulk said, hands up in a show of submission. 'Please, Odo! You are my brother, my companion, my friend.'

Odo took a deep breath. 'No, brother. You are right. Let us take a cup of wine. We'll drink to our ambitions, and to our arrival in Jerusalem.'

'Yes,' Fulk said. 'Whenever that may be.'

'Early next year, I believe, brother. Early next year.'

Civitot, Wednesday 15th October

While Fulk was glad to have his brother back, he felt it would be politic to keep away from Sybille for a while. He had no wish to cause another argument. The thought that if Odo had died while riding down to Xerigordos, their last words would have been those of enemies was enough to leave a cold unease in Fulk's belly. Still, their enmity was healing. He would not willingly pull at the scab.

In Odo's absence Sir Walter had come to make more use of Fulk, and Fulk had grown to respect him. Sir Walter was a tough, uncompromising old fighter who took time to assess men, but once he felt he knew their measure, he valued them. Fulk was new to the world of battles, but he had a shrewd head, and Sir Walter appreciated his wisdom when negotiating with Greek merchants or bringing a general discussion around to his point of view.

The next morning was bright and clear. It was hard to believe that any danger existed, with the sun gleaming on the waves sluggishly slapping against each other out to sea.

Fulk would remember that morning for the rest of his life. He was listening to Sir Walter discussing food transport with

Greek merchants, all clad in rich silken robes that Fulk privately suspected they would not have been able to afford before they started supplying the pilgrim army, when a sudden commotion came to their ears. There had been no news of the enemy since Odo's arrival, and while many of the men in the camp were preparing to pack and march to meet the Saracens Odo had warned of, there was little urgency about them. But suddenly there was shouting and fearful voices, and Sir Walter held up a hand, his head cocked. The man before him continued extolling the virtues of his grain over that of other merchants, a fact hotly disputed by the others, so Sir Walter nodded to Fulk, who stepped before the merchant as Sir Walter walked from the pavilion, bellowing for an explanation of the noise. Fulk made it clear that the negotiation was adjourned, and hurried out to see what was happening.

A rider was cantering towards them, his horse flecked with foam and sweat. He swung from the saddle and hurried to join them, panting his news breathlessly. A party of Saracens had found some pilgrims only a few leagues from the camp. This man had been in a copse at the time, and witnessed the appearance of the Saracens, the capture of the Christians, the separation of the youngest from the main group and the beheading of the others. He was the sole survivor. While he spoke, the army's commanders arrived to hear his words. He had to repeat his tale three times as more and more men came to listen.

Godfrey Burel leaned forward to the breathless, grieving messenger. 'How many in the party?'

'Only some hundred horsemen. Not more, I think.'

'And they rode back where?'

'East and south. I saw them go, and as soon as I could, I came back here. I couldn't do anything to protect them, sir! I was alone. If I'd tried—'

'You did nothing wrong,' Sir Walter said. 'It was better that you brought news of this attack to us.' He turned to the other commanders and Fulk could see his face was twisted with concern. 'We must send to the city and ask for reinforcements. Someone must tell Peter the Hermit, too. He must come back at once.'

'He didn't come back yesterday, when he was told about the men killed at the castle.' Looking up, Fulk saw it was Godfrey Burel. 'Why wait? If we do, they'll likely wipe us out! We've no defences to speak of, and the idea that we, the army, should sit on our arses is mad. It's not what I came here for! We all travelled here to fight for God. He will protect us if we take the initiative. I say we march at once and attack!'

Fulk saw Alwyn shake his head. The Saxon had walked to join the gathering when the messenger appeared, and now he spoke with ill-contained frustration. 'If you march to them, you will be slaughtered. Kilij-Arslan has a large army, and if he is approaching you may be sure that he will have collected together all his vassals to destroy us. Better by far to evacuate this place and wait for—'

'That is the word of a Byzantine!' Godfrey said contemptuously.

'I am a Saxon, not Greek! I have seen their host at first hand. I know these men; I have fought them. They have an awesome army.'

'I don't know why you are here! All you want to do is avoid battle. Not me! I'm a foot soldier. I don't need a knight's belt and spurs to give me courage. I have enough of that already. All I need is a spear and a sword and shield, and I can go and kill all the Saracens you want! I say we go to them!'

'Oh, really? And what would be your strategy?' Sir Walter said sarcastically.

'What strategy do we need? God wants us to throw these heathens off His Holy Land, so all we need to do is find them and

385

He will help us with the rest. We find them, and we fight them until they're all dead.'

There was a cry of 'God wills it!' and others took up the call, with *'Dieu le veut!'*

'God prefers to help those who think through their actions first!' Sir Walter snapped.

'What, are you scared of a fight? These are heathens, not Christians!'

'It matters not! One Christian may fight ten thousand, but even with the courage of an Achilles or a Hector, he would still be overwhelmed,' Alwyn cried.

'If you have courage, you will march now!' Godfrey said. He turned and held his arms wide, speaking to the men of the army who had joined the ring about the bickering commanders and were now listening with interest. 'Look at these *distinguished* knights, my friends! Look at them! All cautious and wary in the face of the enemy's advance. All would have you think that they were the boldest, bravest, most honourable men, and yet they want to remain here. Well, let them! I have a spear and a sword, and I'm happy to walk out now and fight any number of these Saracen scum! Who will march with me?'

There were many bellows of support, and more than a few catcalls and jeers at the knights, and Alwyn felt a rising anger and panic to hear them. His mind was bent to Jibril and Sara. If these fools wanted to throw themselves needlessly against the army now massed against them, he would not see his servants slain needlessly.

Nearby, Sir Walter bristled to hear the foot soldier's declamation and stepped forward, raising both his hands over his head. 'Listen to me! *Listen!* If you march out to war like this, without preparation, without knowing the size of the enemy, without knowing his line of march, without knowing *anything* about him, you will be slain!'

'That is heresy!' Godfrey countered. 'If God wills it, we cannot fail!'

'God will not bend Heaven and earth to help those who do nothing for themselves!' Sir Walter shouted as the crowd broke into loud insults. There was a sneer from one of Godfrey's men, and Sir Walter shoved him in the breast, his hand going to his sword. Instantly Godfrey and three of his companions had their hands on their own weapons, and it was only when Alwyn stepped between them, pleading for an audience, that the two parties broke apart.

'My lords, noble knights, pilgrims all! Let us not do the work of our enemies for them! Do we want to commit murder here? Focus on the real enemy! They are out there, perhaps marching to meet us even now. Sheath your swords and keep them ready for the Saracens!'

'And what will you do if we march?' Godfrey demanded.

Alwyn looked at him with disdain and held up his savaged hand, showing where his finger had been shorn away. 'I will march! I will march at your side, but only if Sir Walter tells me that the time is right. I would not willingly march into a trap. Would you?'

'I march for God. If He wills it, I put my faith in Him.'

CHAPTER 31

Civitot, Wednesday 15th October, 1096

'Fulk, walk with me,' Sir Walter said. He led the way back to the pavilion, where the merchants still stood hopefully, and the guards hustled them from the tent. 'Fulk, I need to you take a message to Peter, telling him all that has passed today.'

'No, Sir Walter. I am your servant, but I will not run from this battle like a coward. If I go, it will be late tomorrow or the day after before I could return and I would be too late to take part.'

'Someone must warn the Emperor.'

'Not I. I will remain at the battle until we win or I die.'

'Your commitment does you honour. Very well, I will find another.' He sighed and stared through the open tentflap. 'The foot soldiers insist on marching at once. So be it. They may be right. Even if I were to delay and wait to seek for the Saracens, in all likelihood they would find us first, and in that case, we may well be destroyed. If we march out, at least we may bring them to fight on ground of our choosing.'

He was about to continue when there came a call at the

pavilion's entrance. Sir Walter barked, 'Enter!' and Sir Roger walked in, ducking beneath the doorway.

'Sir Walter, I would be glad if you would accept my sword at your side.'

'I would be honoured. Will you take my commands?'

'Yes. I would be content to ride at your side, but if you prefer, I will swear allegiance to you now.'

'Kneel, then,' Sir Walter said.

Sir Roger was surprised, but he bent his knee and turned his face to the ground, holding up his hands. Sir Walter placed his own about them and took Sir Roger's oath, before helping him to his feet.

'Sir Roger, I wished to have you swear your oath, rather than agree to ride at my side, because I may have to give you an order that goes against your instincts.'

'I can swear to you that I would never need to be ordered to fight!'

'That,' Sir Walter said with a little smile, 'was not my fear. It is possible that the battle will go so badly for us, that I will have to command you to retreat from the battle.'

'Sir Walter, I could not.'

'Sir Roger, you *will*, if I deem it necessary. I may desire you to leave the field and bring news of the disaster to the Emperor and to Peter the Hermit. This would not be a matter of cowardice, but an act of courage that may help to ensure that the next pilgrims will be better advised. I will ensure that my clerk gives you a letter confirming this agreement. If we are too sorely pressed, we will need someone to bear tidings to the Emperor.'

'Surely you could do so yourself?'

'Me? No, I will not be able to do so, for if I were to be seen leaving, the battle would become a rout in moments and all our men would be slaughtered. But at least if you return and tell of the tactics and methods of these Saracens, some good may come of our deaths.'

Fulk felt a cold chill to hear his words. 'Do you think that we could lose?'

Sir Walter had forgotten Fulk was still there. He took a deep breath. 'Fulk, if I were marching this army against a force led by the King of France, or the Holy Roman Emperor, I would know that my plan must fail. A bickering force of pilgrims, pitted against the martial power of the King or the Emperor, must surely collapse. These Saracens are not so powerful as a Christian ruler, of course, but we do not know their strength, only that your brother told us there were countless thousands. He could be wrong, and this force that beheaded the Christians might be only a scouting party; but I fear that it is the precursor to the main army, and if that is correct and the host of the Saracens is near us, we can only put our faith in God and fight with all our strength.'

'What if we fail?'

'That is easy. If we fail, we die.'

Sybille was mostly recovered now. For that first day she had been weak and feverish, and although she had improved with rest and water, she was still very weary. Guillemette was convinced that she was so enfeebled because she had spent so much time looking after her daughter during the weary miles to reach Constantinople. Now that Richalda was fit and well again, after resting here in the camp, at last Sybille had been struck down herself. It certainly seemed more an attack of complete exhaustion, rather than a sun-fever.

'You should let me get him,' Guillemette had said during that first afternoon. 'Let me fetch Fulk. He should know you are like this.'

'Why? If I am dying, what good would it do him? Better that he doesn't see me like this,' Sybille said.

'He cares for you. He would wish to comfort you.'

'He is not my kin. It would be unseemly for him to be here. I am a widow, not a concubine. I am in mourning still. Having a single man come to see me now would not be right.'

Guillemette was sure that Sybille was not trying to be hurtful, but that word, *concubine*, stung, nonetheless. She had to take a deep breath before she spoke again. 'If you die and you do not allow him to see you, how would he feel? You do not think of him at all?'

'I do, yes,' Sybille said. 'But if I call him to come to me when I am unwell, what would that achieve? You think I don't care about him, that I am heartless? I *do* care, and that is my agony. I cannot trust myself with him. I yearn for him, but I am still a widow, and I may not show my feelings for him.'

'You are on pilgrimage, and—'

'And what? You think that makes any difference?' Sybille hissed. She grasped Guillemette's forearm, making Guillemette wince. 'Listen to me! I set off with a husband all those months ago, and now I have nothing! Do you think I want to lose another man? If I give my heart to Fulk – what remains of my heart – there will be nothing left if it is broken again!'

'He wouldn't—'

'I don't care about fidelity! What if he dies? Who knows which men will die, which will live? Perhaps, if we do reach Jerusalem, then I can think again, but now? Now, I do not dare fall in love. It would kill me!'

Guillemette recalled that conversation now. The camp was astir, with pilgrims gathering belongings, women packing food for their men, some of them preparing themselves for another march, and she looked across at Sybille. She was sitting with

Richalda, playing. A nervous smile was on her face, as if she feared breaking down at any moment.

Richalda looked up as Mathena walked past, a basket full of loaves resting on one hip. 'Are we going soon?'

Guillemette smiled at her, and looked at her mother.

'No, my sweetheart. I don't think we want to see another battle, do we?' Sybille said. 'We would only get in the way of the men, wouldn't we?'

'Others are going, aren't they?'

Guillemette looked at Sybille. She sat with a rigid tension in her muscles that spoke of her terror at the thought of another march towards slaughter. Sybille looked as though seeing another battle would send her raving. Guillemette sighed inwardly, but leaving Sybille and her child behind alone was unthinkable.

'Some are, Richalda, but I don't think it's very sensible. Do you? I think we would do better to remain here and prepare to welcome the men back, once they have won their battle.'

Alwyn stood and watched as the knights and their men-at-arms went to their shelters to begin to prepare. He saw Sir Roger hurrying from Sir Walter's pavilion a little later, and felt the acid in his belly at the sight. Alwyn still wanted to kill the man, but he must not, lest news of his act came to the Vestes' ear.

But in a battle, sometimes it was possible to kill a man and others not realise.

With that thought he hurried to his own tent. Even as he went, the camp was erupting into urgent activity. Men were rushing about – two barging into Alwyn and making him mutter under his breath. They were gathering their weapons and stores for two days or more. No one knew how long this might take. Women hurried to the springs and wells, filling leather flasks and costrels, hurriedly packing their few goods, while children screamed and bickered at the sudden, unaccustomed busyness. Wailing came from one side of the camp as men took leave of their womenfolk, while in other groups the women shouldered weapons along with their husbands, prepared to stand or die beside them.

Alwyn paused, standing still as the men and women hurtled about him, watching them with perplexity. They were not fearful! There was an air almost of a feast day about the people, as though they need only turn up at a battle for God to deliver the enemy to them. But Alwyn remembered the battle at Hastings and the other at Dyrrhachium. He could see all the bodies littering the ground at both, and he knew that although God could certainly destroy any enemy He wished, a man would be well advised to shift for himself if he wanted to live to see the victory.

Soon, he feared, most of these men would be dead. That thought settled like lead in his mind as he continued on his way.

At the flap of his shelter Sara was waiting for him, Jibril behind her, both staring out at the activity with fear.

'Sara, pack your things. You must return to the city. Take Jibril with you. I am called to battle.'

'I will not go.'

'You have to. I need you to look after Jibril,' he snarled.

Jibril sank back inside the shadows, but Sara stood her ground, blocking his way inside. 'I will not go,' she said.

Alwyn glared at her, then began to throw all his belongings into a small sack. 'You have to go, woman. I go to fight in a battle, and I may well die there. If I die, you will be safer back in the city than out here. The army may wipe out these foolish pilgrims, and then they will come here and rape and kill all the women. You understand me?' He looked up, then dropped his sack and took her by the upper arms. 'You have to leave here, or I will not be able to fight. I cannot go to battle knowing that you are at risk here.'

'If you know I am here, you will fight harder,' she said defiantly, her chin raised. 'I stay here.'

'What of Jibril?'

'I am ready.'

Alwyn turned to see that his servant had bound a long knife about his waist, and now he stood determinedly, waiting. 'I will see to your horse and polish your sword. I am a good servant. You need me with you.'

Staring from one to the other, Alwyn felt his eyes smarting. 'You fools!' he said, and then smiled, turning away to wipe at his cheeks so they could not see the tracks of his tears.

Odo ran to the shore after hearing the news of the army's imminent departure. Jeanne was there in her usual place near a great black rock at the water's edge, and he hurried to meet her.

'My lady, we have wonderful news!' he said.

'Yes?'

'We have found the enemy army at last! We shall ride to them and, with God's aid, we must defeat them!'

Jeanne's face paled. 'But you told of the vast size of their army.'

Odo had no doubts. 'God must succeed, no matter how powerful the enemy. This will be the last great battle, during which the forces of the heathens must be utterly destroyed, and then . . . Jerusalem!'

'You are sure of this?' Jeanne said.

'Woman, you don't understand. When the forces of God stand against the heathen, God's people must inevitably win,' Odo said condescendingly.

'I hope so. I am scared, Odo. I fear losing you, and being all alone. What would happen to me then?'

'You need not worry yourself, maid. I won't give you up so easily,' Odo said. 'I will be back, and when I am, I will protect you.'

And then, I will marry you, he promised himself, looking down tenderly. He wanted to kiss her, but he dare not. Not until they were married. Otherwise his desire and passion could overwhelm him. Better by far to remain chaste for now.

Fulk rode with Sir Walter, while Odo rode further ahead with the scouts. Sir Walter's company included Sir Roger and his men, and a scowling, unhappy Alwyn, who glowered at the surrounding hills like a man being taken to the gallows, Jibril trotting at his side.

There was an air of suppressed excitement in the host as they rode out from the camp in six columns, each of them marching under a proud, glittering banner. Men had spent their spare moments stitching their pilgrim crosses more securely on their breasts, while squires and servants spent their time polishing and sharpening all the various weapons that the knights needed. The noise had been deafening. For Fulk it was a relief to be marching at last.

The army marched with the slow determination of men who wore thickly padded gambesons or heavy coats of mail. The knights were the most heavily weighed down, with their mail coverings and heavy steel helmets, but the ordinary foot soldiers were forced to bear all their own equipment. Only a few had the aid of a donkey. Most of the pack animals had been eaten on the way to Constantinople or here at Civitot.

Fulk rode on through the dust with his head hunched, eyes slitted against the grit. Every particle that entered his eye seemed to scour the surface of his eyeball like the point of a dagger.

'Smile, boy! You may never see a sight like this again,' Peter of Auxerre chuckled at his side. He seemed impervious to the clouds of dust rising all about them.

'Smile?' Fulk's eyes were watering unceasingly. 'At what? The sight of a division of men walking? I would smile if there were a pretty woman to smile back at me. But this? All I can feel is my eyes being worn away with every blink.'

'You need to take life more simply,' Peter said. 'Look at him. He has a sense of humour.'

He pointed to a priest who rode back down the column with a beaming smile on his face, assuring all who would listen to him that this was a glorious day to die, that God Himself would welcome with open arms any one of the pilgrims who died on the battlefield, because their presence here meant that they would die without sin. 'Killing heretics is no crime! It is the path to eternal life! Slay as many as you can, and know that every wound on your body will be blessed in the sight of Christ! God Himself will reward you, all of you!'

Fulk watched the cheerful priest with bemusement. 'He is very confident of God's thoughts.'

'I would be prepared to wager that the good priest has been supping at the communion wine,' Peter said. 'With the Masses said for all these men, there can't have been much left over, but he may have thought to drink it all to save it from the Saracens, in case they did break through us.'

'Will they, do you think?' Fulk asked. He had to repeat his question.

'Mayhap. If it looks like they will, we'll just have to put our faith in our nags and hope they can take us to safety.'

Fulk nodded. It was not the most reassuring reflection.

It was as they came over the side of a small hill that they saw the Saracen army planted on the road before them.

'Look at them!' a man blurted.

Peter puffed out his cheeks. 'Today we earn our bread, boys,' he said.

*

Alwyn puffed out his cheeks to see the mass of men in their path. In his mind's eye he saw again the Normans at Dyrrhachium, their flags fluttering softly in the gentle breeze, their armour grey-brown with rust, but these Moors were not formed of the same clay. These men were proud warriors, and they stood out against the ground like sable-clad giants. Their limbs gleamed when the sun struck them, shining brightly in his eyes as if reflected by ten thousand mirrors. Helms shone like pure silver, and their flags were not the dull, sun-bleached linens of the Normans, but silken banners which gleamed and flamed.

'Good gracious God,' one of the men murmured, while others were muttering the Paternoster.

'Jibril, I need you to return to Sara. Go to her and tell her that if I do not return by dawn tomorrow, she must take you to the sea and return to Constantinople. You must go to the palace and speak to the Vestes and tell him the size of this army. Do you understand me?'

'Yes. But I stay here with you. Your servant . . . your squire.'

'No. I need you to run to Sara. Right now, Jibril. Do not delay.'

Alwyn watched as the lad trotted away, darting between the horses and mules of the army, until at last he saw the slender figure breast a little hill and disappear behind it.

'Right, then,' he said, and tugged at his sword belt, pulling his gloves a little tighter, checking the long knife in its sheath and thrusting it home again. 'At least you're safe, Jibril. God help all of us.'

At the outset, all Fulk knew was utter dread. The enemy was so numerous, so vast, that he felt deep in his bones a cold certainty that it was impossible for him to survive this clash of arms. All across the valley before him was a wooded area, but beyond that there stood an army so massive that he could not hope to count the men. It would be like trying to count the ants in a disturbed nest. The sun glinted from lance-tips, helmets and gleaming mail, while silken banners and flags rippled over their heads, but he still had the impression of black beetles, perhaps because of the menace that the horde represented. It was a scene of colour and pageantry, but that did not detract from the ominous threat emanating from the ranks of men and horses.

His belly seemed to turn to liquid slops, and he had to clench his buttocks in an effort to save himself the ultimate embarrassment. He could not help but look for Odo, wondering if his brother felt a similar emasculation, but Odo was staring ahead fixedly like a huntsman watching for the quarry before releasing his hounds. For an instant Fulk resented Odo's calmness, but then his attention was distracted.

There was a movement as the Christian divisions advanced. At either flank, squadrons of Saracen cavalry moved out away from the main army, while individual riders from each company rode back to the centre of the Saracens, to where a great banner danced in the wind.

Sir Walter observed these and pointed them out to his commanders. 'Look! They report our appearance. They have good systems of control and communication, then, which means that banner is the place where their leader rests. He is the man we must remove.'

Alwyn muttered, 'They are well versed in all forms of warfare.'

'Aye, they are a professional army.' Sir Walter was silent a moment as he sat on his massive destrier, his men clustered all about him. Then he looked up and around at the men nearby. 'Gentlemen, good knights and common men, this is the moment we have sought. We came here to seek the Saracens and destroy them so that we could continue on our way to Jerusalem. We have found the Saracen army, and it is a great army. We could hardly have expected to find so magnificent an opponent, but it matters not, for we have God on our side. No man may stand against us while we have Him with us.'

Near his left side, Fulk could not help but think that when Godfrey Burel had said the same, Sir Walter had not been so convinced, but he knew his knight was attempting to build the spirits of his men.

Now Sir Walter continued more loudly: 'All of us shall ride today into history, for who will forget the charge that won Jerusalem for God? You will all of you win great glory today, and you shall be a source of jealousy for all those who did not join us. They will feel themselves dishonoured, those who stayed at home and so missed this opportunity for renown. So ride hard, be bold, show your Christian courage!' With that, he called out to the foot soldiers, bellowing a similar message of boldness and courage. Finally he beckoned his priest forward, and the men all bent their heads as prayers were spoken.

As the priest made the sign of the cross and finished, Sir Walter lifted his head. He cast a look to left and right. 'We shall ride onwards at the trot, my friends.'

Fulk felt his horse begin to jog forwards before his legs or hands could give the command. His beast knew what was expected of it, and he was riding straight towards the Saracens at the far right wing.

The horses at both flanks were already breaking into a canter, and Fulk heard Peter grunt in approval.

'What?' Fulk demanded, crouching low and trying to maintain his seat. He was unused to riding at any time, and sitting atop this rocking, jerking creature was almost as alarming as facing a Saracen on one. Trotting was hard enough; the thought of galloping was as terrifying as jumping off a cliff.

'They know what they are doing. Send out the horsemen with bows first, to soften up the front. Poor devils don't realise what they're facing, though, if they think that their little arrows will hurt the knights!'

Fulk saw what he meant. As the horses rode on, the front ranks of knights began to charge, their lances lowering as their destriers took up the gallop, but just as it looked as though the Saracen horsemen must be speared like so many boars in the woods, Fulk saw the Saracens disperse, fading away into clots of ones and twos, some running along the front of the knights, some running along their flanks, while others turned tail and ran, and over the thunder of the Christian hoofs, Fulk heard blood-curdling screams and shouts, as though all the demons from Hell had been set loose on the field of battle.

He heard the bright, clear tones of a horn blown, and saw that ahead the pennons and flags were lowered, and realised that Sir Walter and his knights were beginning their charge. Peter did not follow immediately, and Fulk looked over at him, but Peter pointed with his chin at the knights. 'Let them ride on ahead. We're to hit the enemy as a second wave, then give the knights spare spears and remounts.'

A squire whom Fulk vaguely recognised bellowed a command, lifted his fist holding a lance, and pointed it after the knights. Fulk could hear nothing but the blood surging in his veins and the pounding of his heart. The air was full of dust and grit, and he coughed and spat. He had never felt so alone as he did now, in this mass of men and horses with roiling clouds of fine sand obscuring the sight of the Saracens. To his alarm the beast beneath him began to increase his speed, and settled into a brisk canter along with all the others about him. Then the squire urged his mount into a gallop, but even as he did, three knights came hurtling back towards them. All three were wearing tunics that had been slashed and torn, the shield of one was dented and had a huge notch hacked out of the top, and a second had an arrow protruding from his flank.

Two took up fresh lances and joined the men. The knight with the arrow in his side remained, his head low – he reminded Fulk of a panting hound sitting after a long chase – while the army flowed about him like river water about a small rock.

Fulk felt his beast pick up speed, and now he was forced to crouch lower, feeling the saddle rise and club his buttocks with every pace. He heard the low growling roar of the Christian fighters as they gave their battle cries, and the lances were lowered as a line of Saracen horse appeared in front of them, and then the Saracens seemed to separate and disappear, and he realised that they were allowing the Christians to pound onwards without finding any of them. At the same time he saw a man in front of him struck by three arrows, and he reeled in his saddle, then fell. A second man shrieked and hunched over as an arrow struck his neck. His spear point dropped, hit the ground, and he was catapulted from his saddle by the spear's butt under his armpit. A third man was hit and fell instantly, while two more men were flung from their horses by arrows.

At last Fulk realised that Saracen bowmen were riding parallel with his company, loosing arrows with abandon as they rode. He pointed to them, shouting at Peter, but others had seen them, and broke away from the main group to chase after the Saracens, who immediately took flight. Before Fulk could give a jeer of pride to see the Saracens ride away, he saw them turn, inexplicably, and loose more arrows over their horses' rumps. They were as accurate with their bows in retreat as they were at the charge, and another Christian was tumbled from his mount. The man behind him had his horse hit, and it collapsed, head falling, snapping its neck with a horrible crackle even as the rider was thrown. He landed on his head and didn't rise again.

Fulk watched with horror, and realised that there were more Saracens behind him. They had ridden behind the Christians, and had all but encircled Fulk's companions as well as Sir Walter's. Their retreat was sliced in two by a knife of Saracen steel. 'Peter! *Peter!* They're behind us!' Fulk screamed, but he didn't know if Peter heard him or not. Peter was lifting his sword to cut at an unhorsed Saracen on the ground, and as he did so Fulk saw his opponent raise his bow and loose an arrow into Peter's face. His head was thrown back, and as Fulk stared in appalled fascination, Peter fell back against his cantle and rode away, already dead.

CHAPTER 32

Three miles from Civitot, Wednesday 15th October, 1096

Alwyn drew his sword and stabbed at the nearest Saracen, but missed. He was too out of training for this, he thought. Hacking at another man, his sword bounced from the man's armour, and almost rebounded into his own thigh. He decided to use the point and try to break through his enemy's armour, but it was not easy. Saracen armour was noted for its strength, and he could not break through the man's mail. The man kept up a steady series of blows aimed now at Alwyn's head and now at his belly or thighs, and in the flurry of strikes Alwyn found it hard to block and parry each. A lucky stab sheared into the man's cheek and he cried out once, then fell, to be trampled.

Alwyn had a moment to breathe. He had seen Sir Roger earlier; the young knight was beset by enemies on all sides, and Alwyn found himself praying that he might not fall, so that he could himself strike the final blow. He could ride up behind the knight and assail him from behind while he was engaged by Moorish knights. Then, as he fell, Alwyn would tell him why he had attacked him, remind him of the name of his father among the English, and leave him to die in the dirt like the . . .

Alwyn was struck a great coup from behind, and he fell forward. His opponent aimed a cut at his neck, and Alwyn jerked aside as the sword fell, shearing through his horse's neck and lodging there. As the man tried to wrest his blade free, the horse reared, and Alwyn shoved his sword at the man's exposed armpit. It slid into the Moor's chest with ease, and the man toppled from his horse even as Alwyn's steed crumpled with blood spraying from his nostrils. Alwyn had time only to kick his feet clear of the stirrups and throw himself aside as his beast fell dead.

There were men and horses all about. From the ground, it seemed as if he was in a forest of hoofed legs. Men rode past, battering at each other with their great swords ringing. A knight rode at him to stab him with a sword, but recognised he was no Saracen at the last moment and instead swung his blade to smite another man. Alwyn gripped his sword in both hands, praying for a miracle.

'Don't let me die here,' he prayed, and quickly kissed the cross of his sword.

There was a shout and a thunder, and he looked up to see a Saracen aiming an arrow at him; he commended his soul to God, for in that instant he knew he was looking at death itself, but then a man rode up behind the archer and brought a sword down on the man's head with such violence that Alwyn saw it slice halfway down the Saracen's forehead. The arrow flew wild, and as the knight wrestled to free his sword, Alwyn realised it was Sir Roger.

His sword free once more, Sir Roger saluted Alwyn and rode on.

Alwyn pursed his lips and returned to the fray.

*

Some ranks behind Fulk, Gilles felt his blood surge to be in battle again. Sir Roger had been pensive as they rode towards this place, but as soon as they caught sight of the enemy and the call to battle was heard, all hesitation and irresolution were washed away. It was good to see that all the hard-learned lessons of Sir Roger's youth had mingled with his experience on the journey. They had given him confidence in himself and in the men about him.

Riding at his side, Gilles looked about him. There were so few of them now, with only Eudes and Guarin remaining from the original guard and Lothar, the tall Rhinelander, loping along with them. It gave Gilles a fleeting sadness that they were all gone.

He felt no fear of his own death. He would be happy to rejoin the others in Heaven, if that was his fate today. For now, all he felt was the elation that came with the end of anticipation. As he spurred his mount to the canter along with his knight, he felt a thrilling in his breast and a broad smile washed across his face. He glanced at Lothar, who maintained a stolid glower in the face of the enemy, but when he looked across at Gilles, the Rhinelander too began to grin, and the two bellowed their excitement as the horses began to lengthen their stride, shaking their heads, the roar of the wind deafening them and making them blink.

The lines before them were pelting ahead now, and Gilles saw them slam into the ranks of the Saracens: initially the heavy knights, while their squires and men-at-arms formed separate lines behind them, so that the attack was a rippling like the sea rushing the shore, first one, then a second, then a third, and the Saracens were washed away like the sands. Yet always there were more of them. Their forces were vast, an unimaginable number, Gilles thought, and he was preparing to gallop when suddenly a flight of arrows came, black as a murder of crows. Gilles felt one strike and bounce from his shoulder, but to his left a horse dived to the ground with an arrow in his head, flinging his rider to the ground as a large force of Saracens appeared on the right. There was a terrifying moment of panic, but then Gilles saw Lothar rise in his stirrups and remove a Saracen head with one sweep of his sword, and Gilles roared, charging the nearest riders with his spear. He struck one man, and saw him crumple like a roll of parchment struck with a club, before aiming at another. There was a jerk at his arm as the tip caught the man in the breast and he too fell away, and Gilles realised that his lance had sheared off. All that remained was a four-foot stump with a vicious point of splintered wood.

A Saracen rode at him with his sword upraised, and Gilles thrust the remains of his weapon into the man's face, sending him tumbling backwards. Gilles threw the stump of his lance at another man and drew his sword, looking for Sir Roger, Guarin, Eudes or Lothar, but it was already impossible to see them in the press. There was only a mass of men, thrusting and stabbing at each other, seen through the hot dust that rose in choking swirls to blind them.

In the confusion Gilles was dizzy, wondering in which direction the main force was and where he was pointing now, but the onrush of Saracens was too powerful for him to get his bearings. He found his horse being forced back, while he blundered about with his sword, flailing to protect his beast and himself as weapons slammed at him, bruising him beneath his mail and padded gambeson, feeling the jarring of heavy blows on his helmet. He felt his arm tiring, the dusty breath tearing at his throat, but then there came a scream like a banshee and suddenly three men were felled from his side, and Lothar was there, his sword whirling in his hand. The Saracens held back from that, but one man darted forward with an arrow nocked to the string, and would have let it fly but for Eudes. The man-at-arms was too far away to stab the archer, but he swiftly pulled out his long-bladed dagger and flung it. It missed the man's face, but sliced into the palm of his hand, making him shriek, but also cutting the bowstring that cracked like a breaking rock, one half slicing neatly up the archer's cheek and into his eye.

As he was trying to pull the blade from his hand, Eudes reached him, took the knife and stabbed the man in the throat. As he did so, Gilles and Lothar reached his side. Guarin was nowhere to be seen. Gilles wondered whether he had fallen.

'They have surrounded the others,' Eudes said, pointing with his bloody dagger. 'The whole of Sir Walter's force is in there.'

Gilles could see the banners of the knights rising over the pennants and flags of the Saracens who blocked their path. More arrows were directed towards them, and he swatted at them irritably, like a bull flicking his tail at flies. 'We cannot break through this many.'

'If we stay, we must be killed,' Lothar said. 'Where is Sir Roger?'

'By God's blood!' Gilles said. There was no sign of him immediately. And then he caught a glimpse of a warrior battling like a berserker, his sword held two-handed as he dealt blows on all sides from his destrier. There was one man at his side, and Gilles recognised Guarin. 'There!'

Sir Roger was failing. He could feel his strength ebbing as he blocked, slashed and stabbed. The sword in his hands was slick, the grip growing slippery as blood dripped down the blade and ran onto his fist and the hilts, but he could not surrender. His father would hear of his death, he thought, and his soul would be forever saved. That was a glorious prospect. Guarin was with him, laying about with his sword while the Saracens kept on battling, but then Sir Roger saw Guarin turn to him. There was an arrow at his belly, and as Sir Roger urgently tried to go to him, another arrow struck the man's throat and he slid from his horse.

'No!' Sir Roger bellowed. He could only stare as Guarin landed heavily on the ground, his hands at the arrow in his throat at though trying to pull it loose, and then his hands fell away.

He was dead. There was nothing Sir Roger could do for him. He felt an arrow pluck at the tunic at his waist, spinning away as it hit the mail beneath, and turned to ride down the archer before he could pluck a fresh missile. The archers here needed space, he realised. If they were pressed hard, a determined cavalry attack could crush them, but first a man had to catch them, or hold them against a river or rockface. If they had an escape, they would melt away before the knight's charge. This one spurred his beast and turned to run before Sir Roger could catch up with him. He turned in his saddle and drew a fresh arrow, but then the man began a loud keening wail, slumped over his horse's rump. And behind him, his sword still covered in the archer's blood, was Gilles.

'Sir Roger, we have to get you away from here.'

'No!' Sir Roger snarled. 'I'll not retreat in the face of these heretics!'

'If you don't, you'll die!'

'I will not!' Sir Roger said, staring about him. And then he saw Sir Walter. There was a momentary gap in the press, and he saw the knight clearly, battling with three Moorish horsemen. Sir Roger saw Sir Walter's helmet turn towards him, and felt shame to see the leader of the pilgrim army so beset. He spurred his mount, bellowing his war cry, but even as his beast began to surge forward, he saw an arrow strike Sir Walter in the face, and then he was hidden from view. The men moved, the battle flowed onwards, but the window into Sir Walter's plight was gone.

'*No!* Sir Walter!'

'Sir Roger, please! We must go!'

'What of the rest of the men?'

'Perhaps they have retreated to reform the charge, sir?'

Sir Roger nodded vaguely. His heart still thundered with the thrill and fascination of the battle, and now his eyes were all over the field, seeking his friends. 'There are some over there. It looks like a pilgrim banner,' he said.

For Fulk, at least, from the moment he saw Peter die, the day became one of confusion: gaping mouths, fierce excitement and visceral horror.

Fulk wanted to go and stop Peter's horse, but already events were overtaking him. More Saracens were riding about the encircled knights and men, and although the foot soldiers were trying to reach the knights to defend them, the Saracen horses were too swift, darting in close to loose an arrow or two, then retreating as speedily before a man could try to attack them in his turn. They kept up their incessant waves of archers riding in, wheeling about, riding away, and each time more men would fall from the Christian side.

'This is madness!' Fulk screamed, and stared about him, unsure what to do, where to aim his mount, how to attack the enemy. That was when the Saracens burst through the Christian flank and hacked its way into their midst. He saw a black-bearded heathen screaming in his unintelligible tongue, his curved sword cutting all about, before a lucky arrow struck him down. A Christian rode past Fulk, his mouth wide, his eyes terrified, his throat gaping from a sword-cut, blood spraying and covering Fulk. He wiped his face hurriedly, in time to see a man in front of him turn; as he opened his mouth to bellow, his face became bloated, as if inflated like a pig's bladder. An arrow had slammed into his skull. A man stood up in his stirrups, staring all about him, then peering at the ground, where his arm and sword lay. He looked more peevish than upset.

Fulk felt someone tug at his arm. It was his brother.

'We have to escape,' Odo said. 'If we stay here, we shall be cut to pieces!'

Fulk nodded, staring at the chaos all about. He understood his brother, but while his mind was considering his words, his body insisted on remaining still and watching, as though he was impervious to danger. He gazed at the carnage, seeing men hacked, beaten, punctured by arrows, knocked by slings, trampled by warhorses, and the shock sank deep into his bones. He felt heavy, unthinking, dull and leaden in the face of this remorseless horror.

'Brother!' Odo shouted, and slapped his face. 'Fulk! Wake up! Come with me!'

Odo could see that his brother was befuddled. It struck him as strange, for here, in the middle of the battle, Odo felt in his element. His mind was clear. The sight of the enemy simplified everything, reduced every decision to the basic one: what must he do to survive so that he could carry on with God's plan? This was simplicity itself: he must kill or die. He must fight his way clear, before making his way back to the shore and safety. If he were to die, he knew that God would take him to Heaven, so he had nothing to lose, but he yet had a duty to live, in order that he could fight on.

He was a soldier of Christ: a warrior of God.

Fulk looked lost. It brought a pang to Odo's heart. He saw how Fulk blinked, gazing about him at the carnage, as confused and lost as a child.

'*Brother!*' Odo cried again, and slapped him again with his leather-gauntleted palm. 'Fulk, in God's name, bestir yourself!'

Fulk's eyes turned to him, his eyes full of tears. Odo would have to speak with him seriously later. Fulk was weak. He was Odo's brother, but this indecision was unforgivable. Fulk must harden himself or be lost.

He pulled the reins of Fulk's horse and spurred his own mount. Fulk watched, appalled, as the pilgrims were cut down, but a pair of horsemen, whether Christian or Saracen Odo could not tell, passed between the brothers and the injured and dying, and as though a rope had been snapped, Fulk returned to the present, shivering. Odo felt a flare of contempt, but he swallowed it. He tossed Fulk's reins back to him, and flashed a coldly encouraging smile.

He had his lance still in his hand, and as they rode towards the Saracens behind the army, he stabbed at an archer. The point took him in the breast with the full force of Odo and his mount behind it. Odo felt it skip over a metal plate, and then catch. With a sickening lurch, it punctured the man's mail and was in his body. There was a greasy little movement as it entered the man's ribcage, moving on until it caught on his backbone. The man said nothing, or else Odo's ears were so used to screams that one more was unnoticeable, but then the man was thrust from his horse, and Odo's lance was free again. In an instant, he saw another man grab the horse and mount, and he thought it must be a Saracen and was about to swing his lance at him, when he suddenly realised that it was Alwyn. The Saxon nodded curtly to him, and turned his own mount's head to join the two.

Odo heard a roar that seemed to make the ground shiver, and Lothar rode past him, his sword held high, riding full pelt for a pair of Saracen archers. One had an arrow ready, and loosed it, but the other stared in horror at the sight of the Rhinelander and seemed transfixed. Lothar's blade caught his arm as he tried to nock a fresh arrow, and then he reversed it to smash the cross into the other archer's face.

An arrow passed close by Odo's head, and he crouched lower, spurring his beast to greater efforts. There was an archer before them, but he was fumbling for a shaft as Odo reached him, and the grey blade of his sword almost beheaded the man. Then they were past, and lying low over their horses' necks as they reached the woods and fled through them, listening as the noise of death and slaughter faded behind them.

As they reached the far side of the wood and set their horses' heads for the camp at Civitot, Fulk finally could not hear the battle any more. He felt safe for a moment, and the party stopped for a few moments. Gilles and Eudes stared back the way they had come, as though looking for pursuit, while Lothar grimly inspected the notches in his sword's blade. Sir Roger looked almost blown. He sat in the saddle hunched over, looking much older than his years.

Fulk drew a deep breath. 'We made it!'

'Made it?' Alwyn said. 'You realise what the Saracens will do when they're finished with our people? They'll come straight here.'

'Here?'

Odo could not believe how his brother had been so unmanned by the battle. 'Of course, Fulk! They'll come to kill the rest of the Christians! What else would you expect from heretics? They'll want to find the camp and destroy it.'

Fulk's face suddenly hardened. That was when Odo knew his brother was worth rescuing. Fulk was committed to the pilgrimage, just as was Odo himself. He smiled and clubbed Fulk's shoulder with his fist. 'We shall survive this, Fulk!' he said.

'Sybille! We must save her and the other camp followers,' Fulk said.

Suddenly the bile was harsh and bitterly stinging in Odo's

throat. 'But we have to escape this place and rejoin the other pilgrims at Constantinople,' he said.

'I saved Sybille once before; I will not leave her to suffer death here!' Fulk shouted.

Odo felt a lurch in his breast. Fulk would throw his life away for the whores and misfits at the camp. He was no brother. Fulk had not the divine inspiration that burned in Odo's heart.

Fulk was not worthy of the pilgrimage.

CHAPTER 33

Civitot, Wednesday 15th October, 1096

The seven men, with three others they found on the way back, were the first to clatter into the town beside the shore, and the old men and women glanced up in surprise as they rode past, making for the main encampment, yelling to all who would listen to them, 'The Saracens are coming!'

'Don't be a fool!' a woman called. 'They'll meet our men soon enough. The army will stop them!'

'Woman, they have cut our men to pieces. We are all that remains!' Odo snapped. He saw her grimace of sardonic disbelief turn to shock as she took in the sight of Sir Roger and the others, and realised what he was saying. Shouting and yelling warnings, he continued after the others.

'Quick! The Saracens are coming!' Fulk called to a group of women chatting at a cookpot, but they merely stood and gaped at him and the others as though their warnings made no sense. Fulk tried to wave them on, to persuade them to start to move, but it was no use. They could not comprehend their danger. How could

414

they, he wondered. If he had been in their position, it would be hard to believe that so vast an army could be eradicated utterly in so short a space of time. These women must think that Sir Roger and the others were all guilty of drinking burned wine. It was inconceivable that God could have allowed His host to be slaughtered.

In the end, the companions rode to the little harbour. There was a small boat there, and Fulk gazed at it with hope. 'Sir Roger, there is a ship. We can send messengers to Constantinople and ask for help. I will stay here, but I have one request: a widow, Madame Sybille, please take her and her child with you.'

'I will remain,' Sir Roger said. 'I fled that battle; if I do not stand and fight here, I will be dishonoured forever. Sir Walter asked me to make sure that news of the battle was taken to Peter the Hermit, and that I will do, but I will stay to protect the pilgrims here, or die trying. Gilles, you go and tell the Emperor and any others who will listen.'

Gilles shook his head. 'Not me. Send another.'

'Lothar? No? Eudes, what of you?'

To his surprise, Sir Roger found that all his company were unwilling to leave the town without him. In the end, he turned to Fulk and Odo. 'You will have to go. I leave it to you. Tell any who will listen how this enemy fights. Tell them that the enemy's tactics are to rush in with bow and arrow, and then retreat, loosing missiles even as they ride away. You must tell them so that future armies know what they will meet.'

He wheeled his horse, staring about him, and instantly his eyes went to the old tower. 'We have to go there, I think. It's the only defensible place here. Gilles, come with me. You others, go and tell all the women, children, old folk, to help barricade it. Odo, Fulk, Godspeed.'

*

415

Alwyn rode with the Normans, resentful at the turn of events. Sir Roger had saved his life, and that meant Alwyn was in his debt. Honour obliged Alwyn to help the man, to protect him. It left a sour taste in his mouth.

The tower was a square block with the familiar Greek castellations, such as could be seen throughout the Empire, but it was in poor repair. Although since the news of Xerigordos had arrived, some men had begun to attempt to rebuild the worst of the ravages of time, still the tower was a solitary building in a land of broken walls and half-demolished houses. Yet the walls of the tower itself did appear to be strong. They were a yard or more thick at the base, and enclosed an area of some fifteen yards by twenty.

'It will have to suffice,' Sir Roger said.

Gilles nodded, and as the first of the older pilgrims began to make their way to the building, urged on by Eudes and Lothar, he rode to the farther side of the encampment, where he saw more people.

'We must make this place defensible,' Sir Roger said, and climbed from his horse. 'Help me.'

Alwyn remained on his horse. 'First I have to tell you something.'

'Be quick, then!'

'I intended to kill you. You are my enemy and the enemy of my family.'

Sir Roger peered up at him. 'What are you talking about?'

'I am English. You and your people killed my father and my uncle. Your father slaughtered my people.'

'And you think that matters now?'

Alwyn stared. 'You think this is a joke?'

'I think there are other things to worry about.'

'I would have killed you today, but you saved my life. I must repay that debt, but when I do, I will seek revenge for what you and your father did to my family.'

There was a sharp cry, and Sir Roger's attention snapped over towards the sea, but he could see nothing. He looked up at Alwyn, and then slowly gazed out across the pilgrims' encampment again. 'I honour you for bringing it up, man, but do you not think we could see to our defences now, and save this conversation for later?'

Alwyn felt his mouth twitch into a half-grin. This Norman was likeable, he admitted. 'Aye. Let's get this place ready to receive the remaining pilgrims.'

As Sir Roger and the men trotted away, Odo glanced at his brother. 'Fulk, I need to find—'

'I know: Jeanne. Let's go and fetch her and Sybille.'

Odo felt embarrassed. 'Jeanne is a good woman.'

'I am sure of it, Odo. She deserves a little good fortune.'

'Because of her journey?'

'That as well,' Fulk said. 'Guillemette told me a little about her. They have neither of them had much luck in life. You will be good for her.'

Odo shrugged. 'I will try to be.'

He spurred his horse towards the sea while Fulk rode on to the camp where Sybille had her tent. Fulk would bring Sybille, but Odo was not going to worry about that for now. The main thing was to find Jeanne and rescue her.

Jeanne had always loved the sea. She had told him so. He remembered that time when they had first spoken, and she had said she would marry her husband by the sea and he had sworn to himself that he would be the man she married. He wondered on the way what it was that Guillemette could have said about her. It made him frown that Fulk knew more about her than he did, but then he put the thought from his mind.

He saw her now, a solitary figure sitting on a rock near the

417

water, and he rode to her filled with joy that he might at least save her. 'Jeanne! *Jeanne!*'

She turned and he saw her break into a smile at the sight of him. She slithered and slipped down from her rock and was at the foot of it as he reined in.

'The Saracens are coming,' he said. 'You need to come with me, Jeanne. I have a boat and I can save you. I'll take you to Constantinople with me. You'll be safe there.'

'But . . . what about the others here? I must get—'

'There's no time. We need to hurry. Come with me. I will marry you and protect you, and when we reach Jerusalem we can—'

She had blanched. 'Marry? I cannot marry you, Odo.'

There was no debate about her words. She was entirely certain. Odo felt his face harden. 'I thought you loved me; I thought I made you happy!'

'You do. But I cannot marry you. I am married already.'

Odo felt that his world had shattered like a dropped pot. A terrible emptiness consumed him. He heard a loud roaring in his ears that all but deafened him, overwhelming even the waves crashing on the beach. 'Married? To whom?'

'My husband in Sens. He made me . . . he made me do things I didn't want, so when the pilgrimage was announced, I came away with Guillemette and the others.'

'Guillemette? The whore?'

Jeanne lifted her chin. 'She is my friend.'

'How could you be a friend with—' That was when he was suddenly struck with the enormity of her confession. 'You mean, you are a whore too?'

She coloured. 'I am a pilgrim, just as you are. Any sins I have committed are between me and God, not you.'

'*No!* No, no, no,' he said, stumbling backwards, hands held up as though to stem the words flowing from her.

418

So *this* was what Fulk meant. She was another draggle-tail! Fulk was laughing at him! His own brother had known that he was wooing a woman who was a common whore and, worse, a woman already married. Jeanne had polluted him, his mind, his soul. He had wanted to give her everything, but she had taken it knowing her soul was befouled.

'*NO!*'

In that moment, all love was burned away by the heat of his anger: the love for this woman, the love for his brother, both were scorched away like hair in a flame. There was no space for affection in the emptiness of his soul, only hatred.

'I'm sorry,' she said. There was a flash of sympathy in her eyes, a spark of compassion, but he was repelled by it and by her. To think that he, a warrior and leader of men for God, could have been taken in by this . . . this witch. She would have polluted him and brought the pilgrimage to destruction and ruin. Look at the events of today – already the pilgrim army was destroyed, even though he, Odo, had been given God's own mark of approval. And God had saved him from the disaster of the ambush, only to allow him to come here.

But God had shown him her evil, shown him Fulk's betrayal. Fulk should have told him what Jeanne was, but instead he kept the information to himself like a miser hoarding gold. Fulk was a heretic, surely, to have concealed this news.

He stared at Jeanne, but saw only a foul, disgusting agent of the Devil. She was a whore. She should not be here with devout pilgrims who sought to bring about God's victory on earth. She should *never* have been here.

There was a roaring in his ears as he grabbed her and put his arm about her neck. He didn't hear her short scream, which was instantly stilled as he clenched his arm and began to squeeze. All the while he recited the Paternoster in a whisper. He hoped that she would be forgiven. He loved her, after all.

She struggled, so he drew his dagger and thrust it into her until she stopped.

Fulk found Guillemette with other women at the river's edge, trying to wash their clothes. It was not efficient, and the tide kept rising up the river's mouth, but it was better to have clothes that smelled of brine and sea weed than those that reeked of sweat alone.

Guillemette looked up at the sound of his horse, and her relief to see him alive lit up her face. 'Fulk, are you uninjured?'

'You must come with me. Right away! Where are Sybille and Richalda, and Jeanne? Where are they?'

'Richalda and Esperte are over there at the tower, playing. Why?'

'What of Sybille?' he asked, following her pointing finger. He didn't see her face fall.

At one time, there had been a wall enclosing the whole port, and the squat, Byzantine tower was all that remained of the corner where two walls met. All about it were loose rocks and rubble. He saw Sir Roger and Alwyn up on the walls, staring back the way they had come.

He said, 'Get ready to leave. The Saracens have cut our army to pieces, and they will be coming here next.'

A woman grabbed at his stirrup. 'Was my Piers there?' Another fell to her knees. 'My Karl – did you see him? A tall man, like . . .'

There were many others crying out to him, seeking a comforting word, something they could cling to: a mere hope. 'I don't know, mistress. I don't think many escaped,' he said. 'I'm sorry. I must go! Get to the tower. You will not be safe here in the open.'

But before he rode off, he bent down and whispered urgently, 'There is a boat, Guillemette. I won't leave you here. Tell

Mathena, and Jeanne if you see her: gather your things and make your way to the port. And *hurry*!'

Guillemette stared out to the sea as he rode off towards the tower to find Richalda and Esperte, but then she sighed, grabbed a few clothes from her pile, and wrapped them into a ball before making her way to the camp at a brisk trot. Mathena hurried to grab her belongings and follow her. Guillemette could see Fulk at the tower with other men, and as she reached her part of the camp and began to thrust the little food and possessions into a bag, Roul appeared.

'Roul, where is Sybille?'

'She went towards the rocks over there with Gidie, to see if they could catch a crab or fish,' Roul said, pointing towards rocks nearer the harbour. Something in her expression made him hesitate and frown. 'Mistress?'

'The men are all dead. The Saracens are coming here. We have to leave. Some will stay in that tower, but as many as we can, we must help escape. There is a ship . . .'

Roul's face had fallen. 'The whole army?'

'You must help, Roul. Fulk is fetching the girls.'

Roul said no more, but began to gather his pack and threw the strap of his scrip over his neck and shoulder. Guillemette shook her head. The rest of their belongings were too few and worthless to worry about. She rolled the last of the clothes into a tighter ball, thrust them into the bag, and looked about for Fulk. He was riding back with Richalda sitting before him, Esperte clinging on behind.

'Sybille and Gidie went to fish,' she called as he approached, pointing towards the cluster of rocks.

He nodded, helping the two girls down. 'I will go and fetch them. Hurry! Make your way to the port!'

*

Odo had carefully laid Jeanne's body on the sand she loved so much, and crossed her forearms over her breast. Her eyes were staring up at the sky, and he left them open. She would like that view, he thought. She was so lovely, even now she was dead. He only hoped that her soul would be free and find redemption after the catastrophe she had brought upon the army.

He didn't mount his horse, but instead walked it back towards the harbour. The roaring in his ears was growing quieter. It was much like the sea in a storm, but now it was diminished. In it he thought he could hear the bellowing of demons in Hell, furious that they had failed to catch him. He was disorientated, confused, as if he had been drinking wine for a week, and his steps were careless. Tripping, he almost fell flat on his face.

Fulk had known about this, his own brother had known and not told him, not warned him.

On the way there was another group of rocks with many pools. He saw movement ahead, a man and woman clambering over the rocks: it was Gidie and Sybille, he saw. She was no whore, Fulk had told him. Rather, she was the unfortunate victim of disasters herself. Her husband dead, her money all gone. She would be glad of an escape. She did not deserve to be left behind. Of course, Fulk wanted her, but Fulk could never remain loyal to any one woman. He was always looking for the next entanglement. Besides, he did not deserve her. He had kept news of Jeanne's background from him. With Odo, she would have a better life.

Odo deserved her.

'Mistress, you must come with me,' he said when he was closer.

'Why?'

'The Saracens will be here at any moment. We have to escape and bring news of this disaster to the Emperor.'

'Disaster? What do you mean?'

Gidie was looking at Odo's sleeve. Odo glanced down and saw the blood. He wiped at it ineffectually. 'The army is dead. They ambushed us and have killed or enslaved the whole army.'

'My God! What of Fulk?'

Odo looked at her. She was a fine woman, he thought. She was Christian and faithful, and God could not object to her. 'My brother was with me in the battle,' he said. She seemed to totter, and he reached forward to steady her. 'Mistress, you must come with me. I will look after you.'

'Fulk dead?' she whispered.

'Come quickly!'

The old man nodded to him and took her arm. 'I'll help. If you can save her, so much the better.'

Odo nodded, and mounted his horse. Gidie helped her up to sit before Odo, and Odo put an arm about her belly.

'What of Richalda?' she said distractedly.

'She will be in the boat,' Odo said.

'No, I have to have Richalda!' Sybille shouted, and struggled to free herself.

'Mistress, I will get her,' Gidie said placatingly. 'You go to the boat, swiftly as you may, and I will see you there. Master Odo, take her there. I will bring Jeanne.'

'Hurry!' she called after him.

Odo spurred the horse on and they reached the boat in little time. When Odo stared back towards the camp, he could not see the man. It was a relief at first, but then he saw Gidie. He was at the shore, near the rock where Jeanne had been sitting. Where she still lay.

He rode on, the hoofs clattering down the stones to the pier, and there he set Sybille on the ground. The shipman was by his little boat, and Odo pointed. 'Go to it, mistress. I will fetch Richalda and any others.'

She nodded dumbly, and he turned his horse and set it at the ramp from the pier again.

Gidie saw Jeanne almost as soon as he left Odo. The body was lying just at the edge of the water, and when he hurried to her, he saw the iridescent colours of the water about her, and realised it was her blood colouring the waters.

He sank to his knees at her side, and put out a hand to her throat, but with her eyes wide like that, and her blood staining the sand, he had no hope of finding a pulse. 'Poor maid,' he whispered. She was so like to his own dear Amice, that he felt his heartstrings tugging.

There was the sound of hoofs drumming on the sand, and he looked up in time to see Odo appear.

'Master Odo, I am sorry, this woman is dead,' he said. All knew that Odo and she had been handfast.

Odo rode up without breaking his mount's pace, and Gidie realised that he had his sword unsheathed. He gaped as Odo lifted his weapon, but then he threw himself aside, and the blade went wide. Gidie shouted, 'Man, what are you doing? *I* didn't kill her!'

On hearing his words, Odo let his sword drop. Gidie thought he looked wild-eyed, a little mad, and reminded himself that Odo had until a few scant hours ago been fighting in a battle in which he had seen all his comrades slain. It was no surprise that he stared about with agitation.

'I have to go!' Odo said. 'I have to tell the other men about this so that we can have more men come. Yes, that's what I have to do.'

'What about the woman's child? You can't go without her.'

Odo looked down at him as though seeing him for the first

time. 'Child? Yes, her child. You must fetch her to the port. Leave poor Jeanne here. Hurry!'

Gidie nodded and rose, setting off for the tower.

He had only gone a few paces when Gidie felt the blow on his head and he immediately fell down to the sand.

CHAPTER 34

Civitot, Wednesday 15th October, 1096

Fulk heard a shout, and glanced towards the tower to see Gilles and Eudes waving frantically. When he looked over his shoulder towards the battlefield, he could see that a cloud of dust was rising, black against the sky.

'Quick! To the tower! There are men there who can help,' he said.

'What of my mother?' Richalda asked plaintively.

'She will be safe,' Fulk said. The dust was not so thick that it could be produced by a large force, he thought. Perhaps it was raised by a scouting party. 'I will make sure of that. Come with me and I will take you to her.'

Roul had already told him where Sybille had gone, and Fulk was keen to be away, to take her to the ship and see her safely aboard, but she would never leave her daughter behind, he knew. But he would not go with them. So long as Richalda and Sybille were safe, he would be happy. He would remain here with the other pilgrims, rather than leaving them to their fate. He held out his hand and Richalda looked at it a moment, then took hold and climbed up behind him, holding tight to his belt.

Even as he stared, the first men appeared, but they were not the fierce, dark-skinned and bearded warriors he had feared, these were the rag-tag remnants of the pilgrim army. Thirty, then another twelve, and then dribs and drabs, running with the drunken, stumbling gait of the exhausted or terrified.

'Roul! Make sure as many of these women get to the tower as possible. I'll be back soon,' Fulk said, adding, 'Hold on tightly, maid,' before spurring towards the men at an ungainly canter. Roul nodded and picked up a long-handled war hammer, weighing it in his hands while he urged the women to hurry.

To Fulk's surprise, he saw that one of the men was Godfrey Burel, the Hungarian leader of the foot soldiers, who had done so much to persuade Sir Walter to take the battle to the Saracens. 'Godfrey, how many men are with you?'

Burel's eyes snapped up to him. There was no terror in his face, only an all-consuming rage, Fulk saw. 'Mayhap I have a few hundred. Not a man more, I'll swear. Those heathens cut us off. They rode in between me and the rest of my men and slaughtered them all, the cowards! They wouldn't fight cleanly, but rode round and round, letting their arrows fly until the men were all slain.'

'Did they not chase after you?'

'I don't suppose they thought we were worth the effort,' Burel said with a curl to his lips. 'They were too busy cutting the fingers from bodies to pull off rings, and searching the knights' bodies for gold, or stealing the best harnesses from the dead horses, the devils!'

'As soon as they have done with that, they will be here to find us,' Fulk said. 'They wouldn't wipe out the main army for no reason. They are here to demonstrate that any army sent against them will be utterly destroyed.' He glanced up as more men arrived. There was a steady stream now, and they began to make their way to the tower. All could see it was the only defensible building.

Burel looked at the sea. 'We will die.'

'No. We will build what defence we may. Go to the tower,' he said. 'It is the only place with walls here that could hold most of us. See what needs to be done to secure it. Tell these people of the danger. They wouldn't listen to me.'

Burel agreed, and soon had his men hurrying across the ground towards it, shouting at the people all about as he went, trying to persuade them to join him.

Fulk was away again. He rode across the old encampment towards the beach. From there he would ride faster along the sands to the port, he thought, but as he approached the water, he saw the two bodies. 'My God! What treachery is this?' he demanded.

He dropped at the side of Jeanne, telling Richalda to stay on the horse. The incoming tide was about Jeanne's head now, but her hands were still chastely placed over her breast. When he looked at Gidie, he was surprised to hear a stertorous breathing. Quickly, he rolled the man over. His head was a mass of blood and he was unconscious, but alive. Fulk pulled him to a sitting position, crouched before him, pulled both arms over his own shoulders, and tried to stand. It was fortunate that Gidie was old and wiry, for lifting his dead weight would have been impossible, were he heavier. As it was, it took three attempts before Fulk could stand. At the last attempt, Gidie grunted and mumbled and tried to stand. He retched, and Fulk sourly told himself that if the fellow puked over him, he would leave him here.

'Where is Sybille? Gidie? Where is Sybille?' he demanded.

'Your brother . . . he has . . . her . . . She's . . . at the harbour . . .'

After a struggle, he managed to get Gidie into the saddle and climbed up after him, lifting Richalda up to the pommel, then holding the recumbent figure in place while the horse trotted back towards the tower.

At the top of the sands, Fulk stared out to sea. He could see the ship sailing away over the water towards the city on the next coast. His eyes turned to the harbour, expecting to see Odo, and for a while he stood confused, wondering what could have happened to his brother, whether he had been attacked, or was still searching for Jeanne, or . . . but then a cold certainty struck him as he turned to sea again and stared at the ship.

'So, Odo, we are deserted by you,' he said. There was a quick, hollow despair in his heart at the thought.

Alwyn left Sir Roger at the tower and hunted for Sara and Jibril. He found them at his shelter, and he spoke little, commanding them to leave everything but food and water. They must go to the tower, where everyone else seemed to be heading.

Sara began packing, her manner slow and precise as she gathered up Alwyn's few belongings.

'Woman, leave it! Leave it all!' he snapped. She turned to look at him with surprise and hurt in her eyes, but then she saw his urgency and began to throw a few more items together – bowls, a spoon, some twine – and when he took her by the arm, she looked at him with fear, but left the rest.

Alwyn looked about them carefully. Jibril was at his side, gripping a lance and cleaver he had found in another shelter, and Alwyn set off to the tower with them both at his side. Jibril looked terrified, and Sara took his hand in hers. She reached for Alwyn's left hand, but he snatched it away. He hated anyone touching it. It made him conscious of his deformity. Sara was hurt, but she held his gaze and deliberately took hold of it again. He glared at her, but set his jaw, and gradually his fierce expression softened, and together, hand in hand, they trotted over the plain.

'Hurry!'

Fulk rode back with the urgency of rage driving him. On the way he met the women and Roul, and he explained what had happened.

'We have no choice. We will all have to join the rest of the men in the tower. It will have to serve as our fortress.'

Guillemette nodded. Esperte was clinging to Mathena, and Richalda was sobbing, repeating, 'I want Mother!' over and over again, while she was passed down to Guillemette, who held her and tried to calm her, stroking her head and murmuring gently to her.

Fulk rode with them, still clinging to Gidie as he went, but all the way he could see only the vessel crossing the water towards Constantinople. His own brother had deserted him: him and these others, whether for cowardice or some other motive he could not comprehend, but it left him desolate.

At the tower he dismounted, pulling Gidie from the beast. Alwyn was at the gateway with his servant, and they helped him half-carry, half-drag the man inside. Guillemette followed with Richalda, and the others hurried in their wake, Roul bringing up the rear.

Just inside the entrance he found Burel, who stood with his arms akimbo and glared about him. 'This is your idea of security, is it? Not even a gate!'

'Have your men bring rocks and stones to block the doorway,' Fulk snapped. 'If you have others to spare, set them to finding any weapons lying about the camp. Arrows, bows, knives, slings, extra rocks: *anything*!'

Burel stared at him a moment longer than was necessary, but he began to bellow at his men as soon as he felt he had shown the correct disapproval of being ordered. Soon a stream of women and old men was coming towards the tower. Fulk walked inside the tower, eyeing the walls and wondering how long they would survive a dedicated onslaught. He found Gidie being ministered to by Sara.

'My head hurts. I didn't expect to have this when I set off.'

'It's been a few miles since Sens, old man,' Fulk said. 'You have more miles left in you.'

The old tranter looked up at the sky and winced. 'I think you and I would have been better served if we'd stayed behind, eh? Will I live?'

'Someone has tried to open your pate and spill your brains, but you have the luck of the devil, so probably you will live!'

'Someone?' Gidie looked at him sharply and shot a look at Fulk. The sudden movement made him wince. 'Yes, of course.' He closed his eyes.

Fulk was about to ask him what he meant, when there came a shout from above. Sir Roger was pointing.

'Here they are!'

They arrived in a solid mass of men and horses, bursting into the encampment like a pack of wolves seeing a flock of sheep. Fulk shouted to those outside to hurry, to get to the security of the tower, but it was already too late for many. The Saracens rode into the clearing at the gallop, the archers bending their fearsome bows and sending lethal darts into all who looked threatening. The old were cut down, with only some young nuns, children and women left alive. They were snatched and thrown over Saracen saddles, kicking and screaming, while more riders came with their fearsome curved blades, lopping off heads and

limbs. With no armour or shields to protect them, the pilgrims
stood no chance. Fulk gripped his sword and would have rushed
out to try to save some of them, but he felt Godfrey Burel's hand
on his breast.

'Go out there, and you'll die. You know that. You won't save
a single life, but you'll throw your own away for no purpose.'

Fulk stared. It felt as though he was peering into Hell. He
saw an old crippled man trying to escape the riders by hurrying to the tower, but then a lance-point appeared in his breast
and he was thrown high into the air as the rider flicked him
from his weapon. A pair of dames who could not have been
younger than fifty were herded together by three laughing
men and cut to pieces, while a child was run down by a large
horse and trampled into the mire. Fulk had to gulp back a sob
at the sight. It went against everything he had ever learned
or thought to stand back and watch this slaughter. He felt as
though he was himself responsible for their deaths, as though
by watching from the safety of the tower, he was colluding
with the murders.

Godfrey Burel shook his head. 'It's not worth it. Stay alive and
protect the poor souls in here.'

Lothar nodded. 'God sent us here not to die senselessly but to
free His people. The people inside this tower depend on us: you,
me, and all the other men-at-arms.'

Burel and Lothar were right. If he were to run out, Fulk would
die needlessly. Fulk nodded curtly and turned his back on the
slaughter. There was nothing he could do out there.

The tower was a different matter. He clambered over the
rocks laid in the gateway where two men, who were stonemasons
and had experience of building dry-stone walls, were working
swiftly. Soon they had three layers of rock, each reinforcing the
last, with shields inserted between to spread the effect of any

attack, and behind this the two built a hefty buttress to support their walls from rams. Satisfied with their efforts, Fulk took the stairs to the upper level and peered out. An arrow hit the rock of the battlements a foot from his head, and he flinched, but it gave a dull *tock* sound and pinged away.

At the base of the tower a number of Saracens were already milling about on their horses, casting bemused looks up at the walls, one or two dismounting and airily sauntering to the gate itself with a swagger in their steps. Fulk saw a boy clambering up the stairs weighed down by a great rock that must have weighed almost as much as himself. Taking it, Fulk carried it to the wall above the gate. Peering over the edge, he felt a brief belly-swooping horror at the height, but then saw that a helmeted Saracen was at the gate with a spear, and appeared to be thrusting it at the stone wall to see if he could move it. Fulk waited until the man leaned forward to prod again, and then held the rock out over the wall and let it go.

There was a short gasp of agony, and when he looked again the man was lying on the ground. His shoulder and upper chest had been smashed by the rock, and he was writhing in pain, moaning in shock. Another man on the walkway saw him, and grabbed an arrow to send it down and end the man's life, but Gilles was already there. He pushed the bow away. 'Leave him. While he suffers, the others will not want to come close, except to try to rescue him. Keep your arrow trained on them as they come to save him.'

Fulk frowned. 'That is not necessary, is it?'

Gilles pointed to a pair of men hurrying forward. The archer drew back his bow, and took aim on the target. He loosed his missile and grunted with pleasure to see the first man fall with a squeal.

Burel was nearby, his thumbs in his belt. He strolled to Fulk's side, peering down, and said, 'Were you out there today? I saw them cut down Sir Walter Boissy-Sans-Avoir. He died hard, and they hacked him about into little pieces. Feel no pity for them: none of them deserves it.'

CHAPTER 35

Civitot, Wednesday 15th October, 1096

Fulk left the walls when day gave way to night, and made his way down the stairs. The whimpering man was still before the gate, but his comrades were not willing to risk lives to help him. Instead, as his pathetic cries for help grew quieter, they bent their efforts to sending arrows over the battlements and into the tower's huddled pilgrims. Arrows flew, and although many missed their mark, striking the walls and flying away again, some few did bounce off the walls and thence into an old man or woman.

The people were huddled together for warmth as the sun went down. The arrows that fell among them were a terror that few were prepared for. They tried to keep closer to the walls, but that was little protection, for all too often the arrows would strike a wall and run almost straight down it. Fortunately, these had little energy left to penetrate a body deeply, but every so often a shriek would puncture the evening quiet, and the women and a couple of old men would hurry to help them, teasing a hideous barb

435

from a wound, or snapping off a shaft and pushing it forwards to avoid doing more damage. Three women and one boy died from bleeding when arrowheads sliced through arteries.

'How are you?' Fulk asked Guillemette.

She was using a damp cloth to cool a man who lay shivering and weeping as a large barbed arrow was being removed from his thigh by Roul. Gidie the tranter sat in the corner of the wall nearby, watching with his eyes narrowed. His head was covered with strips of linen but his face was dreadfully pale. Fulk wondered whether he would survive from the blow – and then realised that it was unlikely any of them would escape this tower.

'I am well,' she responded. 'But I would be glad of fewer arrows flying over the walls.' She looked up at him and smiled weakly. 'How are you? You look terrible.'

'I will live,' he said. 'Though I could sleep for a week or more. Where is Richalda?'

'There,' she said, pointing with her eyes at a low building beside the gate itself, little more than a shelf that struck from the wall, with a thin thatch of leaves of some sort. Someone had constructed it to give shelter to animals, perhaps sheep, from the sun and worst elements, and now a pilgrim had added to its protection by throwing blankets over it. All the smaller children had taken their residence beneath it as the best means of protection that they had. Every so often they huddled together as a fresh missile struck the blankets, the smaller children whimpering.

Fulk walked about the tower, then made his way to the upper walkway, deep in thought. Now that he had time to think, perhaps Odo had made the better choice. He had taken Sybille because she was there at the port, clearly, and he had saved her at least. If their roles had been reversed, Fulk would have saved Jeanne, clearly.

436

Sybille: the mere thought brought her face to mind. He could imagine her here, could almost feel her warm arms about him. She had never looked more beautiful than in the moonlight. Her face seemed to have a luminous quality, her eyes meltingly wonderful. He could imagine her hair coiling about her shoulders and forming ringlets. He wished she had not been so recently widowed, that he should get to know her just as her husband had died, when she was in mourning. How long ago was his death now? He could not remember. It was outside Belgrade, and that was weeks ago, but not long enough. To try to woo her would be disrespectful to her husband's memory and must hurt her feelings, but he did think of it. He thought of little else.

What was the point of considering such a matter when they could be taken by storm next morning, and Fulk slaughtered with the rest? This was not the time to think of taking a wife. He must work out how to escape and make his way to her in the safety of Constantinople.

There was no obvious attack forming from the Saracens, and Fulk returned to the ground. He spoke words of support to the injured, and reassuringly to the women and their children, saying the ship had escaped before the Saracens' attack, and the Emperor must surely come to ease their plight. When he reached the children under the little shelter, an arrow landed, quivering, in the ground beside him. He picked it up and studied it, then passed it to Richalda. 'Keep this. There is no better good luck symbol than the arrow that didn't hit you,' he smiled. 'You will be safe now.'

When he left to climb back up the stairs, he hesitated halfway and glanced back at Guillemette. When their eyes met, she held his gaze, not a whore measuring a client, but a weary woman who had seen too much death and wondered whether she would live to see another day.

437

Civitot, Thursday 16th October

The attacks were renewed early the next morning.

They heard the Saracens at their morning prayers, and Fulk wished that the pilgrims had a priest with them to give a response to the heathens' mournful wailing. The clerics had all perished in the battle, but there was a man who seemed to remember many of the words, and since no one was there to tell him not to, he recited several of the prayers. Although he was not qualified, the familiar words were soothing to the Christians.

As the sky began to lighten in the east, Fulk was nodding at the upper wall, sitting on the boards of the walkway, his back against the cold stone. He jerked awake, filled with a conviction that something was amiss, and stood warily.

'*They attack!* All men, all men, to the walls!' Sir Roger bellowed. He was at the upper walkway, and Alwyn saw men shaking their heads to clear them of their dreams before hurrying to the knight's side.

Sara was near, and Alwyn sent her below to help with the injured, away from danger so far as was possible. Jibril was already gathering up arrows, ready to supply the archers on the walls. Taking a quick pull of brackish water from his leather flask, Alwyn made his way to the top of the wall and stared out.

On the plain before the tower he could see the sparks and glows of the Saracen fires, and he frowned to see them, wondering why he did not see men moving about among them. He would have expected to see men walk before the fires on their way back from their prayers. But then he realised.

The Saracens had come in the darkness, silently stepping forward, and now they were already at the gate. He could hear them moving about under him. He took up a stone and placed it

438

on the battlements, rolling it forward and over the lip. There was a thud, but it was the sound of a rock striking gravel and sand, not a man. He picked up another and pushed this forward a foot to the right, pushing it gently until it toppled over. This time he heard a scream.

Arrows flew past him, and he ducked back as they smacked into the castellations or hissed by. He grasped another rock, not an easy task with his broken hand, and set it on top of the wall. Men were with him now, and he saw Roul taking up rocks in both hands, hefting them and putting them on top of the wall ready to push them over. An old peasant woman was at his side, pulling rocks from a pile and rolling them towards Roul.

Alwyn pushed her away. She was too old and feeble to do more than get in the way of the men. He saw Fulk and called to him. Fulk hurried to his side and was soon helping, lifting large pieces of rubble to the walls. Arrows flew all about them as they worked, and more and more men were arriving on the walkways as they struggled. Alwyn bent and lifted, feeling the muscles in his back and arms complaining. He straightened, and as he set the stone on the battlement, he saw an arrow climb from the army below him. It appeared to aim, seemingly, straight at him. He could not draw his eyes from the thing as it hurtled straight for his face. There was almost a sensation of relief to see it. His struggles would soon cease, he thought, and then, as though by a miracle, it dropped a matter of inches, and struck the rock he had placed on the wall. The missile sprang away, and Alwyn stood like a statue, his mouth gaping, and for a moment he felt as though his heart had stopped; he had been so convinced that the arrow would strike him that life seemed impossible. An urgent call brought him back to his senses. Near-death or not, there was work to be done. He bent again and, as he lifted another rock, he saw a ladder.

For an instant, befuddled from the shock of the arrow, he wondered why there was a ladder there; it was an incongruous sight, and he gazed at it with bemusement before his brain awoke to the danger, and he screamed for help, flinging his stone at the first of the men to climb the rungs. It hit the man on the cheek, and he snarled as he came up the last rungs.

Alwyn fumbled to pull his sword from its scabbard. The cross was caught in his tunic, and in his panic he could not think to release it. Luckily Lothar was already at his side, slamming the pommel of his own weapon into the man's face, sending him flying. While arrows smacked into the stonework, Lothar grabbed a heavy rock and dropped it down the middle of the rungs. It struck one and bounced, plummeting down to strike a man's leg and shattering two of the ladder's rungs. Another man began to negotiate the ladder, slowing when he reached the broken rungs, ducking as Alwyn and Lothar threw more rocks at him. Then Roul came running. He had a broken spear in his hand, and he pressed the shaft against the topmost rung. As the men below climbed the ladder, he pushed. Alwyn put his own weight behind him, and the two gradually saw the ladder swing away from the wall. It swayed, with men at the feet desperately pushing it back, but then Lothar had a lucky shot with a rock that broke the forearms and hands of three men at the right of the ladder, and in another moment the ladder was past any balance and crashed back, knocking down several men. One was hit by a splinter of rung that opened his breast from collar to belly, and he fell back, staring at the blood.

There was a shout of despair at the next wall, and Alwyn saw that a ladder had successfully disgorged Saracens, who were even now spilling out over the walkway. Alwyn bellowed, and saw Fulk turn to him.

Fulk was at the far side, but he saw the danger. He had three archers near him, and turned them. The three sent shafts at the ladder. One man at the top of the ladder was hit full in the face, and he fell back instantly, clearing those behind him. Then Fulk was running full tilt at the men on the walkway. The first had a spear, but Fulk struck it with his sword held in both hands, one hand on the blade, shoving it left and up, and running his sword down the shaft until the blade met the man's fingers, taking them off, so furious was his charge. Fulk swung the cross up and into the man's face, knocking him down into the tower's interior, where old men and women set about him with their knives, while Fulk continued on.

A pilgrim was in front of him, trying to hold off two Saracens, and Fulk joined him. He felt a curved blade clash with his own, and he was shocked by the man's strength, but then Alwyn was at his side, and his furious attack made the man flinch and draw back. Fulk stabbed, catching the man at the side of his neck. A mist of blood erupted, and the man put his hand to the wound, knowing that he was mortally wounded. He fell to his knees, and Fulk kicked him down, stabbing at his throat to end his pain. The other man had been hit by an arrow and killed, and now Fulk was at the ladder where more men were climbing. A spear lay on the walkway and Alwyn took it up, stabbing a man at the top of the ladder, then pushing it away from the wall while Lothar flung heavy rocks at the men at the ladder's base.

And then, as suddenly as it had begun, it was over. Men on the walkways went from Saracen to Saracen, picking them up and throwing them over the wall.

Fulk slumped against the wall, eyeing the retreating enemy as they dragged or helped limping comrades back from the assault. All about the base of the tower he saw broken spars and rungs of the ladders, while men groaned and whimpered amid the mess.

Lothar and Roul grunted with the effort as they picked up a

quietly moaning Saracen and rested him on the battlement. They pitched him over, and Fulk listened for the thud as he landed.

'How many assaults like that can we withstand?' Fulk said.

Lothar shrugged and peered over the wall, ducking as an arrow slithered past, narrowly missing his brow. 'As many as they throw at us. The Pope said, "God wills it". Let's hope he's right.'

Alwyn went about the bodies, stabbing each in the throat to ensure they were truly dead. With the help of a white-faced Jibril, he hauled them up to the battlements and cast them down outside the walls. It had been a hard morning, and the stench of blood and faeces from opened bodies lay heavily up here. In Alwyn's mind the memories of past battles haunted him. At one he had lost his father and uncle, at the other his friends.

Jibril stood at his side, attentive as a mastiff, and Alwyn ruffled his hair. As he did, he felt tears threaten at the thought that this battle could see the end of his servant.

'Master?' Alwyn turned to find a young woman holding out a skin of water. He took it gratefully and drank, passing it to Jibril when he had had enough.

'Thank you, mistress,' he said as Jibril tipped his neck back. It was a large skin and unwieldy, and he spilled much over his face, making Alwyn laugh. 'What is your name?'

'I am Guillemette,' she said. Her eyes were up on the walls, watching Fulk.

'You know him?' Alwyn said after giving her his name.

'He walked with me part of the way from Sens.'

'He's a good man.'

'Yes,' Guillemette said, and then she reddened. She smiled at Alwyn fleetingly. 'You were not with our army.'

'I came here many years ago. I've been living here in

Constantinople,' he said. He liked the way that she made no comment on his ruined hand or his scarred face. 'I was a warrior for the Emperor, but now I just trade in the city.'

'You have a kind face.'

He laughed. 'You are a swift judge! Perhaps I'm good at concealing my true colours!'

'No, I think you're kind.' She smiled again, but just then there came a horn's blast, and Alwyn took the skin from his boy and gave it back to her. 'We must go. Another attack is forming.'

'Be careful!' she said impulsively.

He turned and smiled at her briefly, and then he was off up the stairs once more.

Lothar, Fulk and the remaining men were hard-pressed for the rest of the day. The assaults on the walls continued, and the garrison was forced to rally at different points of the wall through the heat and dust. The arrows flew continually, steel-tipped with barbs that dug into flesh like a tick and would not give up their purchase easily. There were some men who were trained and experienced in digging out the vicious weapons, but as the day wore on, more and more men were forced to stumble down the stairs to where priests and the women were praying and trying to help the injured. Before midday the whole of the ground area was a dense mass of injured men and women. Only when the sun began to sink did the Saracens draw back, to sit and sing and dance at their great fires.

As dark flooded the land, Fulk left the walls and went down to see the people. Lothar sat where he was, watching Fulk walk from one person to another. Sir Roger was still standing. His face was smeared with blood, and he was constantly clenching his left hand and bending his elbow from where a maul had almost crushed it, but he remained alert.

Down in the tower's courtyard, Lothar saw that, although most of the pilgrims were generally anxious, they kept their spirits up with prayers and singing. It was the children who concerned him most. Many sat, their eyes wide with fear. All had experienced death already on this pilgrimage, but now, seeing the dread on the faces of their mothers and friends, the full horror of their position was made clear to them. None of the adults expected them to survive this. Richalda sat clinging to the support of the shelter, a rough bough of some straight wood, and Lothar saw Fulk go to her and squat at her side, talking gently. Gradually the child released her grip and put her arms about his neck instead. He settled her on the ground beneath the shelter to rest.

Not all were so transfixed with fear. Some boys, who had been forced to sit and keep hidden during the worst of the attacks during the day, were up now, and playing catch with stones. It reminded him of when he had been young and such simple games had entertained him too, and he smiled. Close by them was the body of an old man who had been unlucky and struck by an arrow, but they did not seem concerned. Their attention was, for now, fixed on their game.

Nearby was Gidie and other men with more vicious wounds. Guillemette and other women were with them, washing their injuries and giving them water to make them as comfortable as possible. As he watched, Guillemette stood, tucking hair beneath her coif. She saw his glance and smiled wearily before bending to another patient.

He felt a hand on his shoulder and looked up. It was Mathena. She smiled.

'You fought well,' she said.

All at once the fighting of the day came back to him, the screaming men trying to stab or slash at him, the arrows, the

444

bodies, and his voice was thick with exhaustion. 'It was a hard battle.'

She had a little thickened pottage in a wooden bowl and passed it to him. 'You must be hungry. You need your strength,' she said.

He took a little, but then looked beyond her to Richalda. The girl sat with her knees to her chin, her eyes half-closed with weariness and despair. Lothar passed the bowl to Mathena. 'I will eat again before long,' he said. 'You give this to her.'

Mathena nodded.

'You have been safe enough?' Lothar asked.

'The arrows came down here, but we were safe from the worst of them. The children have suffered. They all know that they could die, and . . .'

Lothar put a hand on hers. 'Do not think of it.'

'I can't help but think of it,' she snapped, pulling her hand away. Then she relented and took his hand in hers again. 'I know that one of these Saracens would take my little girl Esperte for their concubine, or sell her at the slave markets.'

'You have heard of such things?'

'There are many here who know all about these people. They mutilate their prisoners, force the men to accept their faith and cut off their manhood, and if the men refuse, they are beheaded. We women, if we are attractive in any way, will be raped and sold as whores. We know our fate.'

'With the protection of God, hopefully that will not happen,' Lothar said.

'You will protect us?'

'As I hope to reach Heaven, I will.'

She gave a small sigh and took his hand, touching it to her brow. 'I thank you for that,' she said. 'But I must beg one boon.'

'You need only name it.'

'At the worst of times, if it comes to it, I beg that you do not let me or Esperte fall into their hands. Save us from that, I pray.'

Lothar had a sudden chilling vision of the two Jewesses and their dead child. He shook his head. 'Mistress, I do not think—'

'You have the strength, Master Lothar. Please, if they come and will take us, please kill us both. Don't let us be taken into captivity by them.'

At last Lothar understood the two Jewesses at Rudesheim. They had been terrified of being taken and raped, and would seek death before that dishonour: Mathena's fear was the same as the despair of the Jewesses. Suddenly he felt a welling sympathy for this woman, but also for the two Jewesses. And he wondered now at their courage. He covered her hand with his own and smiled down at her.

'I will not,' he promised.

Civitot, Friday 17th October

The next day the assaults came quickly. Ladders were used, and a great beam that the Saracens had slung beneath a roof of wet hides, which they used to beat at the stones of the pilgrims' makeshift gate.

Every thud of that beam reverberated in Lothar's head like a hammer. It would not have been so bad if it had been regular, but it was not. There would be two or three in set intervals, but then a man would fall injured and the beat would slow, and gradually pick up once more as more men filled the gaps. It set Lothar's teeth on edge. He wanted to have an end to this incarceration, and an opportunity to leap among his enemies and fight them honourably. But for now it was a case of struggling with ladders and men, hurling any missiles that came to hand and occasionally meeting a man in hand-to-hand combat, battling with swords, or struggling with a man in a wrestler's grip, smelling his breath and sweat, hearing his breath rasping in his throat, avoiding the head-butt, trying to knee him in the ballocks, biting, scratching, holding the other man's weapon away with main strength while trying to stab him with his own.

Twice he had to be saved by other men. Once Sir Roger had to thrust his sword into Lothar's opponent's throat, another time it was Alwyn who clubbed his enemy about the head with his sword's pommel, but on both occasions Lothar was aware of his growing weakness. He had been fighting for too long and his body craved sleep. His reserves were too low for him to continue. He must succumb to the next Saracen who reached the wall. But even as he had the thought, he saw again in his mind's eye the Jewesses – and Mathena and Esperte. He would not fail Mathena: he had sworn an oath, but he could not kill her yet. The idea of cutting her slender throat was unbearable. Yet if he could not kill her, he must himself remain alive.

It was that determination that kept him fighting. As a new man climbed to the top of the wall, Lothar lumbered to his feet and pushed and hacked and stabbed until that man too was sent tumbling backwards to the ground.

Then there was a flurry of running men, and ladders and grapnels were flung against all the walls. The pilgrims bellowed for help, and ran to each of them, Alwyn ringing sparks from the walls with a hatchet as he tried to cut a rope, others hurling the remaining few rocks into the faces of the attacking parties while bowmen tried to ensure that every dart met a target, but soon there were all too few even of them, and still the Saracens came on.

Lothar took his sword in both hands as the first Saracens reached the castellations. He swore loudly in his own language that these sons of whores wouldn't pass him today, and stepped onto the wall itself, keeping his legs close to the battlements so that an attacker would find it hard to strike them, and from there he belaboured all the men coming up his ladder. Alwyn was at the other side of the ladder, and he dealt death like a Viking. Lothar caught his eye at one moment and he could have taken his oath that Alwyn was smiling like a berserker.

There was a surge, and the men running up the ladders started to make headway. Lothar was separated from Alwyn and he felt his courage begin to fade as he realised that the pilgrims in the tower could not hold back the Saracens for much longer. He cut and battered with his sword, but for every man he wounded, two more climbed to the battlements and came over the wall, teeth bared in ferocious determination, their blades keen and deadly. Lothar had to give way, gradually retreating until he was with Sir Roger.

'We are lost,' Lothar muttered.

'Then we will sell our lives dearly!' Sir Roger snarled.

Lothar barely heard him. His attention was focused down into the middle of the tower, towards Mathena. She was there, embracing two terrified children. Her eyes met his and he felt their glance like darts piercing his heart.

He must go to her; he had promised. On hearing another scream he shuddered as though an arrow had struck him, and lurched towards the stairs.

Alwyn clubbed a bearded, screaming face, snatching his arm back to slash the sword across a second, but there was little they could do to stem the tide. There were so many of them, the tower's small guard must soon be overwhelmed.

A curved sword passed so close to his belly, he could feel the steel catch his shirt. No matter what he attempted, he and the rest were pushed back. There was barely room to swing their weapons, the press was so great, and ever more and more men were pouring over the walls. They could not slow the onslaught.

He saw Lothar break free of the rest of the group and take the steps down towards the women and children. It made Alwyn stare, wondering what the man was doing, where he was going, and as he did so a blow struck him on the side of his head. He collapsed to his knees, then all fours, feeling as though a fustian sack had been tugged over his head. The light was dimmed, and all noise became deadened, as though the battle was happening a long way away.

The clash of arms was all about him, the clatter of sword against armour or hammer against helmet, the thud of weapons striking skulls. A face stared up at him. It was a young man with blue eyes, but he was unmoving in a pool of blood. Alwyn looked up at the men struggling about him, and saw a Saracen beaten back, a lucky thrust piercing a weakness in his mail, and then more of the enemy were pushing him aside to attack. Alwyn felt the warm, greasy wash of blood on his face.

There was a high, keening cry, and he looked up to see Jibril trying to break through the men to Alwyn's side. A Saracen gave a casual flick with his wrist, and Jibril's breast and belly were opened. A second, and the boy's throat and shoulder gushed. The boy's face showed surprise rather than pain, and he collapsed, toppling over the edge to fall down into the centre of the tower.

'NO!' Alwyn roared, and clambered to his feet. He had his sword in his hand and tried to stab at the man who had killed Jibril, but there were too many others there, too many swords, axes, war hammers, and he was pushed back and back, always retreating. This must be the end, he thought. The Christians could not survive such a massive onslaught.

It was then, when he was at his last extreme of effort, that a clear, bright sound could be heard even over the battle: a horn blaring outside the tower.

It was as if the stream of men was instantly dammed. The pressure of new men appearing over the top of the wall ceased, and suddenly it was a matter of only those who were before him who were battling on. Alwyn saw men climbing the wall and descending the ladders, running away. He gave a roar of victory and slammed his sword against his opponent's, and barged into him, bodily shoving him over the edge of the walkway, so that he fell with a scream to the ground below. Another bearded face was in front of him, the man who had killed Jibril, and he span his sword into the fellow's face, beat at him, kicked, screaming all the while, until the man fell, tumbling. There was one last man, a youngster of only maybe fifteen or sixteen years, who stood on the wall with terror painted on his face. He dare not try to climb down the ladder, but he was petrified with fear to be confronted by Alwyn.

Alwyn screamed, his sword raised, rushing at the boy. But then, as he hacked down, he saw, as if in a dream, Jibril's face staring at him from this boy's. It was enough to snap the maddened frenzy in his mind. He drove the sword to the stone wall at the boy's side, striking great sparks when the blade struck.

He was exhausted. Jibril's death had broken his heart. He could not kill another here, now. 'Go!' he said, and motioned with his fingers. The boy stared at him with terror, not daring to turn his back. Sir Roger came up, full of bile and fury, his weapon ready for the killing stroke, but Alwyn put out his hand to stop him. 'There's been enough killing,' he said. 'Let this one go.'

The boy looked at him, and bent his head as though in gratitude before disappearing from sight.

'What has happened?' Sir Roger said.

In answer, Alwyn pointed.

On the sea, their sails puffed like pillows of goose-down, came the Imperial fleet, and on each deck was the bright, clear sparkle of armour.

BOOK EIGHT

Liberation
and Betrayal

CHAPTER 36

Civitot, Friday 17th October, 1096

At the prow of the fourth ship in the Byzantine fleet, Odo stood proudly clinging to a rope, basking in the glory of his new position.

The crossing had taken little time. He had hurried to see Peter the Hermit as soon as the boat docked, running to the city gates and demanding access. Peter realised the enormity of the disaster as soon as Odo broke the news, and took Odo straight to the Emperor where, amid the finery of the Greek court, servants and nobles alike had stared at Odo's blood-stained face and tunic with appalled horror, the ladies holding perfumed cloths to their noses, the men keeping well away so their expensive silks would not be stained or smeared. But the Emperor was different; he had understood.

He was a figure of great presence. Not as tall as many of the knights Odo had known in France, he seemed taller because of his broad shoulders and rich clothing. On his head was his crown of gold, with a huge emerald at the front, and a sapphire and ruby flanking it, while his tunic was of golden cloth that shimmered. At his breast were more rubies and sapphires, and a man was sure to feel overwhelmed by such a display of abundant riches. His hair was so dark it was almost black, as was his thick beard, although that was shot through with silver. But more than the vast wealth, Odo found himself taken by the Emperor's eyes. They were like pits of such depth that a man could drown in them. When he fixed them on Odo, it felt as though he could stare straight into his soul and see the doubts and guilt beneath.

Peter began by summarising the campaign, and then motioned to Odo to speak.

'Your Majesty,' Odo began, bowing low, 'I was with the company that rode to Nicaea and thence to Xerigordos.' He quickly told of the attack, the Saracen siege, the escape and urgent flight back to Civitot, the march to meet the Saracens, disaster, and return to the shore. 'I have no doubt that my brother and all our friends will be dead or enslaved, your Majesty. But if there is any hope of their rescue, I would beg that you send men to effect it.'

The Emperor appeared to consider for a while, and then motioned to a scribe and issued his orders. He was distressed to hear of this disaster, he said. The peoples of Christendom had rushed to his aid when he had asked them, and now it was time that he did what he could to support the people who had thrown their lot in with him. He commanded a general, Constantine Euphorbenus Cataclon, to take an army to seek out the surviving Christians and bring them back safely.

Odo left the audience chamber elated. He had never been in such company, and to have spoken with the Emperor himself, and to have been heard by him, was thrilling, all the more so because he was acting for the benefit of God. This must surely provoke the lazy Greeks into joining with the pilgrims to win Jerusalem.

He returned with Peter to the lodging where the Hermit had been stationed, and there he found Sybille waiting.

She had not spoken more than a couple of words in all the journey back from Civitot, and she sat now, her hair bedraggled from the sea air and dust, her tunic marked with stains from the boat. Odo recalled her misery with compassion, considering that now she had lost her daughter, no doubt, as well as her husband. It had been so difficult to persuade her to leave the harbour. He had been forced to tell her Richalda was dead, and she had sat on the deck sobbing as though her heart would never mend. She was struck with despair to know she had lost everything: just as he had. She and he were united by bereavement.

There was a simple resolution, he saw, and he begged a moment more of Peter the Hermit's time. He spoke at length, and at the end of it he and Peter went to Sybille.

'Sybille, I feel I must offer you what support and aid I may,' Odo said. 'You have lost your husband and daughter, and we have both lost Fulk, I fear. You are here in a strange land without any means of providing for yourself, and I feel sure that my brother and your husband would have wanted to see you cared for. I will marry you, and I hope that I can comfort you in the days to come.'

'Will you have this man as your husband, woman?' Peter asked.

Sybille shook her head. 'No, no, I cannot! I am in mourning, and—'

'Mistress,' Peter said gently, 'you have no option. This is a good man. He will protect you and bring you safely to Jerusalem, where you can pray for your dead husband and for this man's brother. If you do not, what will become of you? You are here in a strange city, and you could remain, but with no trade or income, I ask again, what will happen to you? If you come with the new pilgrim armies to continue the pilgrimage to which you are sworn, no man will protect you. There will be hardships for all, but at least as a married woman you will have the comfort of this man and his protection.'

He continued much in the same vein. She looked from him to Odo, but in truth, she heard little of what was said. Prostitution, she heard, or cooking or sewing, but more than likely, she would be left in the wake of the army, unable to keep up, unable to feed herself, unable to find water. She would fall behind, and her bones would whiten in the sun. It was not to be borne, Peter said.

She did not, afterwards, recall the actual oath. But her hand was taken and she mumbled some words, and then she was taken away to a separate chamber to consummate the marriage. She remembered the expression of pain and exultation on Odo's face as he arched his back. For her there was no pleasure, no joy. Her body could be taken by him, but all she knew was an overwhelming emptiness. She had lost her husband and her daughter. All her friends were no doubt dead. Perhaps Odo could give her life some meaning, but she doubted it. She was only a husk of the woman she had once been.

But Odo was aware of none of that. He was convinced that her awe of being married to him was all that stilled her tongue. She was proud to have him as her husband, as she should be. Odo would lead men in the assaults against the heretics, and he would become as beloved as any prophet, even Peter the Hermit himself. She was fortunate to be bound to him. He was marked out for greatness. Only today Peter had nominated him to be his own captain with the pilgrim forces which would soon be gathering. A man of Odo's courage and determination, Peter said, should be rewarded.

*

They could see the Saracens marching away as they approached the coastline, and Odo felt the stirrings of trepidation. His eyes were drawn to the place where he had left Jeanne. There was a ripple of cloth, he thought; perhaps her body still lay there. No, surely not. The tides would have pulled her out to sea. Would Fulk's body be near? He didn't want to see it if it was. Fulk had his weaknesses, but he was Odo's brother, and Odo hoped his end had been swift. He could not regret his actions: God willed it; yet, while Odo forgave Fulk for deceiving him about Jeanne, Fulk would still have been a threat to the entire pilgrimage. His sins would cause the failure of God's ambition. That could not be permitted. However, Odo was torn. He wanted to think his brother was safe.

He sprang into the waves with the first of the men, walking up the sand while the army of Constantinople gathered and formed ranks preparatory to marching up the beaches.

The sight that met his eyes was enough to make him stop and gape. Smoke rose from hundreds of fires that had been left by the departing army, but more than that was the reek. Some was caused by sewage from the tens of thousands of pilgrims who had been camped here for so long, but over that was the stench of death. Many hundreds of pilgrims who were old, weak or who had fought against the Saracens lay dotted about the camp, their bodies bloated and blackening in the sun. The smell of rotting flesh pervaded the whole place.

As the tramp, tramp, tramp of booted feet marching in step came to him, he heard a sudden noise. It was a rumbling, like many rocks tumbling over and over. It came from the old tower, and he heard a captain in the army shout an order. Instantly skirmishers went to scout and see if they could find the source, darting forward with shields and spears up in case of ambush. Some ran to take cover behind rocks, where they waited with javelins up at the ready, while more moved forward. A group of archers trotted up and took position nearby.

Odo moved to join them, and was there when the last rocks were pushed away from the doorway, and the first of the hollow-eyed men, women and children clambered over the devastation.

Gidie could not hear what Lothar was saying at first. The Rhinelander seemed to be talking about some sort of defeat, while at his side Alwyn wearily rubbed his eyes. There was a hellish whistling noise from somewhere, and Gidie's skull felt as though it had been broken open and his brains exposed to the air, but when Fulk appeared and with a broad smile on his face helped Gidie to his feet, the old tranter slowly rose, wincing and hissing as he did so.

The tower's interior was a mess. Bodies of pilgrims had been taken to the farther corner and neatly laid out, while the injured stayed here, nearer the gateway. Saracen bodies were dumped unceremoniously in the middle of the ground, where they had fallen when pushed from the walkways above, and stabbed by the women down here to make sure they were dead. Around them were piles of faeces where the pilgrims had defecated.

As he gazed about him, he saw Alwyn cross over to Sara, and both stood staring down at Jibril. Sara put her arms about him, but Alwyn seemed scarcely to notice. The old man's eyes were glistening.

The children seemed to be screaming and shrieking, but less from terror, more from joy. Only a few, like little Richalda, did not join in the general jollification. She sat huddled in the corner of the wall beside a supporting beam.

Gidie walked to her slowly on legs that threatened to pitch him into the dirt at any moment. He held out his hand to her, and she looked up at him as if without recognition. It was some moments before she took his hand and stood with him. She tentatively put her arms about his waist and rested her face against his belly. It made his heart melt.

Fulk walked through the gates into the sunshine and held his face to the sky. It felt like a rebirth, after being held in that hellish tower for so long. He allowed the cool breeze to wash over him, and it left him refreshed, as though it was wiping away the dirt and foulness of the last days. When he opened his eyes again, he found himself staring at a gleaming barrier of Byzantine warriors arrayed in steel and leather, shining in the bright light.

And then he saw his brother.

Odo stood near the door to the tower, his hands on his hips as he surveyed the battlefield.

'Odo!' Fulk shouted.

'Brother!' Odo said, and his face paled, and then he smiled. 'Fulk, I'd thought you were dead! It never occurred to me that—'

'That I could live if you sailed away and left me here?'

'That wasn't it! I saw the enemy coming and I had to go and find help. And look at this! I brought an army, and the mere sight of them drove away the Saracens!'

Guillemette came out, and with her were Lothar, Mathena and Esperte, blinking. Odo saw the blood on Guillemette's tunic. 'What, has she been—'

'She has been nursing the injured through the battle,' Fulk said. He was too weary to maintain his anger. 'She and the other women have been courageous, helping the men when they were wounded. But Sybille wasn't here. You had her.'

'She was in danger. I thought she might be killed. I thought you were dead, my brother.'

'You sailed away and deserted me.'

'I had to get news to the city, as you know. We were instructed to do so. When I saw the enemy riding to attack, I knew I had to go immediately. You know I had no choice. And yes, I saved Sybille. It was the hardest thing I've ever done,' Odo said. 'And I've sworn to protect her,' he added more quietly.

'Good,' Fulk said, but there was a harshness to his tone. He would never forget the sight of the boat sailing from the coast, deserting him and the others. For now, he was too weary to think of the time it had taken for the Saracens to arrive after he saw the vessel sail away.

'I must be gone,' Odo said, hearing a shout. 'I will return soon and see you.'

He was off like a hawk called to the lure, and Fulk watched him go. He was unsure that he would ever be able to trust his brother again.

'He survived, then,' Gidie said as he appeared at his side.

'Yes. He was fortunate.'

Gidie nodded. He saw again Jeanne lying in the surf, the smear of blood all about her, and he saw Odo, his sword raised ready to strike. 'Yes,' he agreed, 'very fortunate.'

On board ship

Odo was fêted on the ship as he and the first of the pilgrims made their way back to Constantinople. The wounded and the women nursing them were being loaded on the next ship as Odo's slipped her moorings and set sail.

Sir Roger applauded his swiftness in taking the message to Peter. 'Without you, we would surely have died. We must reward you.'

'I have my reward already,' Odo said. He was quiet momentarily, but his pleasure meant he could not keep the news from this man. Sir Roger had been with him in Xerigordos. He was his friend. 'You see, I have married. I saved one of the ladies from the town when I left to find help. She was at the beach, and ... well, I didn't want to leave her behind to be killed, naturally, so I brought her with me.'

'Who is this fortunate lady?'

'A lady from Sens called Sybille. She was travelling with her husband and daughter. Her man died, sadly, at the Hungarian border, and while I know a man should not seek to marry a widow so soon after her bereavement, Peter the Hermit agreed that it was better for her to have a protector while she continued on the pilgrimage.'

'Sybille?' Lothar said. 'Was that not the woman your brother was hoping to marry?'

'Yes, and if I had only known that Fulk would live ...' Odo said. He looked over to the horizon as he recalled the rage, deep in his soul, when he realised Fulk had been laughing at him, at his infatuation with Jeanne. It had been a terrible acid eating at his heart. If only God had taken Fulk, instead of letting him survive the tower at Civitot. It would have been better all around.

He wondered how Fulk would receive news of his marriage. It mattered little. It was God's will. But Odo hoped that Fulk would feel a little of the desperate anguish Odo had known when he had understood what Jeanne was, when he saw how his brother had laughed at him for falling in love with a *whore*.

Yes, it would have been better if Fulk had died at Civitot.

He brought his gaze back to Sir Roger. 'Naturally, if I had known that Fulk would survive ...' What? Would he not have married her? No, for she was his prize. Sybille was God's gift to him, a reward for his integrity and piety. But God's kindness did not stem the flow of tears. 'However, I thought he was *dead*, and thus I had a responsibility to save her from death or worse on the journey.' He looked down into the hull of the ship, where Richalda and some other children sat anxiously. 'At least I can bring her good news of her daughter.'

Sir Roger looked at him, his head shaking. 'My friend, what have you done?'

'I deemed it best.'

'Many a man will justify an act by saying that,' Gilles said. He met Odo's fixed glare impassively.

'It was not his fault, surely,' Sir Roger said.

'Perhaps,' Gilles said. 'But it would be best to be away from here before your brother learns you have married his woman. I expect him to be angry when he learns of it.'

Odo spoke coldly. 'He must learn to accept it.'

Lothar listened to them talking, but his attention was fixed on the receding coastline.

He could think of nothing except his promise to kill Mathena and Esperte. Mathena's desperation to see herself despatched swiftly and with honour, and the same determination of the Jewesses, put Odo's action into perspective, Lothar thought. He could all too easily condone a marriage to save a woman from peril. He threw a look towards Mathena. It was mad for a woman to come all this way on her own. There were so many. Although these women might have the desire to see the Holy City for themselves, they were not as hardy nor so strong in a battle as men. He was not certain of the motives of such women – especially those who had brought children.

He pulled his eyes away from the women and listened to Odo and the knight once more.

Sir Roger was leaning on a rope. 'I hope it will not lead to difficulty between you and your brother.'

'I did not come here to see to his hurt feelings, but to win back Jerusalem,' Odo said. 'Besides, he will cope. He is not so pious as a man on pilgrimage should be. Sadly, my brother is lecherous – more so than any man I have known.'

'He is a man, when all is said and done,' Sir Roger said. There was nothing unusual in a man pursuing his natural desires. 'At least he will be forgiven his crimes if he reaches Jerusalem.'

'That is my fervent wish,' Odo said. 'God knows, he has many sins to atone for.'

On a different ship, Fulk spent his journey sitting with his back to his ship's hull, eyes closed, enjoying the feeling of the cool breeze on his face. After the hellish experience of the tower, seeing so many men slain for no advantage to either side, it was good to be rocked by the waves here. The ship creaked, the ropes holding the sails groaning and cracking as the wind changed, but there was a steadiness to the noises and the calm, unhurried commands from the ship's master.

He could still smell the stench of death about the tower. It lingered in his nostrils, no matter that as soon as he could he had dunked his head in the sea and washed his arms of all the blood that caked them. Death was a part of him now. His experiences had marked him for battle and dealing execution. He longed for a sight of Sybille, a chance to speak to her once more, as though that could eradicate the memories of horror. Richalda was still quiet, leaning against Gidie as though he was her grandfather, and Fulk thought he could win a little favour with Sybille, were he to return Richalda to her. It was a good thought. He could imagine Sybille's joy at being reunited, especially since Fulk had helped to protect the girl through the worst of the fighting.

Sybille would appreciate his efforts. Perhaps she would consider his protection for the rest of the journey? Even after the last days, that thought brought a smile to his face.

Constantinople

Gidie was happy to give up the child to Fulk when they reached the harbour and could disembark at last. Dusk was falling, and he felt old, too old for this life of hardship and toil. He stood on the solid paving of the harbourside for a while, stretching his back and feeling the crackle of the scab breaking where his pate had been broken. It hurt badly, a soreness that was close to nausea when he stood, but he was determined, and he knew what he must do.

Odo had tried to kill him.

Gidie had thought it was because Odo saw him with the corpse and assumed Gidie himself had killed her. But as he lay in the tower while the fighting raged all round, he had been struck by the way that Odo had spoken so little, by the way that his face had hardened like a wooden carving, and by the way that he had struck Gidie down when Gidie had been walking away, thinking that Odo knew him to be innocent.

Now Gidie wondered not whether Odo had struck because he thought Gidie was guilty, but in order to conceal his own crime.

Odo had murdered Jeanne and tried to kill Gidie in case he should realise.

Gidie waited until Fulk had left the ship, and then he rose to his feet, his legs wobbling. The whistling noise was still in his ears, but it was abating slightly, and his legs grew stronger as he made his way down the gangplank and began to push through the press to follow Fulk. The harbour was packed with returning pilgrims, soldiers embarking to join others at Civitot, a squadron of cavalry which were skittishly waiting to be walked up a broad gangplank, and the usual mess of sailors and dock workers rolling barrels, coiling ropes, patching nets and eyeing the pilgrims with disdain or contempt.

Gidie forced his way onwards, thrusting himself through the people like a ship passing through flotsam. As he moved, he kept a close eye on Fulk up ahead. A pair of men approached Fulk, and he had a brief discussion with them. They seemed to want to take Richalda, but Fulk would not allow it. He was determined to carry the child to her mother, and no one would steal that pleasure from him.

Another man appeared, and this time Fulk bent his head respectfully. It was Peter the Hermit. He motioned to the girl, and reluctantly Fulk allowed her to go with the two men, while he spoke with Peter.

'What does Peter want with Fulk?' Lothar said. He had joined Gidie and now stood at his side, staring after Fulk.

'I don't know,' Gidie said. The two men with Richalda were walking away quickly now. 'You stay here and watch Fulk. I'll be back soon.'

He set off after Richalda. She was hard to see with all the people about, but one of the men was tall, and bore a coif of pale linen that was clearly visible as he moved through the crowds. Gidie trailed after them, and as they left the harbour and walked about the walls of the city, passing close by the Golden Gate and on to a mass of tents and pavilions, Gidie saw that they meant the child no harm.

But then, at a large shelter, with a flag fluttering outside it, which bore a red cross, Gidie saw Odo.

The man had a grim expression on his face. It looked much like that which he had worn when he had tried to kill Gidie.

Gidie watched as he took Richalda from the two men. Then he followed Odo to another, smaller tent.

Lothar waited until Fulk was alone.

The short figure of the Hermit was easy to miss in the throng

467

of people moving all about, but two of his bodyguards remained near him, and Lothar could easily see them looming over the folk all about. It was only when they turned about, and he saw that they were following Peter, that he stepped forward to find Fulk.

'What did the Hermit want with you?' he said.

'Lothar? You startled me!' Fulk looked surprised to see him. 'Peter was asking how the battle at Civitot was, how many we lost, how the Saracens fought. His men took Richalda to her mother. He insisted that I needed a rest, rather than going to search for Sybille.'

'Perhaps he was right,' Lothar said.

'I wanted to present Sybille with her daughter,' Fulk said, staring over the heads of the men nearby as though he thought he might find Sybille here in the crowd. 'I hoped to see Sybille again.'

'Perhaps the Hermit was right. Surely it is better that Sybille be reunited with her daughter without interruptions from an admirer?' Lothar said.

Fulk nodded slowly as he absorbed this, and Lothar felt like a traitor. He glanced over in the direction that the Hermit had gone, and he frowned quickly. Lothar was a warrior. He believed in speaking the truth, and in honesty and integrity. That the Hermit had taken the girl spoke to him of deceit. Peter must know that the two brothers were estranged, first by Odo's leaving Fulk and the others behind while he took the last ship, and then by his stealing Fulk's woman to be his wife. Lothar could not imagine a worse betrayal.

'Come, Fulk. Let us find a place to drink a cup or two of wine?'

'Yes,' Fulk said, but his eyes still roved about, searching for Sybille.

*

468

Sybille was sitting with some sewing in her lap, not that she could concentrate on the needlework. It was not the gathering gloom; her eyes stared sightlessly at the wall of the tent as though she could see through the canvas to the harbour, and thence to the narrow waters and away to Civitot, where she felt sure that her daughter lay dead.

She had accepted Odo's proposal of marriage against her better judgement. She had no feelings for Odo. He was not made from the same mould as Fulk. Fulk was exciting in a way that she could not explain, and as kind as an uncle. She had the feeling that he would make a good father to Richalda. But now both were dead. As Peter the Hermit had said, it was unlikely that she would find another man so willing to take her as Odo. Odo was a gift from God. He would look after her and protect her on the way to Jerusalem, and once there, Peter had said, she would find her life infinitely happier, for Jerusalem's streets flowed with love; it was a Heaven on earth, he had said. She hoped so, but she doubted it.

When the entrance of the shelter went dark with shadow, she flinched, but then she saw Odo and gave him a small, bleak smile.

'My love,' Odo said, 'I have wonderful news for you: Richalda is alive, look!'

Sybille felt her heart pound with something like agony. The idea that Richalda could be alive still had been in her mind all these last days, but she dared not submit to their temptations, as if to do so would put a curse on the dream. She gave a low moan almost of grief as her child appeared in the doorway, and held her arms wide. Seeing her, Richalda threw herself forward and into her mother's embrace. Odo watched with a smile to see the pleasure he had brought to these two.

'How did you survive?' Sybille asked, holding her daughter's face between her palms as though disbelieving her own eyes and thinking that the girl was a dream brought to torment her.

'Fulk and Roul took me to the tower,' Richalda answered brokenly. She pressed forward again and hid her face in her mother's shoulder. 'They fought the Saracens and saved us. All of us.'

'Fulk?' Sybille's face froze. She looked up at her husband.

'He survived. He must have run to the tower as soon as he might,' Odo said.

'But you said he was dead! How ... I wouldn't have ... If I had thought—'

'Wife, be still!' Odo said. 'We are wedded, and the marriage is consummated. We can do nothing about that. We have made a sacred bond.'

'But Fulk lives!'

'And if we had known that ...'

Sybille stared at him. He was pained, she saw, and she realised the hurt that this would give Odo as well as Fulk. Odo knew that of the two brothers she had been most fond of Fulk. Fulk would be terribly hurt, and there must be a dreadful rift between the brothers. All because of her.

'I am so sorry! I should have waited until we knew. I should have realised.'

'Enough! You are bound to me, wife!' he said, not unkindly.

'Of course. I am sorry,' Sybille said. She hugged Richalda tightly, but when Odo looked across at her, there was a look she did not recognise in his eyes. If she had described it, she would have said it was a covetous, greedy look.

He smiled at her, and she returned it, but there was a cold doubt in her heart. She felt ungrateful, for this man had saved her life. He had brought her away from the hell of Civitot. She owed him her life. She should be grateful.

But she could not lie. When she looked at Odo, she was repelled.

CHAPTER 37

Constantinople, Friday 17th October, 1096

Outside the tent, Gidie was surprised to see Sybille appear. She walked out with Richalda, and made her way down to the bank of the river, where the pilgrims and the poorer city folk would congregate to wash their clothes. Sybille clung tight to her daughter, and crouched at the side of the water, tugging Richalda's tunic over her head and seating her in the water before washing her face and body, crooning as she did.

Gidie walked to her. Sybille glanced up as he approached, anxiety in her eyes until she recognised him. 'Gidie! My friend, I am so glad to see you!'

'And I you, mistress. I am happy that you are well,' he said with a smile.

Sybille used the hem of her tunic to wipe her daughter's face. 'My Richalda is returned. How could I not be well?'

'Odo has told you of Fulk?'

'Fulk is alive, yes,' Sybille said. Her voice was quieter.

'It is fortunate we survived.'

'Odo told me that the Saracens came and attacked.'

'Did he?' Gidie said, and then it burst from him: 'Did he tell how he knocked me down and left me for dead? It was Fulk who saved my life.'

'Odo did that?' Sybille whispered, and then Gidie told her all.

Sybille stood at the water's edge, staring down at the lapping waves. In her mind she could see Fulk's face, his mouth smiling but his eyes filled with sadness and hurt, while Odo was beside him, leering. It was impossible not to believe Gidie. His words carried the force of conviction.

Her legs almost refused to support her. She tottered and almost fell, and it was Richalda who took her hand and steadied her. 'Mother? Mother, you're scaring me!'

'Don't be upset,' she said, but her words carried no weight. She felt as insubstantial as thistledown blown on the wind. It was a curious sensation, almost dizzying, as if she was already floating, and she wondered if this was what death felt like.

Gidie had told her he wanted to kill her husband, but she snapped, 'You want to die? If you harm him, the Hermit will have you executed within the hour!'

'Then what may I do?' he demanded. 'The man tried to kill me. You expect me to allow him to get away with that?' He pulled his dagger from his belt and held it up. 'I may be a peasant from the countryside, but I know what honour is!'

She had persuaded him to do nothing hasty and left Richalda with him. As she walked, her strength returned to her, until she had made her way back to the tent just as Odo was leaving it. Now, standing in Odo's path, his words came back to her. The old tranter had more sense of honour than Odo.

Eyes blazing, she confronted him. 'Is it true? You killed Jeanne, and then tried to kill Gidie too, and deserted Fulk? You married me, letting me think that I was in your debt for rescuing me, but all the while you were lying!'

'Wife, who told you all this?' Odo said. He smiled soothingly and tried to embrace her, but she whirled out of his reach.

Sybille had been doubtful, but now she studied Odo with a horrified certainty. His manner, his aloofness, were proof. 'You left my Richalda there: you left her behind on purpose! She is only a child; she could have been killed, but you didn't care, did you? Why, because you wanted me without any impediment? Or was it to make your brother jealous? To hurt him? Do you think Richalda and I are mere playthings, for you to pick up or discard as you wish?'

'Woman, you are hysterical.'

'I've learned my husband is a murderer!'

'Woman, you will be silent,' Odo said. He didn't try to move closer, but spoke more quietly. 'You are my wife, and you cannot accuse me of a crime. You will not bear witness against your own husband. And I will not have you shouting at me in the roadway like this. It is shameful behaviour.'

'I will shout your guilt from the rooftops if I—'

His fist caught her chin, and she was flung back, falling on her rump in the roadway. Both elbows struck the ground at the same time, and she remained there, stunned, while Odo crouched beside her. To her surprise there were tears in his eyes.

'You think I wanted this? I wanted to protect you, from *Fulk*! He isn't a good man, he's too driven by his passions. Can't you see that? He lied to me – *me*! He let me think Jeanne was a good woman, but he lied, tricking me, making me think she was suitable as a wife. When all the time he knew she was married and a . . . and a *whore*! I have a sacred duty here. I will help guide the armies to Jerusalem, to save the Holy City. That is my duty and my honour. And you must help me. We will not speak of this again, my wife. What is past is past. I have no regrets.'

'You murdered Jeanne,' Sybille whispered. 'And tried to kill Gidie.'

'It was all most unfortunate,' Odo said. He stood again, gazing about him, and then he wiped his eyes and smiled down at Sybille. 'But it is all resolved now. God is guiding me, you see. He approves, and He will see us safe to Jerusalem. Now, settle yourself, wife. I must go and speak to the Hermit.'

Sybille refused his proffered hand, and eased herself to her feet. She dusted herself down and gingerly touched the point of her jaw where his fist had caught her, and then felt her elbows. Both were grazed. Odo made as though to embrace her, but she averted her face and stepped back, away from his encircling arms. He scowled, lifted his chin haughtily and made his way to Peter's pavilion while she made her way back to the river where she had left Richalda. There were scores of children playing in the water here, giving shrill cries as they splashed and cavorted, the droplets of water catching the dying sun with sparkles and flashes.

'Did you speak to him?' Gidie said.

'Yes,' Sybille said, and looked about her, suddenly lost as the enormity and horror of her position struck her. Her eyes felt as though they were about to well, but no tears came. The horror was too great for weeping. She reached for Richalda and hugged her close. 'Dear Heaven! What will become of us?'

After leaving Sybille and her daughter with Guillemette, Gidie went in search of Fulk, finding him with Lothar at a small tavern near the harbour. He took his seat on a low wall and accepted a cup of watered wine, draining it with gratitude. The others were in a sombre mood.

He stared from Fulk to Lothar, unsure how to tell Fulk what he knew. Fulk was unaware of Odo's murder of Jeanne, and Gidie did not know how he would react on being told that his brother had killed the woman before taking Sybille. Glancing at Lothar, he held out his cup to be refilled, and then held it in two hands like a priest preparing for Mass while he tried to find the words to tell Fulk.

Lothar snorted and spat. 'There are more armies on their way here. Men from all over Europe are flocking to God's banner.'

'Is that what Peter has said?'

Fulk nodded. 'Yes. He said that there would be a need for men to go and scout the land from Civitot to Nicaea. We are to leave in a few days, when we are prepared.'

'Will your brother come with us?'

Fulk looked up. 'I don't know. Peter may want him here – he finds Odo useful, I think.'

Gidie stared into the cup as though he might find an answer there. 'Master Fulk, when I was knocked down at Civitot, you chose to believe that I was struck by a Saracen. But I was not.'

Fulk peered at him. 'I don't understand.'

'I said nothing because I could scarce believe it myself, but it was your brother who struck me down.'

'No, you are mistaken, Gidie,' Fulk said with a chuckle. 'Why should Odo do a thing like that?'

'At first I thought it was because I had found Jeanne at the water's edge. Perhaps Odo reasoned that I must have killed her, I thought. But the expression in his eyes was not rage and venge-fulness. It was more like fear, and a cold determination.'

'Hold!' Lothar said, raising a hand. This was too much for him to absorb. That Odo could have taken Fulk's wife was dreadful, but to do so after murdering Jeanne as well . . . that was incom-prehensible. 'You say that he killed his own woman? Do you know what you are saying?'

'He killed Jeanne, and sought to remove the one man who

could have witnessed the death – me. He knew I would guess he had killed—'

Fulk shook his head violently. 'No! You are wrong, my friend! Odo? He *loved* her. When I left him at the harbour, he was going to fetch her, to bring her here to safety, just as I was going to seek Sybille.'

'He saw me and tried to ride me down. I reasoned with him, and I thought I had got through to him, but then, when I turned away, he attacked me. It was he who did this,' he said, touching his scalp.

'You are confused, man! It was the blow to your head. Odo wouldn't do a thing like that – not attacking another pilgrim like you for no reason, nor killing Jeanne.'

'A man can change. Especially after the bloodshed we have seen on our way here.'

'Odo is a pious man. He wouldn't attack you. He couldn't.'

'You trust him?'

Fulk nodded. 'Yes.'

'Would you still trust him if he had taken Sybille from you? If he had married her?'

Fulk grinned quickly, but then, as he took in Gidie's serious expression, a terrible blankness came over him. He shook his head. 'No – don't even jest about such a thing. He couldn't have . . .'

Lothar felt Fulk's eyes on him and looked down and away, ashamed to see Fulk's distress.

'It is true,' Gidie said. 'I am sorry.'

Fulk climbed to his feet, stumbled, then frowned. It was impossible! Gidie must be lying! He turned and launched himself at Gidie, his hands bunched into fists, pulling back his right to beat Gidie until he admitted it was all untrue, that it was made up. 'You will take that back! Odo would not steal my woman! He couldn't!'

Lothar caught his fist in the air. 'Fulk! Why would Gidie

lie to you? I did not have the words to tell you that Odo had taken your woman, but it is true. He has married her. I swear, I was going to speak, but I was searching for the moment. As for his attack on Gidie . . . I had not heard this before.'

Fulk shook his head, tore his fist from Lothar's grasp, let go of Gidie's shirt and stared about him, his eyes wild. If Odo had done that, and then took ship from Civitot, it meant he had deserted Fulk there; it meant he deliberately left Fulk to die. His own brother!

Gidie was speaking. 'I'm truly sorry, Fulk, but it's true. I heard him. Odo married your woman as soon as he got her back here. While we were fighting for our lives, he took her as his wife. I heard them.'

'No, no,' Fulk said. Gidie's words sounded thick and almost incomprehensible. 'He couldn't do that to me. She would never have agreed.'

'They thought you were dead,' Gidie said. 'But that doesn't explain why he tried to kill me first.'

'No, you must be wrong!'

'And now we are to be sent back, you say? Perhaps Odo has spoken to Peter and persuaded him to send us all so that we can die in the lands over the sea, just as King David sent Uriah the Hittite to be slain so he could take the man's wife. Perhaps your brother will wear a penitent's garb if you die.'

Fulk suddenly clenched his fist and lifted it. Lothar grabbed it again, but Fulk was not attempting to punch Gidie. He knew now that Gidie was speaking the truth.

'Enough!' Lothar said again, but Fulk had already snatched his hand back, and set off at a run towards the pilgrim camp.

Heinnie and Father Albrecht were directed to a large pavilion, and there they found the Hermit and many of the leaders of the pilgrims. There were several priests sweltering in their heavy, religious garb, and men-at-arms and knights clad in light tunics against the heat.

Born in the Rhineland, Heinnie found the humidity oppressive here at the coast. It was good that as the sun dropped, the temperature fell with it, but it was still appallingly hot. The moon's reflection glittered and twinkled, offering the balm of cooling waters, but few of the pilgrims were of a frivolous enough bent to go and bathe. Heinnie determined to go and avail himself of the water at the first opportunity.

'You are very welcome,' Peter the Hermit said after Albrecht and Heinnie had been introduced. They exchanged the kiss of peace, and Heinnie stood back to allow Albrecht to speak directly to the Hermit.

While they spoke of the army of Hugh de Vermandois and the other men who would soon arrive, Heinnie kept his eyes on the ground at his feet. He could tell she was still near, and if he were to turn, he knew that he would see the column of smoke, roughly woman-shaped, with a dark, cowled face. Only he could see her, hear her footsteps; only he was aware of her presence, but he felt as if she was as plain as a live woman. He knew she was invisible to all but him, but the fact only served to increase his sense of isolation. She was his personal guilt, a symbol of his offence.

Albrecht had tried to ease his loneliness, but although the priest was knowledgeable and worldly wise, early on Heinnie had decided to keep his secret. The priest might well support him, but other soldiers would not.

He stared out over the sea. Somewhere out there, beyond the horizon, lay Jerusalem and his salvation.

Then a wild man appeared, and he was startled from his reverie.

*

Fulk ran in a fog of confusion. He wanted to see his brother; he wanted to demand the truth.

Anger and resentment at the injustice of Odo's behaviour swarmed in his head like flies about a corpse: every explanation he could conceive was smothered by suspicion and jealousy. Sybille was *his* woman. How could his brother have stolen her from him?

He passed the great gates of marble, and continued on over the sandy soil towards the pilgrim camp. Silken flags showed where the camp's commanders abode, their soft, fine fabrics snapping and fluttering in the breeze from the sea. Fulk did not notice their gleaming material. All he knew was that his brother must be there.

The pavilion was a tall structure with space for twenty men beneath it. Fulk saw Odo at the rear, standing with Peter the Hermit looking over the shoulder of a clerk at a wooden table while he laboriously wrote on a long scroll. There was another priest nearby, and a pilgrim with a scarred face whom he didn't recognise.

'Odo!'

Fulk could not hide the raw pain in his voice. He wanted to speak, to beg for an explanation, but the words wouldn't come. Instead he held his hands out like a supplicant.

'Brother!' Odo said.

'Odo, I ... Tell me it's not true! You haven't taken Sybille and—'

'I married her; I had to, to protect her,' Odo said, and gave a thin smile.

Fulk felt his smile like a bolt from the sky. In it he saw the truth of all Gidie had said. At first he felt a numbness, like a man who has been struck on the head whose legs begin to wobble before he collapses. Then he felt rage thunder through his veins. There

479

was a mist of blood between him and Odo, and he grabbed his dagger almost without realising, moving forward and making to jump at his brother, but before he could, the pilgrim gripped his wrist and held him. He struggled and fought, and tried to punch the man's face, but the strange priest took hold of his arm. Fulk shook him off and, swinging a fist, he felt it connect with a man's face, but then a blow struck his head and he toppled to his knees and fell into an abyss.

Gidie hurried in the wake of Fulk, and now, as Fulk collapsed, he and Lothar reached the group.

'What, will you kill him, like you tried to murder me?' Gidie shouted at Odo. He set his hand to his knife, but as he did, he was grabbed by bodyguards to the Hermit, and forced at spear-point to stand still. Lothar found his way blocked by three guards, each of whom eyed him with the suspicion of farm dog watching a fox.

'Leave him alone!' Gidie cried out as a man kicked Fulk in the upper body. A spear-butt slammed into his belly.

'Shut up!'

Gidie bent over, retching, while Lothar called to Peter and Odo, 'Masters! We are friends to Fulk. Let us take him back to our camp, and we shall ensure that he is kept safe until we leave this city and continue on our pilgrimage.'

Peter turned and frowned at Lothar as though trying to place his face. 'He is mad, you understand? How will you ensure that my friend Odo is secure from his violence?'

Lothar looked at Odo. 'He is Odo's brother. This is a madness caused by his grief. I am sure that Odo would not want his own brother's blood on his hands?'

'It would scarcely be Odo's fault if his brother were executed for a violent attack on him.'

'But Odo would feel the blood on his hands all his life,'

Lothar said. 'Odo would carry that on his soul for the rest of his days.'

Peter glanced sadly at Odo. 'It is not only Odo who would feel the sorrow. But I have to weigh up the danger to the other pilgrims, were we to lose Odo to a madman's attack. I cannot risk that.'

'At least hold him. This madness will pass.'

'No. I shall inform the Emperor and ask him to deal with the fellow,' Peter said. He held out his hands wide, as though an invisible cross had them gripped, shook his head mournfully, and said, 'Fulk, I shall pray for you. God forgive you!'

That was when the men gripping Lothar's arms pulled him away. Gidie was trying to speak, but he managed only a gasping croak before a fist struck him in the mouth and he was still.

Peter the Hermit stood at Odo's side as guards gathered up Fulk and bound his hands. 'My son, I am so sorry to see this!' he said, rubbing his hands with distress. 'That your own brother should draw a knife against you! It is terrible. Terrible!'

'He is your brother?' Heinnie said.

'He cannot cope with the thought that I married my wife,' Odo said calmly. 'He wanted her for himself.'

'Oh,' Heinnie said. He glanced at Fulk. Even now, unconscious, Fulk bore a look of despair. Heinnie felt a quick sympathy for him. He had lost Lothar and now knew how wrong his actions had been; this fellow had lost his brother. They were both alone, and both because of a woman.

'But for a brother to lift his hand against his brother, while we are on a holy pilgrimage!' Peter said. 'That is unforgivable.'

'It is sad,' Odo said. He looked down at Fulk, and he did feel a pang. They were brothers, and he felt a lingering affection, but it was not strong enough to erase the pain Fulk's duplicity had instilled. He hardened his heart. Fulk had betrayed him. He deserved his punishment.

'He must be deeply offended. You should not have married your wife so swiftly,' Peter said. He began washing his hands – Odo thought he looked fretful, like Pilate making his decision. 'I should have urged more caution.'

'I married her to protect her. He should accustom himself to the fact. It is a judgement on his past life.'

Fulk heard their voices as he groggily came to consciousness once more. He gazed about him, blearily at first, but then the last minutes returned to him and he tried to climb to his feet. A man placed his boot on Fulk's back and pressed him down once more as Peter the Hermit eyed him with sadness.

'My son, you must forgive your brother. He behaved with the best of intentions, I assure you.'

Fulk burst out, 'He took my woman as his wife, and he—'

A boot struck his flank and Fulk subsided, pain reaching out like a star with points of poison to stab his armpit, hip and spine. As more boots kicked at him, he felt a rib crack, and curled into a ball to protect his head.

He would have continued. He would have told Peter that Odo had murdered Jeanne, that he tried to kill Gidie, that he betrayed those left at Civitot and deserted them, but as he looked up into Peter's anxious eyes he knew it was pointless. The Hermit would brook no further dispute: he was convinced of Odo's honour. If Fulk were to accuse his brother and Peter declared Odo innocent, under the law, Fulk must pay the penalty of the false accuser: he would be executed.

'This is God's judgement of you, Fulk,' Peter said sadly. 'You must learn to accept His grace and accept your fate at His hands.'

Hands grabbed Fulk beneath the armpits, and he felt himself lifted. When he glanced back, he saw that Odo had taken his sword and stood now staring after him as he was half-carried, half-dragged from the pavilion and along the roadway, the stones grazing his knees. As he heard the noise of the sea grow louder, and realised that he was being taken towards the harbour, a fresh blow struck his head and he passed into a blessed unconsciousness, far from his brother, his worries and all alarms.

Gidie came to with a cool cloth on his brow. Looking up he found himself peering into Guillemette's eyes. She smiled down at him, then lifted one eyebrow and shook her head slowly. 'You poor fool.'

'I wanted to stop him. I tried.'

'I know. Lothar told me. You should not have told Fulk what had happened, though. It was too soon.'

'He had to know; he had to know what sort of man his brother has become, what he did to—'

'What Odo did to you and to Jeanne, yes. I understand,' she said.

'You don't understand!' he said savagely. 'You can't! He tried to murder me!'

'You think I don't understand?' she said, and there was a cold, fierce tone in her voice. 'Jeanne was my friend, Gidie. I walked all the way here with her, saving her from her husband, and just when she needed me and my help, I wasn't there to save her! She died because I left her!' The hand on his brow shivered with passion. 'I failed her.'

'And I will not fail to avenge her. I have to – not just because of what he did to me. He is mad, and there's no telling what he might not do while in charge of the pilgrims under Peter.'

She shook her head. 'You're in no state to threaten him. Not with your head in this state.'

'Then when I am recovered. I cannot accuse him. Peter will listen to no criticism of his favourite adviser; that would only result in me getting thrown into gaol alongside Fulk.'

'There must be someone you could tell,' she wondered.

'Who stands equal to Peter the Hermit? If he rejects an accusation, that is an end to it. I could not even speak to the Emperor. Only Peter and Odo seem to have the Emperor's ear.'

She was silent for a moment. Then, 'What do you think will happen to Fulk?'

'Peter said that they will let the Emperor decide.'

'Decide what?'

'Whether he lives or dies. And Odo said nothing to protect him.'

She squeezed out a fresh cloth and replaced it on his brow. 'At least wait until your head is better,' she said. 'You are in no condition to avenge anyone just now.'

He nodded and closed his eyes, but he was determined that he would take the first opportunity to kill Odo.

CHAPTER 38

Constantinople, Friday 17th October, 1096

Fulk came to slowly.

He was in a dark, cool, dank chamber that stank of rats and piss. His hands were bound, and a chain ran from his wrists to a ring set in the wall. He lifted his wrists to his mouth and tried to ease the cords, but he failed. The hemp was chafing both wrists, and the weight of the chain made movement painful as the fibres irritated his sore flesh. He rolled over to kneel, keeping his hands on the ground to stop the irritation as far as was possible, and studied his surroundings. There were three walls of stone and a small entrance in the fourth that held a low doorway that was blocked by a gate of steel rods set in a frame. It looked immovable, but with the chain Fulk could not reach it in any case.

Rolling again, he sat with his back to the wall and rested his hands in his lap, wincing as the rope moved about his wrists again. Blood was trickling slowly from his left, and it took an effort of will not to wipe it away. Every movement was painful. Better by far to remain still and let the blood trickle until it dried.

Occasionally a breeze wafted in and circulated about the cell. When it did, he snuffed it like a dog scenting prey. He could smell the sea, a salty tang, the odour of rancid fish and entrails, and he wished he were outside again, free. But that would not happen. Peter and his men had contained him here, and that must mean that he was to be held and punished. He had spoken of Sybille, and he had gone to Odo with rage and hatred in his heart. At the least he could expect to be flogged.

He barely cared. Sybille was lost to him. Without her, life lost all savour. The idea of continuing to Jerusalem had lost any attraction. He had nothing to offer to that great project. Where he had been keen to fight the enemies of Christ, now he was merely weary. Whatever the punishment Peter the Hermit saw fit to impose, he would endure it. And then, when all was done, he would set his face to the west once more. He would return to his homeland, to Sens, and he would put aside all thoughts of Sybille. Odo was dead to him. They were no longer brothers. He would go home and set up his own smithy somehow, forget about the pilgrimage. If God could do this to him, He did not want Fulk to make the journey.

Drawing up his legs, Fulk set his brow upon his knees, screwing his eyes tight shut against the urge to weep.

That evening a bowl of rice and a cup of water were brought to him by the gaoler, a man who was already past his thirtieth year, and who was clad in better clothes than Fulk would have expected on a merchant at home. He assumed the man acquired the clothes of those executed from his cells.

The thought made him wonder where his sword was. Odo had picked it up, but he hoped Odo did not mean to keep it. Somehow he doubted he would ever see his weapon again.

He put the sword from his mind. It was the least of his concerns.

Constantinople, Saturday 18th October

Guillemette and Mathena were kneeling at their small cookpot. It hung over a little fire and the smell of pottage was enticing. Esperte was sitting under the lip of their shelter, which was little more than a cloak slung between four sticks, while Gidie, his head bound with a dirty strip of linen wound about his skull like a cap, stood guard nearby. He glanced over and ducked his head when he saw Sybille approach, leading Richalda by the hand. She gratefully sank to the floor when invited.

'What is it?' Guillemette asked. Their march had long since dispelled any animosity between them.

Sybille began to speak, but quickly her throat clogged and the words wouldn't come. Instead her eyes filled with tears, and she broke down into sobs as she tried to explain.

'It is decided! The Emperor has approved the death warrant. They will execute Fulk!'

Guillemette gasped. 'Who will?'

'Odo told me. He was gloating as he told me! Peter the Hermit sent Fulk for judgement to the Emperor, and he is keen to execute any malefactor, just to show that here his law holds sway.'

'Will Odo speak for his brother?' Guillemette said.

'Him? Odo made no sign he would dispute the Hermit's right to see Fulk killed.'

'Odo is a devil,' Gidie said. 'I will kill him.'

'No, Gidie!' Sybille said. 'You mustn't! This is a pilgrimage! You must not act against Odo.'

'I have to! He slew Jeanne and would have killed me too!'

'*No*! You must not do anything that could threaten your soul. Odo has committed offences as we know. He will pay for them, but not at the expense of your soul.'

'I must have my revenge. God will understand.'

'So I will lose you as well as Fulk?' she demanded tearfully.

Gidie winced. 'Odo has to be killed, if he is not to bring the whole pilgrimage to disaster! How could God want him to lead us, when Odo cannot even be trusted to protect his own brother?'

Guillemette nodded slowly. She stirred the pottage idly, while her mind worked. Then she abruptly climbed to her feet.

'Where are you going?' Mathena said.

'I won't sit here while a good man gets killed.'

In truth, Guillemette had little idea what she could do. At first she was walking to speak with the Hermit to beg for Fulk's life, but as she walked, she found her legs growing more reluctant. The Hermit was an austere man, and although he could be persuaded by the pleas of others, it was unlikely that a reformed prostitute would win favour in the eyes of a man who still considered Odo to be the soul of honesty and piety.

Who else, then? She had thought she might go to Odo, but discarded that idea quickly. He had made his views about her all too plain on the journey here. Besides, Odo's action in marrying Sybille spoke of little respect for Fulk. No, she must think of someone else. But she had no idea who else could help. Sir Walter would have supported Fulk, she was sure, but he had been killed by the Saracens.

Then she remembered the tall, scarred man at the tower: Alwyn. He had kind eyes, she thought, and he had lived here in the city for long enough, he must surely know someone who could help her.

But how could she find him?

She was at the edge of the pilgrim's encampment when she saw a slight figure ahead of her. Surely that was the girl who had been with Alwyn in the tower while they endured the siege? She was sure of it! Guillemette quickly set off after Sara, hurrying in the gathering gloom.

Sara was making her way along the edge of the pilgrim camp, and suddenly ducked down under a shelter of thick material that had been securely pegged down in military fashion. Just in front of it a small fire blazed. As Guillemette approached, she saw Alwyn sitting beside it, staring deep into the flames. He looked up as she approached.

'Mistress,' he said, 'last time I saw you, you offered me water. Would you accept some water from me in return?'

'Gladly!' she said, and sat across the fire from him. When Sara brought a mazer of fine polished wood, she sipped gratefully. 'Master, I crave your help.'

'Anything,' he said, and leaned forward when she began to speak.

BOOK NINE

Flight

CHAPTER 39

Constantinople, Thursday 23rd October, 1096

On his first morning in the cell, the Saturday, Fulk had been still awake, stiff and unrefreshed, when the gaoler appeared, standing in the doorway peering at him. Soon Fulk had a plate of dried, flat bread that wanted to break his teeth, and a small pot of water that tasted brackish and foul.

On the Sunday, Fulk had woken to find a jug of weak wine and a platter with some fresh flat bread and cheese at his side. He sat staring at it for a long time, half-asleep, thinking it was a dream. The sight of a cockroach on the plate spurred him to eat, rather than deterring him. With the first taste he realised he was voraciously hungry, and he consumed the food eagerly. It was enough to send him into a doze for much of the day. That evening he had a meal of broiled chicken meat, cold rice and some thickened food that was rather like mashed swede with spices added.

He spent three days in this manner, then on the fourth he was woken by a stone striking his head. Blearily he opened his eyes and yawned, and saw Lothar and Alwyn at the doorway. The early morning sun gave them a golden glow, almost like haloes about their heads.

Alwyn jerked his head. 'You need to leave here. Now!'

In answer Fulk held up his hands. 'If you would unchain me, I'll be happy to.'

Lothar pulled out a knife and strode to him. The blade sliced through the cords that bound his wrists like a razor, and Fulk stiffly climbed to his feet with a grimace as his hands developed pins and needles. He felt befouled, and his feet were uncomfortable, his legs weak, as he followed after his friends.

'What did you do to the gaoler?' he whispered.

'We bribed him, but only a little,' Alwyn said matter-of-factly. 'He didn't see much point in keeping you here. Besides, he's a Greek. He saw no reason to hold you here on the say of the Hermit. He was happy to take our money.'

Lothar peered out through the doorway, then moved on, beckoning them to follow. When Fulk joined him, he saw that they were near the gates to the harbour. Lothar held up a hand, and when Fulk peered around his shoulder, he saw a number of pilgrims standing at the harbourside. A young woman with a simple shift bound at the waist with a leather belt padded past them on light, bare feet, and Fulk recognised Sara. She walked to Alwyn as though she had not a care in the world, and bent her head as she spoke. 'There are many guards but they are to protect the ships from pilgrims, not to search for one man.'

Alwyn nodded and soon the four were striding along towards a ship.

'Where are we going?' Fulk said.

'You cannot remain here. We are to sail to spy the land for the armies that will follow,' Lothar said. 'We shall return to Civitot and thence ride to Nicaea and beyond, if we can.'

Fulk stopped. He gazed down. His feet were unshod, and he

had no weapon, not even a knife. 'Look at me! What use can I be to you? My friends, leave me. You go on; my pilgrimage is over.'

Lothar had halted, and he gave Alwyn a quick look. 'Fulk, you must come with us.'

'There is nothing for me in the Holy Land. I should return to my home, not go seeking more adventures.'

'Fulk, if you remain here you will be killed,' Alwyn said. 'You have been reported as a troublemaker to the city authorities, and you will be executed.'

'Who would do such a thing?'

Alwyn exchanged a glance with Lothar, then back at Fulk, his head lowered. 'Does it matter? It could have been the Hermit, your brother, or even someone else whom you have upset. What does it matter? The city is determined to maintain order, and with so many armed pilgrims, and more armies on their way, the Vestes and the Emperor both fear riots and lawlessness. It is in their minds to produce a few bodies to demonstrate that the law here holds sway over all: city folk and pilgrims alike. You will be a strong example. You must come with us.'

Stunned, Fulk allowed Lothar to take his arm and lead him onwards. At the harbour they were stopped by seven heavily armoured guards, who demanded to know what they were doing there.

Alwyn drew himself up to full height, then allowed his head to drop, his chin jutting truculently. His eyes narrowed, and his thick, greying hair moved with the breeze as threatening as the Medusa's snakes. 'Do you know me?'

'Yes,' the leader admitted.

'Who do I work for?'

'The Vestes.'

'And you know I could have you flayed for delaying the Vestes' commands?'

'Yes . . . sir.'

'We go to that ship, to sail to Civitot and scout the lands for any survivors and see whether we can find what the army of Kilij-Arslan does – whether it has returned east or lies in wait. Would you have the Vestes deprived of that information?'

'No, sir.'

'Then get your rabble out of my way!'

The soldiers retreated, and Alwyn glared at them a moment longer before striding along the harbour wall.

At the farther end of the harbour there was a small vessel with a sun-burned crew, and Fulk followed Alwyn to a ladder. Sara sprang to it and went down it as agile as a squirrel. Alwyn went next, and then hands were helping Fulk. On the deck, he stood in a state of confusion. To have been liberated from that cell was more than he could have hoped for, but now the bright sunlight was giving him a headache, and he was filled with a weariness that came more from misery than his ill-treatment.

'Fulk, try to rest,' he heard, and Alwyn clapped him on the back. The older man peered into his eyes. 'I am sorry how things turned out,' he said.

'There is no reason to dwell on the past,' Fulk said. He stared about him. 'Odo is not the same man who left Sens with me. This new Odo is someone I do not know; he has lost all feeling for me and his friends.'

As he spoke the ship came to life. Orders were bellowed, and shipmen went running up the ratlines to the sails, while others loosened the ropes holding the hull fast to the harbour. More commands, and the ropes were pulled in and neatly coiled, and long oars were used to shove the vessel from the stones of the wall. More sweeps appeared along the ship's sides, rising and waiting while a drum began to beat. In time to the beat the oars dropped into the waters, pulled and rose again, and the ship began lethargically to move away from the city.

Fulk sat with his back to the mast and ignored the rest of the party as they crossed the straits. It was only when the ship reached the far shore at Civitot and the other men had disembarked that he rose to his feet.

He moved stiffly along the gangplank and made his way up the harbour. From there he walked slowly up the sands until he could see the tower where he and the others had fought to hold the Muslims at bay. All about him there was a bustle of barked orders and competent busyness. Along with Lothar and Alwyn there was a party of some thirty men who had come to help scout the lands, and some were settling on the beach repacking food and other items while others helped disembark horses and pack animals. More ships were coming with additional soldiers.

Fulk did not speak when Lothar joined him, but remained stock still, staring at the land before him. In his mind's eye he could see the men being hacked down by Saracen warriors, the spear-points penetrating the people running away, the hideous curved swords moving so apparently easily, taking off the heads of their victims. He could hear the screams, the solid *whack* of arrows striking flesh, feel again the horror and despair.

'Fulk, my friend,' Lothar said. 'Do not mourn.'

'How can I not? She has been stolen from me. Even if Odo dies, I cannot marry her now. Legally I would be trying to wed my sister. Odo has taken her from me, and there is nothing I can do about it.'

'No, so concentrate on the things you can do.'

'Like what? I am a broken man!'

Lothar's voice held a sharper tone. 'There are others in the pilgrim army who have lost everything: men and women and their children lie here. You can smell them! Their bones are being picked clean. They lost all in the struggle to get here and fight for their faith. You were bold enough to come here for that same purpose. So God is testing you now: perhaps for a greater purpose. Who can tell?'

'What more does God want of me?' Fulk spat.

Lothar grabbed his arm and pulled him round. The big Rhinelander glared deeply into his eyes. 'Look! You see nothing. *Look* at this place! It was a Christian land, and now it is stolen. What would you have the people do here? Submit to the invaders, or fight to win back their freedoms?'

'What do you want of me?'

'Help us! Pray! Renew your vows to God to serve Him on this holy pilgrimage; remember that there are others here who need your help. You have suffered, and your woman too. So do what you may to serve those who have yet to come. Help guard them.'

Constantinople

It was late afternoon when Odo heard of Fulk's disappearance. The sun had faded outside, and through the tent's walls he could see the light from a score of campfires.

He was coldly furious that the gaoler at the harbour could have allowed Fulk to escape, but while speaking to the man he concealed his anger beneath a cold, haughty demeanour that he felt was more suitable when dealing with fools.

Peter the Hermit had been more astonished than irate when he heard that his prisoner had been released. He closed his mouth, white with vexation, and politely asked that he be taken to the Vestes. Before leaving the camp, he told Odo that he would find out where Fulk had gone, and would ensure his arrest. 'We cannot allow heretics and malcontents to go unpunished,' he said as he left.

To Odo's mind the Greeks of Constantinople were incompetents. They demanded an army to come and liberate them from the vile depredations of the Sultan and his hordes, but when the Christians arrived to give them aid, the Greeks deserted them, driving them over the straits to lie mouldering on the shoreline. When the Christians attempted something wonderful, the Emperor did nothing to help until their armies had been wiped out, and only when a mere few remained did he send ships to rescue them.

And now Fulk had been released.

He should have been punished. Peter was right. And yet in the midst of his righteous anger, Odo rejoiced at the knowledge that Fulk was free. He felt almost physically torn, caught between indignation that Fulk had escaped, and joy that his brother was saved from the rope. It left him feeling strangely empty, his belly twisted.

Back at the tent he sat on his stool. Plates of fruit and some cheese were set before him by Sybille on the chest they used as a table, but he had no hunger. He stared at the chest. Inside was . . . but no. He wouldn't think of that now. Looking at his wife, Odo saw that she had little appetite either.

She knelt on blankets beside the boards that constituted their table, picking at the fruits on the wooden trencher, Richalda at her side.

'Wife, are you not hungry?'

'My appetite is not strong today,' Sybille said.

'Fulk has escaped from the cell where he was held.'

'He has escaped?' Sybille said.

She looked up at him with a face as pale as new linen, and Odo shivered suddenly as though he was looking at a wraith. There

499

was a germ of hope in her eyes. A hope that was unbecoming in Odo's wife.

'He is said to have made his way from the city.'

'Where will he go?'

'Back to our home, I expect. He will return and tell tall tales of the people he met, the women he loved,' Odo said carelessly. 'He was ever a keen collector of women.'

Sybille looked away but said nothing.

Odo could not help himself. He gave a sour grin, adding, 'He enjoyed many of the women in the pilgrimage. I think he only chose to come when he heard how many women were joining. He was always keen on Guillemette and the other women.'

'He is a good, kind man.'

'When he saw how it would give him an advantage, perhaps.'

'That is a spiteful thing to say about your own brother,' she said.

'Woman, look at me!' Odo said. He disliked the way that she would avert her head when she objected to what he said. She was as recalcitrant as a mule on occasion. 'Fulk is my brother, and I know him well. Too well, perhaps. I know you were fond of him, but do not make the mistake of thinking you were special. You were one of—'

She stood. 'I have a headache. I will go for a walk.'

'You will remain here while I am talking!' Odo shouted. 'I am your husband.'

'Yes,' she said quietly. 'You are.'

'What does that mean?'

'Nothing, husband.' She stared at him for a few moments, her eyes red-rimmed, he noticed.

'Come back here!' he shouted, but she had already left the tent. He stared down at Richalda, who remained squatting on her haunches, meeting his gaze with fear. Odo tried to smile at her, but his lips felt as if they would rip with the effort. Instead he rose and stalked after Sybille.

Civitot

Lothar's words were to come to Fulk again that evening.

They had lighted a fire in the rubble and mess of broken arrows, and Fulk and his friends sat about it. Outside the walls two other fires served the rest of the company, and one group had begun to sing and dance, swaying to the music.

There were dark patches in the dirt, but Fulk and the others avoided looking at them. They indicated where someone had bled to death.

Alwyn had passed about strips of salted beef that had been dried in the sun, and they were chewing the tough meat. When they threw logs onto the fire, sparks were thrown up into the air. Fulk didn't watch them, he kept his gaze fixed to the glowing heart of the flames, and all the while he mulled over what Lothar had said.

He still believed that he should go back home, but something in Lothar's words made him feel guilty, as though he was deserting others who needed him. When he had set off with Odo from Sens, he had sworn the same oath as the other pilgrims, to come and release Jerusalem. So many of them had died, the bodies were impossible to count: scores in Hungary and along the route to Constantinople, and now thousands of the survivors had been slaughtered only a few miles from here at the latest battle.

News of these disasters must have reached home, surely, yet still more men were on their way. More pilgrims determined to do their best for God, and perhaps die in the attempt. Their willing sacrifice made Fulk's urge to leave the pilgrimage and return home seem petty and shameful. Yes, Odo's theft of his woman was abominable, but Fulk had not come all this way to find a wife. Perhaps he should look on this as a pilgrimage for his own redemption.

Alwyn was sitting with Sara. He stood now, and beckoned Fulk to join him. He took Fulk away from the camp and the ribald humour of the troops.

'This is a good land,' Alwyn said. He waved a hand vaguely. 'Christ was born over there, and it was blessed by his feet. It is worth fighting for.'

'Perhaps so.'

'Have you prayed for God's help?'

'No. I have no words. I need a priest to help me.'

'Then we will find you a priest. You have to be comfortable with yourself.'

'You think I'm not now?'

Alwyn looked at him from the corner of his eye. 'I arrived here many years ago, before this,' he said, lifting his horribly disfigured hand. 'At the time I came because I had no home. The Normans under Sir Roger's father killed my kin. So I and my friends came here to join a new army. We hoped that we would succeed in protecting the Empire of Byzantium from the Saracens. Yet all my friends were slain and this was done to me.'

'I know.'

'But you don't know how it hurt me. I was injured, looked down on for surviving the battle in which my comrades had perished, and when people saw me in the street, children would stare at me with revulsion. At first, some people helped me, but after weeks had passed, I was no longer an injured hero to be admired, but a pitiful beggar to be kicked from the path. I was a reminder of failure, you see. No one wanted to be reminded that our army had been kicked in the teeth by a force of Norman donkeys.'

'And your point?'

'Only this: I understand you and the torment of your soul. You have lost everything here, but you have a home in Sens. You can scuttle off back. I couldn't. When I came here, I knew I could never go home. I have none. Perhaps that made life easier for me to accept after our failure at Dyrrhachium. I had nowhere to retreat to.'

'Like a coward, you mean?' Fulk said coldly.

'You can take it how you wish. If that is how it feels to you, perhaps so.'

'I am no coward!'

'No,' Alwyn said. 'I don't think you are. But you would desert us and the pilgrims to come.'

'What use am I?'

Alwyn lifted up his hand again. 'Do you think I never wondered that myself?'

'You fought for the Empire,' Fulk said, peering into Alwyn's eyes. 'That means you have a home here.'

'I did. I was born a free Saxon in Wessex. I lost my home there even though I thought God was on King Harold's side. But He protected William of Normandy instead, and my people were slaughtered. So I came here and made Constantinople my home. Now I have lost that too.'

'Why?'

'The Vestes threatened me. He told me I must behave well towards the Normans like Sir Roger there, or he would sell my Sara into a brothel and see Jibril enslaved.'

'That is why you brought her with you here?'

'Yes. It showed me that no matter how hard I worked for the benefit of my new home, I was never fully accepted. With Jibril dead, I have cut the shackles again. I am free, once more. And I choose the direction of my life from here. I shall go to Jerusalem.

Perhaps to die, but at least I will have tried to serve God. If I gave Him any reason to despise me before, I will wash away my sins before my death. I will die in Jerusalem or in the attempt to reach it.'

'And I should too?' Fulk said. He did not keep the sneer from his voice.

'You can run home on your own or help your comrades. You may die, but at least you will die doing God's work. The choice is yours.'

Alwyn left him soon after that. And it was as he walked back to their campfire that Lothar's words came back to Fulk: 'Serve those who have yet to come. Help guard them.'

Perhaps, he thought, there was a meaning to his life still.

Constantinople

Odo could not find her. Sybille had moved westward, and he walked about the rough encampment until it was fully dark, long past the blaring of trumpets that heralded the barring of the city's gates. Eventually he made his way to the shoreline, where the fishermen held their nets and the rank odour of fish guts left to rot in the sun hung like a heavy miasma over the land. He followed the coast back towards the city, slowly making his way through the shelters and tents of the pilgrims until he found himself back at his own.

'Woman! Where did you go?' he demanded, seeing Sybille at the door to his shelter.

'I wanted fresh air,' she said.

'I called you back.'

'I know. I didn't want to come.'

'You are my wife.'

'You do not own my heart!'

He lashed out. It was not hard, it was merely an instinctive slap of his open palm, but in the enclosed space it sounded as loud as a hammer on a shield. Both stood stock still in the aftermath, she looking away, he staring at her, while Richalda gave a high squeal that seemed to go on forever.

They remained there for many heartbeats. She did not put a hand to her cheek, but stood staring at the shelter's wall. Then, she turned to face him as her cheek began to redden. 'My husband only struck me once,' she hissed. 'Only once, because he loved me and did not want to offend me. You do not love me.'

'I married you to protect you,' he said. 'There was never mention of love between us.'

She walked past him to her daughter, shushing her and sending her outside. She spoke with her back to him. 'That is true enough. And there will be none.'

Turning to face him, he saw a tear trickle from her right eye as she spoke. He watched it course from her lower lid, moving slowly to the flat expanse of her cheek, where it traced a snail's path to the crease where her mouth used to widen into a smile. He longed to touch it, to lick it away. She had never looked more desirable.

'Let me—' he began.

'Don't *touch* me!' she spat.

'What?'

'You do not want me! What, did you only wish to hurt Fulk? You succeeded, I am sure. But you killed my heart at the same time. You do not love me and I *despise* you! You are weak, a coward, and—'

This time his hand was not open. He bunched his fist and hit her in the belly, hard, so that she fell backwards, and then he was on her, and throwing her skirts up, prising her legs apart, entering her while she slapped ineffectually at him, until he gripped her wrists and held them down over her head. She thrashed and bucked, but he would not let her go until he was spent, and then he pulled away from her, standing and adjusting his hosen and tunic.

'Tomorrow, woman,' he said coldly, 'I will lead a party to find my brother, and I will make sure that the orders of the law are carried out. He will die for his heresy. You will never see him again. Grow accustomed to that.'

He went to the flap of the door, then faced her briefly. 'You are my wife now. You will obey me.'

As soon as he had gone, Sybille moved to her knees and rested there for some time, her hands on her belly. His punch had seemed almost to pass through her, crushing her stomach and womb. The rape afterwards had left her bruised, sore and humiliated – worse: *defiled*. He had broken her with his vicious act of possession.

She climbed to her feet. It was hard to walk to the tent's flap, but she managed it by clutching at the tent pole on her way. She clung to it like a staff while her heart hammered, fearing that she would be sick, and then had a thought. She sank to the ground and opened a chest. Inside she saw the wrapped package. She took it from the chest and held it to her breast before rising and stiffly walking from the tent and out to the pilgrim camp.

Two men called to her as she went, but her tragic expression stopped them. With her hands on the parcel as if holding it in place, she walked through the other pilgrims. They could have been as insubstantial as wisps of smoke to her. No one was of any consequence. She was unaware even of her own daughter, who trailed along behind her like a loyal hound.

'Guillemette,' she called, as she approached the little shelter where the women were huddled. Roul was lying nearby, and he climbed to his feet at the sound of her tone.

'Mistress, I . . .' Guillemette saw her expression, her stiff bearing, and the way that her hands remained on her belly. 'God's pains! Come here, Sybille!'

Sybille gave one choking sob, and fell into Guillemette's welcoming embrace as the tears came.

Gidie was startled awake when Guillemette shook his shoulder roughly. He looked up blearily at her. 'What? It's not dawn yet, is it?'

She stared down at him. 'You have work to do, if you want to thwart Odo's plans and save Fulk's life.'

CHAPTER 40

Civitot, Friday 24th October, 1096

The sight was enough to make all of them take pause.

They rose early, before the dawn, and set off to begin their journey. Lothar was leading the way with Alwyn when they had travelled the league or more from Civitot and found themselves on the field of death. They could smell it long before they came to it: a stench of putrefaction that clung to their nostrils and stuck cloyingly in their throats.

Fulk gazed about him as he rode. The scene was familiar, yet only vaguely, like a place imagined in a dream. The last time he had been here, the dust of battle had been in his eyes and throat, and the whole area had looked different. But now he longed for that blanket of obscurity. It would have hidden the horror.

Fulk came to a place on a hill from where he could see the battlefield. It was, he thought, the vantage point where Odo had gone to view the ranks of the enemy. Now the place had become a scene of horror.

At the top, there was a mound of bodies. Not a mere wall or

heap, but rather a monstrous hill of the dead, clad in shreds and tatters of material, the remnants of hosen or tunics. Many were showing pale and white where the corpses had been picked clean to the bone. Even now, foul birds hopped and flapped, so gorged with carrion that they could scarce fly. Wild dogs, rats and other creatures scuttled.

Nearby stood a pyramid, neatly stacked, of heads. A hideous warning, were one needed, that the Saracens would fight to the bitter end to defend this land. These were the heads of those whom the Saracens thought were unfit for slavery. He heard a sudden intake of breath, then a loud scream of horror as Sara caught sight of the grisly scene. Fulk glanced back towards her, surprised at her reaction. Lothar was with her, blocking her view, murmuring to her and helping her onwards.

Fulk was irritated, and then upset to the point of grief. He should *himself* have felt revulsion. The sight would only a few months ago have caused his belly to heave and brought on a fit of weeping. But now? It struck him as a sad sight, a horrible sight, but where his heart had once beat to the rhythm of his emotions and his empathy for others, now it worked to a different tune. He could look at the figures, and see only numbers. There were too many to mourn, too many for whom to feel compassion. One person lying dead at the roadside was a source of sorry sympathy, but the sight of this multitude was ... overwhelming. It left his soul untouched.

It was many miles before the odour of death left them, and even then Fulk felt keenly the need to bathe, as though the foul stink had sunk into his flesh.

Constantinople

Odo did not give his wife a glance when he left the tent that morning as dawn was breaking.

He had no need of her, nor the squalling child who moped about the tent and looked so miserable, cowering when he glanced in her direction. She had been the same since he chastised her mother. Sybille had no understanding of the pressure he was feeling. In the last week, since he had first been forced to slap her, he had been busy with Peter the Hermit, negotiating supplies from the Empire, planning the onward march of the new pilgrim armies about to arrive. It was difficult, but he had ignored her sulking. It was her fault he struck her; he *had* to. As her husband he had a duty to discipline her. And now, since he had made love to her last evening, he hoped she might come to her senses. True, she had not been a willing partner, but she was his wife; surely she would come to appreciate his command and authority over her, given time.

As he had pulled on his clothing, she had watched him with eyes as dead as a fish's, and he was disgusted. She made him feel befouled, as though he had done something wrong. It was unreasonable! If he had not rescued her, she might even now be lying among the dead at Civitot. She should be *grateful* to him; he had saved her life. What could Fulk have done? Pulled her inside that tower with him, to sit and wait for the arrows to sleet down on her head? Yet she still preferred Fulk to him. Perhaps she would come around before long. When she realised that his brother had always been a feckless womaniser, she would learn to appreciate Odo. If only ... but no, he refused to think of Jeanne. The horror of the nearness of his escape from her was enough to make him shudder. To have married a whore and bigamist!

Now he had need for speed. He must find and capture his

brother. The thought was thrilling, but terrifying. How would he react when he saw Fulk's face? Would he be able to act resolutely? He pushed his doubts to the back of his mind. God would see to it that he had sufficient resolve.

After speaking with Peter the Hermit last afternoon, he had asked to take Roger and Gilles, as well as a force of twenty pilgrims who had been blooded over the miles, and a squadron of cavalry from the Byzantine army who were said to know the territory. At the harbour, Odo looked at these Byzantines suspiciously. They were *turcopoles*, the mixed-blood sons of Greeks and Turks, or Seljuks who had been baptised. He had heard that they were as reliable as the *kataphractoi*, the heavily armoured shock troops of the Byzantine army, and with their lighter armour the turcopoles should be more helpful as a supporting force, but he still distrusted them. They were foreign to him with their dark faces and odd language.

'You will need to hurry and find your brother,' Peter said. He had come to the harbour to bid Odo farewell. 'There are armies from all over France on their way now. I need you at my side, not hunting down this renegade.'

'I will be back as soon as I may,' Odo said.

'Do so. I am lost without poor Sir Walter de Boissy-Sans-Avoir; I relied on him. And now, without him, I rely on you, Odo. When the armies come here, there will be much to do, negotiating to cross the waters and make our way to the Holy Land. We shall have to fight almost every step of the way, and I need you at my side. Return soon.'

'I shall,' Odo said, taking the Hermit's hand and kissing his ring.

He strode from the Hermit to the gangplank, and walked headlong into Heinnie and Father Albrecht. 'My pardon, sirs.'

'You are in a hurry, friend,' Heinnie said.

'I go to hunt a man over the water.' Odo recognised the pilgrim and priest who had witnessed Fulk's assault on him.

'You go to the lands of Rum? Let me join with you, master. I am keen to cross the water!' Heinnie said. The sound of steps behind him was stilled, and he could almost imagine the wraith leaning forward and listening to his conversation. Oh, to be away from her! He was desperate to be over the water and on his way to Jerusalem on his personal pilgrimage!

Odo glanced at him, taking in the strength in his arms and upper body, the purpose in his eyes, and nodded. 'Come with me.'

Plains before Nicaea, Saturday 25th October

Fulk and the men had been riding through the first half of the afternoon in a land of lush, low hills when they heard the sound of cantering, and Fulk whirled his mount about, staring back the way they had come. His heart leapt, thinking it could be a party of Saracens, and he felt the bile rising at the thought of another action.

Behind them, and approaching rapidly, creating a dust storm of its own, was a swift-paced horse. Fulk peered into the yellowish mist, trying to discern what lay at the heart of it.

Lothar and Alwyn trotted to come level with Fulk, while Sara remained behind a screen of other riders.

'One rider?' Alwyn said.

'Yes. Not being pursued,' Lothar said.

'It looks familiar,' Fulk said, his eyes closely narrowed. 'Who . . .? It's Gidie!'

The three allowed their horses to amble forward to meet the man as he drew to a halt, panting. His mount was lathered and foam-flecked, and his head dropped as soon as Gidie stopped, looking as though he was close to collapse.

'What is the urgency?' Alwyn said. 'You have nearly killed your brute.'

'I was sent by Guillemette to find you if I could,' Gidie said. He looked about him at Lothar and Alwyn as though he doubted them, but then concentrated on Fulk. 'Sybille went to her to say that your brother has come here to hunt you with a strong force. He will capture you and take you back in chains, or kill you here.'

'Why would he do that?' Lothar rumbled. 'Is it not enough that Fulk has been driven from Constantinople?'

'I don't know. But I know this, Fulk, Sybille was injured before she came to warn Guillemette.'

Fulk's face hardened. 'How so?'

'He punched her,' Gidie said. He saw the anger in Fulk's eyes. 'I think he hit her in the belly, and he ...'

His reluctance to speak told Fulk all he needed to hear. He clenched his jaw and made fists of both hands. 'Where is he?'

'I came by an early ship and rode at speed. I slept as night fell and was up with the dawn. He would have taken ship soon after, but it depends on how long his party rested overnight. He will be some leagues behind me, I think.'

'Good. I will ride back to meet him.'

'He has a force with him, Fulk. If you go back, they will capture you,' Gidie said. 'You know what that will mean. They'll execute you on the spot.'

Fulk nodded slowly. The thought that Odo could have molested the woman Fulk loved was like acid in his heart, eating slowly into his soul. 'I came here on pilgrimage thinking it would be an adventure, some excitement from my boring life, but I've known nothing but death and misery. Now my own brother wants to take me back to Constantinople to be executed. Well, if God wants me to die, so be it. I will not see more men injured or killed to protect me.'

Lothar scowled. 'You will give up?'

'Give up?' Fulk snarled. 'I have no woman, no brother – nothing! If God seeks to take my life as well, I submit to Him. But if He gives me leave, I swear, I will dedicate my life to winning Jerusalem and to holding it for Him. I will commit my life to His glory.'

Gidie hawked and spat, then shrugged and cast an eye up at the sky. 'Aye, well, it's all a bastard, but there's no point riding to your death. You might as well wait here with us if you won't have your mind changed. There is one thing you may want, though.'

'What?'

Gidie reached down. Bound to his saddle, beneath his left thigh, was a long package wrapped in muslin. 'Sybille thought you should not go abroad without protection. She sends you this.'

Fulk took the package and smiled at the weight. He untied the thongs binding it and unwrapped his sword. Drawing it, he held it up and admired again the steel with its silvery patterns. 'Thank you, my friend.' Just gripping the weapon seemed to send a calmness into his breast, and suddenly he had a feeling of hope. He reversed it, gripping the blade in both hands, and repeated his oath. 'If I am allowed to live, I will dedicate my life to winning Jerusalem and holding it for God, protecting His pilgrims to the end of my life. This I swear on the cross.'

He kissed the cross of his sword, and as he did so, he felt as though God Himself had looked down and approved.

Sara sat with Alwyn. She had little idea where he was intending to take her, but she was happy to be with him, wherever he led. Staying at the house would have been unbearable with him gone, now that Jibril was dead. The young slave had been a fixture of her life for so long that she still often thought she heard him pattering along on his bare feet, and would turn to call to him, only to realise that there was no one there.

Alwyn was the one permanent rock to which she could hook her life. He had taken her as a slave many years ago, and she had become his concubine gladly. She had been terrified of his injuries when he first bought her, but over time she had grown fond of him. He was a kind master, for all his accustomed gruffness.

'Where shall we go?' she asked him now.

He was sitting with his back to a rock, and he glanced up at her question. 'Go? Onwards, I suppose. There's nothing for us to go back to. The Vestes may take you from me; and me, I don't know what he'll do with me.' His old eyes stared into the distance for a while. 'I'm sorry, Sara. You should have left me years ago when you had the chance, when I offered you your freedom.'

Her heart sank at those words. 'I did not want to leave you. I was happy to stay with you.'

'You don't know what lies in store for us.'

'No more do you,' she said. She sat cross-legged at his side. 'You are going to journey now. I will be with you. I can cope with a journey.'

'You foolish child,' he said. His hand sought hers, and she realised with a shock that it was his injured one. She gripped it tightly, and when she looked at him she saw that tears were running down his cheeks as he gruffly said, 'But thank you.'

It was late in the afternoon that Fulk thought he could see a vague swirling of smoke in the distance towards the coast. It was several miles away, and it appeared over the low, rounded hump of a hill as a mist, but as he sat and watched, he was sure that it grew. It was a force, and a strong one at that.

Should he give himself up to the men pursuing him and submit? If he were to fight, it would affect all these other men.

515

They did not deserve to be dragged into his fight. They should not be forced to die for him.

But surrender was impossible. The more he considered the idea, the more he rejected it. Besides, he had made an oath to God. He would not willingly be forsworn.

He rose and stretched. His fate would soon be decided. He patted the sword at his side. It felt natural there, a part of him. He had borne it over mountains, plains, and over the sea, and now it was welded to him like a new limb. Since his rescue from the cell he had felt diminished without it, and now it was returned he felt like a man who had lost a hound which had returned. It felt like a faithful friend.

Setting his hand on the grip, he pulled gently. There was a slight friction at first as the swatch of lambswool at the top gave up its grip, and then it slid out smoothly. He studied the pattern on the blade, admiring the weight and balance, the precision of the workmanship, and suddenly an unaccountable sadness washed through him.

The appearance of the men coming to capture him meant he might never grip this hilt again, that he would neither see Sybille nor Jerusalem, that he would never again share a pot of wine or ale with friends. All would be taken from him if he surrendered himself and this weapon. He would die.

He shook his head. It was too late to worry about such things. Pushing his sword into the scabbard, he glanced back towards the pursuit. The force was approaching at speed now, the cloud of dust in the air growing, and Fulk could see the twinkle of metal glinting in the sun. He sighed and turned to make his way down to rejoin the others.

But before he could pass more than a few steps, Alwyn came hurrying up the slope. 'Fulk! Over there! Look!'

CHAPTER 41

Plains before Nicaea, Saturday 25th October, 1096

Fulk gazed at him with befuddlement. 'What? I can see them coming.'

'No! Not Odo and his men! Look *there*!'

Alwyn flung out his hand towards the north and east. Following his pointing finger, Fulk saw a second cloud of dust. It was almost as close as Odo's party, and Fulk stared at it with surprise. There were no other men supposed to be out here. His party with Alwyn was the first of the scouting groups, and Odo had followed close on their heels to catch Fulk. Nobody else should be out here.

That was when he realised what it meant. There was a Saracen force coming towards them, perhaps engaged on the same task: scouting the land to learn what their enemy was up to.

'Christ's pain! Come on!' Alwyn said urgently, and together the two slipped and skidded down the hillside to where the rest of the men and Sara were waiting. They were soon in their saddles, and Fulk pointed towards Odo and his men. 'Quick! We must warn them and prepare!'

Sir Roger de Toni rode slumped in his saddle. The crossing had not been easy, and the force had ridden only as far as the battle-field on the first day before being forced to camp. They had tried to move far enough from the scene of carnage to be free of the odour, but the wind had changed in the night, and he had woken to the stench assailing his nostrils as though it was a living thing trying to choke the air from his lungs. After that, he had been unable to sleep again, and he wore a dejected air. When he came seeking adventure and knightly opportunities, he had not thought much of the deaths of others. Killing and war were his life, after all; and yet the smell and sight of putrefying corpses was more shocking than he had expected before coming here.

They were riding quickly, cantering along a valley floor between green hills that had small flocks of sheep, the remnants left after the depredations of the pilgrims who had died here. A couple of turcopoles suddenly spurred their mounts and rode, shrieking, into the midst of the sheep with their light lances. Both speared lambs, flicking their wrists to fling the creatures high into the air, off their lance-points, to lie bleating piteously behind them. The two continued, chasing more.

Odo saw them kill their first prey, and bellowed at them to come back, but they ignored him and continued their slaughter. Sir Roger watched with a lacklustre eye.

'At least this night there will be fresh meat,' Heinnie said.

Sir Roger nodded. He was not sure of this 'Heinnie'. The man seemed competent, but he was as nervy as a virgin in a brothel. He kept peering around, over his shoulder, as though looking for something.

'Perhaps we shall find them soon,' Heinnie said.

'Unless they have been killed already by the enemy,' Sir Roger grunted. He was unsure that he wanted to catch Fulk. He rather liked the man. From all he had seen, Fulk was both likeable and dependable, precisely the sort of pilgrim that Sir Roger would have wanted to have join his party.

Odo had slowed their advance to a rapid trot while he waited for the two wayward turcopoles, and Sir Roger drew his leg over the saddle's crupper to ease his muscles and joints.

Father Albrecht at Heinnie's side murmured, 'I am sure that will not have happened.' He narrowed his eyes as he gazed ahead. 'The Good Lord has sent us here to do His bidding and Odo is a most devoted servant of the Lord, so—'

'What's that?' Heinnie exclaimed suddenly, standing high in his stirrups.

Sir Roger stared. 'Dust? A dust cloud?'

'A strong party of riders, from the look of it, and they must be travelling fast.'

Odo pulled a face. 'It's my brother! He must be riding back to challenge us!'

'How would he know we are here?' Sir Roger wondered.

'You don't know my brother,' Odo snarled, and then bellowed at the two turcopoles once more. They were collecting the bodies of the sheep they had killed, binding them by the throat and slinging them over their horses' withers. Their commander, eyeing the signs of riders, shouted a command. Hearing his shout, the two looked up quickly. One dropped a pair of lambs, and was about to return to them when his companion snapped at him. He nodded and left them, hurrying to his horse, remounting swiftly, and soon the two had rejoined the main party as the squadron of turcopoles took their position in a column to the left of the pilgrims. Sir Roger glanced at Eudes and Gilles, testing the sword in his scabbard and wrapping his reins more tightly about his left gauntlet. Eudes looked at his ease, while Gilles glared at the hills all about as if daring them to harbour danger.

Heinnie sat still, once more appearing to listen to a voice only he could hear, and Sir Roger gave a fleeting frown. 'Is there something the matter?'

'Me? No, Sir Roger. No.'

Sir Roger moved his shoulders irritably. It was plain to him that Heinnie was not happy, but then, who was? He was hot and uncomfortable with the thick, quilted padding of his gambeson beneath his mail, and he could feel the sweat trickling down his spine, but better that he should be discomforted than die of a stab wound. He gripped his lance more tightly as Odo led the way to the front of the valley at a cautious trot, all eyes ahead on the pass in front of them between two low hills.

Suddenly the first men appeared, and Sir Roger heard Gilles give a very unchristian oath at the sight: it was a glittering company of Saracens, all clad in black, with glistening steel helms and mail, riding at a brisk trot. Those at the front wheeled about, moving to the flanks, and the remainder of the contingent was suddenly exposed, a strong force of some hundred or more. Flags and banners flew in the mild breeze, and the riders halted, while a group of men trotted to the front.

'Good God in Heaven!' Father Albrecht murmured.

Heinnie heard him, but watched impassively. He had a lance in his hand, and though he was unpractised with such a weapon, he was confident he could hit his mark, so long as the spirit of the girl didn't distract him. The Saracens were preparing themselves for battle with rousing shouts, and then a roar went up as a fellow rode up and down the front rank, urging the men to great efforts of courage. Although they had no knowledge of the language, his meaning was plain.

'You go, do the same,' Heinnie said urgently to Albrecht.

'Me?'

'These men need to know God is on our side. They need a prayer! Go give them one!'

Albrecht took another look at the enemy, and Heinnie thought he might decide against it, but then he trotted forward, and turned to face the Christians. *'Pater Noster,'* he began, and the whole company, turcopoles and Franks, began to mutter along with him, as they had at a thousand Masses before. When they reached the 'Amen', Albrecht rode back to Heinnie, giving him a shaky smile.

'And now,' he said, 'may God bless us all!'

Suddenly there was a shout from the Saracens, and the front men bent as they spurred their beasts, and soon all the host was moving towards the Christians, the flanks riding faster, overtaking the body of the force, and in an instant the first arrows were slicing down into the Christian soldiers.

Sir Roger lowered his head, gave a bellow and spurred his horse. A party of three was before him, and he sent his beast straight at them, Gilles and Eudes at either side of him. It gave him a warm feeling to know that these two were with him. The turcopoles had wheeled and deployed in line abreast, and now joined his charge, a solid phalanx behind Sir Roger. When Sir Roger glanced behind him, he saw that their rapid deployment had taken Odo by surprise, and he was left stranded with Heinnie and Albrecht behind the turcopoles, whipping and spurring their horses to keep up.

With a crash Sir Roger was in the midst of the Saracens. Two flanking ranks of bowmen hurtled around and past them, and the flights of arrows were fierce, slamming into the men, sometimes pinging off mail or helmets, but many finding their mark, and men disappeared from view in an instant, falling from their saddles.

He had his target, and pelted onwards at the gallop even as his enemy rode towards him. Sir Roger huddled tight in his saddle, tight like a fist, his lance high until the last moment, when he let it fall and saw it take the man high in his breast, piercing him through and through, the lance snapping with a crack that Sir Roger felt in his elbow and shoulder, but then he had his sword out, and he was battering at another man with it, his horse biting at the other man's as the blood lust and rage filled rider and beast together.

Arrows, arrows from everywhere; from before them, from behind, arrows slamming into mounts and men, striking shields and sticking; a storm of arrows that made a man want to shrug his head down into his shoulders and cower away, but Sir Roger fought on. He was aware of a man attacking him on his left, but then Eudes was there, and beat the man away, only to give a sudden yelp that was so like a dog's, Sir Roger thought his horse must have crushed a hound, but then Eudes slumped in his saddle and Sir Roger saw an arrow protruded from the back of his neck, buried deep in his spine. Eudes fell forward and over his horse's neck and Sir Roger saw him no more.

'Pull back! Withdraw! They are too strong!' Gilles roared.

Sir Roger bared his teeth. 'You think I am a coward? I will not run from a fight!'

'Then you will die! There are too many! They are far too strong for us!'

Sir Roger heard a man say, 'God will not let us fail!' and turned to see Albrecht and Odo. It was Odo who had shouted, and now he lifted his sword high and screamed, *'Dieu le veut! Dieu le veut!'*

It was as he cried the second time that Sir Roger saw the

arrow. It slammed into Odo's left shoulder, and Odo was spun about. He almost dropped from his beast, and clutched at his injured shoulder with his hand still grasping his sword. Glancing at the arrow, he paled and turned a waxen green colour, and Sir Roger bit his lip, but he could not leave him to die. This man was God's chosen leader. 'Retreat! Pull back!'

Their way was blocked. The archers at the two flanks had encircled the force, and now rode up and down behind the turcopoles, loosing arrows into their midst and cutting off their retreat.

'Too late!' Gilles snarled, and thrust at another Saracen. 'Every man must do the best he may.'

Fulk and the others came to the head of the valley as the battle surged, and he gazed down at his horse.

The beast, like all the others, was hot and weary after their journey, and now Fulk must demand that it run again. He glanced at Alwyn, but the older man had eyes only for his woman, who was riding at the rear of the company. Alwyn called to her. 'Sara, ride up that hill and stay out of sight. If you can, ride back to the coast and wait for a ship.'

'No. I am coming with you.'

'You cannot ride into battle, woman!'

'If I stay behind and you lose, I will be taken as a slave and concubine. I would rather die with you.'

Alwyn snapped a look at Fulk and gave a half-grimace of apology. 'Sara, if you join us, I will be worrying about you all the time and I will be killed. Keep away from the battle, I beg you, in God's name!'

She glared, but turned her mount and set it to the nearer hill.

Alwyn pulled his mail shirt's throat so that the back of his neck was better protected, gripped his sword in his good hand, and wrapped the reins about his left wrist. 'Ballocks!'

Seeing his grimace of determination, Fulk drew his own sword and raised it high over his head. 'Courage! My friends, we ride to save Christians! We ride to protect pilgrims! Ride with me now, and Godspeed us all!'

Sir Roger had several arrows stuck in his shield, and it was growing unwieldy. He quickly drew his sword down the face of it, cutting off all the arrows to two-inch-long splinters. A man rode at him from the left, and he rammed the hedgehog shield into his face, then stabbed down with his sword where the man's mail met his collar, and felt the blade sink in deeply. He pulled it from the sucking flesh and whirled his beast, searching for an escape, but there was none. Only a seething, heaving mass of men and horses.

And then he heard something faintly over the clamour of battle: a series of screams and bellowed war cries. Suddenly the press about him was lessened, and he lifted his own sword and shouted, 'We are rescued! To me! To me! We shall win this day!'

He saw Gilles turn to face him, but then they were all battling again, pressing forward, pushing at the men in front of them, while Sir Roger could see Fulk and the others battering at the men between them. An arrow flew past Sir Roger's ear and slammed into the face of the man in front of him, who gave a shrill scream and fell, and then there were only two men between Sir Roger and Fulk, and they were knocked down.

'Never has a friend been more welcome!' Sir Roger said, grinning.

'I thought Odo was here to capture or kill me,' Fulk said.

'Yes, but now you have saved us, you must be honoured. I will see to it.'

'Perhaps after the battle?' Fulk suggested with a smile.

The fighting was soon finished. The sudden charge of the

reinforcements under Alwyn and Fulk had shattered the confidence of the remaining Saracens, and they drew back, some few archers trying to loose arrows in retreat, but the turcopoles were fleet on their fast, light mounts, and soon the Christians had won the field.

As the turcopoles went from man to man on the ground, ending the suffering of the injured and saving those they could, Fulk saw Odo being carried to the shade of a blanket thrown between two trees. He was very pale, and Fulk hurried to his side. 'Odo?' he said, but then stopped at the sight of the blood.

'Fulk?' Odo was pale and weakened from loss of blood, and when he bared his teeth, it was less a smile and more like a snarl. 'I am here to capture you.'

'And instead I rescued you and your men.'

'You must come back with me.'

'You're in no position to force me, Odo,' Fulk said coldly.

'How does it look?'

Fulk kept his eyes on his brother's face. 'Little more than a scratch.'

'Will I be able to knead dough again?'

Fulk pulled a grin. 'What? I know you're only a mediocre baker, but even you can't use this to escape work. You need a more sensible excuse.'

'You're a dreadful liar,' Odo said, and closed his eyes. 'Do you have any water? I'm parched.'

'I'll get you some,' Fulk said. He turned and went to fetch the skin from his saddle. Soon he was propping Odo's head up while he set the spout to his brother's mouth. Odo coughed a little, but then peered up at Fulk. 'I hated you for what you did.'

'What did I do?'

'You never told me about Jeanne.'

525

Fulk's mouth fell open. 'You mean you didn't realise? I could tell she was a . . .' He stopped. The thought of Jeanne having been murdered was still too painful.

'I had no idea. And now it's irrelevant. I lost her.'

'You *killed* her, Odo!'

'I had to. I could not allow the pilgrimage to be harmed by one woman's unchaste behaviour.'

'You murdered her – how will that affect the pilgrimage?'

'But it was too late,' Odo said, as if he had not heard him. 'I tried to remove the cause of the Lord's dissatisfaction, but it was plainly too late. Our Lord had decided that the pilgrimage was not worthy, and destroyed it.'

'You blame all those deaths on one woman?' Fulk said, disbelieving. 'Why would He turn his face from those most devoted people to His cause just for one woman's misbehaviour?'

'She was married, man! She should never have left her home and her husband!'

'He was a bully and trickster. He beat her and sold her to his friends.'

'But he was her husband.'

Fulk shook his head. 'Everything is black or white to you, isn't it? Good and evil – there is no graduation. People are not like that, Odo. We all struggle.'

'I wouldn't expect *you* to understand, Fulk. There is too much worldliness in you. You should submit to God.'

'Relax yourself, Odo, don't overtax yourself.'

'Yes, yes. You're right,' Odo said. He shot a quick look towards the arrow in his shoulder. 'It is not very serious, is it?'

'You'll be fine,' Fulk said quickly. He could not look at it.

'I am sorry for what I did, Fulk,' Odo said after a while.

Looking up, Fulk saw that Gidie was nearby, watching Odo intently. 'For killing Jeanne? For stealing my woman? For

526

attacking Gidie? For seeking to capture me so you could execute me? There are many things for which you should feel remorse.'

'I did what I thought was right.'

'Aye, well, if I hear that you have mistreated Sybille, I will . . .'

'What, break my head?'

Fulk stared at him coldly. 'Don't test me, Odo.'

Just then a man with a shock of white hair and the emaciated look of a man who had lived in the sun without nourishment for too long, arrived with a bloody leather bag which he dumped beside Odo. 'How bad is this one, then?'

'I shall go,' Fulk said as the barber began to frowningly study the wound, cutting away the spare material to display the angry, puckering skin clinging to the bloody arrow. He pulled his bag nearer and tugged out a pair of pincers.

The man caught hold of his arm as he tried to walk away. 'No, you won't. I'll need help digging this one out,' the man said.

Fulk found he had no words to excuse himself. He stayed.

Lothar walked with Alwyn, both leading their horses to the lines set out at some distance from the battlefield where the beasts would be able to rest without the smell of blood to distress them.

Alwyn was quietly smiling to himself. Sara had already returned and was helping to fetch water for the injured, and Alwyn had a conviction that his world was improving. He was coming to the conclusion that she would make a better wife than concubine.

For his part, Lothar was glad merely to be uninjured. He had seen the body of Eudes as Sir Roger and Gilles went to find him. He had died quickly, so the knight had said, but afterwards he had been terribly trampled and broken as the battle raged over his body, and the men had to wrap him in his cloak to pick him up and carry him away from the dead Saracens for a proper burial.

Sir Roger would not leave him with the corpses of his enemies to be picked over as though he was no better than them.

They left their horses with halters tied to ropes slung between low trees, and Alwyn went to find Sara, while Lothar stood patting his beast for a while, stroking her warm flanks and murmuring soft comforting sounds to her. She had been terrified in the battle, and only her innate obedience had allowed her to bear it. Now there was still an occasional tremor passing through her body, but she was growing more calm.

'She looks a good beast.'

Lothar was suddenly stock still. He knew that voice: he would know it anywhere. 'Heinnie.'

'Yes. And if you will accept it, I willingly offer you my apology for Rudesheim. I rue the day I saw that town.'

Lothar turned slowly. Heinnie's voice had sounded genuine, but Lothar found it hard to believe. It was, after all, Lothar who had scarred Heinnie and left him bleeding in the dirt. 'Your face has healed,' he commented.

Heinnie's hand rose to the wound, red and raw in the sun, and Lothar watched his hands in case Heinnie should reach for a knife. He was always known to be deadly accurate at throwing knives. 'Yes, the flesh is healing well. But my soul is still . . . broken.'

'How do you mean, "broken"?'

'Walk with me, Lothar.'

'Do you mean to fight me again?'

Heinnie looked at him. 'I have forgiven you this scar, Lottie. How can I do else? Please, walk with me.'

Lothar glanced at his horse, but then nodded. There was little enough that Heinnie could do to him, and Lothar was confident he could defend himself against any threat Heinnie might present. 'Very well,' he said. After they had crossed past the horse lines and were strolling up a shallow incline, he glanced at his companion. 'How did you reach here? Did the Count come? Is he at the city?'

Heinnie seemed not to hear him. Instead, he walked with his head tilted slightly, his left ear over his left shoulder. His face held a sadness that quite touched Lothar. When he spoke, it was in a muted tone. 'Do you hear anything?'

'The wind, men talking, birds, the horses at the lines. What do you want me to hear?' Lothar asked.

After a few more paces Heinnie gave him a look. 'I hear things all the time. Things I should not hear. Perhaps I will stop hearing them if I reach Jerusalem. I don't know.'

Lothar peered at him warily. Something in Heinnie's voice sounded like panic held on a tight leash, like a mastiff held away from other people.

'What do you hear?' he asked.

'Steps,' Heinnie said. He threw a look at Lothar. '*Her* steps. I have heard them every day, every night . . .'

'The Jewess?' Lothar said, and involuntarily cast a glance over his shoulder.

'She is there now. I can hear her. When I look, there is a . . . a sort of mist. I cannot look too closely! Our army was defeated in a town called Moson. Did you pass it?'

'No. We headed over the mountains towards Rome.'

'I saw her there. She was in an alley. I just thought it was some . . . but it was her. And behind her, her brother. They have been with me ever since. All the time.'

Lothar sucked at his teeth. He had heard of superstitious sailors, but never before had he heard of a hard-headed Rhineland mercenary being so scared. 'She is there now?'

'Yes.'

'What will you do? Would a priest help you?'

'I cannot tell anyone. I will go to Jerusalem. Perhaps there she will forgive me.'

'What then?'

'I will stay there and dedicate my life to prayer and the protection of Christians. I will offer my life as penance, if she will just grant me a night's sleep,' Heinnie said.

Lothar was at a loss. Heinnie had been a friend for many campaigns, and Lothar had an urge to put an arm about him, yet still the memory of anger and hatred because of the murder of the girl and her brother lay heavily on him; now there was an added revulsion with this story of a ghost.

He was still there when Sir Roger appeared. The knight was quiet, and nodded in their direction. 'Master Lothar, you are well?'

It was the oldest greeting known to a warrior: the acknowledgement of life and survival. 'I am well, Sir Roger. You are also uninjured?'

'Yes, I thank God. Although now, of all my men, only Gilles is alive. Eudes died in the battle. I will miss him.'

'I am sorry to hear it.'

'A priest is to speak some words over his grave. Would you come and join us?'

'I would be glad to. I will miss him also.'

Heinnie nodded, and walked a little way with them towards the shallow grave scraped in the dirt near the valley's floor. Then he walked on, past the little group with Father Albrecht as the priest began to intone the *viaticum*.

But as he left, Lothar could have sworn that he heard something; faint and almost drowned out by the sound of wind in the grass, he thought it was like the slapping of a sandal many yards distant.

Lothar felt a sudden piercing chill that made him shudder. The sound seemed to follow Heinnie.

CHAPTER 42

Plains before Nicaea, Sunday 26th October, 1096

Walking and leading his horse for some miles to rest it, Fulk was grateful when Lothar joined him and walked at his side.

The captain of the turcopoles had been slain in the battle along with several of his men, and those who had survived had suffered a number of greater or lesser injuries. Three who had been more grievously wounded than Odo had already perished, and now their bodies were bound to their horses like bags of grain. They would be buried at the coast, rather than delaying the journey to bury them. All the men felt the same fear: that the scouting party they had bested might reappear at any moment with a stronger force behind it. Meanwhile those with the worst injuries had been tied to litters which were being dragged along behind their horses. Odo himself was on one. He was hot and growing delirious with the pain of his shoulder, but Fulk knew there were excellent surgeons in the city. Odo would recover well enough, he had no doubt.

Lothar said, 'You know your danger if you go back to

Constantinople? You will be taken and, because you ran from the gaol, they will execute you.'

'Yes.'

'You are fixed on this course?'

'What would you have me do?' Fulk said. It was not a question framed from despair, it was based more on serious enquiry. He was genuinely intrigued to hear what Lothar would suggest. 'I had thought to return to my home in Sens, but there I would be reviled for cowardice and not seeing the pilgrimage through to the end.'

'Then do not give up on the pilgrimage.'

'If I remain at Constantinople, I will be executed.'

'Not if you are protected by a powerful man.'

'Who would protect me from the Hermit and the Emperor?' Fulk scoffed, but Lothar was perfectly serious.

'If you come with my friends Heinnie and Father Albrecht, you will be safe. They came here with the army of Sir Hugh de Vermandois – you know who he is?'

'Of course! He is the brother of our king.'

'And as a royal prince of France, even the Emperor would think twice before insulting him. If you are under his protection, you will be safe.'

'And you think this can be arranged?'

'You will soon be a part of the army of Sir Hugh, and then you will be safe.'

Civitot, Monday 27th October

Fulk had made his mind up while riding here: he must accept Lothar's suggestion.

The decision was easy to make, especially when he had met

Father Albrecht and spoken with him. He took Mass with the priest on the Sunday and, with Lothar there, told him all that had happened, save mention of Odo's murder of Jeanne and attempt to kill Gidie. They were matters for which Odo must himself confess and seek forgiveness. It was not Fulk's part to accuse. To do so could cause suffering to Sybille, and he had no wish to see her endure more pain.

Fulk was glad of Lothar's company as they reached the harbour. The Rhinelander's stolid calmness was reassuring, and a strong counterweight to Heinnie's nerviness. At every sharp sound, Heinnie seemed to spring into the air, and when there was none he spent his time listening acutely for something that only he could discern.

There were two fishing boats in the harbour, and over the water Fulk could see larger ships tacking over the waters, some heading towards them from Constantinople.

Fulk made his way to the horse dragging Odo's litter.

'Odo, the ship will be here soon,' Fulk said.

Odo was lying on a litter, his injured shoulder a source of constant pain. 'I am sorry, brother. You must surrender. Come back with me and accept the judgement of the Hermit.'

'Odo, I'm sad to have made you unhappy. I am sad that you thought I tormented you over Jeanne. It was never my intention. I just thought you realised what sort of woman she was. But I can never forgive you for stealing Sybille.'

Odo grimaced. 'I did what I thought best.'

'Like you did with Jeanne.'

'Yes.'

Fulk clenched his jaw till his teeth ached.

Odo continued, 'A man has a responsibility to keep his wife obedient. She should be submissive and ...'

'Did you assault her?'

Odo looked at him, and a little smile played at his mouth. It looked like a sneer. 'I have had to chastise her. She is my wife. It is my duty.'

Fulk stared at him. 'What has she done to deserve that?'

Odo smiled. 'She has argued with my decisions. I have a right to expect her support. I will have it. And her love.'

Fulk saw a malevolent gleam in Odo's eye as he spoke. It was vengeful and cruel. Odo was determined to hurt Fulk. He would take Sybille when he wanted, and she would suffer torments at his hands, and Odo would ensure that Fulk knew. *And I shall have to live with that pain and jealousy for all my days.*

'Odo, we shall never be friends again.'

Guillemette was at her little cookpot, stirring, when she heard a voice call to her, and she looked up with a smile of relief when she recognised Gidie. 'You are back! Did you find him?' she asked with barely suppressed anxiety.

She had seen Gidie go with apprehension, fearing that he would be riding into great danger, but after Sybille's urgent warning, Guillemette was convinced that someone must go to alert Fulk. The sword was proof, if he needed it, of the message's veracity. But after Gidie had gone, she had a terrible fear that he would not come back either. He and Fulk would die on that horrible shore in the land they called 'Rum'. It was not to be borne.

'Yes, he found me,' Fulk said. He was a pace or two behind Gidie, and now he stepped around his companion, smiling to see how Guillemette stood gaping at the sight of him. 'And I think I have you to thank for my freedom now.'

'But – but you should not be here!' she said.

'I have been freed from the dangers by friends,' he said. 'I am safe now.'

'What of Odo?'

Gidie looked at her as he squatted by the fire. 'I have not killed him. But I will, when he is recovered.'

Fulk put his hand on Gidie's shoulder. 'Leave him, my friend. My brother is injured, and is no fit target for your ire.'

'You may wish to forgive him, Fulk, but I cannot.'

'Then at least promise me that you will avoid him. Do not challenge him here, Gidie. It can only lead to your destruction. Besides, perhaps his injury has beaten some sense into him.' Fulk told Guillemette of his flight, meeting Gidie, and the battle in which he and his men rescued Odo's company. 'Father Albrecht was keen to inform everyone here that it was only my holy zeal that rescued him and the pilgrim party from annihilation, instead bringing God's divine vengeance on the heretics,' he grinned. 'It is good to have so vocal a supporter. And now, because of that, I am to be placed under the protection of the Christian armies.'

Guillemette smiled. 'That is good,' she said.

'Your pottage smells good.'

'I have no need of food from others now,' she said, looking at him very seriously.

'Maid, I had no intention of asking any favours for—'

'I am glad to hear it!' she said sternly.

He eyed her fondly. She was a comfort to him. She caught his eye and gave a quick frown, as though he was ogling her bosoms, and he reddened instantly and looked away. *Ridiculous!* he told himself. *You've seen her naked, and she you, many times since leaving Sens.* But there it was. They were here on a holy march, not for the enjoyment of the natural pleasures, but for a more stern task.

'May I sit here awhile?' he asked.

'You would like some of my food this time, then?' she said with a chuckle.

'Yes, if you have enough to share; but really, all I want just now is your company.'

She laughed then, and Fulk thought it was a wonderful sound. But then he thought of Sybille, and he felt his heart weep.

All the while Gidie sat quietly nearby. But he had not forgotten Odo's acts, and nor could he forgive them. He yearned for revenge.

Heinnie stayed up late that evening. He spent it talking quietly with Lothar. He could tell that Lothar was uncomfortable with him; perhaps because Lothar felt that Heinnie could not truly have forgiven him for that terrible scar; perhaps because Lothar did believe Heinnie about the Jewess following him.

It didn't matter to Heinnie. All he knew was, he must fight his way to Jerusalem, and there make his peace with God. He had to make it there. Without God's forgiveness, he knew that the Jewess would drag him down to Hell and make sure he suffered for every blow, every thrusting of every rape, every moment of agony and terror she had endured before her death.

When Lothar rolled himself in his blanket, Heinnie felt her again, like a witch peering over his shoulder, and he covered his face in his hands and began to sob.

At the same time, Sybille was sitting in her tent, rocking her daughter as Odo snored.

Men had brought him here on his litter, and carried him inside on it, helping him to Sybille's bed. He looked at her as he was brought in. Sir Roger was with him, and the knight told her how brave her husband had been. He had been at the forefront of the fighting, he said, and it was a cruel chance that saw him so injured.

She thanked him, but as he was leaving the shelter he paused, glanced back at Odo, and told her quietly that he hoped Odo and Fulk were reconciled. Odo had accepted that his brother was entitled to remain in the pilgrimage, and Fulk was to march with Sir Hugh de Vermandois for the rest of the journey.

Sybille nodded, expressed her thanks, and turned just in time to see Odo's smirk of satisfaction. It was a sight to chill her heart. Odo was not reconciled, no matter what he might say to others.

She had thought – no, hoped – that she would never see him again, that he would die on the shores of Rum, that a Saracen arrow would find his heart. It had been so close. Only a few inches away and he would be dead now. It was tempting now to pray for his death, that his wound might prove fatal, but a look at him told the lie to that. He was healing well.

And she was bound to him for life. Till death parted them.

She prayed it would come soon.

CHAPTER 43

Constantinople, Friday 14th November, 1096

Odo was satisfied with his recovery. The first week after his injury at the battle, he had thought he might die, but the second week he could feel himself improving daily. Although his wife was unresponsive and cold towards him, Peter had expert physicians visit him, and now he was feeling strong again.

On that Friday he rose early and made his way to the chapel where he celebrated Mass with Peter the Hermit and many of the senior knights in the pilgrim army. Every day more and more men were arriving, and at first Odo was impressed to see how the camp about Constantinople was growing, but more recently Odo had become aware that the new arrivals were not as respectful as they should be.

There was nothing that was obvious at first glance. It was a fact that Peter seemed less welcome in the Emperor's presence than before, but there were men such as the French King's brother and other noblemen. At first Odo had thought it was merely that: the need of the Emperor to spend time with the men who were most important in the growing army, but then Odo heard sniggers and quiet comments when he or Peter passed by newcomers, as though they were the source of amusement.

Today, walking back to his tent, he heard a man laugh, and although he turned swiftly, he could not see who was responsible.

Angrily, he made his way to the tent and lifted the flap. His wife was inside.

She was wearing a tunic of some light material that set off her pale skin perfectly. She sat still, her hands in her lap as he entered, staring at him fixedly.

'Wife, you look most appealing,' he said with a mild smile. His mind was still dwelling on the chuckles he had heard outside. It was almost as if he was a figure of fun. Not that anyone who had heard of his exploits could believe such a thing. He was the figurehead of the entire pilgrimage – Peter had told him so.

She said nothing to his pleasantry, and he looked at her as he sat down on his palliasse. He patted the bed beside him, but she gave no indication that she had heard him or seen his gesture.

'Wife, you must grow to accommodate yourself to the situation. We are man and wife, and there is nothing we may do to change that. What, will you not speak? This sulking is unbecoming a wife. Come, fetch me wine and let us sit together as a man and wife should.'

'I will not be a wife to you,' she said. Her face was set into lines of determination.

'You are my wife, woman.'

'I will remain here when the pilgrimage continues.'

He frowned. 'Wife, you should be by my side. It will be better for you to be a part of the pilgrimage, and ...'

'I will join a convent. Richalda can come with me. You will release me, and I will devote my life to prayer.'

'No, I cannot,' Odo said. 'I need you at my side.'

'I will *never* be your wife! Let me go.'

Odo rose and felt the rage filling his breast. 'Woman, you are my wife. I do not give you permission to leave me. That is an end to it!'

She remained where she was. 'I will not be a wife to you. You have stolen me from the man I wanted to marry, but you will not have the pleasure of my body or soul. I *despise* you!'

He felt something snap in his mind. 'You *bitch*, you will respect me and do as I say, or in Christ's name, I swear I shall destroy you!'

'Kill me, then,' she said. 'Like you murdered Jeanne when she rejected you, or like you tried to kill Gidie, or your own brother!'

He did not even recall the blows later. A mist of blood seemed to appear before him, and he was aware of clenching his fists, trying to stop her talking, battering ... and then, when it dissipated, Sybille lay on the floor before him, moaning, curled into a ball, rocking gently. Odo was dumbfounded; he shook his head, took a step backwards. He dropped to his knees and put his hand out to her. She whimpered and withdrew. There was blood, blood on her face, at her mouth, and she clutched at her belly.

It was horrible. For all the passion of his words, he wanted her to love him. There was no point in a marriage that was only a battlefield. 'How can you not love me? Why do you not want me? I don't *understand* you, woman!'

Then it was that the answer wormed its way into his mind.

It was Fulk, of course. He must have been wheedling his way back into her affections. Fulk could not bear to think that Odo could have won his woman. Any woman must love Odo, naturally. As the man at the right hand of Peter the Hermit, any woman would desire him. The fact that Sybille hated him must be because Fulk was pouring bile into her ears. Odo should have fought harder for Fulk's punishment after his attempt to injure him. When they had returned, Fulk had ingratiated himself with Hugh de Vermandois and his men while Odo lay recovering. By the time he was able to walk again, Fulk was fully rehabilitated. There was no opportunity to bring Fulk to justice.

Odo had not pursued his brother, and now his kindness was to be repaid like this!

He moved to Sybille, but she crawled away from him. 'Don't touch me! I hate you!'

Odo stood again. He shuddered to hear the hatred in her voice. She rolled over, a sob escaping from her throat. Then he turned and stalked from the tent.

He would find his brother, and he would kill him.

Gidie was with Guillemette when Odo appeared.

Guillemette saw him first, and she tried to distract Gidie, but before she could try to send him away, Odo was with them.

'Where is he? Where is my brother?'

Guillemette stood her ground. 'He is not here. Perhaps you should go back to your pavilion and sleep it off.'

'You think I am drunk? I am drunk on the deceptions and betrayals of my own brother! He is working to take my wife from me now, and I swear he will fail!'

Guillemette scowled. 'He has had nothing to do with your wife. Sybille has not seen him since he returned from Civitot with you, when he helped save your life.'

'You are lying, woman! What would I expect from a whore!'

Guillemette recoiled as he clenched his fist and held it before her threateningly.

Gidie was already there, and he grabbed Odo's forearm. 'You want to murder her like you slew Jeanne? You are a weakly *coward*, Odo! If you want to fight, fight me – but this time, fight like a man, don't try to stab me in the back again!'

'You don't know what you are talking about!'

'Really? I saw you with Jeanne, remember? And then you struck me down and fled Civitot. You left me and your brother there to die, didn't you?'

Odo pulled his hand away and grabbed at his sword, sweeping it out in a flash of silver and grey steel. Gidie had only the dagger at his belt, and he pulled it out, but already Odo was stabbing at his belly. Gidie leaped back, trying to avoid the blade, but as he went, his heel caught a stone, and he fell back. Winded, he looked up at Odo as the blade swung up.

Then Guillemette hurled a ladle-full of pottage into his face and Odo screamed and wiped at his eyes.

Fulk saw them as he returned to Guillemette's camp. He saw her fling the boiling liquid at Odo's face, and saw Odo turn to try to stab her. Fulk ran forward as Gidie rolled and caught Odo's heel, pulling him down. Odo fell, swearing and cursing, and dropped his sword. He had it again in a flash, but now Fulk was there, and he held out his hands placatingly. 'Odo, brother, stop! What is this about?'

'You have poisoned her against me, haven't you? You couldn't bear the fact that I won Sybille, so now you are seeing her and trying to turn her from me! I won't allow it!'

'I've not seen her, Odo. I have neither spoken to her nor seen her since we came back here.'

'I don't believe you!' Odo was on his feet again now, and he suddenly lunged at Fulk.

Fulk had to retreat. 'Odo, man, stop this!'

'You should have died for trying to kill me before. I won't let you escape this time!'

Gidie was clambering to his feet, and Odo saw him. He gave a snarl, and hacked down with his sword. Fulk barged into him, his palm striking Odo's injured shoulder. He screamed, and his blow was sent wide. Odo faced Fulk, and now Fulk could see the hatred in his eyes. It was horrific, like seeing a demon staring at him from his brother's face. 'Odo!' he cried, but then he had to draw his own sword as Odo slashed at him.

Fulk managed to avoid that, but Odo's weapon stabbed quickly at his lower belly; Fulk knocked his blade away, and then blocked a fresh hack at his head, and he used his weight and momentum to push Odo's sword to his right. Odo spat in his face, and Fulk blinked away the spittle, but then Odo kneed him in the groin, and Fulk bent double. Too late he felt his sword free as Odo pulled his own away, and then he was shoved away by Gidie. Gidie had his own sword now, and he attacked like a berserker, his blade whirling and dancing in the sunlight.

But the training with Peter of Auxerre on the long march had given Odo experience and fast reactions. Fulk saw him block one attack, and saw how Odo placed his feet. From that he knew his brother was about to launch himself at Gidie, and that his Damascus blade would whirl and cut from the flank. It was how Peter had trained them. There was nothing Gidie could do to defend against that assault.

It was a preemptive act; nothing more. Fulk sprang forward to stop the blade from sweeping into Gidie's torso. His sword was up at the right height to stop the blade, but then the pain from his cods made him lurch with agony, and as he did he felt the point of his sword seem to slither, like an eel sliding over ice, and a moment later he felt the clatter as the hilt of Odo's sword struck his own. Gidie was safe, and Fulk tried to grab Odo by the shoulder, to disable him before anyone was hurt, but even as he stared, he saw that the length of his sword was buried in Odo's torso. His stumble meant that Odo had taken the full force of Fulk's thrust in his breast.

Fulk fell to his knees and screamed, '*No!*' as Odo fell back, two paces. His hand went to Fulk's sword-hilt as though in wonder, and then he gave a cough. He collapsed like a castle of sand, Fulk's blade still trembling in his chest.

EPILOGUE

Askanian Lake, Nicaea, dawn, Thursday 18th June, 1097

The sun glistened from the wave tops, from the limewashed buildings, and from the steel all about him. Helmets, mail, lance and spear-points were points of bright reflection, like a galaxy of stars twinkling before him, and the effect was blinding. Fulk had to narrow his eyes.

Under his feet the deck rolled, and he was forced to clutch at the man beside him, a tall, dark-skinned turcopole with the patronising manner of a Greek nobleman in the Byzantine court. The man looked down his nose at Fulk, but Fulk did not react. He had more than proved himself in recent months. There was not a Greek in the Byzantine army who had seen as much fighting as Fulk in the past year. All he knew was, he was glad to be leaving Constantinople at last.

The ship was wallowing now as it approached the shoreline. Horses below and in the other ships were neighing, some wildly, and there was a brief scream as a man was crushed by a falling destrier.

Fulk looked over the men with him. He was a part of this new force, an army ready and prepared to conquer the Holy Land and release the city of Jerusalem from the hideous rule of the heretic Saracens. The people would be grateful to be told that they could soon expect to be released from their near-servitude.

It was a huge host of men. Some said that there were more than fifty thousand, others that this was an underestimate and the numbers were nearer eighty thousand. Fulk had no idea, but the men of the army seemed as numerous as the grains of sand held in a fist. It was hard to believe a man's eyes when he saw them gathered together. There were the vassals of Duke Godfrey de Bouillon, of Bohemond of Taranto, of Raymond of Toulouse, Tancred of Hauteville, and Baldwin of Boulogne. An almost incomprehensible number of men-at-arms, with their ranks boosted by pilgrims like Fulk.

They were outside Nicaea now, besieging the ancient city that had been so important to the Christian faith. Kilij-Arslan had declared this city as his capital in his pride and foolishness, and now the heretic was learning that the Christians would not suffer their lands to be stolen. While the army fought at the landward side of the city, Fulk and this naval force had portaged their ships over to the lake, and were now sailing to the western walls. There they would soon help destroy all opposition.

Peter the Hermit was at the poop, ridiculously excited to be travelling with this army, like a child with a new toy, Fulk thought sourly. Sybille was back at the shore with Guillemette and the rest of the camp followers. He had avoided her since Odo's death. He never wanted to see her again. It was too painful to see her, to think of his brother's death. Poor Odo! Fulk missed him every day. His only memory was of that look of hatred as he fought Fulk at the encampment outside Constantinople. It was a look Fulk would never forget.

He had to forget Odo, to set aside the man who had grown to so detest him that he had tried to kill him. Instead Fulk concentrated on the other people. The men and women whom he had met on the way. Over to his left was Gidie. The old tranter was smiling grimly now, staring forward towards the city they were about to assault.

Farther on Alwyn and Sara clung to the ropes holding the great sail. She had sworn never to leave his side again, much to Alwyn's displeasure. Even now, she was with him. As he watched them, he saw Alwyn put his arm about Sara, holding her as the ship rocked. Alwyn looked ten years younger than he had when the Vestes had held his boy and woman against his good behaviour. Fulk stared at him, thinking that if a man were to see Alwyn and himself side by side, they would think Fulk was the older of the two.

It was a peculiar thought. Only a few months ago Fulk had been a careless, wayward young man. He had no thoughts in his head other than where his next cup of wine would come from, or which maid at a tavern would be most likely to welcome his advances.

It had all changed when the Hermit had come into his life. That day had heralded his first sight of Sybille, and it had betokened the beginning of his search for adventure. How ironic that he should have found so much adventure! He would, if he could, have returned to those days of peace and comradeship with Odo.

Odo; his friend, his ally, his brother. The man who had discovered a new, masculine form of religion for himself, who had become so intolerant and distrusting that he had cut himself off from Fulk, nurturing a hatred that was incomprehensible to him. It left Fulk feeling guilty, perversely, as though it was Fulk's lesser conviction that had led to Odo's extreme conversion to the concept of holy war, which had invariably led to Odo's death.

547

And now Fulk had the guilt of his death added to the weight of the burden he had to carry.

'Will we soon disembark?'

It was Heinnie. He was close by, clinging to a stanchion, while Lothar stood before him, a smile on his face as he stared at the approaching coast like a hound snuffing the air.

Lothar pointed. 'Yes, soon we will be there. The ship will be glad to throw us off and return to the sea! This vessel is like a bird in the sky, in her element. If the ship had a soul, it would rejoice to be here on the water.'

'I am glad it makes you happy,' Heinnie said. He was staring ahead too, but Fulk was sure that his attention was not forward. The man had some secret that he would not share with Fulk. Lothar had said that he was not mad, but would not elaborate beyond that.

Fulk considered the man briefly, but then found he was looking past Heinnie. It was as if he could see all the others who had first joined this pilgrimage: Benet, Josse, Peter of Auxerre, Jeanne and many others, dead now and lying in shallow graves, or none, over the hundreds and hundreds of miles. He could see them distinctly, rank upon rank, people laughing, crying, or weeping. They had planned to come and free Jerusalem. None had so much as seen the Holy Land, let alone the city.

Perhaps that would be his own fate, Fulk thought.

The ships were approaching Nicaea. Suddenly, arrows sleeted down as the archers found their range, and men shrugged their shoulders, as though they could shrink under the protection of their helmets. Shields were raised, and arrows plinked from metal bosses or whacked into the leather, canvas and wood.

Yes, perhaps he would not see the Holy Land, but whether he did or not, he would fight while he could.

He had nothing else to live for.

AUTHOR'S NOTE

It was while I was researching my Templar Series that I first began to read about the Crusades.

The story of the tens of thousands of Christian men, women and children who made their way over thousands of dangerous miles to join in a fight between faiths was inspiring then, and since looking into the different Crusades, my respect for these people has not diminished.

It is true that few, very few, of those setting out on the grand pilgrimage to Jerusalem had even a faint inkling of the dangers that they would encounter on their journey. Their way would be beset by brigands and outlaws, as well as organised armies keen to dissuade these enormously disruptive and dangerous religious fanatics. They would be forced to suffer hunger, thirst and the risk of death or slavery. For all the honeyed words of preachers like Peter the Hermit, their paths would not be easy.

During the writing of this book it became clear that there were some areas of confusion about travelling times to cover certain distances, about dates for certain encounters, and not least about the acts committed by Christians against other Christians.

For those who are keen to learn more, I cannot recommend highly enough that readers go to books that have been published on the subject. Although there are many sources listed on the internet, it is necessary to consider what the motivation is of the author concerned.

The Crusades were a cataclysmic series of wars over (in the Holy Land) some two hundred years. They were largely responsible for waves of anti-semitism that led to the medieval slaughter of Jews and the German genocides of the Second World War. The hatreds that grew between Muslim and Christian were exacerbated and have grown in recent years.

The internet has given access to a vast amount of information. Sadly, some of the information is skewed, censored, or plain wrong – but when it comes to religious matters, I suggest that the reader has a duty to be dubious about much of the information presented. Much will have been put up in support of one or other religious line of thought and will be as misinformed as the propaganda spread by Peter the Hermit and his companions.

My advice would be to go to a library and look at books such as: *Dungeon Fire and Sword* by John J Robinson (Michael O'Mara Books, 1991), *Armies of Heaven* by Jay Rubenstein (Basic Books, 2011), *The Crusades* by Thomas Asbridge (Simon & Schuster, 2012), or (for a briefer summary) *The Crusades* by Geoffrey Hindley (Constable and Robinson, 2003), or *Crusades* by Terry Jones and Alan Ereira (BBC Books 1995).

For a more in-depth study of impacts and effects of Crusades and Jihadism, I recommend Karen Armstrong's *Holy War: The Crusades and Their Impact on Today's World* (Macmillan, 1988). I also heartily recommend Norman Cohn's *The Pursuit of the Millennium*, which can be found in many versions since the original edition in 1957.

For those who want to look at specific areas of the history I've set out in this book, I can recommend *Harold: The Last Anglo-Saxon King* by Ian W Walker (Sutton Publishing,

1997); *The Siege of Jerusalem* by Conor Kostick (Continuum, 2009); *Byzantium: An Illustrated History* by Sean McLachlan (Hippocrene Books Inc, 2004); *Roger II and the Creation of the Kingdom of Sicily* by Graham A Loud (Manchester University Press, 2012); and if you can get it, a copy of Gibbon's *The History of the Decline and Fall of the Roman Empire* – my copy is an elderly Folio Society edition. For a good examination of the distances covered and the time taken (as well as the confusion of languages, coinage, and customs) I would suggest you find a copy of *The Itineraries of William Wey* by Francis Davey, published by The Bodleian Library, University of Oxford, 2010.

This is not intended to be an exhaustive list, but these are the books I turned to routinely while trying to sift the sands of information and come to a conclusion about conflicting dates and locations.

Although I always try to get to the facts of any events I write about, sometimes the histories just do not agree. Of course, the most egregious errors are those posted on the internet. If I pick up a book – let us take the last example above: *William Wey* – I will know that the author has put his or her name to that piece of work. I can be sure that it will have been read by an editor with either a knowledge or interest in that period or subject. It will have been read and fact-checked by a minimum of one copy editor. Then it will have been proof-read by a professional who has some understanding too – they tend to be picked for that reason and matched with books that would be relevant for them. These give me confidence that the book, when published, will have factual merit.

Compare that with a blog or posting on a site where there is no validation, other than, perhaps, the good will of the poster, and you will see why I still go to efforts to find printed books that are published by professionals.

My key advice, however, is not to look at any piece of work with an entirely uncritical eye. The events portrayed, whether described by a Christian, Muslim or Jew, will carry the perspective of that religious belief system.